Saving Grace

Saving Grace

Annie Jones

ALABASTER
BOOKS

SAVING GRACE
Published by Alabaster Books
a division of Multnomah Publishers, Inc.
© 1998 by Annie Jones

International Standard Book Number: 1-57673-330-0

Cover illustration by Deborah Chabrian/Artworks
Cover design by Brenda McGee

All Scripture quotations, unless otherwise indicated, are taken from
The Holy Bible, New International Version © 1973, 1978, 1984 by
International Bible Society. Used by permission of Zondervan
Publishing House. All rights reserved.

Also quoted: *The Holy Bible,* King James Version

Alabaster is a trademark of Multnomah Publishers, Inc.

For information:
Multnomah Publishers, Inc. • PO Box 1720 • Sisters, OR 97759

Library of Congress Cataloging-in-Publication Data
Jones, Annie, 1957–
Saving grace / by Annie Jones.
    p. cm.
    ISBN 1-57673-330-0 (alk. paper)   I. Title
    PS3560.045744S28   1998   98-28170
    813'.54–dc21   CIP

98 99 00 01 02 03 04 05 — 10 9 8 7 6 5 4 3 2 1

For my dear friend, Melanie O…"Guess you had to be there, huh, Mel?"—and you were!

For Lynn B.… I'd tell everyone how you kept me sane a few times, but then that might make some people question how good a job you did!

For my own prayer circle…your faith and strength have held me up when I could not have gone on alone—thanks for being there, 24/7.

For my mother, Ida Maxine Barrett Shorter, whom I still miss every day.

And for my husband, Bob, who is my very best friend.

Prologue

Moonlight, as blue as her mood, cast a cool light from the large upstairs bedroom windows over Naomi's heirloom wedding-ring quilt. The moon, looking like a silver coin tossed high into the darkened sky, beckoned her. Gently she folded back the quilt, lowered her bare feet to the hand-loomed, old rug that had once been her grandmother's, and tiptoed across the room.

The brass lock made a precise little click as she flicked it open with one finger. The wood of the window frame groaned in protest, then gave way to her effort and nudged upward enough to let the fresh, fall air inside. It tingled in Naomi's nostrils as she inhaled deeply, her eyes shut.

It was the last week of October in New Bethany, Tennessee. The autumn colors had peaked, and now every good gust of wind brought down a flurry of yellow, orange, brown, and sometimes red to spill out over everything below. Often on a tree-lined lane the blanket of leaves would be so thick that it became impossible to tell where the lawns left off and the pavement began.

When the Bible says the streets of heaven are lined with gold—this is what I picture.

Naomi could practically hear Mama say those words. Just the thought of Mama made Naomi's chest tighten and her throat close. She felt like a little girl again, small and not quite sure of the things that lay ahead of her. This time, though, Mama's hand could not take hers and make everything all right.

Naomi missed her. No matter how old or wise—or how many wonderful, terrible, or fascinating things the good Lord had in store for her—Naomi would always miss Mama until she herself went on to be with Jesus in heaven. And to make matters worse, the women she had come to look upon as a second family—women who had stood beside her through Mama's death and whom she had seen through their own triumphs and turmoils—now seemed distant and beyond her ability to reach. The saddest part was no one seemed able to do anything to stop it.

Naomi clenched her fist and rested her forehead against the glass of the window. They were so different, these friends... with almost nothing in common but their faith. Even in that, they attended different churches, yet they had become friends through their struggles to revive the tradition of the prayer tree. Friendship had blossomed as they faced loss, found new loves, squabbled a little, and laughed a lot. And the prayer circles had survived.

This year three new trees stood in the community grove next to the small apple tree she, Rose, Gayle, and Mary Lucille had chosen the year before. However, while their little sapling and the seeds they planted in the new prayer groups seemed to be flourishing, their friendship was not.

Naomi understood it. Time and the demands of everyday life had taken a toll...it was only natural that the four of them would drift apart.

Naomi sighed deeply, and her gaze wandered to her bureau. The moonlight reflected on a white envelope: Gayle's invitation for Naomi and the others to the Splendor Belle Gala at her country club tomorrow night. It was obviously a last-ditch attempt to keep them together, to strengthen their ties. Either that or—

Or it was a means to say good-bye.

Naomi choked back the urge to cry, her heart aching. She hadn't felt this alone in this new hometown, the place she'd returned to eighteen months earlier, since Mama died.

"Buffalo Gal won't you come out tonight?"

Naomi started and stared out the window. She turned quickly, hoping to find her husband of three months still lying in their bed, sound asleep. She hoped the image singing up to her from below was a mirage. The rumpled pile of quilt and linens on the empty bed said otherwise.

"Taylor Boatwright!" Her pulse thrumming, Naomi tried to decide if she was more shocked, upset...or totally charmed by her husband's behavior.

With one petulant tug, she hoisted the window open as far as she could. A cool breeze whipped at the open collar of her cotton gown. "What on earth are you doing on the front lawn, Taylor?"

"Well, it seems the last couple nights the only thing that interests you is whatever's out this window. I thought that might as well be me." He folded his arms over his dark blue robe and smiled up at her.

"Have you lost your mind?"

"No, but I seem to have lost your focus. That doesn't speak well for someone married such a short time. Tell, me, what is it out this window that you find so fascinating?"

"The lunatic on my front lawn."

"There's a lunatic out here?" He feigned surprise, gazing about him in first one direction, then another. "Where? I haven't seen one."

"Then maybe you should come inside and I'll show him to you—I do believe I have a mirror in here somewhere."

"I'd rather see myself reflected in your eyes." He folded his

9

hands over his chest, playing it up big. The breeze ruffled his brown hair, giving him a tousled look—which only made his act more appealing.

"Reflected in my eyes, my foot." She clucked her tongue to keep from seeming to give in too easily to that beguiling Southern charm of his. She loved her husband, loved him like no other man she'd ever known, but there was still something in her that would not let herself surrender her trust too easily to any man. She had to show some spunk to guard herself a little, even if only in jest. "You are going to see yourself reflected in the shiny side of a frying pan if I have to come out there and drag you back inside for your own good."

"I'd rather you chase me round the block with that frying pan, Nomi, than give up before I find out what's making you so blue these days."

Even from this distance she could sense the mischief in those gorgeous blue eyes of his. She could certainly see the deep lines that fanned out over his taut cheeks and framed his grin. Years of working in the sun, caring for grounds and trees and shrubs and gardens with his family nursery, had left his face tanned as leather. Taylor Boatwright, in her humble opinion, was an enchanting mix of gentleness and toughened masculinity. Those were the traits he was displaying now, a subtle demand that she share her thoughts with him…a gentle urging that left no room for doubt as to what he wanted and expected.

"I've just been thinking about how much I miss Mama." Taking a precarious perch on the windowsill, Naomi hunched her shoulders enough to put her face in the open window frame. She kept her voice quiet, relying on the stillness of the late hour and the straight drop down to carry her words to him. "And maybe even more so, how I miss my friends."

"You'll see them at the Belle Gala."

"Yes, I know."

"Then that's all that's bothering you?"

All? To her it seemed huge. She inhaled the brisk air as a breeze ruffled the curtains and stung her cheeks. If only it would whisk away the sense of impending loss crowding her emotions. "Yes, that's *all.* It's nothing about you or the children, if that's what you're concerned about."

"Good to hear that. You know, when a man's married only a few months and his wife starts spending her nights stargazing instead of snuggled up asleep next to him, he starts to feel a little... put out."

"Well, you look put out all right—like a cat for the night." She waggled her finger at him. "If you are feeling neglected, then shutting yourself out of the house is hardly the way to remedy that, sweetheart."

"Lot you know." His smile never dimmed. He stuffed both hands in his pockets and rocked back and forth in his wool-lined slippers. "I've left the front door open."

"On a blustery fall evening like this? Why it's liable to—"

Wham!

"Blow shut." She tried her very best not to giggle.

"Guess this means you're going to have to come climb down from your tower, fair maiden, and rescue me."

"Guess again." This time a light laugh escaped her as the absurdity of the moment took precedent over her doubts and difficulties. "You were the one who was supposed to fix that door so it wouldn't lock behind us. Looks like now you are reaping the fitting harvest of your own procrastination."

"Yes, but I only came out here to cheer you up. At least you could show me some mercy for that." He spoke it like a man who had no doubt that she'd relent and let him back in.

"Well, I'll tell you what."

"What?" His grin grew wider. Clearly he expected some kind of mushy confirmation or show of appreciation for his actions.

"It worked." He'd get his show of appreciation and then some, but first she was going to have a little fun. "Because seeing you locked out, stranded on the front lawn in your night clothes? It surely has cheered me up to beat the band." She slipped from the sill and pretended to start closing the window.

"You'd better come down here and let me in, darling wife of mine, or I'll be forced to start up my serenading all over again." He gulped in a big breath as if ready to belt out another chorus.

"And you had the nerve to ask *me* for mercy!" She laughed outright.

"Buffalo Gal—"

"Now, stop that! Stop it right now." It wasn't his voice she objected to so much as the situation. "You're embarrassing yourself."

"I'm not one bit embarrassed." It was revoltingly true. He looked as relaxed as a man settling into his favorite easy chair. He gathered another breath and launched into song again. *"Buffalo Gal—"*

"Then think of your daughter. If you wake up Ashley this way she will be totally humiliated by your behavior."

Taylor shrugged. "She's fourteen. The very fact that I exist seems to be a source of perpetual mortification to her. What's a little bit more at this point?"

Naomi cringed. While she and Taylor's daughter, Ashley, had reached an understanding—even begun to form a fragile friendship for a while—the new marriage had put a strain on that. All was not smooth between them, and this kind of thing would not help matters.

"Buffalo Gal—"

"Oh, all right. Hush up. I'm on my way down there. But it's out of respect for Ashley's feelings and to save you from becoming the talk of New Bethany like poor old Grace Grayson-Wiley."

"Ol' Grace? Whatever made you think of *her?*" he called up before Naomi could step away from the window.

"I don't know. Timing, I suppose." She gazed up at the autumn sky. "You know, it's this time of year that just about everyone in town who knows her story thinks about her."

"Sure, now and again they turn their thoughts to her, but do they ever turn their hearts to her? Do they ever try to do anything to see if they can help the poor old girl?" He snorted in disgust.

He had a point. People did just talk about Grace. They talked about her and *gawked* at her. Even Naomi had done that. But who had extended the hand of Christian love to the elderly woman? Naomi could not think of a soul. Not one soul.

If only…

Her eyes widened. "Oh, Taylor, that's it!"

"What's it?"

"The solution."

"What solution?"

"The solution to bringing the circle back together. Taylor Boatwright, you are a genius! A pure, unadulterated, I-could-kiss-you-for-thinking-of-it *genius!*"

"Well, you can't kiss me unless you come down here and let me in—and when you do that, maybe you'll be so kind to explain to me what you have got up your sleeve, my precious partner-in-life. Because from the tone of your voice I can tell you're on fire with some kind of scheme and I've got the feeling it's something that no one is going to talk you out of."

One

wilight fell over the gathering at the Bethany Heights Country Club as gentle as a blanket spread over a slumbering babe. The band, a local conglomerate of brass and strings, electric guitar and drums, plodded its way through "The Tennessee Waltz" as autumn leaves tumbled down now and again from the canopy of trees above the large courtyard. The air, crisp with the chill of fall, carried the earthy tang of wood smoke from some homes in a nearby holler to mingle with the scents of fine food, ladies' perfumes, and a traditional apple cider punch with cinnamon sticks simmering in it.

Rose Holcolmb inhaled slowly, as though she could somehow take it all in and hold onto it for dear life. She longed to store it back as a hedge against the coming chill of the inevitable. This moment, this feeling, this precious time tonight might well be the last time she and Lucy and Naomi and Gayle were all together as friends.

"It's a lovely party, Gayle, sugar. Thank you for having us." Even to her own ears, Rose's accent, which had always been thick as bees on a honeycomb, sounded abundantly Southern. Maybe it was the nostalgia of the early November evening, she thought, that swathed her words in soft, Southern congeniality. Or perhaps she could blame the atmosphere of the generations-old tradition they had come to observe.

The annual Splendor Belle Gala, held since before the Great War of Northern Aggression on the first Saturday night in November, was the closest thing a small town like New

Bethany, Tennessee, would ever have to a debutante ball. Generations of the town's young women from only the finest families had, in their senior year of high school, been trotted out in their finery to be shown off to "society," such as it was. And society gathered to inspect and approve those select few whom all expected would one day run the Junior League, the PTA, and the Hospital Auxiliary.

That was how it was done, Rose noted. That was how it had *always* been done. New Bethany was not a place to go tossing away convention and custom because it no longer suited modern thinking and lifestyles. No, in this town one did what was expected of one, even if one had to grit one's teeth like the steely smile of a bear trap to get through it.

Still, Rose had to admit, even New Bethany could not deny that an event like the Splendor Belle Gala had grown terribly passe. Bethany Heights Country Club, which had hosted the gala for some thirty-seven years now, had gladly begun over the last decade to make subtle changes. Now the "Belle Gala," as everyone called it, was *the* primary fund-raising event for the holiday season. The idea was that even a quaint or antiquated custom might be endured, possibly embraced, in the name of raising money for a good cause. In this case that cause was a fund that was drawn upon by several reputable charities throughout the tri-county area.

This year, Gayle Shorter Barrett and her husband, Ted, had "sponsored a table"—which meant they'd written a check that would have crippled the budgets of most folks in town in order to feed and entertain eight guests. Everyone knew they could afford it, of course, and not just because Ted's law practice was booming or because he came from money to begin with, or even because the couple had sent their oldest daughter off to an exclusive all women's college. Everyone knew the Barretts could afford such luxury because of whom they chose to invite to share their table—not a client or judge or a person with political aspirations in the bunch!

Gayle and Ted Barrett had blithely squandered—yes, *squandered* was the word Rose had heard generously bandied about—the price of sponsoring a table at the Belle Gala on Gayle's *friends.*

Tiny white lights twinkled around the country club's towering columns and from the topiary bushes placed discreetly here and there on the grounds. They blurred in the corners of Rose's eyes as her focus became the three women: Naomi, Mary Lucille, and Gayle.

Heaviness weighed down Rose's heart, making it hard for her to swallow. She touched the rounded collar of her beaded jacket and wished she had thought to bring her handkerchief instead of leaving it in her pocketbook back at the table. If her escort for the evening, William Boatwright, had been at her elbow, she might have sent him to fetch her bag. But since the menfolk had all formed an ad hoc armchair coaching staff for their beloved Tennessee Volunteers football team and the women had excused themselves to escape the subject, she supposed she'd just have to do without her linen hankie.

Rose shut her eyes for a moment to blot out the sadness that threatened to overwhelm her. When she opened them, she gazed onto the swirl of girls in shimmering gowns and their tuxedo-clad young escorts. Suddenly she felt very old. "I can't believe it's been forty years since my own Belle Gala."

"Twenty-one years for me," Gayle whispered.

"Thirteen." Mary Lucille braced both hands on the rail and leaned out just a bit, as if drawn inexplicably toward the scene. The tiny lights around them gave Lucy's pale blond hair a silvery-white sheen. The expression on her round face was dreamy and distant, giving her an almost ethereal glow. "How can that be? Thirteen years?"

"I know how you feel," Rose murmured. "I have no idea where the last forty years have gone. In my heart I still feel young and vibrant and ready to embrace whatever the future will bring, not at all like the world-worn woman who looked back at me from the powder room mirror a few moments ago." That woman, she thought, had not only been a wife and mother but was already a widow with two grown daughters of her own. That woman had sold the huge, old, stately home—where she had raised her children and held quaint teas, lavish dinners, and elegant parties—and moved into a two-bedroom condo that was just the perfect size for her alone. And, of course, for the occasional visit from her girls. That woman had more experiences behind her than there were left ahead.

While she had the faith to face that fact, Rose did sometimes worry that she'd played it too safe for most of her life. Born right here in New Bethany to parents who adored her, she'd worked for a time while living in the Grayson Boarding House and then married well. The rest just sort of took care of itself.

Yes—her lips pressed together—she'd had it too cushy. She hadn't dared enough or done enough.

She swallowed hard and reached for her handkerchief, then remembered again that it was in her pocketbook. Well, why did she need a hankie anyway? Dabbing at your neck with a monogrammed linen hankie was an old lady's affectation! That was not for her, not yet. Rose Holcolmb still had lots of life left in her, thank you very much, and tonight was a lovely night full of romance and promise, just as it had been for her so many, many years earlier.

Straightening, she looked at the young people mingling and

laughing, glorious in the fine bravery of youth. She edged forward as all time melted away for her. "Don't you just feel as if you could step off this old veranda and into that crowd and just be one of them again?"

Gayle cocked her head, her tailored black gown at odds with the curls of her soft, layered hair and the faraway gleam in her eyes. "Yes. I feel like I could just shrug this middle-aged lady's body off like some sturdy overcoat my mother made me wear and show everyone that that's not the real me. I feel like it couldn't have been so very long ago that I was one of them, that if I closed my eyes and got my courage up and just went out there, I could be one of them again."

Lucy murmured something indistinguishable in agreement.

Gayle held her breath, then let it out slowly as if she had drawn in the essence of the moment and it had revitalized her. "You know, inside of me there's still that part, that eighteen-year-old girl, so sure, so ready, so poised on the verge of…everything."

"Me, too," Lucy whispered, her hand at her throat.

Rose smiled. Of all of them she surely felt the passage of time most severely. "I think I feel that most on nights like this, when the evening is just saturated with memories of being young and beautiful, of how it feels to catch a young man's eye, to place your hand on his arm."

"Oh, and the thrill of that sense of anticipation…you know, before the evening starts? When you're waiting at the door, peeking from behind the curtains, trying not to let him see you. He strolls up the walk all cockiness and ill-fitting suit, with a corsage box he doesn't quite know how to handle shifting from one hand to the other and…"

"Oh, stop it, please!" Naomi put one hand over her eyes in a show of high drama. Her short black curls flipped over her fingers and fell against her thick gold wedding band, where the sapphire and diamond sparkled. "Ya'll are scaring me." She aimed a jaded look of amusement at them all. "All this talk about lost youth, waiting for your beau to come and sweep you away, and being feted once again at the Belle Gala?"

Lucy blinked at her.

Rose and Gayle exchanged confused looks.

"It's creepy." Naomi over-articulated the words, then shook her head. "I don't know whether I'm looking at my dear, wonderful friends or the beginnings of a support group for women suffering from Grace Grayson-Wiley syndrome."

"What's that supposed to mean?" Gayle crossed her arms over her chest, challenging her friend. Much as she loved Naomi and despite all they had been through together, Gayle was not in any mood to put up with Naomi's irreverent attitude tonight.

"You figure it out." Naomi folded her own arms in mirror image of Gayle. "It doesn't take much imagination to make the connection."

"Then I must be a quart low because I don't get it." Lucy tipped her head to one side. "What have any of us got to do with that loony old lady, Grace Grayson-Wiley?"

"Well, you were all waxing nostalgic about the Belle Gala—" Naomi made an open-handed gesture, encouraging Lucy to put the pieces together.

Gayle rolled her eyes. This was supposed to be a special night, a precious memory, *not* a time to dredge up local legends and make unflattering comparisons. Gayle loved Naomi like a sister, but like sisters, they could surely get on one another's nerves.

"You know the story, Lucy," Naomi prodded. "The Belle Gala, Miss Grace wanting to be escorted to the ball again?"

Lucy shook her head.

Gayle sighed. Wasn't this just like Naomi, trying to lead things off in a ridiculous direction—one that either gave her something to joke about or prompted others to do things they would normally never consider? Like Rose was doing right now, seemingly quite content to abet this departure from the lovely mood of the evening to talk about that crazy ol' Miss Grace.

"Lucy, sugar, haven't you heard the talk about Miss Grace?" Rose's fine eyebrows raised in surprise.

"Only that she's not quite right—" Lucy dropped her voice to a harsh whisper and gestured toward her own temple "—in the head."

"Well, so you *do* know." Gayle took Lucy's arm and turned her toward the festivities again. "Wasn't it fascinating—and a dreadful shame, of course? Now, Mary Lucille, tell us about when you were—"

"Oh, my dear, you *have* to hear this." Rose took Lucy's other arm and turned the girl back toward Naomi again. "It's just too...too...mythical old South, the stuff that makes us, as Southerners, well...who we are."

"Absolutely." Naomi threw up one hand then huddled in close, her voice lowered to imply a delicious tidbit. "And this is the *perfect* time to hear it, as it was over fifty years ago, on this *very* night, that loony Miss Grace had her date with destiny." Naomi waggled her eyebrows, which added both comic punctuation and played up the strange flavor of the oft-repeated tale.

"Nuh-*uh*." Gayle slashed her hand through the air. This had to stop and it had to stop now. Otherwise the whole ambiance of the night—the first time they'd all been together in such a long time—would be disturbed beyond repair. "You are not going to retell that whole miserable fable, Naomi Beauchamp Boatwright. Why, everybody in this town has heard that sorry saga about a million times by now."

Lucy poked her lower lip out. "I haven't."

"You have to remember, Gayle," Rose, who seemed totally caught up in Naomi's merriment as well as the mystery and romance of Grace's tale, said, "Lucy is much younger than we are. People don't pass along these silly old stories about their neighbors like they used to. They have better things to do with their time now. They watch *Hard Copy* and *Entertainment Tonight* on the TV—so they can pass along tales about total strangers."

"Oh, well, I'm sorry Lucy is too young to have been around when all we had to do to amuse ourselves was tell scary tales by firelight." Gayle tightened her arms over her chest and lifted her chin. She noticed her words came out clenched and a bit flippant—more so than she had intended. She forced an understanding smile, trying to temper her acerbity with humor. "'Course that was what we did directly before we bolted the fort gates, snuffed out our beeswax candles, and crawled into straw mattress beds come sundown."

"You had a straw mattress?" Naomi played into Gayle's sarcasm with a little of her own. "*I* had to sleep on cold, bare dirt…"

Gayle's smile broadened. *See what a good sport I can be?* she hoped her expression read.

"With my whole family…"

"Very funny," Gayle drawled.

"And the hunting dogs…"

"All right, Nomi." Gayle felt her smile stiffening. "I get it. I'm put in my place, now if you would just—"

"And a pig—"

"Knock it off already!" Gayle knew when she had lost a point, which—as she had known since they were girls—was just about always with Naomi. Even so, she made her concession with an earnest laugh. "Just tell Lucy the story of Grace Grayson-Wiley, would you?"

"Why, I'd be glad to Gayle, if you're sure that's what you want?" Naomi's expression was gleeful.

"Oh, please." Gayle said it in that way they called "slopping sugar," which meant it was just too sweet to be believed.

Naomi laughed, then moved even closer. Rose and Lucy followed suit but Gayle chose to hang back just a bit.

"See, Lucy, it was just after World War II," Naomi began. "The Grayson family was in tatters as they had lost their only son, Grace's brother, early on in the fighting in the Pacific theater."

"Uh-huh." Lucy nodded to show she'd grasped the situation.

"To make matters worse, that winter Grace's father had succumbed to pneumonia after a long and torturous illness, leaving only her mother, her baby sister, and Grace to care for what was left of generations of grandeur now fallen into decay. The family fortune was beyond restoration by then. All that remained was their heritage, the house and lands—*and* Grace Grayson's ability to latch onto a man who could restore their honor, social standing, and financial security."

As she listened, Gayle shifted her gaze from the party to the small knot made by her intent friends.

"So, you see—" Naomi held up one finger "—and it's imperative that you understand this…the family's entire future rested squarely and irrefutably on the shoulders of the petite eighteen-year-old Grace. She *had* to go to the Belle Gala to meet and mingle, with hope to win the marriageable intentions of the only kind of man that could save her family from their predicament."

"Wow." That Lucy identified with the pressure of measuring up to family expectations shone clearly in her eyes as she fixed her complete concentration on Naomi.

The lights, music, and soft sounds of the crowd blended into the background now even for Gayle as she lowered her head to catch every detail Naomi spun out for them.

"Now, this being just after the war, no one expected the kind of grand finery that had been—and would again be—the hallmark of the Gala festivities." Naomi gestured as she spoke, her tone a peculiar mix of the northern phrasing she had acquired in years of living in Maine gilded with a renewed Tennessee accent. "So it was that the lack of money did not hold Grace back, nor did breeding as she *was* a Grayson, and they were among the first citizens and founders of New Bethany."

"They're shirttail relations of mine, you know." Rose angled her chin up just a bit and her hand fluttered near her throat as though holding some unseen feather fan.

Naomi glanced at Gayle in a knowing way and winked. Gayle reined in the impulse to giggle. She had to admit there was something about hearing this tale that made her feel like a teenager again. Probably because when they were young, she and Naomi had many times driven very slowly by the old Grayson place and tried to spot the house's lone occupant, knowing they'd probably have swooned with fear if they'd ever so much as seen a rabbit in the road.

"Yeah, yeah, money and social standing weren't issues." Lucy tapped the toe of her pump. "So, did Grace go to the Belle Gala or not?"

"I'm getting to that," Naomi said. "While Grace might have

been forgiven not being feted in a new gown or that her parents were no longer able to present her properly, one thing did stand between Grace and the Belle Gala she so desperately needed to attend."

"What?" Lucy's mouth hung open even after the word had left her lips.

"Time."

"Time?" Gayle's brow crimped down over her eyes. "What do you mean time?"

"Like Cinderella turning into a pumpkin at midnight?" Lucy offered.

"Oh, no, nothing like that." Naomi gave a backhanded wave. "I guess I should have better said *the* times. See, this was the nineteen-forties. There was a rigid way of doing things, so Grace could not simply go on her own—like Cinderella—to the ball. Oh, no, she had to have an escort, and not just any man would do. She had to have a fellow of high moral fiber and unimpeachable character."

"She did?" Lucy's forehead creased.

"Well, of course, Lucy." Rose laid one hand on the young woman's shoulder. "Since Grace did not have a father to, um, *assure her honor,* she would have to make sure herself that everything remained above reproach."

"Oh." Lucy blinked. Then her eyes grew wide. "Oh!"

"Trouble was, because of the times, she couldn't simply ask such a man to take her." Naomi lifted her shoulders in an eloquent shrug. "Of course, she could hint and wheedle and flirt within the limits of decency, but he would have to issue the invitation on his own."

"Besides, if there really was a guy like that to take her to the Gala, she wouldn't have to *go* to the Gala to meet a man like that." Lucy nodded as she reasoned it out aloud, then her

25

shoulders slumped forward. "Poor thing."

"Well, somehow she did find a man willing to take her. At the last moment, a friend of her late brother's—so it was said—stepped forward purely out of a sense of duty, and she was set."

"Good." Lucy sighed with relief.

"The night of the Splendor Belle Gala came, and Grace Grayson stepped into a stunning satin gown made over from her mother's wedding dress, so the story goes."

"Ooh, I hadn't heard that." Gayle narrowed her gaze on Naomi, but in her mind she could almost see that dress. She could not imagine, however, the old woman she had seen most of her life only in nervous glimpses *in* that dress. No, she could only picture the hunched over Grace Grayson-Wiley, with a tuft of white hair trailing out from beneath a straw hat, in the ankle-exposing polyester pants and voluminous housecoats that were the old woman's trademark. Still, it was enthralling to think of Grace as young and beautiful, vulnerable, and yet ready to do whatever she must to save her family.

"So, there she is," Naomi continued. "On the night that could either make or break not only her own future but that of her family and the home they called Sweet Haven from ruination, Miss Grace puts on the corsage her gentleman friend had sent out to the house earlier in the day, and she waits. The clock strikes to tell the time he is supposed to come, and she waits."

Lucy drew in her breath in a tiny gasp, then held it.

Gayle found herself holding her breath too.

"Grace gets anxious. She decides to go out to her porch swing for some fresh air. Perhaps she will even see him coming up the walk, tall and handsome under the canopy of yellow leaves from the arched branches of the towering sweet gums. And she waits." Naomi paused for effect.

Gayle could almost count the precise number of silent beats Naomi would take before going on. Two...three...four...

"And waits."

Lucy's gaze darted first to Rose then to Gayle, then back to Naomi's face.

Naomi wet her lips. "And—"

"Oh, I can't stand it!" Lucy squeezed her eyes shut, her hands in fists at her side. "He didn't come, did he? That awful, thoughtless, should-have-known-better-than-to-trust-one-of-their-kind...*man* stood poor Miss Grace up!"

"Exactly." Rose let out something between a huff and a sigh.

"That's right, Lucy," Naomi confirmed. "He stood her up."

"How awful." Lucy hugged her arms around herself, making her cranberry-colored velvet gown bunch across the middle.

"How awful, indeed." Rose's quiet monotone foretold what each of them except Lucy already knew.

"Grace lost everything that night, her chance to help her family, her self-esteem, her...how shall I put this?" Naomi ruffled her fingers over the top of her black curls, looking pointedly away from the group for a moment before clearing her throat and meeting their gazes again. "She also lost her...shall we say, fragile grip on reality, that night."

"Fragile grip on...? Yeah, right." Gayle laughed at the melodrama Naomi had infused into what had been common knowledge around town all their lives. "She lost it. Flipped out. Bought a one-way ticket to the funny farm. Elvis had left the brainpan, darling."

All three of Gayle's companions gaped at her, and she bit her lip. Perhaps she had gone a bit too far. She met Naomi's eyes and winced, opened her mouth to form some kind of apology for her tackiness when her old friend spoke instead.

"Don't you go trash-talking the king, little lady," Naomi said in a poor imitation of a familiar husky Memphis mumble.

There was silence for a moment, then Lucy broke into a giggle, followed by the rest of them.

"We really should not be laughing at poor Miss Grace's misfortune," Gayle reminded them, trying to regain her composure.

"Oh, we're just laughing to clear away the tension, sugar." Rose smiled and patted Gayle's arm, her eyes filled with an odd kind of intensity. "It has nothing to do with Miss Grace and everything to do with us and how stilted and testy...*cautious*, I guess, we've been with one another all night."

"Preach it, Sister Rose." Naomi hugged the older woman. "We've been more prickly than porcupines with one another tonight."

"It's just been so long," Lucy said softly. "I think we got out of the habit of being friendly."

"But we're not any less of friends," Naomi hastened to say.

"Oh, no," they all agreed, heads nodding, setting their fancy hairdos and glittering gowns moving.

"Just out of practice." Rose reached out to give Lucy's arm a squeeze. "And I, for one, am a bit ashamed of having let it happen."

"We never should have stopped." Naomi leaned back against the railing.

"Stopped what?" Gayle studied her.

"The prayer circle, the meetings, giving ourselves to something better, something higher...serving God." Naomi did not quite meet Gayle's eyes.

"Now, just because we're not in a prayer group together this year does not mean we've stopped serving God." Gayle bristled. "I am still active in my charities and church as much as my family responsibilities allow. Lucy and Rose hold open the day

28

care free of charge on the nights the group with young children meet, and you…you're a new wife and mother to a teenage girl. That alone should notch you up closer to God than ever before. As I recall I spent most of my Mathina's thirteenth and fourteenth years in almost round-the-clock contact with God Almighty."

Naomi laughed. "You have a point. Still, I think there's something we really ought to consider…"

"Never happen, Mr. Boatwright. Never happen." Ted's voice drifted across the veranda, and the women turned to see the men framed by the country club's massive doorway. They were jovial but had that air about them that every woman recognizes on sight as meaning they'd had enough of the monkey-suits and the dog-and-pony show. They wanted to go home, prop up their feet, and watch TV.

"Looks like my evening is drawing to a close, ladies." Gayle waved to her husband.

Lucy looked at her in dismay. "Already? But it's early yet."

"Well, you're welcome to stay as long as you like, honey," Gayle insisted. "But I think we'll be leaving soon. Ted's been feeling out of sorts lately, nothing really wrong, just easily tired and not bounding back from simple things like he used to. Of course, I want you all to know this has nothing to do with the fact that the man is forty-two years old. This is not an age thing, this is a *health* thing, and he reminds me of that one hundred times a day or more."

Rose and Naomi laughed in appreciation.

"We'll probably go soon, too." Rose directed the comment toward Naomi, since they had all come in one car.

"Aw, no." Lucy pouted a bit. "Really?"

"What can we say, doll?" Rose grinned. "We've hooked up with a bunch of party poopers."

"Oh, men!" Lucy crinkled up her nose.

Gayle thought about asking if there was trouble between Lucy and her new beau, Dwayne, but since the men had all started making their way across the wide veranda toward them, this clearly was not the time. Instead, she joked, "Well, I guess Miss Grace just didn't know how good she had it all these years without them."

"Oh, that reminds me." Lucy tucked her straight blond hair behind her ear. "Whatever became of Miss Grace? She must have finally married at some point."

"She was married briefly and lived away from New Bethany for a time—about the same time I lived at the boarding house," Rose explained. "But her husband died, and she returned home and folks took to calling her 'Miss' again, you know the way some do as a means of mollifying the elderly. 'Miss Grace,' as if she were still some sweet, young thing."

"What about Sweet Haven?" Lucy turned to Naomi. "I recall you saying your mama was born there, right?"

"Yes, that's true, but that was before Miss Grace herself was born. After Miss Grace's mother passed on it seemed Miss Grace hatched one scheme after another to keep the old place in her hands." Naomi stepped back. "You know the lands were sold off years and years ago. It's all developed now. Matter of fact, Rose's new condo is not far from there."

"That's right," Rose said. "In fact, if we took the country roads we could drive by what's left of Sweet Haven on the way to take me home."

Naomi jerked her head around to look at Rose. "Now, there's an idea. It's perfect timing, too, because I was thinking maybe we could—"

"Oh, Naomi, no. You wouldn't." Gayle shook her head, her hand at the neckline of her black gown. "It's just...too tacky."

"Yeah, well, so am I." Her friend grinned like a cat who ate the canary. "What do you say, Rose, shall we make the drive by tonight and see for ourselves?"

"See *what* for yourselves?" Despite her age and her size—Rubenesque, to put it tactfully—Gayle thought Lucy had a way of coming off like a child when she was peeved or upset. "I don't understand any of this. Why would you want to drive by that ratty old Sweet Haven tonight of all nights?"

"It would *have* to be tonight, Lucy." Naomi's eyes grew round, her voice hushed. "We didn't tell you about the result of Miss Grace's break with reality. You see, on the anniversary of her fiercest disappointment, on the night of the annual Splendor Belle Gala, to be precise, Miss Grace…relives it."

"She… what?" Lucy grimaced.

"She reenacts the whole event every year—*each* and every year for the last fifty-something years," Gayle confirmed. "She steps into that old party gown, puts on a corsage, and goes out onto the porch swing to wait for a young man who is never, ever going to come."

31

Two

"Where *is* he?" Lucy tapped the toe of her pump on the curb, then gave the valet a wincing smile.

The young man folded his arms behind his back military style, his gloved hands open but fitted together.

"My date," she found herself explaining, as if she needed the fellow to understand that she was not lurking on the steps of the Bethany Heights Country Club all alone, skulking about, muttering to herself. That image, far too close a comparison to Miss Grace Grayson-Wiley for Lucy's liking, gave her a quick shiver. So, as further evidence that she did, indeed, have a date, she added, "Dwayne. That's his name. Dwayne Cobb."

The valet, outfitted in a brown and gold polyester uniform that had not been in style since the eighties, nodded stiffly in her general direction.

"He'll be here directly to pick me up. He insisted I wait here rather than walk with him out to the back lot, of course." She smoothed down her lifeless, blah-blond hair in a half-hearted imitation of the pretty girls fussing at their gorgeous tresses. It did not make her feel any lovelier or less awkward. "He'd have waited himself—that is, he'd have used the club's valet parking except that he…"

For one instant, Lucy thought of standing right there and lying. Of pulling herself up in her brand new gown that was supposed to make her feel poised and a bit slinky, but didn't, and *lying* to protect the so-called good name of the man she was seeing. It wouldn't be the first time she'd done as much and for far greater transgressions than anything Dwayne Cobb had done or was likely ever to do. Still, as she tried to form her mouth around what most people would dismiss as a "little creative social gussying up of the truth," she simply could not do it.

"Dwayne's cheap," she blurted out instead. "He didn't want to have to tip anyone. No, that's not entirely the truth, he doesn't seem to mind tipping or picking up the check for that matter, when he's out with the boys. And he's happy to pay a premium price for football tickets—only the best seats for him and his pals—or for whatever electronic gadgetry he has fallen in love with this month."

The valet cleared his throat. If he had any intention of saying something, Lucy did not give him the chance.

"So, I guess it's safe to assume that Dwayne is only cheap when it comes to me—oh, and in this case, you." Lucy offered a smile that she hoped conveyed more apology than her actual sentiment, which was "misery loves company, so let's both of us be mad at that jerk, Dwayne."

She pursed her lips. "I suppose it's tacky of me to say it right out in the open like this, but there it is. It's the truth and I can't back away from it. Dwayne Cobb can be one selfish, stingy, thoughtless man. Not that he doesn't have his good points, of course. Many, many, *many* good points."

The attendant's eyes glazed over, but apparently he was too polite to stop her. He just nodded again in a way that made him look like he had a neck brace on under his outdated getup.

Lucy strode out to the edge of the curb once more and looked again, stretching up on her toes as though that might somehow give her just enough of a vantage to spot Dwayne's car in the distance. "However, among his good points, promptness is *not* one of them." Lucy had meant the silly, convoluted statement as a jest, but the joke fell as flat as the evening had gone since Dwayne had insisted they leave early, seeing as the rest of their party was gone.

Lucy had tried to explain that of those leaving early, the youngest was almost ten years older than she and more than twelve years older than Dwayne. She all but begged him to stay and enjoy the evening. She'd even tried to share with him a little of her very special feelings about the Belle Gala and about Bethany Heights, the country club to which her parents had belonged until her father's death forced her mother to relinquish her membership. Which was only what the very old and strict club rules regarding widows demanded.

Lucy shut her eyes and inhaled. She could smell the peculiarly soothing scent still clinging to her hair and clothes that was uniquely of this place and, for her, of another more precious time. Stinging chlorine from the reflecting pool mingled with the heady fragrance of imported gardenias, old men's cigars, young women's perfume, and fine food. It warmed her and carried her, if for only an instant, back to a time when she had loved coming here as a young girl with her parents.

She remembered being around eight and feeling special because her mother and daddy brought her here. Daddy called Lucy "Princess" then, and while she knew—even at that tender age—that it was just a show for the other members of the exclusive club, she had cherished the only bits of praise or kindness her father had ever shown her. She recalled that, then and only then, he had told her how pretty she was and how someone as pretty as she deserved the best, just as her mother did. Looking back and knowing now what he had thought her mother deserved—disrespect, heartache, and betrayal—Lucy could understand the double edge of that remark. Still, at the time, it had seemed full of the promise that she could someday earn her father's respect. She had few memories of the club in her teens. Until the night of her own Belle Gala.

Lucy glanced back over her shoulder at the grand entryway of the club, her mind straining to picture her younger self there, dressed in a gown of divine aquamarine taffeta and tulle that showed even her flawed figure to best advantage. But all she could see in her mind's eye was her mother beaming up at Daddy and him looking at Lucy like she was Sweet Corn Queen, a Phi Beta Kappa, and Scarlet O'Hara all rolled into one. It was only an act, she had known that deep in her heart even then, but for just that night she had let herself believe it might be true.

That night, for one shining moment, they had been a family— or so she had thought. Mother was on Daddy's arm, and Lucy was his princess for real. For that one night Lucy had known what it was like to feel good about herself, to feel like maybe, just maybe, someday she would deserve to be truly loved by a man.

Who was she kidding? Pretty girls deserved the best—that's what her father had taught her. Girls who were anything less deserved what they got. Lucy had known on some level that her father had not intended that in such a cruel and personal way…or had she known it? Even now she could not say her father had not meant that as a warning, as a foreshadowing, as a way of laying blame on her for all the hurt and disappointment that he—and ultimately the other men she found in her life—would cause her.

Tears bathed her eyes but did not fall, as if they knew hers was a very private pain not to be shown to the world, ever. Her father had not loved her or cherished her and some small part of her still thought that his coldness was her fault. No wonder she'd always ended up with indifferent or deceitful men in her life. Chubby, plain-faced girls like Lucy deserved no better, or so she had thought. Then she'd met Dwayne.

"You know when I first met him, Dwayne went out of his way to be kind and sensitive." She was talking more for her own comfort than to share with the valet, but she was glad of his nearness so it didn't seem she was having a conversation with herself. "I didn't want to go out with him, but everyone persuaded me… so I went and I really liked him. I liked him a lot."

She strained her neck to see if she could spot his car winding along the narrow path that linked the back parking lot with the front of the club. The headlights of a limousine slashed across her eyes but that was all. She sighed, pivoted, and walked slowly back to where the valet stood.

"I still like him, but he's not the same…not that he's bad or mean or unkind or a cheater like—" She looked away "—like some other men I could name." She bit her lip, knowing she'd said too much, even to someone who did not know her from Adam's Aunt Fanny.

Her father had been a prominent man, and he had flaunted his dalliances with equal prominence. Likewise, Lucy's former boyfriend, Ray Griggs, was well known in his own right for owning a small eatery that was a bit on the shabby side—and for having small, shabby indiscretions.

Dwayne on the other hand had no reputation other than his glory days as a high school jock over a decade ago. Dwayne was not a man of prominence; he didn't own anything but his clothes—even his car was leased. He didn't seem able or interested in holding a job for more than six months at a time, and he still lived with his parents. At twenty-nine that did not add up to a man ready to make a commitment.

What Lucy had initially found endearing in him—his boyish

charm, his willingness to let her make most of the decisions, his carefree approach to everything—now made Lucy wonder if she, in Dwayne, had just found another kind of man she thought she deserved rather than the kind of man with whom she could truly make a life.

Many times she had laid that question before the Lord in prayer and just as many times she had withdrawn it, too afraid to face the answer. She bit her lip again, longing for the days when she had the power and the clarity that came from the prayer circle. How she wished she could go to her friends, gather around the table and laugh and joke and tease—and lay herself open, her real self, for them to pray over and help and love without judging.

But those women had moved on. They all had men in their lives...men who gave them that kind of unconditional acceptance, who supported them, and listened to them. And Lucy was sure that Gayle, Rose, and Naomi thought that she had the same. Otherwise they would be there for her, they would come to her aid and help her. Lucy knew that, just as she knew she could not burden her friends, who were so busy and happy in their new lives, with her silly romantic trials.

Lucy rubbed one open palm over the rich-textured sleeve of her velvet gown, then wrapped her arms over herself until they formed a kind of *X* low over the rounded bulge of her hips and tummy. That did nothing to disguise her figure flaws, but it did somehow make her feel insulated against the sudden chill that had nothing to do with the fall weather.

And Dwayne still had not come.

"Where is he?" Lucy bit her lower lip again, her toe tapping now with all the subtlety of an Irish step dancer.

"Shall I go look for him, ma'am?" The valet's tone rang of formality but just beneath the surface Lucy detected pity ..or was it condescension? Or perhaps just a tinge of desperation in wanting to get away from her and her incessant babbling.…

Shaking her hair back, she straightened and spoke in that detached way her mother had always used with club staff. "No, please don't bother. He's probably stopped to adjust the rearview mirror just so or to listen for an update on the game." Lucy did not know *what* game, but it was a November Saturday in the South: there was always a game, and Dwayne would want an update. "He'll be right along, I'm sure."

"Whatever you say, ma'am."

This time she returned his curt nod, but that did nothing to change her feeling that he viewed her as a pudgy, unhappy, blathering idiot all dressed up and abandoned on the club steps on the night of the Belle Gala.

The notion put her in mind of Miss Grace and the story Naomi had told earlier. Lucy put her hand over her heart. Grace's tale had touched her more than she had let on to the others—more, perhaps, than she had even let on to herself.

Waiting for a man who would never come. That's how Naomi had described young Grace Grayson. How sad, how unfair, how…familiar. Lucy struggled to stand straight and breath evenly for a moment, then swallowed down her emotions and allowed herself to admit that Naomi's words were very much how she might describe herself.

Not that she thought Dwayne Cobb had run off and was never going to return to take her home. No, he'd be here shortly. The kinship she felt with Grace Grayson was much deeper, more symbolic…because Lucy knew that even when the young man she'd been dating for the past eight months drove up to claim her, he still would not be the man she'd been waiting for all her adult life.

And so it was that when Dwayne finally came tooling up in

his two-year-old, leased four-wheel drive, with his tuxedo jacket thrown in the backseat, his tie undone, and the local high school football game blaring from the radio, Lucy marched straight up to him and said, "Dwayne Cobb, take me straight home. You and I are through; whatever romance might have been between us is over."

"Man, am I glad that's over!" Ted slouched into the green brocade wingback chair beside the bed that dominated the room.

"Ted, honey, you're getting all wrinkled."

"Hey, none of us are getting any younger."

"I mean your tuxedo." Gayle laughed at his grumbled words. She moved over to her husband, her open palms pressing gently over his wide, muscular shoulders to ease away his classic-cut, black jacket.

Ted leaned forward and worked out one arm, then the other, enabling her to whisk off the coat.

How she loved this man, Gayle thought as she helped him from the coat. She loved him with all the warmth of a friend, the faith of a fellow believer, and the passion of a lover. While from time to time in their twenty-year union the passion had waned, the friendship and faith had always remained a constant. That proved especially important last year when an old secret, an old love, and Gayle's old insecurities had threatened the life she and Ted shared.

Their love—aided by Ted's wonderful sense of humor and his keen feel for priorities and perspective—had prevailed. Now things were quiet and content again in their home… though sometimes too quiet with their oldest daughter off at college, their son entering his teens and having seemingly been swallowed up by his chaotic room, and their nine-year-old daughter involved in soccer, ballet, and trying to set a record for whispering with friends on the telephone. Still, Gayle couldn't complain. They'd weathered the storm, as the saying goes, and from now on she expected smooth sailing.

She draped Ted's jacket over her arm. It still held his warmth, and she paused to savor the clean scent of him on it. As she drew it in, it seemed to awaken her senses, emotions, and memories. She thought of how charming Ted had been on their first date, how handsome he had looked on their wedding day, how thoughtful he had been when their first child had been born. Time had only enhanced those qualities in him, she thought. Yes, she loved this man and thanked God routinely that he felt the same way about her.

On impulse, she bent to place a kiss on her husband's head.

He flinched.

Gayle withdrew slowly.

"Sorry, sugar, you took me by surprise." Ted reached back without a glance and patted her fingers, which lay curled against the taut cords along the side of his neck.

Gayle blinked down at him, seeing him now not as she envisioned him but as he really was: a grayish pallor seemed to lurk beneath the tan that always lingered long into fall thanks to his love of outdoor sports. Lines fanned downward from the corners of his mouth, as though his face had been set in a grim mask too long and the skin had not quite smoothed out again. His hair, which he had worn in the same style for over a decade, needed cutting—not just a trim, but a good shaping up—and his shoulders had a slump that was not in keeping with Ted's normal carriage or his attitude.

Gayle frowned. Why hadn't she noticed all of this before? Had she been too busy or had she simply chosen to ignore that something was definitely not right with her husband? Her pulse pounded thick and dull in her ears.

Ted seemed not to notice her scrutiny—or even her presence, for that matter—but simply stared off into space, his large hands grinding his fist to his palm between his open knees. He was worried about something, that much was clear, but Gayle could not guess what. Money and work came immediately to mind, and just as quickly she dismissed them.

If there were a problem of a financial order, Ted would see to it. She'd known him too long to doubt that. He would never let it get out of hand enough to cause him this kind of concern. She'd bet her lifestyle on it—in fact, she *had* considering that Ted took care of everything to do with their finances. No, it was not something of that nature that had him glaring into the spacious walk-in closet as if it were some kind of oracle that might give him the answers he needed.

Well, if it wasn't about work or money, Gayle concluded, her heart racing and her stomach turning sour, that only left something of a personal nature.

We're none of us getting any younger. The words he had thrown at her earlier floated into her mind, and she wondered if his mood could be related to that touchy subject—and if so, what did it all mean?

"Ted?" Her voice cracked. She cleared her throat. "Ted, honey, are you all right?"

He sighed as if the weight of the world had him pinned to that antique wingback chair. "Yeah, I'm just dandy."

Tossing his jacket aside, she moved around in front of her husband.

His heavy lids hid his eyes from her view. He kept his head down and to the right. His profile cut a dark contrast against the stark white of his dress shirt, showing his strong jaw set in that way that told Gayle he was in no mood to talk.

But she could not just let this be. She moved closer, her hands clenched together just below the hollow of her throat, like someone staving off a chill. "Ted?"

"I'm just tired, all right?" he snapped. "Can't you leave it at that?"

"You're always tired anymore," she whispered, amazed she could force out even a squeak past the cold constriction in her chest.

"Maybe I'm sick or something," he said more as one might say "Maybe I'll have a tuna sandwich" rather than someone expressing real concern. Then he lifted his head and stroked his chin. "You know I never really have fully recovered from throwing my shoulder out trying that new serve the tennis pro thought would improve my game."

Gayle seized on that weak excuse and relaxed a little. That was all it was, of course, just a general feeling out of sorts, not healing as he thought he should, that kind of thing. She smiled. "Well, you're not a kid anymore, Ted. It takes longer to get over a thing like that when you're forty-t—"

"That's an age, Gayle, not an illness. I said I thought maybe I'm coming down with something, not that I'm falling totally apart." He glared at her through narrowed eyes.

Gayle gripped her hands together, winding them into a knot until the diamond of her engagement ring gouged her knuckle. Ted rarely spoke so harshly to her and never over something this trivial—which could only mean what was bothering him wasn't trivial at all.

She blinked, then searched Ted's face, then blinked again. She wanted to speak but had no idea what to say that would not make him angry or let loose a floodgate of her tears. So she just stood there, willing him to say something.

As if he heard her silent plea, Ted sighed, scrubbed his

hands over his face, then stood. With one staggering step forward, he pulled her roughly into his arms and held her to him as if she were his anchor in a windswept sea. He kissed her temple, her hair, her temple again.

"I'm sorry, Gayle. I'm sorry, sugar. I didn't mean to snarl at you like that. I'm just tired. Really, that's all it is. I'm just very, very tired."

Gayle wrapped her arms around him, her hands flat against his broad back. She felt the rise and fall of his chest in a laborious breath, felt the bone-deep weariness in his body and his being. She combed her fingers back through his shaggy hair and returned his kisses, murmuring tenderly as she did, "It's all right, honey. It's all right. You'll just rest this weekend, then. You'll feel better after that. Everything will be better next week. Everything will be all right."

"Pssst. Pssst. Rose? Rose are you ready?" Naomi tapped lightly at Rose's condo door. She shifted her gaze left to right, taking in the well-lit courtyard, the tingle of anticipation coursing through her almost giddy mood.

"C'mon, Rose, time's a wastin'." She lifted her hand to knock again, but the door swung inward, leaving her fist frozen in the air.

"I sworn, Naomi, this is one of the craziest whims you've ever tried to drag me into." There was a twinkle in Rose's eye and a grin on her lips that belied her protest.

"What's so crazy about it?" Naomi tugged Rose across the threshold by one sweater sleeve. "The moon is full, the air is brisk, my husband and your gentleman friend are safely tucked away in their respective homes. It's the night of the Splendor Belle Gala, romance abounds, mischief is afoot, and Miss Grace

Grayson-Wiley may or may not be sitting out there on her porch swing in her mother's made-over wedding gown awaiting a specter from the past. Don't tell me you're not just itching to go out there and see for yourself?"

Rose's brow crimped down in a show of concern. "You really are just chocked plumb full of nonsense, aren't you?"

"Fun and nonsense." Naomi stuck out just the tip of her tongue and wrinkled up her nose. "Right up to my eyeballs."

"Well, that certainly explains a lot." Rose stepped fully outside. Her door fell shut with a ground-rattling thump behind her.

"Explains what?" Naomi suspected her friend was setting her up as the brunt of a joke, yet she was happy to play along.

"If you are up to your eyeballs in nonsense that explains why you can't see what's what." She jabbed the key in the lock and churned it until the deadbolt clacked into place.

"What's *what*?" Naomi jangled her own keys as they both started down the sidewalk. "I have no idea what you are talking about."

"This!" Rose waved her open hands between them. "When William flat out refused to drive by the old Grayson place on the way to take me home, explaining that that story was all an old fairy tale and held no credence and that it was rude to go out gawking, to boot, that wasn't good enough for you. So you hatch a wild plan, and now we've ditched our dates to go out into the dead of night to spy on some sweet, unsuspecting little old lady who is probably tucked safely in her bed—just to satisfy our own petty curiosities. Don't you think that's just a little bit odd?"

"First of all, ten o'clock is *not* the dead of night." Naomi held up one finger, then another. "Secondly, I've heard Grace Grayson-Wiley referred to as many things, none of them sweet or happy."

Rose chuckled.

Naomi jerked open the passenger door and stared at her dear friend over the gleaming, blue roof.

"And thirdly?"

"And thirdly—" Naomi swung her gaze in the general direction of Sweet Haven. She saw only darkness but she knew the house was out there and so, she believed, was Grace.

Poor, little, shriveled-up Grace, with her dashed hopes and dilapidated house. The story of her loss and the shattering consequences of it had always fascinated Naomi, though for most of her life she had only known the basic outline of what had happened. When she'd told her new husband, Taylor, as much, he'd supplied more details, all of which he'd learned, he'd told her, from his father, who had gone to high school with Miss Grace. The new information shed no light on what had really happened or gave any real insight into the woman. What it did do was whet Naomi's interest even further in the gnarled lady that now lived alone at Sweet Haven.

You know the truth, Lord, that Grace is not the only reason I want to do this so badly. Naomi bit her lip. *But I can't tell Rose about that yet. Not until I know for sure my plan has some merit. Please guide me in my understanding and help us to choose the right course of action should the time come.*

"And *thirdly?*" Rose thrummed her fingers on the car roof.

"And thirdly…" Naomi gritted her teeth, then opened her mouth to say more, then clamped her jaw tight again. She forced out a huff that made a faint cloud of moisture in the evening air. "Do you want to do this or not?"

"Oh, I *want* to do this." Rose popped open the driver's door. "I just want it on the record that what we are about to do *is* a little bit weird, sneaky—and totally none of our business."

"Agreed." Naomi bobbed her head in a crisp nod.

"Good." Rose did likewise. "Now, let's get moving before it gets too late and Grace goes inside."

Three

"Turn off your headlights, Rose."

"Naomi, that's not safe. What if we hit a tree or a small animal or something?" Rose let her big car coast down the dirt road. Now that Sweet Haven was in sight, they did not want to take any chances of scaring off Miss Grace, if she was, indeed, out on her porch. Rose had not expected her stomach to feel so knotted or her mouth to go so dry over the simple little escapade. She *had* expected to find the old house shut up tight and dark, but when she saw the light shining from the large, wraparound porch, her imagination and her pulse had begun to race.

"Just ease your car up into the drive so we can see her better. And put on your parking lights. That'll be safe enough."

"Your ideas are going to get us arrested one day, Nomi, do you know that?" Still, Rose did as requested. "I can see the banner headline on the *New Bethany Morning Messenger* now: 'Local Busybodies Jailed in Late-Night Stalking Incident.'"

"Oh, I keep telling you, Rose, it's not *that* late."

"Funny. Hope you still have that sense of humor when you have to use your one phone call to tell your husband you're—"

"Rose! I saw something move. I definitely saw something on the porch. Now you *have* to pull into the drive just a bit so we can confrim it."

"The only thing I am confirming is that we are getting out of here. It was a silly idea in the first place. I'm sorry I ever got involved." Rose whipped into the drive, with only the parking lights on—strictly, she told herself, as a courtesy to Miss Grace, who might be alarmed at the sight of headlights slashing across the front of her house at this hour.

But then, in that brief moment when they sat facing the stately home that had once been the grandeur called Sweet Haven, Rose *did* see something.

Someone who didn't know any better might have suspected they'd just seen a ghost. The figure seemed so unreal, swathed in pale netting and lace and ruffles from head to tiny feet— which, by the way, dangled from the porch swing like those of a small child. But Rose had lived in New Bethany long enough to know what she was seeing was real.

"We shouldn't have come tonight, Naomi." Rose backed the car up.

"But don't you see—"

"I see we shouldn't have come." Rose gritted her teeth and flipped her headlights back on. She gripped the wheel to make a hard turn to put them back on the road to her condo, fighting a growing sense of shame as she did so. They had intruded where they did not belong. No matter what they knew, or what they *thought* they knew, of Miss Grace Grayson-Wiley's story, Rose did know this: the old women deserved better from two good Christians than being the object of their gawking—especially at what must be for her a private and likely painful moment. "Nothing we found here proves anything, Naomi. That's all there is to it, and I don't want to talk about it anymore."

They drove off in silence, but Rose could not shake the image that, in her mind, was "haunting" the crumbling porch of the old mansion. She thought that as long as she lived she would recall in vivid detail the tiny woman sitting on the porch swing, a coffee cup in her hand, her legs swinging back and forth to create a rocking rhythm.

Grace Grayson-Wiley's dingy, white dress, with it's gaping collar, tight bodice, and an array of bulges that could not be caused by any human body, had looked less like something Grace had put on and more like it had opened up at the neckline and swallowed her whole. The skirt, with its tiers of lace and ruffles, angled out abruptly—as though she was wearing a birthday cake around her hips. Her petticoat hung down below the skirt, something Rose might not have known except that the thing was many, *many* layers of stiff, pink netting that made a lovely transition between the white gown and the old woman's worn, red tennis shoes. A stole had swirled around Grace's arrow-straight back and narrow shoulders and pooled in her lap, rhinestones winking in the moonlight from the frothing tulle. The hat atop the figure's white hair looked part pillbox, part feathered fantasy. It had been set at a forward slant, weighed down, Rose assumed, by the huge glittering brooch and two dove figures fastened to its brim.

The sight should have made her laugh, but how could she do so at someone else's misfortune? Especially when, just at the moment Rose had lifted her gaze to peek in on Grace's long-standing, legendary, Belle Gala tradition, she could have sworn the old gal lifted up her coffee cup as if to make a toast—right in Rose's and Naomi's direction?

"She was out there, I tell you, Gayle. Grace Grayson was on her porch swing, or at least, I think it was her. Anyway, someone was out there." Naomi's simple leather tennis shoes padded lightly over the old blue-and-white checkerboard flooring of Dot and Daughters' Cafe as she rushed up to the table where her best friend waited. "I am so glad you called to invite me to lunch today, because I think I would have just about busted a gut if I had to wait any longer to tell you about what we saw Friday night."

Naomi slid into the booth, plunking down her purse and slipping off her jacket even as she hurried on with her story. "You see, Will got all in a snit when we asked him to drive us by Sweet Haven. Don't ask me what *that* was all about, I don't know, but—"

"Are you ladies ready to order or do ya'll need a minute to look things over?" A raw-boned waitress with hair that looked like an old baby doll's—too frizzy in some places, too perfectly coiled into pin curls in others, and smooshed flat in the back—loomed over their table. Naomi recognized the woman as one of the daughters for which the cafe was named, but she couldn't remember which one.

"I just want the barbecued beef sandwich with the slaw on the side and an order of fries with white gravy." Naomi pushed up her sweater sleeve. "Oh, and iced tea to drink. Gayle?"

Gayle folded up the menu, looking for all the world as though it were a tiring chore to do so, tucked it into the silver holder at the back of the booth, then turned to the waitress. In a voice soft as a purring kitten but cultured enough to lend her words complete authority, Gayle ordered a grilled cheese sandwich and tea.

The waitress told them she'd be out with their tea straight away then lumbered off.

Naomi recognized the stiff-backed reserve in her old friend and knew it meant Gayle was not happy about something. Perhaps she had invited Naomi here for some reason beyond pure friendship—to scold her for marring the idealized reminiscing on the night of the Belle Gala by dredging up old town gossip, for example.

Naomi gulped back a long draw of air and shut her eyes to

focus her concentration. She hadn't come here to get a talking to, nor had she come to argue with her friend. Most of Naomi's life she'd had a rabid curiosity about Grace and Sweet Haven. Now that she finally had some firsthand knowledge of Grace, albeit from a distance, she was not going to let Gayle's prim and proper side tamp down her excitement. Opening her eyes again, she flashed her friend a toothy smile then plunged back into her anecdote full throttle.

"Anyway, the thing is, Will went positively macho-caveman, 'I-said-I'm-not-driving-you-by-there-and-that's-that' on us. I needled him, and Rose worked her feminine wiles on him as best she could with Taylor and me in the backseat catcalling and making kissing noises." She paused to see if that solicited a smile from her lunch companion. Gayle pressed both hands down over a white paper napkin on the table.

Naomi scowled. "But no matter what we tried—and we tried everything short of clunking Will over the head and commandeering his Cadillac—he wouldn't drive past Sweet Haven. Finally Taylor said there wasn't any sense in us riling him up any further and risking giving the poor man a heart attack, this being the night of Belle Gala when every doctor in town, save a large-animal vet and a podiatrist who got weaseled into covering the ER, was at the country club."

Gayle folded the napkin accordion style, making tiny, precise pleats.

Naomi sighed. "The end result of all this was that after we all got home, I called Rose and went back over to her condo so we could go on our own to see if the story was true. And Gayle, I'm telling you, sure as I'm sitting here—it is!"

"Hmm." Gayle nodded slowly as if she were taking it all in, but her eyes did not meet Naomi's.

"Gayle, did you hear me? I just sat right here and told you

that Rose and I saw Grace Grayson-Wiley on her porch last night."

The waitress returned to place two tall glasses of tea before them. "Sandwiches will be ready any minute. Straws?"

"No, thank you." Naomi waved away the offer of two paper-covered straws pinched tight in the women's work-roughened fingers.

"Can I get you anything else?"

"No." Naomi waved her hand again, realized that it looked like someone shooing off a pest, then forced a smile. "No, thank you, we're fine."

Obviously their waitress did not want to leave, but could not find a legitimate way to linger, so she moved on slowly...so slowly that she actually remained within earshot for several moments.

By then Gayle had begun to shred the napkin into long, filmy strips.

Naomi gritted her teeth. Hoping to both exclude the nosey waitress and to draw Gayle out of that grumpy stewing over their less-than-magical gala evening, she leaned across the table and lowered her voice to a whisper. "Like I said, we *saw* Grace last night. That is, I think it was her. You know how the house sits back from the road at the end of that beautiful tree-lined drive? It made it pretty hard to be sure who was out there, but for my money, it looked like little old Miss Grace. Rose wasn't so sure—but even she had to admit we saw someone, and that someone was all dressed up in something frothy and yellowed white."

"Uh-huh." Gayle sort of sighed out the response. The napkin lay in tatters on the table. She picked up one torn strip and tore it lengthwise again.

Naomi ducked her head, trying in vain to catch Gayle's distracted gaze. "I thought the vision we saw must be a giant white rabbit or perhaps a polar bear in a net tutu come to pay his respects at Sweet Haven." Gayle did not even so much as blink at Naomi's outrageous explanation. "However Rose was more of the school of thought that it was merely a quivering tower of shaving cream and toilet paper, as we so often see growing wild in the rural parts of Tennessee. This one had a big old mum corsage stuck on it as a festive fall decoration."

"Um, hmm, yes, I see."

"Gayle Shorter Barrett!" Naomi slammed her open palm down on the chipped tabletop. "You haven't heard a *word* I've said. Ever since I got here, you've been off in your own little never-never land. Now, if you are still pouting because I ruined your trip down memory lane at the Belle Gala Friday night—"

Gayle jerked her head up and the look in her eyes stopped Naomi cold. A shiver of apprehension rippled through Naomi. This wasn't about the Gala or ruining an evening. No doubt about it: whatever was wrong with Gayle was something big. Very big.

Gayle had asked her dearest friend here today for one reason and one reason alone—and it wasn't to pout or to hear about some loony old lady. She'd come because she needed a friend, one who would not judge or dismiss her feelings as foolish but would listen. And who, when that listening was done, would do whatever she must to help. Toward that end, Gayle took in a deep breath, looked Naomi in the eye, and gave voice to the fear she had grappled with all weekend. "Naomi, honey, I think Ted is having an affair."

"An a—" Naomi blinked, her mouth gaping. "Gayle, no. Not Ted. That simply can not be true."

"Obviously it *can* be, because it is." Gayle had no way of preparing herself for the impact saying it aloud would have on her. She'd thought it often enough these last two days, pondered it, dismissed it, then taken it up again and fretted over it some more. But she had never let her fears out and now that she had, they seemed all the more real.

For an instant she considered pushing away from the booth and getting out of there, but her arms and legs felt suddenly too heavy to let her make a clean getaway. Her head spun. Her throat burned. She reached for her glass of tea but found her hand trembling so that she did not trust herself to lift the drink without making the ice clink against the sides, which would only accentuate how very out of control she felt right now.

Naomi must have seen Gayle's hesitant tremor because she immediately clutched Gayle's hand in her own, giving firm squeeze to show her support. "I can't believe it. Ted?" Naomi shook her head. "How did you find out? Were there phone calls from a strange woman? Ted working outlandish hours with only flimsy excuses to cover it? Did you follow him and catch him in the act, as it were?"

"No, no, none of that." None of that indeed, Gayle thought, questioning for the millionth time the line of reasoning which had lead her to this conclusion. "None of those typical things."

"Well, what then? That's a pretty serious accusation to make without some kind of hard evidence, isn't it?"

"I have evidence." Her claim rang hollow, even in her own ears. Gayle tugged her fingers free from Naomi's grasp.

"What evidence?" Naomi hunched forward, her expression fixed like someone trying to force together pieces of a puzzle that just would not quite fit.

Gayle knew how she felt.

"Did you find something? A lipstick smudge? A motel bill?

A love letter from the other woman? What evidence?"

"A feeling," Gayle said with more conviction than she could have supposed she still had.

"A feeling? A…feeling?" Naomi paused a moment, gave her head a sharp shake as if snapping out of a fog, then began to chuckle. She leaned back and spread her arms out across the back of the booth. "You really had me going for a minute there, Gayle, I thought you were serious."

"I *am* serious, Nomi." Gayle used the nickname Naomi's mother always used to somehow underscore to her friend just how serious she was. "I've given this a lot of thought. In fact, I haven't thought of anything else all weekend."

Naomi's eyes grew somber; she folded her hands together. "Well, you sure didn't seem to be thinking this way at the country club the other night. At least you never gave any indication of it, and I'd think if you were having those kinds of suspicions you wouldn't have been able to keep it from us, not after all we've been through together."

"If you must know, I got this notion right after the party." Gayle swept one fingertip down the length of her tea glass. "When Ted and I were alone in our room—"

"Oh, my goodness! You aren't assuming this because he's suddenly not interested in…you know?"

"Naomi, honey, he is not interested in *anything*." Gayle flicked away a bead of water. "This has nothing to do with our intimate relationship. This has to do with him and the way he's acting."

"How's he acting?" Naomi tossed back her dark hair.

"Different." With that one word she suddenly realized she'd summed up the pivotal point of her concerns.

"Different? That's it? Pretty scant substantiation, isn't it?"

"Nuh-uh. No. Not to me it's not." Gayle knotted her hands

in her lap and leaned forward until the table's edge cut across her upper body. Her voice came out in a harsh whisper. "Naomi, I have known this man for half my life and if there is anything I can count on in this world it's that Ted Barrett will always act the same."

"Is that all?"

"Is that *all*?"

"My word, Gayle, the man is forty-two, maybe he's just—"

"Having a midlife crisis? And you don't have to watch too many daytime talk shows or read more than a couple ladies' magazines to know what *that* means."

"Absolutely nothing. And for the record I was going to say maybe he's acting different because he just wanted a change of pace."

"Well, that's a pretty way of putting it, it still adds up to—"

"Nothing."

"Do you think?" Gayle straightened, and the booth seat sighed beneath her shifting weight.

"You know I do, and you know that's why you invited me here and blurted it out like that." Naomi picked up her glass and took a long drink of tea.

Gayle found herself holding her breath, waiting for her friend to finish her explanation. When Naomi set the glass down with a solid thud, Gayle exhaled and wet her lips, then prompted, "That's why I invited you here…?"

"Don't you see, Gayle? You don't really believe Ted is having an affair, and you just wanted me to confirm how silly the idea is. So you tossed it out on the table and counted on me to dismiss it for you. Well, I am." She patted Gayle's hand. "It's not true."

Gayle wanted to believe that. She drew in the aroma of the cafe…pine cleaner mingled with abhorrently strong coffee splashed onto the pot warmer, the occasional waft of cigarette smoke carried through from the back room on the waitress' stained aprons. Gayle wanted with all her heart to be reassured that her wildest fears had no merit. She sighed. "Times like these I desperately miss our little prayer circle."

"I know what you mean."

"I remember last year at Thanksgiving when I needed ya'll so much, and I came dashing into Rose's kitchen all upset and confused. I sought you out because I knew you wouldn't hate me for my past mistakes. You wouldn't judge me, but you wouldn't be fooled by me, either—or take anything less than honest emotion from me. And when I couldn't tell you exactly what was going on, you accepted that and were ready to help me anyway." Gayle swallowed hard, wishing that would alleviate the lump lodged high in her throat. "Just knowing you all would put aside everything for a while and pray for me—I don't think I ever told you how much that meant to me, how much I drew on your strength and faith at that time."

"You didn't have to," Naomi murmured. "That was the beauty of our group. We already knew how much we meant to one another, how much we could count on one another—and we all had to rely on that more than once last year."

"I miss it."

"Me, too."

"We should never have stopped meeting." Gayle wondered if her motives were selfish, stemming out of her concerns about Ted more than for the group as a whole. She dismissed that idea. She really did wish the group had stayed together, no matter what.

Naomi nodded slowly. "I've thought the same thing time and again. In fact, I think we should start it up again."

"But the town already has active prayer groups this year."

"I'm not saying we start up an official group, Gayle, but that we should do something on our own."

A light flickered in Naomi's eyes, which put Gayle on alert: Naomi was cooking something up in that mischievous brain of hers, and she was going to try to drag the whole group into it.

"What we need—" Naomi gestured like the leader of a symphony playing *pianissimo*. Her hushed voiced hummed with excitement as she finished "—is a project."

"A project?" Gayle practically yelped the term. "Like what?"

"Well, I don't know yet—but something will come up, I'm sure of it."

"I've got a suggestion. Maybe we could take up a twenty-four-hour prayer vigil for my marriage." She'd meant it to be a joke, but as the words left her mouth, the old anxiety overtook her.

"Your marriage is fine." Naomi shook her head.

"Do you think?"

"I *know*."

"But still…" Gayle chewed on her lower lip, tapping one fingernail against the rim of her glass. "If Ted isn't having an affair then what is going on with him? Why is he so tired all the time? So, restless, so…unfocused?"

"Hmmm. That's a good question. Have you asked him?"

"Of course I asked him. It was the very first thing I did." Gayle clucked her tongue.

"And he said?"

Gayle finally felt steady enough to take a drink and a little bit embarrassed at her overreaction to this whole mess with Ted. She let the sweet tea fill her mouth then bathe her parched throat with soothing coolness, shutting her eyes to savor it before she had to make herself look like even more of a ninny to her friend.

"Gayle?"

She lowered her glass and swished the liquid around the melting chunks of ice. "He said it was nothing—that maybe he was just coming down with something."

"Well, maybe he *is.*"

"Well, *maybe* he is."

Naomi laughed aloud. "You'll see, sugar. In a day or two that sweet husband of yours will be flat on his back, running a fever, and running you ragged with requests for cold cloths and warm drinks, and whining out 'fluff my pillow' and 'don't leave me here alone, I'm bored.'"

"Gee, you promise?" Under her sarcastic tone, Gayle secretly hoped Naomi's prediction was on the money.

"I reckon." Naomi smiled. "Ted'll be sick as a dog, and you'll be happy as a hog on ice."

Gayle raised one eyebrow and sloshed her tea around again. "Yes, well, that's *always* been my highest aspiration. A hog on ice."

"No, ma'am, grilled cheese on white." The waitress plunked down a small red plastic basket with thin paper rustling around a golden crisp cheese sandwich. "And the barbecue for you. Side of slaw and fries with gravy."

Plunk. Plunk. Plunk.

Naomi looked down at her order as though she had no idea where it had come from and what she was supposed to do with it now that it had arrived. Her face paled.

"I'll be back with a pitcher to refill your tea in a minute. Need anything else?"

Gayle smiled at Dot's eldest daughter with the same measure of grace and refinement she would have shown a member of the royal family. "No, thank you, hon, we're just fine. This all looks delicious." It did, too. For all its greasy spoon tendencies,

Dot and Daughters' had some of the best food in town. "Doesn't this look delicious, Naomi?"

Naomi nodded but the color from her neck to her forehead could have competed with the heavy gravy ladled over her French fries for pasty grayness. "It looks—" She cleared her throat and managed to squeak out the last bit "—just yummy."

Their waitress harumphed and lurched away.

Gayle reached out to put on hand on her friend's wrist. "You okay, sugar?"

Naomi opened her mouth, then shut it again, then opened it, her gaze glued to the food before her. "You know what, Gayle?"

"What?" It would have been rude not to ask, even though she wasn't sure she really wanted to know whatever Naomi was about to share.

"When Ted told you he was coming down with something, I'd have believed him if I were you."

"Oh?"

"Uh-huh—because I think maybe I've got the same thing. I mean, I was tired all weekend and generally out of sorts."

"And now?" Gayle eyed her friend with extreme caution.

"And now it's gotten…suddenly worse. I think maybe I'd better have this put in a to-go box and take it home." She glanced down at her food. "If you don't mind."

"Of course not. If you're not well, you get yourself home and lie down. Can you drive?"

Naomi stood and took a deep breath, then nodded. "Yes, I feel fine except when I look at this food. I guess whatever this bug is, it's in the early stages. Maybe you should head home, too, to check on Ted. Sounds like he had it every bit as bad as I do."

In short order, Naomi and Gayle had motioned to the busboy clearing the table next to theirs, placed their orders in take-out boxes, paid their checks at the counter, and said good-bye in the parking lot, promising to try again after whatever was going around had been around. Gayle climbed into her minivan and drove off.

That was when Naomi realized she'd left her jacket inside. Muttering to herself for her forgetfulness lately, she trudged back toward the door—only to meet with their waitress standing directly in her path.

"Left this." The waitress shoved the jacket toward Naomi.

"Thank you, we sort of had to leave in a hurry."

"Nothing wrong, I hope."

"No…just…" Naomi shrugged, no point going into it with a total stranger. "Um, thank you for bringing my jacket out to me."

"Well, that's the way folks around here are. If there's something nice they can do for another, they'll pretty much always jump in an' do it."

"Uh-huh." Naomi slipped on her jacket, wondering if the woman was waiting around for a tip. It would seem an insulting gesture to make after her observation about doing nice things for each other. "That's what I like about this small town—everyone goes out of their way to be friendly and helpful—most of the time."

The waitress smiled.

Naomi felt in her jacket pocket for a stray dollar bill, thinking it would be good to have ready. Still, she got the distinct impression the woman had something besides a tip in mind.

"Anyway, thanks again." Naomi started to turn away.

"You know ma'am, I couldn't help overhearing you mention Miss Grayson-Wiley's name."

Naomi tensed. "Yes?"

"I just wondered how well you knew the old gal?"

The bald-faced truth—"I don't know her at all, I've just been spying on her"—just did not seem the way to go in this instance, so Naomi flicked a curl away from her ear and smiled. "Well…how well does anyone know Miss Grayson-Wiley, really?"

The waitress nodded and gave a gruff huff of agreement.

Naomi's shoulders eased down in relief.

"I guess the thing is, the reason I asked at all is that, well, she's fired her girl again."

"Her girl?"

"The one that niece of hers had hired to look in on her."

Naomi did not have the heart to admit that she had no idea what the waitress was talking about so she just nodded. "Oh, *that* girl. Yes, the one Grace's niece hired. Hmmm. Well, that's a shame."

"Ain't so much of a shame. Those girls that niece hires ain't never no good. Not a one of 'em lasted more'n six months—not that it would be easy to tend after Miss Grace, no sir. You know yourself, I suppose, that puny runt of a woman can be cantankerous as all get out."

"I can imagine." That was no lie, Naomi could imagine that Miss Grace might be a scrapper if push came to shove—she would have to have been to have survived all these years in less-than-ideal circumstances.

The waitress folded her arms, unfolded them, then folded them again. She was definitely working up to something. Naomi thought about pleading ill and making a getaway while she still could, but the fresh air had cleared away the last of her nausea. Besides, her curiosity about Grace won out over her vague apprehensions.

"The thing is, ma'am, that with the girl gone now Miss Grace ain't got a soul to take her Sunday dinner on Saturdays."

"Her Sunday dinner on—?"

"We fix it up for her here on Saturday, and she warms it over for her big meal on Sundays. Had that arrangement since before my mother retired in '85."

"Oh, really?"

"Usually there's a spare waitress or busboy about who can take it to her until the niece hires a new girl, but with the holidays on us and all, well, I can't spare the help."

"I see." In fact, a very clear picture was forming in Naomi's mind even as they spoke.

"I figured that if you knew her you might be able to help out—or to take on finding some kindly heart to help out—just until January, or 'til the niece gets someone new in." The waitress stubbed her heavy nurse's shoe against the cracked pavement. "She wouldn't admit it, you know, but Miss Grace needs help. She needs someone to look in on her just now and again, someone who gives a hoot about whether she eats or not, whether she's alive in that big old house all by herself or whether she's gone on to her reward."

"Really?"

"Oh, yeah."

"This is so perfect." Naomi didn't know if it was the onset of the flu or her own enthusiasm, but her pulse picked up a bit. "This is exactly what we need!"

"Beg you pardon, Miz—? Sorry, I didn't think to ask your name before."

"Boatwright. Naomi Boatwright."

"Like the nursery?"

"Yes."

"Kin to William?"

"He's my father-in-law."

"Ah-*ha!*" A broad grin spread across the woman's face like the sun breaking slow over a frosty morning. "That's good then. You'll know how to handle Miss Grace just fine."

Naomi wasn't sure how to respond. William could be a bit of a curmudgeon and ornery, too, but he hardly fit into the same category as caring for someone like Grace Grayson-Wiley.

Still, before Naomi could challenge the notion, the waitress had stuck out her meaty hand. "So, you'll do it? You'll look in on Miss Grace for the next few Saturdays?"

Naomi took the woman's hand and returned the firm handshake. "Consider it taken care of."

"Now, you know Miss Grace can be a handful, so I hope you'll have some help…"

Naomi smiled broadly. "Don't you worry. I'll have all the help I need."

"Miss Lew-cy! Miss Lew-cy!" Vhonda Faye Womack, a little bit of a six-year-old with the voice that never seemed to fall below full holler, twanged out in her too-too Tennessee accent. "Baby Ray Junior has went all red in the face and scrunched up, Miss Lucy." Vhonda Faye began hopping up and down on one foot and waving her hands as she beckoned from the doorway. "Even his little ears is all pink on top, and his tiny little mouth is a-movin', Miss Lucy. Miss Lucy, you better get yourself on in here right now before he *busts!*"

On any other day but this Lucy would have calmed Vhonda Faye while strolling placidly over to the infant in question. She would have used her most easygoing tone, cultivated by nearly seven years of owning her own day care, to explain that while eight-month-old Ray Griggs Junior might be working himself up to break loose with an ear-piercing wail, he was *not,* in reality, about to bust. On any other day, that's just what Lucy would have done.

Today? Lucy pushed back one troublesome string of her stick-straight hair—and frowned. Her hair felt wet and matted. She closed her eyes as a dreaded realization swept her.

Finger paint.

Lucy slowly drew her hand away to confirm her fears and grimaced at the red and blue globs of finger paint under her nails and rimming her cuticles. The rest, she could only assume from the dampness against her scalp, remained in a streak plastered from her temple to the back of her head. She gritted out a low groan.

Today, Lucy decided, she would not be one bit surprised if that baby in the next room working himself into a full squalling fit did, in fact, bust.

"Here, Mary Lucille, I'll clean up the paint mess. You go to see about Ray Junior." Rose, who should have gone home twenty minutes ago when they were supposed to have closed up the center, gave Lucy a pat on the back.

"Don't trouble yourself with it, Rose." Lucy shook her head. "You go on home. It looks like Nikki is going to be pretty late picking up her kids and Vhonda Faye, so I'll have plenty of time to clean up. Besides, I'm already a wreck—no sense in both of us having our clothes ruined."

To prove her point, Lucy stretched out the gathered skirt of her dowdy old dress. A reddish-purple grape juice splotch had soaked into the faded lavender T-shirt material and spread into a stain the size of a dinner plate. And now, without meaning to, Lucy had set it off with a nice spattering of paint from her own fingertips.

"I see what you mean." Rose chuckled. "But I still think I'll take my chances and finish the cleanup."

"Rose!" Lucy pinched her skirt between the thumb and forefingers of both hands and waved it in warning.

Rose laughed again and then, in a diversionary tactic so transparent most women could not have carried it off without a stammer or at least a snicker, she tipped back her head and narrowed her eyes. "Lucy, hon? I thought you weren't going to wear those saggy, awful dresses anymore. In fact, I haven't seen you in one since—"

"Since I was dating Ray Griggs." Lucy had bought half a dozen of these dresses when she dated that man, mostly because he said they flattered her. Actually, what he'd said was that these simple, nearly shapeless dresses didn't make her look like she was smuggling hogs in a sack under her skirt—or some such horrid thing. He'd meant that as a compliment, and back then she had accepted it as one.

Lucy scowled. It did not help her mood this day to be wearing this awful dress that reminded her of the woman she had been or that Rose had pointed it out to her. She tightened her jaw but still managed to sound civil when she said, "I haven't worn any of these dresses since Ray left me to marry Nikki, Rose. But I had to today, I didn't have any choice."

"Everything else in the laundry?" Rose walked across the room to grab up a stack of brown paper towels.

Lucy fisted her hands. "If you must know, nothing else fit. I pigged out on snack food and soda all weekend and am now retaining more fluid than the town water tower. I'm bloated and sluggish and look like I'm wearing yesterday's tablecloth. And to top it all off, I have to go in there and tend to the baby of the woman I hired to help me at the day care and the man to whom I devoted four years of my life…the baby that should have been mine but isn't because I stuck to my moral convictions…the baby who's mama is half an hour late—but why should that surprise me when she is *always* late, up to and including all the times she was sleeping with the man I thought I was going to marry."

Lucy didn't realize when her retort had become a rant but she knew it had when she finished and the room felt eerily quiet by contrast. "Rose, I'm—" She took a step toward Rose.

"Oh, Lucy, I understand." Rose opened her arms in an offer of sympathy.

Lucy sighed and took another step, grateful that her friendship with Rose, if not with the others in last year's prayer circle, was still intact. She shut her eyes in anticipation of the comfort of a hug from her dear friend.

"Miss Lucy! Miss Lucy!"

Vhonda Faye's jarring voice pulled Lucy up short.

"I got Baby Ray Junior out of his crib for you and bring him to you." Indeed, she had wrestled the baby from the safety of his crib. Lurching along into the room, she grappled with Ray, whom she held facing forward, both her matchstick arms locked around his middle like someone performing the Heimlich maneuver.

Lucy gasped and rushed toward them. "Vhonda Faye, you should *never* take the baby like that! You're not big enough."

"But I had to, Miss Lucy!" The little girl's whine could have made dogs howl. "On account of he's just about to—"

Lucy heard the baby's strangled gurgle a mere fraction of a second before she saw the milky white liquid, then felt it splatter against her chest, saturating her dress.

"Eeeeewwwww!" Vhonda Faye leapt back to save herself from the sour-smelling fallout so that Lucy, who had both hands securely under Ray Junior's arms, took the whole assault.

Quite in contrast to Vhonda Faye's instinct to distance herself from the sick child, Lucy's well-developed maternal instincts caused her to do just the opposite. Well developed, of course, on everyone's child but her own. Ignoring the stench, the drenched fabric clinging to her upper body, and the warm fluid dripping onto her foot then trickling inside her shoe, she cradled the baby close and began to coo to him, to try to calm his shuddering cries.

"There now, sweet thing, hush, hush. You're all right. You're all right." She kissed his forehead to check for fever. Finding none, she shut her eyes, laid her cheek to his downy soft hair, and sighed.

She heard Rose scrambling to get more paper towels and Vhonda Faye yelling out to Ray Junior's sister, Tiffany Crystal, the details of what had just happened. She heard the door open and close, and sighed again, thanking the Lord that Nikki had finally showed up and could take over the baby's care. Curling the infant closer still to her, she cleared her throat and looked up. "Looks like you got here just in time to miss out on all the excitement—"

There, staring back at Lucy, were the most beautiful brown eyes Lucy had ever seen in a man.

Four

"Gee, if this is what's going on when I've *missed* all the excitement, I suppose I should count my blessings in being held up at the office." The man smiled.

It wasn't his eyes, Lucy decided in a white-hot spark of recognition, not *just* his eyes. It was…She let her gaze trail from his boyish grin to his broad shoulders to his relaxed posture. It was…him.

He wasn't handsome in the sense of someone who could have just stepped off a magazine cover or a professional sports field. No, his was more of a clean-cut, boy-next-door charm that was as much about personality as it was about looks. If Lucy had passed him on the street—as she well might have done in a town the size of New Bethany—she probably would not even have noticed him. Average build, dark brown hair, glasses…nothing to set him apart from dozens of other men around. Still, there was *something*…something that had an immediate impact on her and left her weak-kneed and unable to fully catch her breath.

She tried to swallow, tried to check her breathing, to keep it even and calm…tried to ignore that electrical current that charged the air around this man whose joy-filled eyes and smile went straight for the heart.

Lucy clutched Ray Junior close to her, jiggling him gently. He gurgled and waved his hands, but did not cry or expel anything else, to her relief—though the faint smell of sour soy milk did assault her nostrils.

"Looks like I've caught you at a bad time." He nodded toward the baby in her arms, then laughed—not a nervous, trying to make the best of an awkward situation laugh, but one that came from deep in his chest and reached all the way to the glint in those eyes.

"No, not at all." She murmured the reply without really being aware of what she'd said.

"No?"

She felt her cheeks grow hot and struggled to find a way to make up for her distracted response. She darted her gaze around the room, flitting over the now-tidy row of tiny tables and chairs, the big red and blue tubs heaped high with toys, the paint easels standing silent vigil by the spring meadow wall mural. Comforted by the order of her familiar surroundings, she straightened her shoulders. "That is, it's not a *bad* time, it's more of a, well, routine time. When you deal with young children…"

"Say no more." He held up one hand. "I understand how quickly calm can turn to chaos when you take care of others. I'm a doctor."

A doctor! Lucy could practically hear her mother's approving voice in her head. Not that she was in the market for a man, of course, or that he would be in the market for her—especially in her filthy, fat-day dress and paint-smeared hair.

"Yes, then, you know how it can be." Lucy patted Ray Junior who, now that he had relieved himself of his last meal, had begun to drift off to sleep. "I, uh…can I—"

"Here, Mary Lucille, let me have that baby and get him cleaned up for you." Rose, who seemed to have hustled into the playroom from the nursery without making a sound, reached for Ray Junior. "His mama is bound to be here any second. I'll tend to him, and let you see what the gentleman needs."

Lucy held the baby tight for only an instant before she relinquished him. However much comfort—and camouflage—the infant provided, having a tug of war with Rose over him was definitely not the way to impress any man. *Especially not a doctor,* her mother's voice urged. Lucy handed the baby over, giving him one last kiss to insure she hadn't misjudged his temperature before Rose rushed off.

Now alone in the room with the man, with no baby to provide a distraction, Lucy clamped her arms over her damp chest and shifted her weight. She started to lift her hand to sweep back her hair, remembered the finger paint, and chose, instead, to grip her elbow until her fingertips sank into the soft flesh. "So what—"

"I was—" the doctor began at the same time.

"You first," Lucy suggested magnanimously, since she had virtually no idea what she'd been going to say anyway.

"I was just going to say I'd stopped by to tour your facilities."

"Tour?" Lucy scowled. This was New Bethany. She was Miss Lucy of Miss Lucy's Day Care. Nobody came by to *tour* Miss Lucy's Day Care. Hers was the kind of place that people came to on the high praise of others, not by random selection and the process of elimination. She blinked, wondering if she'd assumed incorrectly. "Tour my day care? Do you mean like a health inspection?"

"No. No, I'm here to look the place over. Personal business. For my kids. I'm trying to find a good day care center for my children."

"I see." She stiffened.

Well, what were the odds of an unmarried doctor walking through her doors and falling madly in love with her anyway? Wouldn't happen. Not to her. Not even on a good day. Not on a flat-tummy day when she had her hair and makeup done to perfection, or rosy, romantic lighting and a million witty, captivating, intelligent things right on the tip of her tongue. The odds were stacked against it happening even on the best day.

"Miss Lucy! Miss Lucy!" Vhonda Faye charged in. "Miss Rose was a-changin' Baby Ray Junior's diaper and he went to squirting like some wild ol' firehose all over the place."

Today, Lucy thought, she not only stood no chance of making a good impression on a man anyway, but whatever impression she did make would not be the stuff of romance novels nor one he'd be likely to forget for a very long time.

"Thank you very much, Vhonda Faye." She caressed the child's chin to reward her for her *helpfulness* then straightened. "You go back in and see if you can help Miss Rose any, okay?"

"Okay, but I ain't a-cleaning *that* up." The child scrunched up her face and marched off, her lopsided ponytail bobbing to her plodding cadence.

"I'll take care of it in a minute," Lucy called after her.

"You're very good with kids."

Lucy turned to find the doctor's gaze holding steady on her, his head tipped just a tad to one side. The intensity in his eyes and set of his mouth made her heart skip, and suddenly she felt he had made a study of her actions and reactions to both the infant waterworks fiasco and Vhonda Faye.

Well, of course he did. He was thinking of putting his children in her care, after all. A man like this doesn't take that kind of thing lightly. Pulling her shoulders up, she put on her best professional demeanor, trusting that she, more than anyone she knew except her own mother, could cover up any stray feelings she might be having and carry on. She pinched at her collar in a gesture that probably better suited an older woman and cleared her throat. "Um, how many children do you have, Dr...?"

"Martin." He held his hand out to her. "Ben Martin."

She looked down for a split second before moving, wondering if she dared let herself touch this beguiling stranger—this beguiling, *married* stranger—for which she had this inexplicable proclivity. *It's a handshake, Lucy*, she scolded herself, *purely a business courtesy. Don't be such a silly-nelly. Just take the man's hand.*

"Lucy Jewell," she introduced herself in a tone as lively as one giving direction to the restroom. "It's nice to meet you, Dr. Martin. I'll be glad to—" She let her hand fit into his, never realizing until she felt the warm *squish* between her palm and his that she still had remnants of paint between her fingers. "Oh! I am so sorry—"

He laughed again and didn't even bother to withdraw his hand from hers, but just held it as intently as he held her gaze. "Don't worry about it, I wash up pretty good."

"I'll bet you *do*." No! She'd said that aloud! She gasped and her mind seemed to short out and all she could think to do was jerk her hand away and wipe it on her skirt. "I mean, as a doctor I'm sure you are very…um…uh…clean."

Oh, yeah, Lucy, you are real *smooth.* Good thing this isn't some single man stopped in for something other than day care business. If that were the case she'd probably make a *complete* fool of herself, she decided with unmerciful sarcasm.

She sighed. As it was, her appearance and behavior had probably only cost the revenue and good references that having a doctor's children there would bring her center.

"Well, I try not to spread too much disease and pestilence in my wake." He chuckled. "Same with my kids. I have two. A boy, almost four, that's Alec, and my daughter, Paige, she's twenty-one months."

"Four and twenty-one months," she repeated in a faraway

tone because she really wasn't sure what she should do with the information. Could it be that this doctor had not entirely ruled her out as a child care provider? She did some lightning-fast calculations as to how two children that age would fit in with the current mix of children at the center. At least, she tried to do some quick calculations, but with the man's near constant gaze…and those eyes, so deep and brown and kind and encouraging…she could not make her mind stay on track.

Lucy clenched her fists, battling back her embarrassment at having such a tangible reaction to this man. She shut her eyes and—all raw nerves, disheveled weariness, and with just enough good manners to sound quite contrite about it—said, "I'm so sorry. Normally, I would happily give you a tour and all the information you might need to make a well-informed decision, but—"

But I don't see how I can possibly take care of your children, her mind wanted to scream out. How could she? How could she see this man on a regular basis and not let her instant attraction to him affect their interchanges? That simply would not be fair, to him, to her, to his children, to the other children—or to his *wife*.

The single, simple word stuck in her chest like a bitter pill lodged halfway. Sad enough she might set herself up to moon over some man who would never really give a girl like her a second look, but the father of two of her charges? She simply could not allow that to happen, not as a good Christian woman, not as a qualified and capable caregiver, not as a frumpy, plump, sympathy-baiting old maid.

And she would tell him as much. Well, not tell him everything, of course, just that she did not see how she could take on his children.

She inhaled deeply. "As I said, normally I would happily

provide you with a tour but I'm afraid that it's just not possible or prudent today." She twisted her hands together, moving her weight from one foot to the other, having suddenly begun to feel like one of her day care babies trying to fudge her way out of the facts. "That is, uh, what with it being after hours and all. And, um, with, well, that is, because of the hectic kind of day we've, uh, had and—"

"Say no more." He held up one hand.

Why hadn't he said that before she started hemming and hawing? But Lucy knew her real anger was at herself for beginning to backpedal. She folded her arms.

"You needn't say another word, Miss Lucy—may I call you Miss Lucy?"

I prefer it to "Foolish, Frumpy, Loser Old Maid," she thought even as she smiled and said, with a graciousness honed in childhood at Saturday afternoon charm school, "Please do."

"Good." He nodded. "Anyway, you needn't bother with the tour or any attempt at salesmanship on my account."

Just as she'd assumed. She doubted the man would put his unwanted pest problem in her care at this moment, much less his beloved Alec and Paige. All for the best, she tried to remember, all for the best. She steeled herself for his outright rejection of her facility and in extension, herself.

"I've already made up my mind about placing my children in your care."

"I suspected as much." She took a step backward and considered it some kind of personal triumph this day that she did not stick her foot in the wastebasket or trip over a wayward toy and land on her well-padded bottom. She held out her hand, hoping to present the air of a model on a game show, offering him the way out with poise and aplomb. "Well, then, if you should decide to—"

"I have decided." His hand grasped hers midflourish, turned it so that he could fit his other hand over hers, and held it there. "It doesn't take a tour or an inspection or even that stack of recommendations I received about this facility to convince me, either. You did that, Miss Lucy."

"I did?"

"Yep. Watching you with those children just now, your kindness and patience, that gentle way of yours that just shines right out from your face and sort of fills up the whole room around you—like a radiance…"

She stared at him, stunned that a man like this would say these things to her and too afraid to actually accept them at face value. No one ever said anything like this to her before—correction, no *man* ever did. Not her daddy nor her boyfriends, not in all their times around her had they ever noticed any such thing about her. Could it be true? Could this man be true? She did not dare hope it. And even if she did, she did not dare cling to it because it really did not mean anything but a passing kindness coming from a married man. In fact, it probably spoke more of him and his basic good nature than it did of her and her…radiance.

"Really, Doctor, I think you're exaggerating a bit, aren't you? You've only just seen me for a few moments—" She tried to pull her hand away.

"A few moments that would have driven other women to a screaming fit, believe me." He would not relinquish his hold on her. "And all right, I will confess I came to New Bethany because I'd heard so much about it and had come to think of it as a sort of haven, a kinder, better place in which to raise my children so I might be coloring you with that same optimistic hue."

She nodded, swallowing hard as she tried to focus on his

words and not the warmth of his touch. "Might be."

"But I don't think so."

"No?"

"No." He shook his head. "In fact I think that I hit the jackpot when I walked through your doors, Miss Lucy. Now, while I know it's after hours for you, I'd like to make an appointment right now to come back another day and finalize the arrangements because I don't think there's anywhere else I'd rather have my children than here. And I don't think there's anyone else I'd rather have caring for them—" those wonderful eyes captured her gaze again "—than you."

Rose eased her shoulders back but it did not work out much of the day's tensions. She guided the car down the long, ambling back road that wound it's way past Sweet Haven and on to her new home. The leisurely route might be just the thing to help her unwind from the overextended work day.

Who'd have thought that she, after practically a lifetime as a homemaker, the quintessential wife and mother, a Sunday school teacher, the twice-chairwoman of every volunteer committee in town, and a renowned hostess for every imaginable charity affair and social event in their small town, would, at this stage of her life, go back to work? And at minimum wage, no less. Rose smiled to herself, savoring the quiet of her smooth riding Caddy after the day of noise and frenetic action at the day care. She loved those kids and, she had to admit, taking a job there had been the perfect tonic to the lack of direction she felt in widowhood and in dealing with her now-empty nest.

Despite marrying at what her mother most delicately referred to as "a well-seasoned age," Rose sometimes felt as if she'd lived all her life as somebody's wife or mother. Not that she didn't love being both of those—she cherished them beyond her ability to put it into words. She would always treasure her memories of her life with her sweet Curry, whom she still thought of and missed quite often even three years now after his death. And not a day didn't go by that she did not pray for and think of her sweet daughters, as well. Stacey, the oldest, who had a job in Atlanta, had been on her own for four years now. Kelley, who had been married last summer to a perfectly lovely young man, had moved to Nashville to set up her own home. Still, no matter how old they got or how far away they went, they would always be the lights of her life, her angels, her treasures, her babies.

But Rose had moved on. She was no longer the woman who had invested so much of herself in the roles of wife and mother that she had allowed them to merge with her given name, so that even her husband, as well as her children, called her their own mingling of *Rose* and *Mommy:* Rommie. It had taken her some time and struggle, but she felt she was finally really untangling herself from a past that no longer suited her or her family. Buying her new condo had been a big step toward that. So had working with Lucy at the day care.

The sky had begun to grow dim now. Much later than she usually got home from work. Every harried moment of the long and hectic day seemed to be seeping into her weary-weighted muscles and heightening the aching in her joints. Rose sighed and flipped on her headlights.

Of course, had Nikki Griggs arrived on time to claim her children and Vhonda Faye, whom she looked after until the child's mother got off work, the day would not have seemed nearly so long. But then again, Rose thought, her mood lightening a bit, had Nikki been on time, they'd have completely missed their visit by that adorable Ben Martin, so it was hard to get too worked up over Nikki's irresponsibility tonight.

Sharp and sudden laughter overtook Rose. "Poor Lucy… poor thing."

The picture sprang to Rose's mind of the younger woman as she'd last seen her, all miswords and mess. Alone now in the car, Rose let herself give in to the kind of giddy laughter that the potent mix of the whole ridiculous fiasco and her own fatigue inspired.

"Poor girl," she reiterated, trying to regain her gentler sensibilities. Forcing aside the ill-mannered impulse to out and out guffaw at it all, Rose cleared her throat and tried to focus on things from Lucy's vantage point.

She shook her head. Life always conspired against Lucy, especially in the presence of men. Or so it seemed. How upsetting for the truly sweet young woman. How frustrating. How…how hilarious!

Rose coughed out a chuckle, knowing it was unkind, unladylike, and un-Christian to let herself give into merriment at her friend's expense. But she couldn't help it—just the image of Lucy, hair streaked with paint and dress blotched by formula and grape juice, trying to carry on a civil conversation with the town's newest doctor brought out the impish little stinker in her. What a way to make a first impression on a man—as only Lucy could.

Fall leaves whirled their way down from the low-hanging branches of the thick trees lining the road. They slapped at Rose's windshield and whistled when they snagged in the wiper blades. Many finally found their way to the road only to come churning back, flung upward by the action of the car's tires.

Drawing in deep the odor of mechanically warmed air, leather upholstery, and the odd mix of paint, baby powder, and canned pasta left over from work, Rose's disposition softened toward Lucy. Such a sweet girl. She only wanted to love and be loved by a decent man and a couple of darling children.

"Is that asking so much, Lord?" Rose rolled her eyes upward for a split second and when she fixed them again on the road, Sweet Haven loomed ahead and to her right.

Sweet Haven. It looked less daunting now in the richness of the autumn dusk…it had seemed almost frightful the other night when she and Naomi had driven past it in hopes of glimpsing Miss Grace in her Belle Gala gown. It also looked less dilapidated now. At night, illuminated by two yellow lights hanging over the wraparound porch that pitched forward at the front steps, the house took on an eerie presence. But now…the stark-white, two-story home with its four chimneys towering over its dull green roof seemed far less formidable and more like the place Rose remembered from her brief time living in it as a boarding house.

They'd only been allowed in certain parts of the house back then: the dining room for meals, the four rented-out bedrooms, and the parlor on Sunday afternoons and holidays. The rest of the home remained closed off and closely monitored by the couple hired by Miss Grace to oversee her property during her absence. She'd been living with her husband in what had then seemed to Rose an exotic urban area back east—Newark, she believed. Even during Miss Grace's brief but tragic marriage— that's how all the women in town of a certain age always spoke of it, "brief but tragic"—Grace had clung to Sweet Haven and ensured it was cared for.

Rose smiled as the car glided on past the entry to the drive, which snaked like a meandering stream toward the house, banked by tall sweet gum maples bursting with yellow leaves. The grounds made the difference, she decided. While darkness had hidden them before, now she could see how carefully kept and surprisingly lush the landscaping around the old place seemed. It made the sagging but still engaging house appear oddly off-balance—like a chipped stone in a platinum setting. Rose frowned thoughtfully. Funny that this old woman who could scarcely care for herself would take such great pains with her landscaping.

Out of pure instinct, not morbid curiosity, Rose told herself, she stole a last quick peek at the house in her rearview mirror. Her eyes honed in on spotting Miss Grace in the side garden, perhaps snipping off the heads of certain flowers for no apparent reason, as the dotty old dear had been known to do. But the garden stood empty, and so Rose sighed and looked ahead.

It was probably not the most benevolent or politically correct thought she'd ever had, but with the very deepest of her heartfelt hopes and emotions, Rose prayed that her friend, Mary Lucille, did not end up like that ornery, old, spry, *nut* of a woman, Miss Grace Grayson-Wiley.

Humming, Rose turned onto the blacktop that would lead her to the condo development on what had once been Grayson land. Her headlights slashed across the white and teal sign proclaiming Bethany Haven Townhomes and she let out a kind of contented, "Aaah."

She had made the right decision in selling the huge house where she had raised her girls and scaling down to her tidy little notch in a row of identical units, all pristine and perfect and energy efficient.

Efficient. That was the watchword for her life now. Cut back and simplified. She did what she pleased when she pleased—eating a sandwich over the sink, if she felt like it, instead of making herself a "proper supper," or staying up until all hours reading or watching television. And no one could tell her to stop, to behave a certain way, or that her actions were disturbing him.

Of course, if William Boatwright had his way, she'd have all those troubles and then some—as his wife.

She stopped at the entrance gate for the watchman to wave her on through. He pointed to the telephone to let her know he was occupied and she gave him a nod to let him know she did not mind waiting.

She had told Will repeatedly that she had no intention of marrying again. Didn't the Bible caution against remarriage, she'd tease him whenever he got too keen on the subject.

"Better to marry than to burn," he had always been quick to quote back to her.

But Rose just wasn't so sure. She'd been married and had gotten it right, such a rare thing, it seemed these days. What assurances did she have that it could occur twice in one life-time? Wasn't it greedy to even want such a thing for herself—especially when someone as wonderful as Lucy could not even seem to get her own turn at marital happiness?

Rose knew, of course, that her case had nothing whatsoever to do with Mary Lucille. Rose was justifying. Justifying because she did not want to think about the implications of marrying again—of losing herself to the role of somebody's wife when she had just learned to embrace her own identity as a person outside of the demands of a husband or children.

The watchman stepped out of his booth and in the flicker-ing light of his small television set, squinted at the decal on her window then flagged her on through the gate. More than one person at church and several of the regulars at her hairdresser's had alluded to the fact that living in a gated community in a town like New Bethany seemed a bit presumptuous. Rose laughed that off. The residents in her small complex were mostly widowed women, and if having some fellow in a blue-and-gray uniform watching black-and-white TV at their perpetually open gate gave them small comfort then what did that matter? Besides, it wasn't as if the place was exclusive or all hoity-toity or as if they were strict about who drove onto their property. Every condo owner was allotted three parking decals, more if they caught the manager in a good mood. Rose had given one to William so he could come in easily to pick her up for outings and had mailed stickers to her girls as well so that they could come and go when visiting.

She rounded the cottage-like clubhouse and its small pool now covered by a black tarp that was sprinkled with fall leaves, then pointed her car directly ahead, ready to slip it into her customary spot right in front of her building.

"Oh, my—" She punched her foot down on the brakes. The tires screeched like a needle skidding on an old record album and the big old Cadillac lurched to a halt that made Rose's head snap forward then upright again. Her pulse made a heavy, stammering beat in her ears as she blinked at the sight ahead of her. "Stacey?"

Could that be her daughter? Here? All the way home to New Bethany, and on a Monday evening no less, with no advance notice? Rose studied the darling little economy car with the Georgia license plates now ensconced in her usual slot. A flutter of movement inside the vehicle indicated a singular, shadowy occupant—then the door popped open a smidgen and the overhead light came on.

"It *is* Stacey." That hard pulse became rabbit fast. Rose felt as if she'd been hurled over a ledge, her stomach dropping and her mind a whir of fears, possibilities, and not wholly formed conclusions. Quickly she backed up, then parked her car a few spaces down.

Stacey had climbed out of her car and stood waiting.

Rose rushed up to put her hands on either side of her daughter's face. "Stacey, honey, are you all right? Are you ill? Have you been hurt?"

"I'm all right, Rommie. I'm fine." Stacey patted her mother's hands then pulled them away from her cheeks. "I'm not sick, or injured, about to become an unwed mother, on the run from the law, on my way to join up with a travelling band of home repair con artists, or *any* other cockamamie things you might could cook up in your wild imaginings."

"Well, thank heaven for small favors, then." Stacey was her mother's daughter—too much tang to her tongue and the inability to suffer fools gladly—or quietly. Rose had to laugh at that while relief at her oldest child's safety immediately gave way to a sort of second tier of concerns. "Then why are you here? Couldn't you call ahead first and let a person know you were coming? And why aren't you in Atlanta? Don't you have to work tomorrow?"

"Well, thanks for making me feel loved and wanted." Stacey tucked her thick, dark hair back behind one ear.

Rose put her arm around her child and gave her a sturdy cross between a squeeze and a shake. "You are loved *and* wanted. I have no doubt that you know that, young lady. You are also a grown woman come home to her mother's doorstep right out of the blue on a weekday evening. If that did not stir up my— what did you call them—my wild imaginings? Well, then, sweetie, I can't fathom what would."

Five

She's moving into *whose* home?" Naomi stared at Rose while they both scooted across the sun-warmed Naugahyde seat to make room for Gayle in the big corner booth at Dot and Daughters'.

"*My* home." Rose clenched her teeth to force the words out. That her friends immediately saw the pitfalls in her predicament did not surprise her, but that did not mean she wanted to go on gabbing about them, either. She nodded in greeting to the latest arrival. "Hello, Gayle, hon, don't you look precious today? Naomi, doesn't Gayle look absolutely precious today?"

"She looks good enough to sop up with a biscuit," Naomi deadpanned, obviously knowing Gayle would fully support the desire to skim over the niceties when she learned that really choice gossip was at stake here. "Gayle always looks stunning and thin and gorgeous and more pulled together than a fat man's belly at a high school reunion. That's why we all hate her so." She winked at her friend and patted Gayle's hand in greeting. "Now stop trying to divert the subject, Rose Holcolmb. Details, woman, we need details."

Rose's stomach lurched. She said nothing.

"Details? About what?" Gayle leaned forward like a cat ready to pounce on some juicy morsel.

"Stacey." Lucy hissed out Rose's daughter's name, which only heightened the sense of mystery in their bringing Gayle up-to-speed on the situation.

"Stacey? Rose's Stacey?" Genuine concern colored Gayle's

expression, and she reached out to Rose, her questioning gaze still on Naomi. "In Atlanta?"

"Oh, it's Rose's Stacey, all right, only she's not in Atlanta," Lucy rushed to add.

"Where is she?" This time Gayle did look at Rose.

She began to shake her head as if to downplay the significance of it all. "She's just—"

"In New Bethany." Lucy gave a sharp nod, her blond hair bouncing as she did so. "She's left Atlanta for good and has come home to live. With Rose!"

"With *you?*" Gayle batted her mascaraed lashes.

"Yes." Rose wished the waitress, who usually tried to get in on all the good conversations, would stick her nose in this one right about now. She flipped open a menu and began bending the already dog-eared corner.

Lucy followed suit, taking the menus and dealing them out to the others like playing cards—part of her perpetual quest to be helpful, no doubt—as she doled out more information to the latecomer. "She turned in her apartment keys—packed her few furnishing in boxes to ship home—the rest she put in her car and drove back to Tennessee."

"We're talking about Stacey? Your grown child? She's moving back in?" Gayle curled her manicured fingers around Rose's wrist. "With all her belongings? In that tiny condo of yours?"

"Yes. That's where I live now, isn't it?" Rose candy-coated the terse reply with a broad smile and upbeat laugh that she doubted would fool a single soul at the table. "So that's where Stacey is going to live now, too."

"Nuh-uh. No, sir. Rose? Say you're not going to allow this. Not for any extended length of time." Gayle's tanned skin looked even more golden and smooth when contrasted with Rose's pale arm. "That can't be good for either of you. Why, where will you ever find the room for her?"

"I'll just find it, that's all." Rose shrugged. "What else can I do? She's my daughter and she's been laid off. She couldn't find another job and used up the last of her savings on rent and food and when that was gone…"

"I see." Gayle tugged the hem of her cotton sweater over her flat tummy. "Now, how old is Stacey, again? I know I used to baby-sit the girls, but I think I've lost track of their ages."

"She has to be about twenty-eight," Lucy volunteered.

"I don't see why that matters." Rose sipped at her water, watching them over the rim of the glass.

"She graduated in the same class as Dwayne." Lucy gave a little shimmy in the seat.

If Rose had to give a name to the youngest woman's movements, she'd probably call it "the superiority shuffle." Not that Lucy was being rude or haughty, but she so seldom got to have the upper hand or be the bearer of premium news to this group, it had to make her feel good. Lucy seemed to have so few triumphs these days, Rose decided to let her revel in this one and not tell her to knock it off.

Yet.

"So, you'd say Stacey still has friends in town, wouldn't you assume, Lucy?" Naomi planted her elbow on top of her menu and her chin in her hand.

Rose glowered at her for egging Lucy on.

"Friends?" Lucy squinted as though doing math in her head. "Sure, I guess."

"Maybe she could hit one up for a job, Rose—or as a roommate." Naomi sounded genuinely hopeful and helpful this time.

Lucy and Gayle murmured their approval of the idea. They began consorting in a free-for-all of further suggestions on the matter in sweet, encouraging tones—talking all at once like small birds chirping for the same worm.

"Maybe she could rent a—"

"I've heard that Outhier's Drugstore is looking for some-one—"

"She really should get out of Rose's hair and—"

"No." Rose slashed both hands through the air just above the chipped tabletop and the silverware all wrapped up like paper mummies before them. "Now, y'all stop it. Just *stop* it!"

The sharp demand silenced them all and caused an eerie quiet to fall over the whole of the cafe as well. That lasted only a moment. Rose stiffened, a vague smile frozen on her face. Seconds passed, and when it seemed clear no further outburst would follow, the gawkers turned back to their own food, com-panions, or reading material.

Lucy, Gayle, and Naomi blinked at Rose, maintaining their silence.

Despite her appearance as a classically aging belle, with her neutral-toned clothes, hair that always looked casually coifed—even if it took a team of beauticians to achieve it—and soft, Southern mannerisms, Rose was not past this kind of behavior. Twenty-five years of teaching Sunday school at the old Antioch Baptist Church before it burned down, a turn or two at running the Christmas pageant had given Rose the battle presence of a seasoned war general. When she used those tones, everyone sat up a little straighter, fixed their undivided attention on her, and definitely, never, ever spoke back.

After having allowed her little display to have its affect on her well-meaning-but-too-helpful friends, Rose flattened her palms on the cool table. She tipped her head ever-so-slightly to one side and resumed her usual dulcet tones. "Stacey only just returned home last night. It's far too soon to be riled up about how much space she'll take up in my condo or how we will get along. She's in a pickle, and I, for one, am proud to be the kind of mama who is there for her children in their hour of need. So, I don't want to hear anymore about this. And, Naomi Beauchamp Boatwright? If I hear one peep out of you about starting some kind of betting pool to name the exact date and hour that I throw my beloved eldest child out onto the street, I'll have your head on a platter as a centerpiece at the Every-Other-Wednesday-Afternoon Gab and Gardening Club. Is that clear?"

"Yes, ma'am." Naomi feigned a sitting curtsey with her gauzy skirt. She dipped her head.

"Now I apologize for that minor eruption." Rose fused with her hair, pushing and patting at the back of her coif with absolutely no consequence. "But I just wanted to make it known that—"

"I think Rose is just the teensiest bit pleased to have one of her baby birds back in the nest again," Gayle sing-songed. She nudged Rose playfully with one shoulder.

Rose bristled in warning not to let this go too far again. "And just what's wrong with that?"

"Nothing. There are times when I think I'd love to have my son back for a while, myself." Naomi flicked open her menu and began to scan the all-too-familiar fare. "Rose, I think you're going to enjoy being someone's Rommie again."

"Well, maybe that is a trifling part of it," Rose admitted.

"Sure, sure," Naomi concurred, but couldn't seem to help adding, "And besides, having Stacey underfoot is an excellent way to keep Will on the string while keeping his marriage proposals at bay."

The truth of that zinging insight stung Rose's pride and set her thoughts spinning. Was she that transparent? Would Will see through what she had thought was a peach of a notion for having her cake and eating it too? She fanned her suddenly burning cheeks with her laminated menu, wafting the scent of perfume and grilled foods into her own face. She cleared her throat and stared at the waitress with a look practically commanding her to come take their orders.

"Naomi!" Gayle clucked her tongue, though her eyes sparkled with delight at the bluntness of the remark.

Lucy giggled.

Rose kept her gaze trained elsewhere but felt she had to say something. "Really, Naomi."

"Really. We all know that manipulating Will may not be the reason behind all this, but Stacey's appearance certainly provides that very tangible benefit." Naomi giggled, too good a friend to let Rose get away with her act for one minute. "So don't you go playing the affronted accused with me, Rose, sugar."

"I didn't—"

"You sure did! Tipping up your nose at me, as if you've caught a whiff of something mildly offensive." Naomi shook her head, smiling fondly.

"Oh, Naomi, anyone can see that Rose did not find your jab honestly offensive." Gayle shot an amused look at her friends and they responded in kind. "But rather, she was feeling a bit *defensive* over the matter with Will. Still, pointing it out like that only proves one thing—you spent far too much time among—" Gayle lowered her chin and her voice dropped to a husky whisper "—the Yankees."

"Now you're just being mean." Naomi laughed.

"No, really, Naomi, that kind of speculation? About the state of my, um, romantic commitments, or lack thereof?" Rose put on her best Southern belle air, which was totally belied by the twinkle in her eye and the wicked lilt to her suddenly thickened accent. "I sworn, my dear, it's just, well, it's too *common* to talk about any further."

If Rose had been wearing a dress, she'd have flounced the skirt—or if she had long, curly hair, she'd have tossed it defiantly. Neither would have had any effect on Naomi and her response, any more than her friends' lame protestations.

"Why is it, do ya'll suppose, that the only time you see fit to reproach me for being common is when you know beyond the shadow of a doubt that I am absolutely, 100 percent, Yankee-sensibilities-not-withstanding...*right*?"

"Oh, that's not the only time we accuse you of being common," Rose assured her, her tone hushed and dripping humor.

"Oh, absolutely not." Gayle gripped her friend by the arm. "Of course the other times are usually behind your back, so—"

"Very funny." Naomi laughed, and they all joined in.

"All right, ladies, enough of this." Rose gave up waiting it out and finally waved the waitress over. "I will admit to you three that Stacey's arrival has come at a, shall we say, *welcome juncture* in things with Will. I'd also be fooling myself if I thought this was anything but temporary—for Stacey as well as for my ambiguous solution to my relationship reticence."

"What?" Lucy screwed up her face like a child trying to comprehend a foreign language.

"Lucy, you know the parable of the foolish man and the wise man?" Naomi narrowed one eye at the stymied young woman. "Where the wise man built his house on rock and the foolish one on sand?"

"Uh-huh."

"Well, Rose is saying that holding off a decision about Will with the excuse of Stacey's moving in is like building her house on the slippery shore." Naomi gave a slow nod. "Sand castle central. The dunes of doom—"

"She gets it." Rose turned to Lucy. "Right? You do understand, don't you?"

"Are you kidding?" Lucy huffed out a cheerless chuckle. "You are talking to the queen of the desert dwellers where romance and that story are concerned."

Gayle reached over and gave Lucy's hand a squeeze, which took the young woman—and Rose, for that matter—entirely off guard.

"Oh, sugar," Gayle's tone was entirely too casual, "don't feel too bad. There probably hasn't been a one of us who hasn't, at one time, felt the foundations of our relationship shift a little. And it made us wonder if the rock we'd built our lives on was as precarious as sandstone."

Rose fixed Gayle with a thoughtful smile. "As someone who has just had her maternal actions and romantic motivations picked apart—and admittedly for my own good because it's given me something to think about—I have to say to you, Gayle Shorter Barrett—" Rose leaned in, one finger raised and with a take-no-prisoners attitude "—we are not letting you get away with a remark like that without offering some kind of explanation."

Graciously, the three other women allowed Gayle to withhold further comment until the waitress had taken their order, clunked down four glasses of iced tea, then scurried off to the kitchen again.

"Well?" Rose emptied the contents of one pink packet into her tea and began to stir, the spoon making a delicate chiming sound against the rim of the glass.

The endless clinking hit Gayle like a mallet striking a raw nerve. She clenched her fists.

Naomi reached over to place one hand atop Gayle's, which helped a little to ease the tension.

"What's going on, Gayle?" Gentle as the prodding seemed, the kindness infused in Rose's eyes, tone, even her posture did not fool Gayle into thinking her friends would let her off-the-cuff crack go lightly by. "Is something wrong between you and Ted?"

"No, there is *not*." Naomi's gaze was on Gayle in a take-no-flak attitude.

Gayle drew some strength from her friend's firm grasp and her even firmer assertion of faith in Ted.

Naomi gave a quick dismissive shake of her head. "There is nothing more sinister going on with Ted than the valiant struggle to fend off that flu bug that's going around."

"What flu?" Lucy shook her head, her brow creased.

"There's no flu bug going around that I know of." Rose leaned in. "Lucy, if there was anything going around we'd have it by now at the day care, wouldn't we?"

"Well, yes, usually." Lucy nodded slowly, clearly uneasy. "Seems like we do bear the first wave of any bug or virus that makes the rounds but that doesn't mean…"

"There's nothing going around…" Gayle's echo was so soft she could scarcely hear herself over the clatter of plates and the hum of midday diner conversation. She rubbed the stiff paper of her napkin between her thumb and forefinger, unable to focus on any of her companions. "No one else is sick or feels like they are coming down with something?"

"I sure do. I've been trying to stave it off for a good week now," Naomi insisted. "Surely *somebody* else is feeling under the weather around town—tired, listless, distracted, sometimes nauseous?"

Gayle perked up, hopeful for some comfort in the answer to that.

The noise of the cafe seemed to swell to fill the moment in which her friend's remained silent. The waitresses, other people, the blue walls, the deep red countertops and glaring red booths, the huge windows framing familiar fall scenes of downtown New Bethany all became a blur to Gayle. A sourness sank to the pit of her stomach. She fixed her entire being for one moment on her friends. Lucy and Rose exchanged glances that said more than any denial ever could.

"You mean this is *not* the flu?" Naomi squeaked out.

Gayle's heart plummeted. No flu. Something else was to blame for Ted's behavior, and she could only fear what that might be.

Another woman? A dalliance, she could forgive, not lightly, but her marriage meant more to her than a man's momentary lapse of honor. She could forgive the man she'd loved for half a lifetime of almost anything, she decided then and there. But what if it proved to be more…and he left her?

She couldn't even contemplate the aftermath of that. The pain, the humiliation, the loss, the loneliness, she couldn't bear to imagine any of it. Nothing in her well-crafted world would ever be the same without Ted and the lifestyle and home they had built together. She would never be the same, she would never get over it and be able to go on.

Naomi's grip on Gayle's wrist, making her watch dig into her skin, brought Gayle back to the immediate situation. Naomi wet her lips, looking a bit greenish-gray beneath her flushed cheeks. "But if there's no flu then—"

"Well, we didn't say for sure there's nothing going around," Rose suddenly backpedaled. "We're running a day care center, after all, not the local chapter of the center for disease control."

Gayle pinched at the napkin in her hand and slowly began to rip off one long streamer. "If it's not the flu then there has to be another explanation, doesn't there?"

"But not necessarily something awful, Gayle, and you know it," Naomi snapped, clearly disturbed in her own right at finding their simplistic hopes about impending illness dashed.

"Of course not, and what does this have to do with Ted, anyway?" Lucy took a long draw on her iced tea through a straw, as though it were a soda pop. "I'm confused."

"Ted's just acting a bit out of sorts lately, that's all," Naomi rushed to reply with self-assured forcefulness. "Nothing to be concerned about."

Gayle wished she could believe her friend. Deep inside, though, she knew that something far greater was amiss with her husband. That something threatened her on many levels. It loomed over her like an oppressive cloud of dread. It waited inside her like a time bomb. It terrified her.

"Of course, Naomi's probably right," Gayle said, as much to realign her own composure as to reassure her friends. Whatever was happening she had no intention of making it fodder for the Dot and Daughters' Cafe crowd. She inched up her chin and straightened her spine the way her mother had taught her—as though her backbone were a string of pearls and she had just tugged the string taut. "Whatever it is, it's nothing to go on about here. Besides, as I recall, Naomi called us together for a purpose?"

She turned to her oldest friend to rescue her from any further discussion of her most private fears and concerns, and Naomi did not disappoint.

"Yes I did, didn't I?" Naomi brightened. "I almost forgot."

"Well, I didn't." Lucy pouted, plucking at the hem of her slimming black sweater, which caused her brilliant new silk scarf to ripple. "I can't dawdle here all day. It may be Rose's day off but I have to get back to work, my staff gets restless if I stay gone too long, and I have an afternoon appointment with the new doctor in town to get his children registered at the day care."

"Ooooh." Naomi waggled her eyebrows. "Tempting as that can of worms sounds to dive into, I guess we'd better not get sidetracked again—yet."

"Mmmm. Worms and sand and stomach flu...what lovely topics ya'll do pick for lunch conversation." Rose grinned. "I do hope yours is a little less...earthy, Naomi, my dear."

"Oh, mine is anything *but* earthy, Rose. In fact, one might call it heavenly—with us acting as the Lord's emissaries."

"Emissaries?" Lucy squinted at Naomi.

"For what?" Rose folded her arms.

"For who?" Naomi corrected.

"For *whom?*" Gayle corrected even further.

"Glad you asked, Gayle." Naomi gave a wink. "And when I tell you this, I know you all are going to be stunned but I do not want any of your preconceived notions to get in the way of giving fair consideration to my proposal."

"Nuh-uh." Gayle began to slowly shake her head. She had enough on her proverbial plate with the future of her home and her marriage in flux, she did not need another one of Naomi's schemes to top it off. "No thank you right now."

"But you don't even know what it is—"

"I don't need to know. That it's your idea and that you have to give it such a big build-up and want to rope us into it is enough." Gayle held her hand up to say that was it for her—she didn't need to hear anything. Her mind was made up.

Naomi opened her mouth to speak but it was another voice that rolled over the gathering like window rattling thunder.

"Well, hey there, Mrs. Boatwright. I didn't expect to see you back here until Saturday afternoon. Howdy, Mrs. Barrett, glad to have you with us again so soon. Saw ya'll come in but I've been too busy in the back to come out and thank you in person again until just now. These the ladies you told me about?" Dawnetta, raised up her chin and without missing a beat from her already random patter, hollered out at someone across the cafe. "That special order'll be out in a minute, R. C., don't you fret none."

"These are the ladies, all right, Dawnetta," Naomi confirmed with a confident nod, though her confidence had waned somewhat after Gayle's reaction. Couldn't they see how much they all needed one another now? Rose needed them to stand by her in her indecision and with her daughter moving home. Gayle needed their strength with her insecurities over whatever was going on with Ted. Then there was Lucy with her—well, Lucy just needed as many friends as she could get no matter what. Naomi felt a swell of sympathy toward the younger woman. But that only made Naomi more determined: her idea would provide what they all needed, if only for a while longer.

To add to the confusion of what she had hoped would be a quiet moment with her friends, the other waitress appeared just then, her arms laden with the food the women had ordered. In a flurry of efficiency, the woman plunked one plate after the other before the proper person, asked if they needed anything else, then spun on the thick heel of her shoe and dashed off, promising to check on them again real soon.

Naomi drew in the smells of the odd mix of breakfasts and lunches burdening the small table—the effect on her stomach being much like the subtle rolling queasiness brought on by driving too fast over a small but unexpected hill. Gayle, Rose, and Lucy all looked at her with expectant faces; Dawnetta watched with an expression of pure satisfaction. Naomi gulped at her squeamishness, no doubt brought on by nerves in this situation, and smiled. "Dawnetta, would you give us a moment, I haven't exactly explained things to my friends yet and—"

"Oh, sure, explain away. I just wanted to come out here and tell you how grateful I am that you volunteered. I know it ain't an easy job, Miss Grace done fired more girls than a dog has fleas and they was paid to do what you're taking on out of the goodness of your Christian spirit." Dawnetta turned, her head shaking but her haywire hairdo moving only on one side as she walked away muttering. "Does my heart good to see someone taking on the ol' gal after so many years of folks disparaging her. It really does."

"Miss Grace?" Lucy's eyes grew big as the lumberjack pancakes swimming in golden syrup on her plate.

"'Taking the ol' gal on'?" Rose quoted Dawnetta's words with a more clipped and calculated tone.

"Did I tell you or what?" Gayle slumped back in the seat so hard the duct-taped cushion did her groaning and sighing for her. "It's another one of your wild ideas you want to drag others into, Naomi. And including Grace Grayson-Wiley, no less."

"Naomi, I don't see how I could, not now…" Lucy looked from one person to another like a pup seeking a pat on the head. "What with the extra duty of taking care of the prayer circle's children and with Ben's—that is with two new babies at the center—"

"And me, with Stacey home again?" Rose shook her head. "Not to mention the holidays."

"And Ted's mysterious *flu*, the source of which I've yet to find," Gayle said it mostly to herself.

But don't you see? Naomi wanted to scream. *Those are precisely the reasons we need to take on something outside ourselves right now.*

"Besides, do you really think we're qualified to deal with someone like Miss Grace? Someone who…" Lucy pointed two fingers toward her temple and bobbled her head back and forth.

"Lucy has a point." Rose's hand darted out and pulled Lucy's arm back down to her side. "At least about our limited abilities to tackle this. We aren't exactly social workers, here."

"Rose! I can't believe you're saying that."

"That's just common sense talking and you know it, Naomi." Gayle adjusted her salad bowl just so. "We're talking about a woman who gussies up in her old ball gown and waits on the porch for a phantom lover—it's positively the stuff of old black-and-white Betty Davis movies."

"Creepy." Lucy scrunched up her nose.

"More than that, it's neither practical nor plausible. Just listen to the sound of it for a moment. The four of us?" Gayle gestured broadly. "Looking after a nut?"

"It's a veritable case of the blind leading the blind," Rose grumbled dryly.

"That's not what I meant and you know it, Rose." Gayle's temper had definitely stretched to it's limit. "It's simply beyond our scope, Naomi. Honestly, have you taken leave of your senses?"

"No." Naomi jerked her shoulders up to challenge her friend's peevish attitude, her own temper somewhat tested. "Have you taken leave of your *sensitivity*? What about your compassion? What about your kindness? I'm not talking about taking the woman in to raise, here. It's just a chance for us to get together once a week through the first of the year—to take her a meal from the diner every Saturday afternoon. That's it, plain and simple."

"Nuh-uh. It's never that simple and you know it, Nomi. In fact, I can sit right here and look into your eyes and know for a fact you don't even *want* it to be that simple." Gayle tapped one finger on the table as if hammering home her point like a fine finishing nail. Her silverware clanked against the edge of her salad bowl as she spoke. "First it'll be taking out a meal"—*clank*—"then doing some errands and maybe taking over some fresh cut flowers"—*clank*—"or a special desert for the holidays."

Before Gayle could land another blow, Naomi grabbed her friend's finger and pressed it flat to the table top.

That did not deter Gayle or soften the cadence of her speech. "Then one thing will lead to another and before you know it that peculiar old elf will have become our little project. She'd become like our very own personal black hole sucking in more and more of our time and effort and even our families would get into the act and then—"

"What's wrong with that?" Naomi bristled.

"Nothing, if that's how you'd presented it in the first place. But pretending that this is just some simple little service we'll be required to perform for a few weeks then hoping—probably planning—that we'd get into it up to our necks? Where's your sense of fairness, Naomi?"

"Well, I…" Naomi cast her gaze downward. She did not do that often, but after having tried to call her oldest friend in the world on the carpet only to receive treatment in kind humbled her. Besides, deep in her heart she knew what even Gayle and Rose and Lucy could not, that she wanted this to happen as much for her own needs as for Miss Grace's—maybe more. She had not acted totally out of compassion and kindness, either, but also out of selfishness and longing to recapture the closeness they had once had, to fill up the emptiness she felt in missing Mama and her friends. "You're right, Gayle. You're right. I'm sorry to have tried to manipulate you all so."

Both Rose and Gayle put their hands on Naomi's shoulders—Gayle in tender atonement, Rose to give her a teasing little shake.

"Let's face it, sugar," Gayle said softly. "You know who you're talking to here. You can't pull the wool over our eyes."

"Of course not, it'd muse our hair," Rose announced, tossing her head back. "And if it's one thing this group won't stand for, it's something ruffling up our hairdos—or our friendships."

"That's why I wanted us to take this on." There was a plaintive edge to Naomi's whispered words. "I thought it would give us a framework to see one another again."

"Do we really need something so contrived as this for that?" Gayle cocked her head, her fork frozen halfway to her lips.

The women all looked at one another, none of them having—or daring to put forth—the answer.

They ate the rest of their meal in a thoughtful quiet, none of them broaching the subject again until Naomi snatched up the check and said, "This one's on me, ladies."

She hadn't said "my treat" because she felt it had been anything but a treat to have her hopes dashed so, even if she could concede that it was greatly by her own doing. Finally, as they stood to leave, she turned to her friends, the women she felt closer to than anyone but her husband and son, and spoke quietly. "I understand if no one wants to take this on at this time, ya'll. I really do. You've all got so much going on now as it is that one more thing…" Her voice broke. It had meant so much to her and letting it go, even though it was the right thing to do, was not easy.

"Anyway, that doesn't change my commitment or leave me with any hard feelings about your decisions. I love ya'll, I truly do, like sisters, and I surely don't want something I thought would bring us closer together to come between us. That said, I'll just remind you all that I'll be leaving the cafe Saturday afternoon at three o'clock to take Grace's meal out to Sweet Haven. If any of you change your minds about joining me, I'll see you then. If not...well, let's just say, we'll see each other when we can."

Six

"iss Jewell?" Dr. Ben Martin poked his head into the day care office. "Miss Jewell, is that you?"

Lucy snapped her head up to find the man's laughing eyes trained upon her. "Um, yes, it's me, I'm...me."

"Good." He chuckled around the word, then stepped fully inside the already cramped room. "I wasn't sure I'd recognize you without the paint in your hair."

"Oh." She ran her fingers back through the silky fringe of her bangs.

"Just kidding." He grinned.

Her heart leapt. "Wha...? Oh. Oh. Yes. Kidding." She managed a limp smile. "I knew that."

If her laughter sounded as weak as it felt, he did not show it. He just pulled out the chair next to her desk and made himself at home, like they were a pair of old pals settling in for a chat.

But they weren't pals. She knew almost nothing about this man except that he'd come to New Bethany to start a medical practice and needed her to care for his children during working hours. She also knew that his nearness made her painfully aware of her femininity—and her failings.

She fumbled with the button holding her jacket closed over her full hips and tummy, suddenly feeling her weight clinging to her, crowding her inside her own body. She fluffed her scarf out as if she could hide the excess her black outfit did not conceal behind the vivid pattern.

"That's pretty," he said softly.

"Um, oh, I…it's just a scarf."

"Well, it's a pretty one. It sets off your eyes."

It made her both blissfully pleased and utterly embarrassed to have him notice her. After all, she had not dressed this way to impress the man. He was a family man here on business. No siree. The only reason she had worn her best outfit—and brand new scarf—was to project a professional image.

Still…he'd noticed her eyes. Her insides turned to absolute mush—not a far journey from the tower of squishy sentimentality she'd become the moment he'd walked through the door. She swallowed hard. "Maybe we should get down to business, Dr. Martin."

"Ben."

"Hmm?"

"Ben," he repeated.

"Ben?"

"That's my name. I'd rather you use it than the doctor label." He waved off the reference.

"Oh, I couldn't…"

"Oh, I bet you could." He raised one eyebrow, just like Cary Grant might have done in some wry romantic comedy. "If you really put your mind to it."

It did not ring of anything flirtatious or inappropriate, but more of an achingly endearing sweetness. The teasing tone, by it's very innocence and the fact that it came before they even knew one another on a first-name basis, made Lucy's breath come quick and shallow. She bit her lip, wondering what it would feel like to play coy and flirty with him, not to lead anywhere but just to savor it for one moment before reality took hold again.

"Why don't you try it?" he asked.

Her eyes widened. *"Huh?"*

"My name. Why don't you try it out?"

"Oh, um…" she cleared her throat. "All right…Ben."

"That's better." He nodded. "I've found my professional title only seems to put up barriers between folks. That has it's place, and being a doctor means a lot to me, Lord knows, but I did move to New Bethany to get more of a sense of belonging to a community. Since you're the first person besides Dr. Glass and his staff that I've met here, I'd like that sense of community to begin with you."

Lucy's breath caught high in her chest. Her cheeks heated, and she crushed the ends of her scarf into a loose ball. This was no ordinary introduction. It went deeper than that, and Lucy, even with her dismal track record of judging men's intentions, knew it. She sensed it in the way Ben's voice deepened, the way he hesitated just an instant before revealing more of himself and his hopes for his new home.

This was an overture of friendship. Pure and simple.

This man was sitting in her office—looking terrific with his tie casually loosened at the neck, his brown hair rumpled, and his glasses just enough forward on the bridge of his nose to allow him to look over the top of the wire rims at her—and asking her to be his friend. Lucy felt stunned. She wasn't worthy of that kind of attention, not from a man like this! And a doctor, no less.

He held out his hand. "Is that all right with you…?"

The unfinished question dangled there between them just waiting for her to take the initiative and fill in the blank with her first name. If she did that, Lucy knew she would be agreeing to more than a means of addressing one another. She gulped in some air through her mouth, but could still smell the scent of antiseptic on Ben mixed with the peculiar blend of peanut butter and pencil shavings that infused her office. She held her breath and eyed his fine, open hand.

He extended it closer to her as if to prompt her into some kind of action.

Just as she had as a child leaping from the high dive at the New Bethany Municipal Pool, Lucy closed her eyes, clenched her jaw, and dove right in. "Lucy. You can call me Lucy."

She wondered if he felt the tremor in her hand as it fit snuggly inside the warm cocoon of his palm and strong fingers. If he noticed her nervousness, he covered for it nicely. "Very nice to make your acquaintance, Lucy."

"Thank you. It's nice to meet you, too, that is formally. Obviously we've…crossed paths before." She grimaced at the memory, then feeling a fool all over again, pulled her hand away from his and plunged into some small talk to take the awkwardness away. "Dr. Glass's nurse is the aunt of a neighbor of the parents of one of my day care babies and I hear she's had an awfully lot of perfectly lovely things to say about you. Though, I don't know what they are specifically, so please don't ask me. I couldn't tell you. I would tell you but I just don't know what was said except that it's *been* said that the man— you, of course—taking over Ol' Doc Glass's practice is a fine, upstanding…"

She was blathering. A blithering idiot. What's worse she seemed to have lost the ability to make herself shut up. Thankfully, her new friend must have sensed her distress and, like a true hero, sacrificed himself by jumping straight in front of the runaway train that this conversation had become.

"Well, if people are going to talk about me, I guess that's the kind of thing I want them to say."

"It's a small town, Ben, and in small towns new folks, rich folks, eccentric folks, wild folks, and doctors are often the next-best thing we have to celebrities." She whisked the back of her hand down her cool, silk scarf but that did not sweep away the physical memory of his touch. Lucy made herself meet his eyes. Despite the thundering of her heart at the emotional generosity that she saw in him she managed to sound quite firm in her assertion. "People *are* going to talk about you."

"I expected as much." He nodded somberly. "I just hope it doesn't have any adverse effects on my children."

"Children?" Lucy blinked then sat back in her chair, suddenly jerked back to reality. "Oh yes, your children. Alec and Paige, right?"

"You remembered." His entire face and posture were alight with pride in his children.

"Well, they are the reason you came here in the first place, aren't they?"

"But you remembered their *names.*" His voice remained hushed. "That kind of thing says a lot about you, Lucy. An awful lot."

"Well, we do aim to run the best day care in town." The breathy quality to her words made her stomach flutter. How could she be acting such a fool, in her own office with the father of her newest charges? What a joke he and his wife would have about her blatant adoration when he got home tonight. That thought stung like an open-handed slap to the face. She'd been laughed at behind her back before—by Ray and Nikki—and while she had forgiven them and moved on, it was not something she would ever want to endure again.

Stiffening, she pushed her seat away from the desk. The metal legs scraped over the dingy tan floor with a deafening screech. She stood. "As I said, I run the best day care in town. One I'm sure will provide the right nurturing environment for your children and make them very happy. I'm sure you and your wife will be very pleased with our service."

"Wife?" Ben stood but his stance remained more relaxed than hers. He crossed his arms, his shoulders at a rakish slant and grinned. "Why, Miss Lucy, I don't believe I ever said anything about having a *wife*. Which quite probably is because I don't have one."

"You...don't?" She blinked as if the entire landscape of her thinking had just shifted like the scene in a kaleidoscope.

He put his hands on her desk and leaned forward—his eyes glittering and his smile downright jammed with mischief—and winked at her. "No, I don't. It's just me and my two children. I've come to New Bethany to make a better kind of life for them than we had in a bigger city. I've come here to create a home and to raise my family by myself. Now, do you think *that* will be enough to provide the locals something interesting to talk about?"

Lucy did not know about the other locals, but the juicy tidbit of information Dr. Ben Martin had just laid on her left her utterly speechless.

"Is my husband around this afternoon?" Naomi held her breath against the moist, dank smell of peat and plant life that hit her like a wall as she breezed into the nursery her husband owned and operated.

"Last I saw him he had a shovel slung o'er his shoulder. Said he was goin' out to work with the Christmas trees." Opal Parks, who had worked for Boatwright Nursery since Moses wore kneepants, jerked her dirt-covered thumb toward the back door and the special crop beyond. With fall in full swing and winter encroaching, the nursery was about to close and would not open up again until early spring, with the exception of a few weeks before Christmas when Taylor ran a cut-your-own Christmas tree venture. "Want me t'give him a holler on the loudspeaker?"

"No thanks, Opal, I'll go out to him." Naomi forced the words out as quickly as she could without inhaling again. She rushed through the musty building, one quick step ahead of the nausea inspired by the pungent odors.

Once outdoors her head cleared again, and her stomach quieted. The sound of the edge of a spade breaking into the rich soil, cutting through grass, and scraping over small stones drew her attention to where her husband was hard at work.

Naomi smiled to herself. Was there anything more compelling and wonderful then watching a man doing what he was best at? Taylor tossed aside the dark soil, paused to wipe his brow with the back of one big, capable hand, then forced the shovel down into the ground again.

Lean and tall, her husband was not the kind of handsome that made women's hearts flutter or their knees wobble. He had that effect on her, though, right from the very start. The first time she had gazed into those striking, honest, blue eyes, she'd lost her heart. When he'd come to show his support of the prayer circles, when he'd promised her dying mama that he'd always care for Naomi, when he'd refused to give up on Naomi and their relationship, she had known he was the man she could make a life with. Naomi placed her hand low on her belly.

The sight of Taylor warmed her right down to her toes, made her heart swell, and stirred something else deep inside her—complete and total dread.

She bit her lip and glanced downward. For an instant, knowing that Taylor had not seen her, she considered turning tail and running away. She could go home, she reasoned, and keep to herself the suspicions she'd formed only moments ago in the cafe—at least until she could confirm them.

She took a shuffling step backward. Her legs felt like lead, yet she managed to move again, her feet carefully controlled and her eyes trained on her husband. She glanced down to make sure she wasn't going to bump into anything, looked up again, then heard the crisp snap of a twig crushed beneath her shoe.

Taylor stopped mid-dig to lift his gaze in her direction. "Well, hey there! What are you doing stopping by in the middle of the day?"

"I, uh…" Naomi gestured vaguely with both hands, her fingers chilled and palms clammy, not sure where to begin—or *if* to begin at all. She met her husband's gentle gaze. All her reservations stilled. "I just came from the cafe and I…I have something I want to talk to you about."

"Ah, right." He laid both hands on the shovel handle and planted one booted foot on the metal edge. "This was the big pitch to try to get the ladies to help you with Miss Grace. Now, don't you tell me, let me just guess at how *that* went over."

Her lips parted to stop him but he hardly took a breath before he surged ahead with his description.

"Let's see, Gayle turned her nose up at the idea. Little Lucy got all flustered at the very notion of going anywhere near the scary ol' gal, and Rose? Hmmm, well, I have to think on Rose's reaction—I'm torn between going with disdain for an impossible, overly idealistic task or unbridled enthusiasm for the generous project." He stroked his chin. "Either way, I'm willing to wager you've come here to tell me to expect you to be occupied for a couple hours every Saturday these next few weeks."

If only that were it. She nudged the rich ground with the

toe of her favorite hiking boots. Her gaze flickered downward, then to her husband again. She shook her head.

"No?" Lines creased his brow and splayed out from his narrowed eyes. "You mean you're not going to be busy on Saturdays? Don't tell me you've given up on the whole romantic notion of helping out Miss Grace and getting the ladies to meet regular again?"

"I haven't given up on that." The thrumming of her own pulse throbbed in her temples. "That's not what I came here to talk about, Taylor."

"You sound so serious, sweetheart." He put his foot down and started to come around the shovel driven into the freshly turned dirt. "What is it? Did something bad happen at the cafe?"

"No, whatever happened, happened long before the cafe. Weeks ago, I'd guess." She tried to sound light but simply could not pull it off. She sniffled despite her sunny smile and tossed back her hair. The sudden movement made her stomach roll.

"What is it? What are you talking about?"

"Taylor, I think…that is, I suspect…" The humid air closed in on her—or were those her own emotions pressing her into a spot where she could do nothing more but blurt out her sudden anxiety? "Oh, Taylor! There isn't any flu going around town!"

She moved toward him, placing both hands on his muscular arm, clinging to him as if he could anchor her against her inner turmoil.

His calloused hands, so rough in manipulating the garden implement a moment ago, gentled on her skin and he let the spade fall away and pulled her into his arms. Folding her fully into the safety of his embrace, his chest heaved in a huff of laugh as he whispered against her hair, "No flu, huh? My, that *is* upsetting news."

"Don't you get it?" She pulled away to look him in the eye. "Don't you see what that means?"

"Less business down at Outhier's Drug?"

"No." She landed a harmless blow with her fist to his chest. "Taylor, for two weeks now I've blamed everything from my extreme tiredness, to my mood swings, to—" She got a whiff of hard work and fresh fertilizer on her husband's skin and clothes and almost gagged "—to these bouts of nausea on the impending flu I was sure was going around town."

"Well, cheer up, sweetie." He lifted her chin with one finger. "Maybe you're just the first one in town to come down with it."

"Yeah, and maybe, just maybe, it's not the flu at all that I've come down with." She met his gaze, hoping her eyes conveyed her deeper meaning better than any words ever could.

"Like what?"

Obviously picking up on subtleties was not her new husband's forte. She flexed her palm against the comforting warmth of his flannel shirt and braced up her backbone. "Taylor, have you ever thought of…well, I know I never even considered it myself, obviously so, or I wouldn't be in this—we wouldn't be—"

"Whoa, Nomi, hon." He held her away from him and bent his knees to put them squarely eye-to-eye. "Go back. Start over. I have no idea what you are talking about here."

"No idea? Why it's perfectly plain to me." She was more curt than the situation called for and snippish and probably just a tinge hysterical, something that grew as she rushed on. "The symptoms, the lack of a flu bug, the fact that we are married and, well, haven't because of our ages taken certain precautions as seriously as we should have…"

"Precautions?" His expression was unreadable.

"Yes, *precautions*. Against pregnancy." She threw back her shoulders and forced the conclusion out in a strained voice. "A baby, Taylor. *That's* what I'm talking about here. I think I'm carrying your baby."

"A…baby?" He looked like a man caught between the urge to whoop with joy or to go and bang his head against a wall.

Naomi knew exactly how he felt—especially the banging your head against a wall part—a nice thick, brick wall. "It's just been so long since I'd had to think about things like babies and preventing pregnancy, Taylor. Why, who'd have ever suspected we'd be this fertile? We're so old for this kind of thing."

"Speak for yourself," he muttered, a twinkle in his eyes.

"This is no time for joking, Taylor Boatwright." Her heart leapt into her throat. Her legs felt a little too liquid to support her much longer. She'd only had to tell one other man this news in her life and that had not gone well at all. Her ex-husband had used her having a baby as an excuse for his self-indulgent behavior, and while Taylor was not like that, the idea of the many changes a baby could bring to a relationship frightened Naomi. Suddenly she longed for her mama and the source of loving guidance she had always been. "I don't see how you can take all this so calmly, anyway."

He shook his head as if unsure what to say to that, his mouth opening then shutting again in his vain attempt to explain his reaction—or lack thereof.

The fall breeze kicked up a spattering of colored leaves and caused one low branch of the nearest evergreen to tickle Naomi's calf. She lurched forward, and in doing so, fit herself completely against her husband, who instinctively tightened his grasp around her waist.

"I don't understand your response to this, Taylor." She lost herself in the tranquility of his amazing blue eyes. "If there is no flu going around and there isn't some other plausible explanation for my symptoms then I'm telling you that in all probability, you have gotten me pregnant."

A woozy kind of half smile crept over his lips and there was an obvious underpinning of pure masculine pride in his eyes, his stance, and the growl of his voice when he put his face close to hers and whispered, "Yes, Nomi, I know that."

A shiver tripped down her spine and even she wasn't sure if it was one of excitement or hesitation. "I don't believe you. You are quite pleased with yourself over this, aren't you?"

"Well…"

"Oh, puh*lease!* Gloat all you want now, but after that macho pride fades *I'll* be the one left huge and bloated and—"

"Beautiful." He kissed her cheekbone, framing her face with his hands. "And I can't wait to see it—to see you all fat and sassy with our little one growing strong inside you."

"Sassy, yes. You can count on that one, mister, pregnant or not. But fat?" For one fleeting moment she could feel her body blossoming with impending life. The sensation had the effect of a deeply banked fire on a miserable day, or snuggling under a plump quilt with her husband, all secure and satisfied.

She laid her head on Taylor's chest, letting the flannel caress her cheek.

She eased out a long sigh before closing her eyes. "Oh, Taylor, lovely as the dream sounds right now, the reality is we'll have a tiny new person in our home and in our lives."

"Yes, we will." He stroked her hair.

"Complete with dirty diapers and 3 A.M. feedings."

"And baby's laughter and itty-bitty fingers and toes and kisses and lullabies—"

"And worries and fevers and feeling too weary to keep up.

Taylor do you realize that by the time this baby graduates from high school, I'll be fifty-eight years old?"

A scowl darkened his tanned face for the first time since the discussion had begun. "Hmmm, I don't know if I like the sound of *that.*"

"See? I didn't think you'd weighed all the consequences of older parenthood before you favored it so."

"Oh, parenthood I like just fine, darling."

"You do?"

"Yup." He gave a nod, his gaze somber and fixed far away before he shifted just his eyes and, with a teasing glimmer, met hers. "It's the thought of being married to a fifty-eight-year-old woman that throws me for a loop."

"Throws you for a—" She pulled way from him. "You want to be thrown for a loop, mister, you just keep talking like that. I'll throw you for a loop, all right—"

"You already have, sweetheart. You do every time you look at me." He tugged her back to him and kissed her cheek, her forehead. "And now we're going to have a baby."

"We are." She wound her arms around him, content to put her worries aside until—

She straightened suddenly. "That is, we are unless there really is a flu bug going around and I truly am one of the first in town to show signs of it."

"Or it could be some other physical problem, you know." Taylor's faced lined with concern. "Either way you have to get yourself to the doctor without any unnecessary delay."

"I'll make an appointment. There's a new general practitioner in town taking over Dr. Glass's practice. I think I'd like to try him."

"Shouldn't you go to an obstetrician?"

"Not if I have the flu." She laughed. "And there is some

small part of me that does cling to faint hope that all this has been the work of some undisclosed virus."

"Really? Why?"

"Because, if there actually is no flu in town, then not only will our family be growing, but poor Gayle's might just be falling apart."

"Do it. Do it, Gayle, just do it." Ted tossed his balled-up suit jacket into the wingback chair beside their huge, dark-cherry bed.

Gayle heard herself gasp more than felt it. The air in the suddenly all-too-quiet room seemed brittle, volatile…as if the least remark would spark Ted's anger. She watched her husband—just held her breath and watched—waiting but unsure of what she expected to happen next.

Ted pushed both his hands back through his thick, sandy-brown hair. He grimaced as if he'd just tried to swallow something the size of a fist. He pinched the bridge of his nose, grimaced again, then sighed.

"I'm sorry, sugar. That came out far more harsh than I anticipated." Ted tugged his tie loose at the neck then pulled at it until the silk fabric whistled as he whisked it free from beneath his collar. "I've just had a hard day, and I feel like the walking dead."

That analogy made Gayle shudder. Still, she told herself, it could have been worse. He could have told her he felt like a man trying to juggling two many things at once or a man who doesn't know if he's coming or going. She would have read plenty into those seemingly innocent cliched excuses. He also could have sat right there and told her he felt like a man about to chuck it all, walk out on his wife, and leave her with the children to raise, the bills to pay, and the rest of her nights to spend alone. He could have said that, she conceded to her inner observer, and that would have been much, much worse.

"You know what I think?" Ted hung his tie over the bedrail, then perched on the edge of the chair where'd he thrown his jacket.

Gayle wasn't sure she *wanted* to know. But she picked up the tie, folded it into a neat rectangle as she always did when she picked up after her husband, and smiled. "What, dear?"

"I like it. In fact, I like it a lot."

"You like what?"

"The whole thing—the whole prayer circle friends reunion tour of benevolence and goodwill toward Miss Grace in her time of need."

"Leave it to a lawyer to puff up a few meal deliveries into a grand gesture and oldies revival celebration." She managed a smile that did not feel forced.

"I'm serious, though. I think it will be good for you to get out of the house a few hours come Saturday afternoons—"

"So, the truth will out." She was testing the waters, but with the semblance of benign teasing. "You really want to be rid of me for a few hours every Saturday."

"Now that you mention it…"

That hurt but she did not show it. "Is that so?" She cocked one eyebrow, using the exaggerated gesture to cover her urge to blink and perhaps puddle up right then and there. "And just why would that be, if I may be so bold as to ask?"

"You may." He tipped his head to her. "That's so, my dear, darling wife, my helpmate in life, and the light of my heart, because…"

He stood and circled her wrist with his fingers, pulling her against him. His teeth gleamed white as a wolf's and his eyelids lowered halfway over his dark, dilated pupils. "If you are out of the house for even two short hours each and every week, that is two hours I am guaranteed you aren't on my heels, staring at me like you expect my head to explode, or something equally awful and entertaining."

"Ted, I—"

"Shh." He put two fingers over her lips, but only for a second before he replaced them with a sweet, hungry kiss that quelled most of her doubts and fears…if only for a little while.

Seven

I can not tell you how much I appreciate your agreeing to go to Sweet Haven with me, Gayle." Naomi wrapped her sweater more tightly around herself. "I really hated the idea of taking this on all alone."

Naomi shuffled her favorite pair of hiking boots over the dingy floor of Dot and Daughters' Cafe. She leaned against the checkout counter. With every breath, she had to fight against the barrage of aromas that assaulted her. She ignored the smoke-filled backroom and the thick, greasy cloud of steam rising up to dampen the ceiling tiles just above the swinging doors leading to the chaotic kitchen. Even Gayle's subtle yet elegant perfume got into the act and conspired to cause Naomi's stomach to turn flip-flops.

"This is one of those 'Don't thank me, thank my husband' situations, I'm afraid, sweetie." Gayle put her back to the cash register while they waited for Dawnetta to bring Miss Grayson-Wiley's regular Saturday order. "I am here today entirely at Ted's behest."

"I ought to just pinch you, you know that Miss Grumpy Britches?" Naomi pretended to do just that, taking the sleeve of Gayle's expensive silk jacket between her thumb and forefinger.

"Nuh-uh, you wouldn't do any such-a-thing." Gayle pulled her arm away, giving that "poor, poor pitiful me" pout that had held her in good stead since they were both teenagers. "Why would you want to?"

Naomi laughed. "Because maybe then you'd have something

real to fuss about instead of fretting about your husband's nonexistent affair."

Gayle frowned.

"Go on, admit it. You know Ted's not the roving kind."

"He's not the catching-any-little-virus-that-comes-around kind either, but that's the only other plausible theory at work here." She fanned her hand before her upturned nose in a gesture that seemed part dismissive, part trying to flit away the staunch smell of the dregs of both the day's coffee and the counter customers. "I'd feel a ton better if one or both of you would just come down with an outright, irrefutable, raging case of this evasive, impending plague you promised you both had."

Naomi bit the inside of her cheek. Until she was sure about her suspected condition, she hesitated to mention it to anyone, even Gayle. If she was wrong about the pregnancy and it was just something simple—the inevitable effects of hormones and age, for example—she'd feel a fool.

This would be a good time, she decided, for that waitress with a penchant for breaking in on conversations to show up. She craned her neck to see if Dawnetta was anywhere near ready with the preordered meal, but saw no sign of the raw-boned woman. Clearly Naomi had to find something to say to Gayle to appease her, but that didn't mean she had to make a full confession.

"While I thank you for wishing all manner of scourge and pestilence on my body—I really do—I have to say that I've begun to think it's something besides the flu to blame for my…feeling mildly out of sorts." There, she thought, that couched the whole delicate matter in good manners and good humor. What more could her friend want?

"Details."

"What?" Naomi blinked.

"I want details." Gayle tapped the toe of her walking shoe like a clock ticking out the seconds. "First you run out of here saying some unknown bug has made you too queasy to even look at your barbecued beef sandwich. You complained of being tired and swore that it must be the same thing Ted had groused about, then you—Oh! Oh, my word."

Naomi tried to speak.

"This *can't* be. Can it?" Gayle reached for Naomi, taking her by the shoulders so she could peer into her eyes. "Oh, dear, oh, no. Nuh-uh. Tell me this isn't so, Naomi."

"*What* isn't so?" Naomi hoped her wide-eyed innocent act was convincing.

"You know what. I'm not going to embarrass us both in this public place by announcing it, but you *know…*" Gayle moved close enough to nudge Naomi with her elbow then began humming Brahms's "Lullaby."

"Really, Gayle." She tried to sound indignant. She didn't want to lie to her friend, but neither did she want to talk about this just yet. So diversion was her best tactic. "Why, that's ludicrous, isn't it? At my age?"

"At *our* age," Gayle reminded her stiffly. "And what's so crazy about that? Women far older than forty are having babies—your own mama was pretty close to that age when you were born, if I recall."

Mention of her mother caused a sudden, unexpected wave of sadness to wash over Naomi. Now she wanted more than ever to escape this line of conversation. "If you're old enough to recall when I was born then you're old enough to know better than to—"

"You are not going to throw me off track, Naomi, not even by making disparaging remarks about my age, which is the same as yours and you know it. Now, confess."

Okay, fine." Naomi threw her hands up. "I confess."

"That's better."

"You *are* the same age as I am and I know it."

"Oh, you are in trouble now, young lady." Gayle's expertly shaped eyebrows slanted in playful warning.

Naomi rolled her eyes. "I am so *not* worried."

"All right, but remember you forced me to do this."

Naomi wet her lips, more curious than anxious about what Gayle had up her sleeve.

"Excuse me, sir." Gayle pivoted to address a man who was just getting up from the cafe lunch counter.

Anxiety began to edge curiosity out of the forefront in Naomi's mind.

"Are you through with this?" Gayle pointed daintily at the platter that he'd been eating from only moments ago.

"Uh, yeah." He scratched at the top of his crew-cut head, a gimme cap—a free, promotional baseball cap from Boatwright Nursery, no less—clutched in his fisted fingers.

"May I?" She made a gesture toward picking it up.

"Uh, I...I guess so." He crammed the hat down on his head and backed away, but Gayle paid him no mind. Instead, she grabbed the platter by the rim, carefully avoiding the splatters of redeye gravy and cast-off gnarled bits of boiled ham and hash browns swirled through with pungent fried onions.

Naomi swallowed. Hard. Unfortunately, that did not quell the riot rising from deep in her belly.

Gayle proffered the platter, a sweet smile on her face. "Spill it now or I'll wave this plate under your nose."

Naomi pointed at her friend and staggered backward until her body pressed against the glass case filled with gum and mints and covered with photos of the staff's friends and family.

"You stick that plate under my nose and I *will* spill it, Gayle, I really will—"

"Confession is good for the soul," her friend reminded her still brandishing the platter.

"And possession is nine-tenths of the law," Naomi shot back. "Neither of which means a thing in this case. Now put the plate down."

"I will if you'll tell me what's going on with you. Otherwise—" Gayle paused to study the remains of the stranger's meal "—Hmmm, is that slimy stuff I see okra? Or is it some kind of kilt greens? I can't hardly tell 'cause of all the lard they used for seasoning…"

"All right." Naomi gulped down bitter acid in the back of her throat. She held up one hand. "All right. Put the plate down and back away from it, Gayle. Then we can have a civilized discussion about this."

"Like there is anything to discuss." Gayle set the platter aside with a sturdy *ka-thunk*. She moved to Naomi with her arms open. "It's perfectly obvious, sweetie, and I'm so thrilled for you."

Naomi accepted the heartfelt hug from her oldest friend. "Actually, I don't see how it *can* be so obvious. It wasn't—it isn't—to me. That is, I don't know for sure if I am pregnant, not for certain. I haven't even been to the doctor."

"Doctor?" Gayle scoffed. "Who needs a doctor for that, girl? That's why they make those nifty home pregnancy tests."

"A home test? I don't know, Gayle." Naomi was hedging. Maybe part of her just wasn't ready to know for certain if she was actually carrying Taylor's child or not. Whether she wanted to postpone the inevitable or to allow herself the luxury of dreaming of the possibilities, she did not know. She only knew she was not ready. "Those tests are not foolproof, you know."

"Well, lucky for you, you're no fool," Gayle teased. "The main reason those fail is human error, I think, honey."

"Which by no strange coincidence is also the reason a lot of people need those pregnancy tests to begin with." Naomi nudged her friend's shoulder. "Human error."

"You're not saying this baby is a mistake, are you?"

Mistake? No she could not stand there and say that the child that came from her love for a truly wonderful man and his love and commitment to her was a mistake.

"A surprise." Yes. That fit. "A great big surprise—if I am actually pregnant, that is."

"Well, there's a way to find out, that's all I'm saying."

"Yes, there is, by going to the doctor. I have an appointment already scheduled."

"When?" Gayle stopped short of outright calling her a liar with the sharp question.

"Tuesday after Thanksgiving." Naomi sniffed a "so there."

"Tuesday after…? Honey, that's more than a week away!"

"Sorry, couldn't be helped. I wanted to see that new doctor, Ben Martin. The one who's bought out Dr. Glass's old practice?" She tried to act casual and chatty and not at all as nervous and wishy-washy about her potential situation as she really felt. "He's out of town with his family next week for the Thanksgiving holiday but is opening his office for business first thing Tuesday morning and I am his first patient."

"Be a lot quicker if we just stopped by Outhier's Drugstore after we get done running our mercy mission out to Sweet Haven, that's all I'm saying."

"I should be so lucky."

Gayle gave her a puzzled look.

"If that really was all you were saying on the subject," Naomi explained. "But I don't believe I've heard the last out of you on it. Nope. Don't believe it for one second."

Out of the corner of her eye, Naomi glimpsed Dawnetta trudging toward them carrying an oversized brown paper bag crumpled closed at the top. The white handwritten bill stapled to one corner flapped with every heavy footfall.

Naomi hurried to get her thoughts out before the waitress could overhear. "I get the distinct feeling I won't hear the end of this until I agree to stop by the drugstore tonight, so purely in the interest of peace and quiet—"

"Don't fret about collecting any money for this," Dawnetta piped up. "The niece pays up once a month, regular as clock-work. But Miss Grace insists on seeing the bill so she knows we aren't shortchanging anybody."

"I'll get one of those tests," Naomi concluded.

"How's that, ma'am?" Dawnetta cocked her head and a corkscrew curl bounced back and forth like an overextended bedspring on top of her head.

"Nothing, nothing." Gayle took the bag from the waitress. She must have slipped the woman a tip just as their hands touched, so discreetly Naomi had not seen it. Wouldn't that just be Gayle's style, Naomi thought as Dawnetta pocketed the folded money and, with as gracious a demeanor as any Southern belle might possess, said, "You didn't have to do that, Mrs. Barrett, but I thank you."

Gayle gave Dawnetta's arm the lightest squeeze then nodded toward the door, her gaze on Naomi.

"That was nice of you," Naomi said as they stepped outside.

"Just common courtesy." Gayle shrugged. "I have the feeling 'the niece' doesn't tack on any gratuity for all the service the cafe provides when she pays that bill. If she did Dawnetta might have extended her the civility of using her name."

Naomi laughed. "True."

"Still, they go the extra mile for Miss Grace, even if they don't earn an extra dime for it. That Dawnetta has a good heart."

"She's not the only one."

"You didn't let me finish." Gayle depressed a button on her key chain, which was aimed at her minivan and a shrill tweep cut through the air. "Dawnetta has a good heart but, of course, what she *needs* is a good hairdresser."

Gayle didn't fool Naomi one bit with that snotty routine. She was deflecting, trying to seem above it all, probably because she was uncomfortable that she was not as outwardly good-hearted to those like Grace Grayson as a waitress in a greasy spoon.

"Well, if that's all she needs—" Being a good friend, Naomi decided to play along "—maybe you can give her the name of your personal groomer. Someone who'd say a thing as catty as that must have an awfully good one."

"Meow." Gayle gave a genuine laugh. "Honest, honey, I didn't mean anything by it."

"I know."

"I think the world of Dawnetta, as I do of all of Dot's daughters. But truth be told, there's not a one of them, their mother included, who could do a thing with the mop of hair God gave them. I don't think saying that makes me catty."

"It doesn't."

Gayle opened the sliding passenger door to place the food delivery bag on the back seat, working to anchor it in place. When she finished she turned to Naomi, who still waited on the sidewalk. "Well, aren't you going to get in?"

"I was just waiting for…well, I really thought that maybe if we gave them a few more…" Naomi sighed. "I just had hoped it would be more than just the two of us taking on the little project today."

Gayle's shoes crunched over the gravel parking lot as she came to her friend and put her arm around Naomi's shoulders. "Hey, don't you mean the *three* of us?"

"Make that the four of us—Lucy is right behind me."

Naomi and Gayle both started at the voice, and looked to see Rose rounding the side of Gayle's van. Rose's face was flushed and she was slightly out of breath. "Sorry to be late but you know we open the center for the prayer circle of young mothers whenever they need us, and today their session went on a bit long."

She turned around and motioned to Lucy to hurry up, then back to Naomi and Gayle. "Well, all right, *all* those young mothers' meetings go on a bit long, and I think we all know who is responsible for them never getting through on time. If I weren't such a refined Christian lady—" Rose pretended to cough into her hand, having fun at her own expense "—I'd call her by name—and a few choice adjectives to boot, especially when I see her taking advantage of Lucy so. And after what she'd already done to the poor girl. Hello, Naomi. How are you, Gayle?"

"We didn't think you were coming." Gayle gave their friend a greeting hug.

Over Rose's back, Gayle's gaze met Naomi's. Naomi raised one finger to her lips and pleaded in silence for some discretion. Gayle winked to show she understood and would honor Naomi's wishes.

Naomi relaxed—as much as she could.

Lucy charged up, clearly aggravated but determined not to go into it. "Well, now are we ready to plunge into this, ya'll?"

"Feet first," Rose pledged.

"Don't you mean head first?" Gayle knocked against her temple.

"Isn't that how we seem to do everything?" Lucy grumbled.

"Not everything," Gayle assured her. "A few things we do *heart* first."

Naomi smiled back at her friend's warm expression. "Feet, head, heart—it sounds like this group doesn't know which end is up!"

"This was your idea, smarty pants," Rose chided her. "Suppose you tell us how we should proceed then?"

Naomi's smile broadened slowly as she took in the sight of all of them together again and ready to do the Lord's work. "How about—" she said, reaching out for the hands of those nearest her "—we do this as it should be done: *prayer* first?"

The women reached out for one another, as they had done so many times before, and held hands. Naomi cleared her throat and began. "Lord, go with us as we attempt this new venture; guide our hearts that we would do this for the right reasons, and show us what we can do to become better servants of you, friends to each other, and helpers for Miss Grace."

They all chimed in with amens, and so their paths were set.

"Git yawselves *off'uh* my front porch, ya'll *hear* me?"

Grace Grayson brandished a bony fist in the window of Sweet Haven's front door. That's all Rose saw of the feisty old lady—all she figured any of them saw. Miss Grace's face and body were nothing more than a distorted blur behind an oval of stained glass that covered the center of the window.

Rose stared at the white and yellow diamond shapes that looked like the leaves of a bowed branch. Then she studied the blue and purple background studded in a few spots where the colors converged with beveled crystal circles. Circles, she recalled, that caught the morning sun and sent rainbows spilling out over the anteroom.

"Beneath the Wings of Angels," the piece had been called by the artist. Mrs. Sable Grayson, Grace's grandmother, had commissioned an artist to create the window sometime around the onset of the Civil War...in the days when the Grayson family still had their fortune and Sable Grayson spent from it freely.

To some in town, this extravagant doorpiece represented the pride and folly of the once proud and wealthy family. A body need only point to this lavish bit of nonsense to explain the Grayson's downfall. How sad that no one saw it as the testament Sable had intended—a testament to the family's love of their home and the strength of their faith in a time of great trial.

Rose studied it a moment longer, swept up in its beauty and in her own memories of having passed by the image daily when she lived at Sweet Haven so long ago.

"Beneath the Wings of Angels."

"What was that Rose?" Lucy edged close enough behind her that Rose could feel a prickle of static electricity from the young woman's fuzzy blue sweater.

"That's what that stained-glass picture is called." Rose looked back on all her friends, who stood huddled on the swayed porch. "I learned the whole history of it when I lived here in the late sixties."

"Oh, Rose! That's right. You *did* live here." Naomi rushed forward, the bag from the cafe clutched tightly to her upper body. "You know Miss Grace. Just tell her who you are, and she'll—"

"Ya'll deaf out there, 'r *whut?* Now go on! Scat!" Grace's tiny fist wagged at them again.

"I hate to burst your bubble, doll, but Grace has no idea who I am." Rose shook her head, feeling the chill of the encroaching late November evening on her neck as her hair swished away from her upturned collar. "She lived in New Jersey, I believe, during that time and protected her precious Sweet Haven by hiring caretakers to run it as the Grayson Boarding House."

"But aren't you always saying you're some kind of relation to the Graysons?" Gayle raised one perfectly plucked eyebrow as if to question the veracity of Rose's former claims.

"Whatever you're a'sellin', I don't want no part of it." Grace dared to peer at them with one squinting eye. "And I can hear ya'll yammering out there, don't think I can't. Scheming is what you're about, I reckon, scheming how you can take advantage of this weak old lady. Well, I'll tell you what, you schemers, you—"

"*Shirttail* relation." Rose knew the announcement was as cool as the damp fall air. She drew a breath and tried not to be so rude as to show her great relief at the lack of strong familial ties to this woman. "Shaky at best, and I never claimed anything closer."

"Well, I may be old, but I'm not weak," Grace called out. "I never been had by schemers up to now in my life, and I'm not fixin' to be had by some today, no sir."

Rose took a deep breath to launch into some lengthy recitation of tenuous lineage connections with more begats than the Bible, who married whom and so forth, but she never had a chance.

"Shirttail or shaky as Jell-O in an earthquake, it's a better in than any of us have." Naomi thrust the bag into Rose's midsection then placed both her hands on Rose's back and gave a light shove toward the door. "Use it."

"Oh, all right. Don't push. But before I risk grave bodily injury I would like to go on record as saying I was not the one who thought this little service project of yours was the best of ideas."

"Ya'll deaf or what? Get on now. Don't make me get out there and get after you." Both of Grace's tiny, knotted fists appeared in the corner of the window like some Victorian drawing of a man challenging them to a round of fisticuffs. "I'll warn you. I may be little, but I'm scrappy."

Naomi choked on a laugh.

Lucy snickered.

"Go on, Rose, I think you can take her." Gayle propelled Rose forward another step. "She may be scrappy, but you're crafty and quick—and you've got us to back you up."

"You have no idea how much comfort that is to me." Rose rolled her eyes, then turned her focus to the door. "Miss Gra— that is, Mrs. Grayson-Wiley? Honey, we haven't come to sell you a thing. We've come to bring you your usual cafe dinner."

"Not so. Not so, you schemer." Still, even as she denied it, Grace inched the door open enough to reveal the tip of her nose. "I have a girl that brings me my meal of a Saturday evening. Brings it to me reg'lar. Rings the bell and leaves the food right there by the door."

"You fired that girl, ma'am. Don't you remember?" Rose tried to sound sweet as pie.

"'Course I remember. I'm not senile."

"No, no. I never intended to imply as much, I just—"

"Like fire, you didn't!" The door rattled a bit, as if under-scoring Grace's own indignity. "You just as much call me senile every time you use that tone of voice, like you was a talkin' to a pouty child or a silly old fool or a…a…a stubborn, snarling poodle who had its teeth sunk into your house shoe!"

Rose started to deny it, then pulled herself up short at the realization that there was some truth in the claim. "Well, if I did sound patronizing, then I apologize from the heart. I didn't mean it that way."

No answer.

All right, if she wants to be that way, Rose thought, then best to give her a taste of it right back. "Still, I might suggest to you, Mrs. Grayson-Wiley, that if you expect folks to address you in some other manner, then you'd be well advised to stop acting like some pouty child or stubborn, snarling poodle."

Tension rose from the women behind her like coffee percolating in an old-fashioned pot, building and almost bubbling up in the tingling quiet. One, two, three, four full, weighty seconds ticked past with not a single sound between them. Then a thin, crackling laughter started low and rolled out from behind the partially opened door.

She wouldn't swear it really happened, but Rose sensed the others exhaling in unison.

"You have yawself a point, Missy. Yes, you do." Grace pulled the door inward just a fraction more, revealing the pink and yellow tulip pattern on her faded housedress, one pale, stick-thin leg with sagging blue jeans rolled up to the shin, and a pair of bright red canvas tennis shoes with a hole in the toe. The woman's face, though, remained hidden by the eerie blue and purple of the stained-glass oval. "But maybe I have reason to snap and bark like some ill-tempered pooch, especially when strangers come sniffing 'round my house. Did you ever think of that?"

"We're not exactly strangers, Miss Grace." Naomi spoke up, moving in behind Rose in what was either a means of getting into position to shove Rose right at Miss Grace at any minute—or just Naomi's way of trying to sneak a better look inside the house. "At least, Rose here isn't. She's some kind of relation to you, ma'am."

"Relation?" Grace squawked. "What kind of *relation?* Not the kind that looks to inherit money, I hope."

"Oh, no, no, nothing like that," Naomi assured the woman even before Rose could. "She's...she's...well, you tell her Rose, how *are* you related?"

"We share a cousin—a distant cousin, I believe—on both our father's sides of the family," Rose explained, her teeth gritted.

"That so?" Grace questioned more than the connection with her tone. "Is that why you're here?"

"No, we're here, like we told you, to deliver the dinner Miss Dawnetta prepared special just for you—just like she does every Saturday."

"Then leave it by the door like my girl does every Saturday."

"Well, now, I believe you are relation to this lady, Rose," Gayle whispered to Rose's back. "Stubborn that deep just *has* to be genetic."

Lucy laughed. "She does sound like you, Rose, like the way you'd handle it from the other side of that door."

Rose lifted her chin to show herself above this common behavior—and this unflattering, but possibly valid, comparison.

"You want stubborn?" Rose realized even as she spoke that she negated everything she'd hoped to rise above with her comportment. "I'll show y'all stubborn."

She stepped forward. "Now that's enough of this foolishness, Mrs. Grayson-Wiley. We are not going to simply plop down this food and scurry off. We are not paid messenger girls. We've made this effort to come here for your sake and to help out Miss Dawnetta, and we deserve to be treated with some measure of civility. Now, we don't expect you to invite us in—"

"We don't?" Naomi's disappointment was clear.

Rose ignored her and went on. "A woman living alone as you do would be foolhardy to do something like that. But I know Miss Dawnetta let you know that we'd be coming out here today.

I also know that you're far too mannered a lady to shoo away legitimate callers without even looking them in the eye."

"I suppose you think you can talk to me that away because you fancy yawself my kin." The doorknob clattered as if gripped with angry force. "But you better know, I ain't impressed by such talk. No sir. I've heard that kind of thing before. You can't imagine how many times someone has shown up on my doorstep claiming to be some form a kin to me— and rightful owners to this house or whatever worldly goods they thought they could bamboozle an old lady out of."

"Actually, I *can* imagine it," Rose said softly and for the first time she felt a real twinge of compassion for the old girl. Maybe they had misjudged her by assuming she was daft or crotchety— and if she seemed those things, perhaps reality and not some overly romanticized fantasy lay at the heart of her behavior. Rose felt a bit ashamed at her bullying tactics. She hung her head. "I can very well imagine how many folks would like to get their hands on this old place and the things inside it. You see, I've lived in Sweet Haven, Mrs. Grayson-Wiley, for a short time when I was a young woman. Back in the days you rented out rooms here as a boarding house."

"You…did?" Suspicion still colored Grace's words.

"Yes, and I know what a special place it is here—" Rose glanced at the intricate artwork that still concealed the old woman's features "—beneath the wings of angels."

Grace's small feet shifted over the dried, wooden floor. Even her slight weight made the old boards creak and complain.

Rose moved the brown bag in her arms to one side and waited, the comforting aroma of hot rolls and fried chicken curling up like steam around her face.

Finally Grace spoke again, her voice brittle and delicate. "Which one?"

Rose blinked, she glanced back at her friends for help but none of them understood the question either. Perhaps, she thought, Miss Grace really was a little senile.

"Well? Speak up!" Grace demanded.

"Which? Which...angel?" Rose finally ventured.

A sharp bust of laughter came in answer. "No, no. Which cousin? Which cousin is it that you say we have in common, Miss?"

"Oh, which *cousin*." Rose sighed in relief. She twisted her neck to repeat to her friends, "Which cousin."

"Yes, which cousin?" Grace echoed.

"That would be Gretta Mae." Rose paused to draw in a breath before spewing out the woman's full name. "Gretta Mae Grayson Mason."

"Gretta Mae Grayson...?" Naomi's disbelief apparently would not allow her to finish it.

"Nuh-uh," was all Gayle had to say on the matter.

"If I were her, I'd have had second thoughts before I married a name like Grayson to a Mason," Lucy muttered.

"It isn't her married name, sugar, it's her given name," Rose explained.

"Gretta Mae. Why I hadn't heard that name since before Granny got the goose!" One of Grace's hands curled around the around the edge of the door. Flakes of old white paint flecked off the weathered wood to fall like fine powdered snow on the old woman's red shoes. Slowly she began to move, her feet shuffling forward. A tuft of hair that looked like a trail of cotton batting pulled loose from an antiquated sofa cushion appeared first. Then her face came into view, her eyes all squinted up and trained most definitely on Rose. "So, you're a Mason, then?"

"By birth, yes. Gretta Mae was my father's second cousin."

Rose smiled sweetly. "I think."

Grace pursed her lips as if in deep thought.

Rose took a moment to study the woman. She wasn't nearly as old as Rose had expected, nor as feeble as her tiny, trembling hands might suggest. She had a staunch backbone and clear eyes that said right out that she knew who she was and she was quite content with it—something many people half her age sadly lacked. And she had a quality that had, for the most part, faded from most modern demeanor. Even with her mismatched clothes, wild, wispy hair, and the hole in her shoe, Mrs. Grace Grayson-Wiley exuded a quiet, unshakable kind of dignity.

"As I recall, li'l Gretta Mae married one of them Henneke boys." Grace cocked her head just so. "Didn't she?"

This was a test. Rose recognized it and found herself grinning something of a wicked grin as she met the challenge with a lift of her chin and a chuckle. "Oh, no. No, she did not."

Grace lifted one shakily penciled-on eyebrow. "No?"

"No, ma'am. Gretta Mae married *two* of those Henneke boys. Not six months after her first husband died in that questionable farm machinery accident, she up and ran off with the younger brother and had a baby seven months later. Premature, of course."

"Of course." Grace returned Rose's grin in kind. "You're family all right. I'm sorry I've been so rude to you all. It's just that I don't open my door to just anyone."

"A wise policy." Rose stepped forward, leading with the bag of food. "But now that you know who we are—"

"Hold it right there." Grace retreated back behind the door again, disappearing entirely this time.

"This is getting us nowhere," Gayle muttered. "Maybe we should just leave the food and—"

"But what about our project?" Naomi sounded positively sorrowful. "We all agreed we'd take Miss Grace on and try whatever we could to help her."

"We agreed to bring her her Saturday supper and sort of check in on her," Rose reminded her friend. "And we've done that. Maybe next week, we'll be able to do more."

"Yes, sure." Lucy put one hand on Naomi's shoulder. "It's like when we have a new child at the day care. We have to go slow, win their confidence, allow them time to learn to trust us. Miss Grace isn't any different than that."

"So, you're all saying we *will* try again?" Naomi tweaked a strand of her black hair between her finger and thumb.

The answers all came at once.

"Yes."

"Sure."

"Certainly."

"Well, in that case…" Naomi made a gesture toward the floor by the door.

"It'll work out all right, you'll see." Rose leaned down to place the bag in the crack of the open door. Adjusting the order so that Miss Grace could not miss the ticket Dawnetta had prepared, she called out, "I'm leaving your dinner, just like you asked, Mrs. Grayson-Wiley."

Suddenly the door swung inward.

Rose nearly jumped out of her skin. Her heart raced and her breathing grew shallow.

Miss Grace stood over her as if out of nowhere.

The smell of lavender and dust and what she could only describe as *age* and the cafe dinner mingled in Rose's nostrils, making her fight off the urge to sneeze. She steadied herself with one hand to keep from falling over backward. "Oh, Mrs. Grayson-Wiley! You startled me."

"Why?" The old woman shook her head a couple times. One or two wild strands of hair continued swaying back and forth for a few seconds after she had stopped. "You knew I was back here."

"She's got you there, Rose." Gayle's voice was full of restrained laughter.

"She *got* me all right." Rose blew out a long, cool breath.

"I just stepped back inside to get you this." She held out her hand with something unseen clutched loosely in her fist. "It's for your trouble."

"Oh, no." Rose recoiled. "We couldn't. We can't. We…really will not accept a tip from you, Mrs. Grayson-Wiley."

"Why? Isn't my tip good enough for you?"

"Well, no, it's not that, it—"

"Then you're too good to take a tip from someone like me?"

"I never said—"

"Don't get all high and mighty on me, Missy. I know who your people are now and I know they're no better than mine are. I am a *Grayson*, after all."

"Well, yes, of course, but we—"

"Then here you go." Grace thrust out her little fist again.

Rose raised her open hand. "But I can't—"

"Oh, just take the tip, Rose," Gayle snapped. "We don't have time to stand here and go through another round of dueling muleheads."

"Why, you taking medicine?" Rose didn't hide her sarcasm anymore than Gayle had.

"No," Gayle whispered. "But some of us do sort of have to get to Outhier's Drugstore before they close up for the evening."

"What for?" Lucy asked.

"Never mind," Naomi said through her teeth, her gaze practically burning a hole through Gayle.

Something was up, Rose decided, and the sooner she stopped arguing with Grace over this tip issue, the sooner she'd find out just what.

"Take the tip," Naomi urged, her cheeks a searing pink. "We'll start a church fund or give it to Dawnetta or something."

Grudgingly, Rose turned again to Grace, sighed and held out her hand to receive the gratuity. Despite her chagrin at the whole incident, she called upon all her training to sound and appear as grateful as possible. "Thank you, Mrs. Grayson-Wiley. I hope you enjoy your dinner."

Grace hummed some singsongy little reply and shut the door with a resounding *whomp*.

As the four of them turned to stroll the short distance from the old wraparound porch to the drive, Rose stole a quick peek at the bounty Grace had bestowed on them.

"One button, three pennies, a twenty-five cents off coupon for hair rinse—make that an *expired* coupon—and several assorted colors and sizes of rubber bands." She relayed the inventory to them.

"Oooo, Rose, next time can I get the tip?" Gayle met their questioning looks with dead-serious humor. "I always need more rubber bands."

"Very funny." Rose snatched up a dull green band and shot it in Gayle's direction. "I'll let you get the tip next time on one condition."

They all came to a stop beside Gayle's van. Gayle pressed the button on her key chain and above the shrill tweep asked, "What's that condition, Rose?"

"That you tell me just what it is you've got to get at Outhier's Drugstore tonight."

Gayle looked to Naomi.

Rose did likewise, as did Lucy.

Naomi, lips pressed tight, went pale. She glared at Gayle, then cast an apologetic smile at Lucy and Rose.

"Never mind, Rose." Gayle waved her hand, her tangle of car and house keys jangling against her thin wrist. "You can get the tip next time. I'll just keep that information to myself."

She opened the door to her van but no one followed suit. They just stood there, all of them waiting, wanting to know more.

"What?" Gayle laughed, but not too convincingly. "It's no big deal. Really. It's just—"

"I'm pregnant." Naomi held her arms out to her sides.

"What?" Rose almost choked on nothing but air.

Lucy whooped and threw her arms around Naomi. "Congratulations!"

"That's a bit early, Lucy, honey." Naomi removed herself from Lucy's hug. "That is, I *think* I'm pregnant. Then again, I may not be at all. That's why we have to go to the drugstore and get a test. I can take it first thing in the morning. Until then, let's just keep this our little secret, all right?"

"You're trusting this group to keep a secret like that?" Rose shook her head, then gave them all a sly wink. "Wild talk like that makes me think you have been exposed to something."

"Yeah, the *love bug*." Gayle pinched her friend's arm, grinning. "We'll keep your secret, all right, you know we will."

"I think it's wonderful." Lucy had a faraway gleam in her eyes. "Just imagine—a *baby!* Aren't you just over the moon about this, Naomi?"

"Well, I don't know, Lucy. One minute I think I'm over the moon and the next—" She looked away and sighed as if the whole world rested on her shoulders "—the next minute I think about all the changes a thing like this will bring to my body, my family, my marriage, to every aspect of my life and I have to wonder if I haven't just gotten myself over a barrel. "

Eight

"Yᵒu two did this just to ruin my life!"

"Well, we live to serve," Taylor muttered to his fourteen-year-old daughter as she ran from the master bedroom. He never took his gaze from the mirror as he wound one end of his gray-blue tie over then tucked it through and pulled it into a perfect knot.

Naomi leaned against the door between the bathroom and their bedroom, the white stick that told the positive test results still in her hand, and watched her husband a moment. She loved seeing him dressed up like this, in a dark suit that hung in flawless lines over his long, lean frame and a white shirt that created an appealing contrast against his tanned skin. She loved the way his rugged features, the familiar creases in his face, and even the roughness of his big, workman's hands were softened just ever-so-much by the stylish trappings. She loved the way he combed and recombed his hair, which he hardly even bothered about during the week, until it lay smooth and shiny against his head. She loved everything about him, and seeing him like this was one of her favorite things about Sunday mornings.

"This doesn't mean you don't have to go to church, young lady," he suddenly called out.

Naomi blinked. The stick in her hand almost went tumbling down to the floor, but she caught it in time. She glanced around then down at her billowy, flannel nightgown and bare feet.

Taylor walked to the hallway and tipped his head back as if addressing the entire upstairs. "Ruined life or not, I expect you to be ready to leave in ten minutes."

Naomi put her hand to her heart. "Gracious, I thought you meant me at first."

He twisted his neck to look at her, then smiled. "I wish it were that easy to get you to change your mind and come with us this morning."

"Hey, I don't miss church very often," she said in her own defense. "And when I do it's because I'm sick or have a really good reason."

He challenged that with a look.

"I happen to have a very good reason today—I just found out I'm pregnant. If the only time I ever miss a Sunday service is when *that* happens I don't think I'll get counted absent too often." She crossed her arms.

He came to her and gave her a hug, ignoring her stiff response. "Point well taken. But still, I thought on this of all days it might be especially nice for us to all attend together."

He pressed his lips to her temple, and she turned her head into his kiss. Letting him fold her into his embrace, she released the tension that had built inside her since Ashley's overly dramatic response to the news of the new baby.

"I don't think Ashley *wants* us all to attend church together right now." She inhaled the scent of his pressed shirt and clean skin, neither of which, happily, had an adverse effect on her delicate stomach.

"Well, I don't know if you've noticed, but this marriage is not about what *Ashley* wants." He pulled her closer, his strong arms like a blanket of warmth enveloping her.

The fabric of his lapel chafed her cheek. His silk tie rustled as she slid her hand down it.

"Maybe it isn't about what she wants but it's not just about what *we* want, either. When we got married we blended two families. It wasn't such a big deal for our sons, what with mine away in his senior year at college and yours just graduated and out on his own. But for Ashley?"

Naomi shook her head. She had had her run-ins with Taylor's daughter before the marriage but eventually they'd found a fragile peace in their bond of having both lost their mothers. Since the wedding, Naomi and the young woman had become friends—as much as any adult can be friends with a girl in the beginning of her teen years. Actually, Naomi had begun to take some comfort in being the object of the eye-rolling, the long, exaggerated groaning sighs, and even the look only a teen can give that makes a person feel they must be something the dinosaurs dug up. That treatment from Ashley meant acceptance—an acceptance that Naomi's latest news flash had probably shattered.

"Ashley seems truly upset by this, Taylor. I worry about how it will effect the family we've been trying to create."

"This new baby is also part of that family, you know."

She did not meet his gaze.

Taylor lifted Naomi's chin with one finger. "Ashley is fourteen years old. She is upset about this today. Tomorrow she'll be put out about it. The next day, still mortified but able to stand it."

Naomi smiled at his assessment.

"Then the holidays will take her mind completely off it until…oh, I'd say after the big Valentine's Dance at school." He brushed a lock of Naomi's hair back off her shoulder. "Then it'll be spring, time to start picking out baby things—clothes and toys and furniture—and I guarantee you this…"

"What?"

"Once my daughter realizes the level of shopping required to get everything ready for a new addition in the house she will be so totally behind this blessed event, you'd think it was her idea that we give her a little brother or sister."

"You really think so?" She touched the taut plain of her husband's cheek with the back of her hand.

"I do," he whispered before placing a kiss on her fingers.

Naomi sighed, knowing she should feel more relieved. She swallowed hard and scrunched up her nose, looking away from Taylor's searching gaze. "I hope you're right. I really would like for Ashley to be happy about this baby."

"Yeah, and after she is—" Taylor put his hands on her shoulders to coax her to look into his soulful eyes "—then maybe you can be too?"

"Are you happy now?" Rose slammed shut the door of her elegant Cadillac.

In the passenger seat, Naomi hunkered down, her shoulders pulled up high. Feeling decidedly not happy, she folded her arms over the strained harness of her seat belt. She crossed her ankles so tightly that the thick sole of one hiking boot squawked against the leather of the other.

"We gave it a shot. What's so wrong about giving it a shot?" She narrowed her eyes at the dimly lit stained-glass window that adorned the front door of Grace Grayson-Wiley's house, a heaviness in her being. "Every year on Thanksgiving Day evening, your church goes out to every neighborhood in town to invite people to participate in their holiday activities, right?"

"Every year for the last twenty years," Rose confirmed as she clicked her safety belt into place.

"So, this year we tried doing the same with Grace. I don't

see any harm in extending the hand of Christian fellowship—"

"Except that what we were extending was our *noses,* right into her business." Rose cranked the key and the engine purred to life.

"Well, as Gayle would say 'Nuh-uh!'" She tossed her head hoping that would add more weight to the denial she did not totally feel. "I never suggested we do this to be nosey. I wanted to be kind. I merely wondered if anybody in this town, that's so happy to gossip about her, ever thought to ask Miss Grace to join in anything."

"I can think of at least one time someone did."

"You can?" Naomi's mood perked up, hoping for an opportunity to learn from a past experience. "When was that?"

"The 1946 Splendor Belle Gala," Rose's expression was deadpan. "And look how badly *that* turned out for her."

Naomi threw up her hands. Why couldn't her friends share her connection to this special project? Especially Rose, whom she had counted on to understand. "How anyone with a name like Rose could be such a stinker is beyond me."

Rose just laughed and backed her boat of a vehicle around, then pointed it down the long driveway.

"Anyway, I managed to leave a flyer on her door with all the dates and times of the holiday events." Naomi sighed. "Who knows, she may just show up at something and surprise us all."

"By *surprise,* do you, by any chance, mean stun and stupefy? Dumbfound and dazzle? Amaze and—"

"All right, already!" Naomi tipped her nose up. "I get it. I get that should Grace Grayson-Wiley choose to show her pruny-but-cherubic face at the Second Antioch Baptist Church, it might shock a few folks."

"A few? Try the whole congregation and everyone they tell

about it—which will be everyone in town." Rose clicked her tongue. "I sworn, if Miss Grace showed her—cherubic? Did you say, cherubic?"

Naomi shrugged to cover her defensiveness. "Can I help it if she reminds me of a mischievous little cherub?"

Rose shook her head. "Anyway, if she should show her *cherubic* face at the Christmas Eve candlelight service, or the All Souls Christmas Sing-Along, or even the children's pageant on the Sunday afternoon before Christmas? Tongues would wag about that for years to come. *Years!*"

Naomi knew her friend's point about Grace's status in their town was legitimate, but she also knew that did not mean they shouldn't strive to change it. "Still, I think it might be good for her—and for them, as well—if she did show up."

"You're absolutely right, Naomi, hon. Just don't pin your hopes on that happening. Especially after the way we were…received tonight."

"We tried." Naomi took some solace in that. "At least we can say that much. I, for one, am glad we did, even if she didn't entertain the invitation in the manner in which it was intended."

"Didn't entertain the…?" Rose grumbled something unintelligible under her breath as she pulled the car onto the dark, back road. "Naomi, sugar, that old woman offered to salt our hides with buckshot!"

"I don't think for one minute she'd have done that, Rose." Naomi let her shoulders slouch a bit and, biting her lip, glanced back at Sweet Haven growing more distant in the back window. "After all, she came around last time we were here."

"Last time we had her supper."

"I don't think she warmed up to us because of the food, Rose. It's not like she's starving in that big old house, you know—unless it's starving for friendship." Naomi leaned back against the seat. "I think the old girl is lonely."

"Yes, lonely for her soundness of mind."

"Rose!"

"I'm teasing."

"You're being mean, and meanness does not become you."

"Since when?"

Naomi uncrossed her ankles and cocked her head, giving her friend a bemused sidelong glance. "Since you've been dating a certain William Boatwright. I do think he's taken the edge off you, Miss Rose Holcolmb."

"Well, any blunt object will do that."

"Too bad that same blunt object can't knock you to your senses," Naomi muttered quite distinctly, just for Rose's benefit.

"What's that supposed to mean?"

"It means…" She twisted in the seat to face her friend and give her a kind and genuine smile. "We missed you at the Boatwright family Thanksgiving today. I really wish you would have come."

Rose shook her head. "No, I just couldn't. What with Kelley and her husband only able to come for a few hours and Stacey entrenched in my house like a seventeen-year-locust digging in for the duration, I couldn't manage it. Besides, I'm not sure I'd have been welcome."

"Of course you would have!"

Rose clenched her jaw. "I don't know. Will and I haven't exactly been getting along famously of late."

"Because he realizes you're using Stacey's presence as a stalling technique?"

"Actually, no. It all started when this whole business with Grace Grayson-Wiley came up."

Naomi blinked, trying to come up with some explanation

for that odd connection. "Really?"

"Oh, yes. If he knew we'd come out here today he'd have a fit."

"That's funny. Why would Will care about us trying to help Miss Grace?" Naomi sat back and listened to the sound of the tires on the rough road. The sound should have lent a lulling sensation to the trip but instead it seemed to agitate, like static hissing on the radio. It kept her from focusing her thoughts and finally she gave up trying to figure out the puzzle with that distracting her. She put her finger to her cheek. "Well, Will certainly hasn't shown any particular concern over *my* coming out here."

"Hmmm." Rose adjusted her hands on the steering wheel, her head tipped to the right and her brow crimped down. "That is odd. He told me he didn't think *anyone* ought to bother Miss Grace. Got pretty cantankerous about it, too."

"Well, maybe he doesn't feel comfortable saying anything to me yet since I'm still new in the family."

"Will?" Rose snorted. "Are we talking about the same William Boatwright? The one I know would happily insinuate himself into anybody's business at the drop of a hat. And tell them exactly what he thought about it, too. Of course he'd couch it in impeccable Southern manners with a twist of wry humor to make it more palatable."

"That sounds like him," Naomi agreed.

"He's probably just getting all territorial on me. Thinking he can tell me what to do, where to go, and who to associate with because we've kept company for so many months now."

"Well, if he thinks that then he doesn't know you very well, Rose." Naomi chuckled. "You don't let anybody boss you around."

"Except you, it seems. I certainly would not have come out

on some fool's errand for very many people—just you, the other girls from our prayer circle and, of course, my daughters."

Hearing herself lumped in with the likes of Rose's daughters caused a bittersweet stabbing high in Naomi's chest. Not a day went by since Mama's passing that Naomi didn't think of her and wish…

Naomi put her hand low over her tummy and dragged in a deep, aching breath. The smell of Rose's perfectly kept car and her subtle cologne sent Naomi's stomach lurching, but she welcomed that. Better a physical symptom to deal with than all the emotional turmoil within her.

She felt Rose's gaze on her as they pulled into the drive of Naomi's home. Naomi swallowed down the acid rising in the back of her throat, batted back the tears that stung her eyes, and sniffled.

Rose wanted to say something to lend some comfort or guidance, Naomi knew. She told her friend not to even try with a quick shake of her head.

"Well, you're home, then," Rose chirped, a bit too enthusiastically.

"So I am." Naomi started to gather her things, using the time to gather her composure as well.

"And I wouldn't worry about that whole Grace thing with Will and me." Rose obviously was making small talk to fill up the awkward silence. "He'll probably get around to giving you a hard way to go about it soon."

"Gee, thanks."

"As soon as he gets used to the idea of your delicate condition." Rose's smile seemed positively angelic.

Naomi unfastened her seat belt and it retracted with a whir. "Oh, he doesn't even *know* about that yet."

153

"You mean you didn't make the big announcement at the family Thanksgiving?"

"No, and I'm not going to make any announcements." She clutched her purse to her chest like a child protectively hugging a teddy bear. "Not until after I've seen the doctor on Tuesday."

"Why ever not?"

"Because…" *Why ever not, indeed?* If only she had a quick, simple answer to that question. She wet her lips, dug her fingers into the supple leather of her bag, and sighed. "Because I'm old, for one thing."

"Oh, yes, you're ancient, my dear. I'm surprised you can still walk unassisted."

"I mean I'm old for having a baby—I'm going to turn forty-one soon." She ran one hand back through her hair, recalling the featherings of silver she'd found here and there over the last year. "I'm not naive, Rose. That automatically puts me in the high-risk category."

"You don't anticipate any difficulties, do you?" Rose put her hand on Naomi's arm, her eyes bright with concern.

"I don't know what to anticipate, Rose. That's why I don't want to say anything to anyone until after my doctor's appointment."

Rose nodded. "You're seeing that new fellow, aren't you? That Ben Martin?"

"Yes, I'm going to be his very first patient in town." She exaggerated an anxious expression.

Rose laughed. "Don't you worry, gal, he's a keeper. New Bethany won't be throwing him back to the city anytime soon. That is, if he treats his patients half as nicely as he does the day care staff—"

"He's been to the day care?"

"Three times now. Twice to check it out personally—don't ask about that first fiasco—and once to let his two kids look around. We passed inspection, and they'll be starting full time beginning Tuesday."

"Kids?" Naomi blinked. "But I could have sworn the scuttlebutt around town is that he's not married."

"He's not." Rose had a gleam in her eye as she conveyed the news. "And whether he's divorced or widowed, he hasn't said, but I do know this…"

"Tell!"

"The last time he was in—the time he came with his kids?"

"Uh-huh?"

"He asked especially that they be introduced to Miss Lucy."

"And?"

"And you should have seen his face when I told him she'd stepped out for the afternoon."

"Disappointed?"

"Crushed."

"Really?"

"Honey, his mood went flatter than a beehive hairdo caught in a sudden downpour."

Naomi giggled. "And how does our Miss Lucy feel about this?"

"She acts like she doesn't care one whit. But I'll tell you this, there's more than one lady from our prayer circle who is right anxious about her encounter with the good Dr. Ben this coming Tuesday."

"Alec! Paige!" Ben Martin bent one knee to put himself at kid-level in one natural, steady movement. "Daddy's here to pick you up—a bit late, but I'm here, now."

The two little ones, whom Lucy had tried to occupy to keep their minds off their father's unavoidable tardiness, squirmed down from her lap, their small feet already thrashing in anticipation of hitting the ground. Almost the second they had deserted her, Lucy felt a pang of longing to hold the adorable pair of Martin children close again. She stood and pinched together the edges of her soft pink cardigan, which draped almost to midthigh and hid a "multitude of sins," as her mother might say.

She smoothed down her cool, silky hair with careful precision. That did nothing to stay the flutter in her chest, which came from the potent mix of the children leaving her side and their father's entering her line of vision.

She'd thought about the doctor quite a bit since their first meeting—and even more so since he dropped the intriguing tidbit that he did not have a wife. What did *that* mean, she asked herself again as she chewed her lower lip. Was the compelling doctor widowed? Divorced?

Her pulse picked up and her cheeks warmed to remember how often she had wondered and worried while he was out of town last week if he had taken the children to spend the holiday with their mother. Had he spent time with her, too? Was there a chance for a reconciliation?

For the children's sake and because she knew it was right, she wanted to hope that was the case. Still, it gave her a peculiar twinge of personal loss to imagine him possibly bringing a remarried wife to New Bethany, a wife who would pick up the kids at Lucy's day care. That was—if he was divorced. If he was widowed, well, that might prove an entirely different situation...

She poked one fingertip through the buttonhole of her sweater and moved to the threshold between her office and the playroom.

Ben Martin spread his arms wide to accommodate the two thundering toddlers who slammed against his body at full speed.

Two-year-old Paige and four-year-old Alec squealed and giggled and threw their pudgy arms around their father's neck. In the darkened, large playroom, their delight practically echoed in the unfamiliar silence. It rang through Lucy's mind, making her feel all the more empty and alone.

She held back from the threesome, one hip cocked against her office doorframe, and watched. The light from behind her cast a kind of glow on the small family unit, which reflected in the depths of Dr. Ben's kind eyes as he spoke in whispers to his redheaded son and blond daughter.

He was a good father. She could tell that, not just by seeing him with his children, but by interacting with Paige and Alec herself. They were good kids, smart and sweet and almost fearless in their curiosity, though familiar with discipline and love—lots and lots of love.

He kissed first one and then the other child on the cheek and laughed that easy laugh that Lucy thought fit him so very well.

She smiled in response to the sound but she did not feel any joy—not like the joy Ben must feel hugging those two bright, beautiful souls and knowing they were God's gift to him alone. And to their mother, of course.

"So, how did you like your first day here with Miss Lucy?" Ben capped Paige's dark blond hair with one hand. "Did you have fun? Did you like it? Are you excited to come back tomorrow?"

"We got three cookies for snack time," Alec reported, sticking up three fingers as proof.

Paige said nothing but solemnly held up one, two, then four fingers.

"They're small cookies and we serve one hundred percent real juice with them," Lucy felt compelled to say.

Ben nodded at her, his lips quirked up in a half smile.

"An' after nap time, after nap time, after nap time, Daddy?" Alec started to stick his finger up his nose.

"Uh-huh?" Ben stopped him with a well-timed hand grab, not saying a thing to embarrass the child but still gently correcting the behavior.

"After nap time, Leonard J. wet Luther B.'s pants!" Alec covered his mouth and giggled, his feet stamping up and down and his knees buckled as if he might just be in danger of dousing his own trousers.

"He what?" Ben released his son's hand and scratched his head for effect.

"The McGuffey twins." Lucy winced what might pass for a smile in the dim light. Feeling rude speaking to them from the relative isolation of her office, she drew in a deep breath. Taking comfort in the familiar smells of baby powder, sundry school supplies, and staunch disinfectant, she crossed the room to where Ben and his children huddled together. Folding her arms, she kept any gestures close to her body as she explained. "Leonard J. had on Luther B.'s spare pants and there was a little… accident."

"Oh." Ben gave an exaggerated nod of comprehension.

Paige mimicked the slow, knowing head bob.

"The kids started laughing at Luther B., 'cause, 'cause, because he hadda change his pants—again. Two times today." Alec gravely held up two fingers this time. "But Miss Lucy stopped 'em."

"She did?" Ben gave her a sidelong glance that seemed to include her in his enjoyment of the story.

"While Miss Rose was finding the extra, *extra* pants, Miss

Lucy let Luther B. sit in her lap, wet pants and all and never even said 'eeeewww.'"

It had to be some trick of the darkness, Lucy thought, that put that admiring gleam in Ben's eye as he grinned up at her.

"I think that's pretty nice of her. Very nice, indeed."

Lucy could not take her gaze from Ben's, and so they remained there for what seemed countless seconds just looking and smiling at one another.

Then Alec's finger went upward, aimed for his nose again.

This time it was Lucy who caught it and gave it a friendly squeeze as if she'd planned that all along. "Well, you know, accidents happen to everyone at some point, Alec. And it wasn't a big deal, not anything that couldn't be made all better by a hug and a quick change of clothes."

"Well, I know both those things always make me feel better even if I haven't had an accident." Ben tucked Paige close to his side, ready to lift her up. He winked at Alec.

"Oh, sure, me too," Lucy played along. It pleased her that Ben supported her handling of the fairly routine problem around the day care—simply because parental support was indispensable, of course. It wasn't as though there was any other, more personal reason, she rushed to tell herself.

"Is that why you changed your clothes before my daddy came, Miss Lucy?" Alec tugged at the hem of her brand-spanking new cardigan.

Lucy cleared her throat. "I…well…I….it was after work and I always change my clothes after work…usually." She fidgeted with the glossy, pearl-white buttons nestled against the fuzzy pink knit. "And it was late, you know, later than normal for me to change my clothes and so I just changed them here."

"With very attractive results, I might add." Ben stood up, lifting Paige with him as he did.

She was blushing like a schoolgirl, she could just feel it, as she murmured, "Thanks."

Ben directed Alec to run and gather his and Paige's coats from the neat little row of hooks on the wall across the room. When the boy had scampered off on his mission, Ben turned to Lucy again. "About that being late, let me apologize again—" He curled little Paige close to him, and she laid her head on his broad shoulder "—but I only have a handful of patients so far and one of them had a very important test run this morning and she had to get back to me with some information so I could have her medical files transferred here from out of state. It was late by the time she got back to the office and I had to write her a prescription or I would have let it wait until tomorrow and…anyway, I really appreciate your staying."

"No problem." She ducked her head, then fully taking in what he had said, jerked her head up again. "Test? That wouldn't by any chance be on my friend, Naomi Boatwright, would it?"

He frowned.

Even with that frown, he still kindled something deep inside her. She just knew it showed on her face, too, yet she felt helpless to do anything but stand there like a perfect clod and gaze at him in doe-eyed adoration.

Ben adjusted his glasses. "I'm bound by the confines of patient confidentiality, Miss Lucy, and really could not answer your question."

"Oh." Well, didn't she feel a total fool? She swallowed, started to fan her scalded cheeks with one open hand, then forced herself to hold off. "I'm so sor—"

"However—" He broke into a thousand-watt grin. "This time I happen to have the patient's permission to share her news. Threatened to torture me with an ice cold stethoscope if I didn't tell you, in fact."

"That sounds like Naomi." Lucy wet her lips. "Well?"

"The test was positive."

"I knew it!" Lucy couldn't help giving a two-fisted victory salute. "A baby! Naomi and Taylor are going to have a baby. I couldn't be happier if it were m—"

She cut herself off before she embarrassed herself beyond repair. Bad enough half the town already knew how badly she wanted to be a mother. She hardly had to go blabbing that fact to Dr. Ben Martin. She reined in her enthusiasm, and while she had never had to address this specific situation at Miss Mavis Adair's School of Charm and Beauty, she felt able to rise to this occasion.

"Well, that's just wonderful." She kept her tones soft and calm, fitting her hands together. "We're going to have a new baby to coo over!"

"I take it Mrs. Boatwright is a close friend?" There was laughter in his voice as he asked it.

"Very." She twisted her entwined fingers. "We were in a prayer group together last year—I guess you don't know about the prayer trees, do you?"

"The…?" He shook his head.

"It's an old tradition in town. Very lovely, really. Just the kind of thing you'd enjoy—the kind of thing you said you came to a small town to be part of."

He stepped closer, his head cocked and his eyes intent. "I'd love to know more."

"Well, there's a whole story about it and then the grove—you'd really have to see that to appreciate it."

He nodded. "Sounds good."

"Maybe we could drive out to the prayer grove one day before it gets too cold, and I can explain it all to you." She had no idea where she'd gotten the gumption to be so bold but now that she had, she didn't feel as scared about it as she would have suspected. She felt downright pleased, in fact, especially when Ben Martin straightened up proud as a peacock and raised an eyebrow her way.

"I'd like that. I'd like that a lot."

"Okay." He was probably just being polite, she realized when he did not try to pin down a day or time. She feigned a sudden fascination with Alec dragging his blue jacket and Paige's lavender one along the gray tile floor.

"Oh, and speaking of Mrs. Boatwright—" Ben hurried to say.

Changing the subject, Lucy thought, *he must really want to distance himself from the idea of going to the grove with me.* She felt stupid and awkward and immature to have even mentioned the idea.

"She told me that you help out with a Christmas pageant at one of the churches?"

"Uh-huh?" She met his gaze under the veil of her lowered lashes.

"And that the kids might still be able to sign up or join in or whatever so they can participate?"

"Oh. Sure, sure. Of course, there's something for everyone. The preschoolers are usually manger animals so they don't have any lines to learn—just have to know how to moo or bah or neigh. And Paige here, she could be in the Jingle Bell Babies—they just sort of stand up in front of everyone and look adorable, shaking big ol' sleigh bells and sometimes singing a word or two of an actual carol."

He laughed.

Mortification aside, his laughed still warmed her.

"Sounds great." He glanced down at his son.

Alec tried to poke one arm into his jacket then suddenly

came to understand that he had to release Paige's jacket in his fist to fit his hand through his sleeve.

"What do we have to do?" Ben looked at her again.

"Well, do you recall finding a flyer left on your door over Thanksgiving inviting you to join in some holiday festivities?"

"Yes, I believe I do."

"Well, all the details are on that—and phone numbers to call."

"Yours?"

"What?"

"Is your phone number listed on the flyer—your home phone, that is?"

This time she'd have given into the impulse to fan herself but the old-style Southern affectation suddenly seemed quite out of place. Still, she wished she knew how to cool her neck and face to help herself better focus on the deeper meaning beneath the doctor's low, almost intimate tone. Intimate in a way that bespoke inclusion and sincere interest.

"Um, no, it's not," she murmured. "My number is—"

"I have my jacket on, Daddy. All by myself!"

They both looked down at Alec standing there with his jacket fastened, each bright blue snap popped tight as it could get into the spot just above where it truly belonged.

Lucy started to help the child correct the situation, quite comfortable as the children's caregiver and their father's new friend in doing so. In fact, after just one extended day with these children and a few scant meetings with Ben, Lucy had more of a sense of belonging than she'd had with anyone in a very long time.

Before she could tend to Alec's coat, though, Ben scooped up Paige's jacket and managed to put it on single-handedly while he patted his son's shoulder. "Good job, son."

Alec beamed.

The sight of the three of them like that drove home to Lucy her outsider status. She did not belong. She was a stranger— worse yet, for a stranger had a chance of becoming more, given enough time. To this family, Lucy reminded herself sharply, she was just the hired help. She slumped her shoulders forward, sighing.

"You were saying," Ben urged as he tugged the hood of Paige's coat into place.

"I was saying…" She looked from Paige to Alec to Ben. "I was saying, don't worry about being late now and then, you're a doctor, it's bound to happen."

"But I don't want you to think I'm taking advantage."

"Believe me, Doctor, I recognize taking advantage when I see it." She didn't have the guts to do anything about it, she thought, but she sure did recognize it. "And this is *not* taking advantage. Still—"

"Hmm?"

"Well, I do have a few parents who would…overstep the boundaries if they knew I was making exceptions for you." She voiced the thought just as it came to her.

"Well, I had thought about getting an after-hours caregiver, you know, someone I could leave the kids with in case of emergency, or if I am running behind picking them up." He stroked his chin.

It was a nice chin, Lucy thought. Strong. Masculine.

"Would you know of anyone you could recommend?"

"Me." Again, she'd spoken before she'd truly thought out her response. She blinked. Well, she'd said it, if she didn't want to feel even more of an idiot than she already did, she had to stick by it, at least for now. "That is, I can do it until you find someone else or…whatever you decide. If you have to work late, for example, I could just take the kids home with me."

"That's perfect. Perfect." He reached toward her.

Lucy tensed, just slightly, but apparently enough to send the message for Ben to pull back.

Paige began to fuss to get down, and he set her on the floor. She promptly waddled over to a tub of toys and began foraging.

"Thank you, really." He seemed not to know what to do with his hands, putting them in his pockets, then on his hips, then crossing his arms. "I'll pay you extra, of course. Double overtime or whatever the going rate is—"

"Oh, no, I couldn't take more money from you!" Her cheeks blanched. "That is, if I took it on as a job then the other parents might feel I should provide the same service for them."

"Yes, of course, that makes sense." He stood there, looking like he wanted to say more but not saying a word.

Lucy wanted to say something, too, to sum it all up and then go home and hide her face for about a week. This man only expected a business relationship from her. He was a cute doctor, for heaven's sake, he wouldn't find anything appealing in a plain, chubby girl like her. Any fascination he had in her ended with what she could do for his children. She was ridiculous to think he could want more.

He shuffled his feet.

She picked at a piece of lint from her sweater. She opened her mouth to speak.

He did the same.

"You first," she suggested.

"No, you," he urged.

Neither began again.

Alec twitched his button nose, then his finger extended upward again.

This time both Lucy and Ben went for it. Twice burned,

Alec must have anticipated the action because he stepped backward.

Lucy's knuckles collided with Ben's, their fingers notched for an instant then he clasped her hand in his large palm. Her stomach flip-flopped; her breath snagged in the back of her throat. She started to pull away but Ben held firm.

"What were you going to say?" he whispered.

"I have no idea," she murmured. "How about you?"

"No idea." He stepped in close to her. "None."

"It must not have been very important, then." Her heartbeat quickened. He wouldn't dare kiss her, she knew that, not with the kids standing right here and the two of them having just met and never—

His lips felt warm—not soft, really, but gentle—and they rested on the back of her hand all too briefly. A cornball gesture, she supposed, but one that spoke volumes without crossing any lines or offending any sensibilities.

Besides, Lucy thought as he straightened away and let her hand slip from his, as long as she lived, no matter how many times some man thought she was not thin enough or pretty enough or smart enough, she would have this moment when Ben Martin made her feel…special.

Nine

ow, why, again, are we spending Sunday after-noon—with only eleven shopping days left until Christmas, I might point out to you—at a children's church pageant when neither of us have children in the production or even attend this church?" Gayle scooted into the empty pew at the very back of the Second Antioch Baptist Church.

The sanctuary lights faded from brightest near the front to almost darkness at the back. The looming, black cross on the white stucco wall directly behind the spot where the pulpit usually stood shone out with it's normal, subtle backlighting. During the course of the pageant more dramatic lighting would give the cross the impression of the blazing Christmas star. Then, by the end of the pageant, when the nativity story had been told and the children stood in silhouette against the blue silk backdrop, the light would fade until the cross in all its starkness stood watch over the scene depicting Christ's birth.

Just anticipating it made Naomi shiver. There were a lot of reasons to come out to this pageant today, she thought, smiling.

Naomi followed Gayle into the back row, her gaze scanning the many familiar faces of the early crowd. On a dreary Sunday afternoon this Christmas pageant was an especially big draw in their small town. That was why she and Gayle had come early, to get a decent parking spot and to allow themselves the luxury of choosing where they wanted to sit.

"We're here to show support for Rose." Naomi plunked

down nearest the aisle, which gave her the advantage of seeing what went on in the foyer and throughout the sanctuary, as well as activities on and just off the altar-turned-stage. "You know from helping out last year how hard Rose works on this thing."

"Listen, if Rose was going to get out there herself dressed like a great big nativity donkey or living Christmas tree, then sure, you couldn't keep me away." Gayle crossed her legs and tugged her skirt hem down at the same time.

Lots of women wore pants these days to church, especially to an informal little event like this, but not Gayle. Even though she had become much more relaxed in her approach to life this last year, her only concession to that new attitude in church was wearing shoes that did not perfectly match her bag. Her manicured nails hissed along the crease of the bright green program that she arranged sidelong in her lap.

Gayle sighed. "But I still don't get why you wanted to go to all the trouble of coming out on a miserable, rainy day like this to hear one more mangled rendition of 'Away in the Manger.'"

"I happen to like 'Away in the Manger.'" Naomi glanced up and noticed the blond head in the row just in front of them. Grinning to herself, she leaned forward enough to make herself heard. "Besides, Dr. Ben's children have parts in the pageant, and you know what that means?"

Gayle leaned forward, fluttering her meticulously arched eyebrows upward. "It means Miss Mary Lucille is here just in case the good doctor should need her assistance."

Lucy went stiff as the back of the pew she pressed her spine against. "I'm here for Alec and Paige. They're new in town and don't have any other family to come watch them and—"

"Any *other* family?" Naomi nudged Gayle. "She's already

counting herself as family, Gayle, you know what that means?"

"'Ben and Lucy sitting in a tree...'" Gayle started in.

"Now, ya'll stop that. Now!" Lucy flicked back her hair to underscore her petulance. "Ben and I haven't even gone on a date. He's just stayed for dinner a couple times when I took the kids home after his work kept him late."

"'K-i-s-s-i-n-g,'" Naomi persisted.

"Shhh." Lucy put a finger to her lips and darted back one threatening glance at them. "Hush."

For maybe three whole seconds Gayle and Naomi shared one thoughtful look.

Around them the other observers moved forward, most of them vying for the few prized seats in the front that had not already been staked out by camera-toting parents, Dr. Ben among them.

Naomi pursed her lips, then nodded to Gayle in gleeful agreement. Taking a deep breath, they chanted on in unison, "'First comes love, then comes—'"

"Then comes me telling Brother Paul that you two can't behave and have to be separated!" Lucy's tone was ominous.

Naomi thought of the church's barrel-chested minister, Brother Paul, with his penchant for blurting out the truth couched in wordiness and peppered with jovial laughter. She could see him strolling down the aisle in that maroon jacket and those green pants he favored for the holidays, sporting some kind of gosh-awful discount store tie given to him by some past year's youth group. Somehow the image did not frighten her.

"Bring him on. We can handle him."

"Sunday! Sunday! Sunday!" Gayle played along, imitating some redneck radio ad, her hand on the pew in front of them and her head bowed just enough so that her antics did not annoy anyone but Lucy, Naomi noted. "The grudge match of the century. Noisy Neighbor Naomi—"

"And her sidekick, Go-Along Gayle," Naomi interjected.

"Take on Polyester Paul, in a duel to see once and for all who rules the back pew."

Mary Lucille scowled, though she clearly had a hard time holding on to it for wanting to giggle just a bit. Finally, she reined in her composure and turned to them. "Y'all are just too funny. Why don't you get yourselves a tour bus and go on the road?"

"You'd miss us something terrible, darlin'." Naomi gave her friend's shoulders a squeeze.

"I'd adapt." The twinkle in Lucy's eye belied her dry delivery. "What *are* you two doing here, anyway? You don't have kids in the pageant and you don't go to this church."

"No kidding." Gayle gave Naomi a "this-is-where-I-came-in" look.

"We came for Rose, to soak in some holiday spirit—and who knows? Maybe we'll be witness to a little Christmas miracle in the bargain."

"What kind of miracle are we likely to witness at the Second Antioch Baptist Church of New Bethany, Tennessee?" Gayle sniffed.

Naomi lifted one of the green programs they'd all been given as they came in, waving it in evidence. "Well, for one thing, it says right in here that they are going to produce three wise *men* as part of the day's celebration. Now if that's not a miracle, especially in New Bethany, then I don't know what is."

"Amen and preach it, sister." Gayle held up her hand for Naomi to slap.

"Is Ted still acting so cross and unbearable?" Lucy whispered over her shoulder, apparently to avoid being overheard.

But the only other people sitting in her pew were a teenaged couple who clearly couldn't have cared less.

"Actually, he's much better. Almost his old self." Gayle squared her shoulders as if taking credit for the change. "But it's that 'almost' part that still disturbs me. I've tried to get him to make an appointment with his doctor but he refuses."

"You ought to get him to see Ben." Lucy's face beamed brighter than the star atop the tree on the library lawn downtown. "He's an excellent doctor."

"Why, Lucy, I wasn't aware that you're his patient, too." Naomi gave a cheeky grin.

"I'm...I'm not...I..." Even in the dim light of the sanctuary the glow of Lucy's blushing cheeks stood out. "Would you two be quiet now? The pageant is about to start."

"Yes, Miss Lucy," they singsonged together.

She twisted around to chide them again, then froze, her already huge eyes growing wider still as she looked toward the door beyond them. "Oh, my goodness! Naomi, it looks like you might just get that little Christmas miracle after all."

"Get yaw'en hands *off*-a me. I mean that. *Now!*" Grace Grayson-Wiley waggled her cherry wood walking stick, menacing one of the greeter's shins with the yellowed rubber tip of the old-fashioned cane. "Been walking on my own since before your daddy was a gleam in *his* father's eye, young man. Leave me to it."

"Miss Grace!" Naomi stood, Gayle right behind her.

Grace glanced up.

Their eyes met, and for one fleeting moment, crotchety old Grace, who had promised to chase Naomi and Rose from her property with a shotgun, smiled.

For the first time since learning about the baby growing inside her, Naomi felt happy, content...and hopeful. Seeing

Miss Grace here seemed just the right antidote to her recent malaise. Naomi knew now that she'd made some kind of impression, that she hadn't reached out in vain. She'd done something good, something that touched a life if only in a minor way. She'd done the Lord's work, something that would have made Mama proud.

Miss Grace had left the confines of her loneliness and the comfort of Sweet Haven to take the first steps toward rejoining life again. It really was, in Naomi's quite ordinary and unremarkable scope of experience, a small holiday miracle.

Then Grace Grayson-Wiley stepped fully into the gently lit sanctuary of the Second Antioch Baptist Church. If one of the Lord's heavenly host had suddenly appeared before those congregated there, it could scarcely have drawn more attention.

A murmur worked its way from the back of the congregation forward until even some of the children playing keep-away with one of the smallest angel's tinsel halos stopped their mischief.

"Look-a there! Look at that old lady done come to our church, Miss Rose!" Vhonda Faye Womack could be heard without benefit of a microphone above the quiet din of people whispering and shifting to get a better look.

The commotion brought Rose out from behind the cardboard inn in Bethlehem.

Will Boatwright, whom Rose had roped into helping with the props this year, stuck his head out from behind a painted palm tree to see what was going on.

Vhonda Faye pointed directly at Miss Grace, who soaked up the attention like white bread sops up warm milk.

"I know who that is, Miss Rose," Vhonda Faye announced. "It's that lady what lives in that big ol' house with the purty window in the door. My mama says she's cr—"

Rose's firm hand covered the lower half of Vhonda Faye's little face quite neatly. In a twinkling of an eye—maybe less—both she and the outspoken child had disappeared behind the cardboard inn and all began to quiet down again.

Grace bowed to the left, the right, then the left again, like the Queen Mum making a much ballyhooed appearance. Then, using tiny, shuffling steps, she made a slow but steady beeline for Naomi and Gayle.

"You came." Naomi clasped her hands as Miss Grace toddled to the last pew.

"Of course I came. You invited me." She motioned for their retreat with her ominous cane. "Why would you do that if you really didn't expect me to come?"

Gayle shuffled backward. Naomi edged along in sidelong steps, her hand slightly extended, ready to catch Miss Grace should those veiny, toothpick legs of hers give out and send her toppling.

"Either help me or get out'en my way, gal." Grace reached out with her trembling free hand.

Naomi enveloped the age-spotted hand in hers, noticing that the older lady had taken the time to apply pearly, coral-colored nail polish and had donned a lovely antique ruby ring. "Here, Miss Grace, come and sit by us. You look very nice this afternoon."

Grace grunted her opinion of the compliment, but Naomi noticed that she patted the mussed black fur collar of her coat as she lowered herself to the seat.

"Let me help you with that, dear." Gayle reached over to help Grace slide the coat off her hunched shoulders.

Naomi carefully laid the cane aside.

"What an exquisite wrap." Gayle sounded entirely sincere, though Naomi wondered how she could possibly mean it.

Naomi remained standing so that Gayle could finish situating the musty-smelling coat against the back of the pew.

"Thank you, young lady. You have lovely manners to say so." Grace tapped Gayle's hand with her bony fingers. "I know it's a ratty old thing but you should have seen how it turned heads in it's day—kinda like me, if you think about it."

She gazed off into space, as though suddenly captivated by thoughts of her heyday. Her wrinkles made a soft drape around her eyes and mouth.

Naomi and Gayle exchanged grins.

Grace fidgeted with the fuzzy wisps of hair floating like thin clouds around the edge of her black hat. She batted away the hat's netting then smoothed down its sleek feather adornments. The long strand of bright blue and gold plastic beads rattled when she brushed down over them. She cocked her little head, crossed her knotty ankles, then finally fluffed the pleated skirt of her brown and deep-purple paisley dress, looking for all the world like a hen arranging herself on her nest. "Fact is, I've made do with this coat a long while because I don't have much use for fancy things these days, seeing as I don't hardly ever go out and about anymore."

"That's right, you don't." Naomi's muttered comment was mostly to herself. "Then how did you get here, today, Miss Grace?"

The old woman directed a sharp look at Naomi. "Oh, *now* you're concerned about that. Where were you half an hour ago? You, who invited me to come to this?" She tipped her nose up, both hands clamped on her pocketbook. "If you invite someone somewhere, the least you could do is show up to carry a body to the place where you have invited them."

"But Miss Grace—" Naomi gave her an embarrassed smile "—when we invited you, you threatened to tenderize our backsides with buckshot."

"Fiddlesticks!" She crinkled her eyes shut and waved the matter off with one hand. "You've enjoyed the hospitality of Sweet Haven plenty often enough to know better than that."

"Enjoyed the…" Naomi cleared her throat.

Gayle hid her amusement behind an open program.

"Miss Grace, you've always made us stand on your front porch and bicker with you through a crack in the door." She put her hand on her hip, determined to stand there glaring down on that cantankerous imp of a woman. "Just how is that 'enjoying the hospitality of Sweet Haven'?"

"Well, I never shot at you, have I?"

"Well, no, but—"

"There you go."

Naomi felt her jaw drop. "There I go? What are you talking about? Are you telling me that your not shooting at us is the equivalent to extending the hand of congeniality to us?"

"Well, would you ruther been shot at, child?"

"No. Of course not."

"So much for that." Grace turned her head away.

Naomi sighed, started to sit, then paused again. "That still doesn't tell me how you got here, Miss Grace."

"I am not entirely without resources, young lady." She wagged one finger. "I called Miss Dawnetta down to the cafe, of course, and she give me your home telephone number. I dialed it up and spoke with a most cordial and considerate gentleman who told me that you'd gone off to the pageant already. When I explained my predicament, he told me not to worry that he'd be straight out to fetch me."

"He did?" Naomi blinked.

Gayle prodded her friend with the toe of one expensive shoe. "Hmmm, maybe New Bethany does have a resident wise man or two."

Grace fanned her neck and sent a cloud of sweet floral day cologne swirling around them. "He come on out to the house right away with his sweet young daughter in tow."

"Ashley?" Naomi hadn't intended that much surprise to register in her voice but she could not hide her interest in the fact that Ashley had conceded to go along.

She glanced around at the folks milling about. Some craned their necks to catch a better glimpse of Miss Grace, others ignored them, having given up the spectacle of the infamous old lady for the greener pastures of town gossip and general speculation.

Naomi sniffled and raised her head. "I mean, was her name Ashley?

"Yes, that was it. Ashley. Darling thing."

Naomi looked frantically around, her eyes narrowed. "So where are they now?"

"They let me out at the front door, and went 'round to find a parking space. That little gal wanted to stay with me, but I wanted no part of that."

Naomi cringed. "Was she rude to you?"

"No, I didn't want her with me because having her helping me like some tottering old woman would have just spoiled my entrance." She lifted her head and shoulders as if posing for a royal portrait. "If it's one thing a lady of my standing knows how to do, it's make an entrance."

"Of course." Gayle nodded.

Naomi glanced around at the curious eyes still fixed on them. "And you made a grand one."

"I know." Miss Grace smiled like a cat full of cream.

Just then Ashley appeared at the door to the sanctuary. Naomi excused herself and went to her stepdaughter's side.

"Oh, hi." Ashley looked past Naomi to where Miss Grace

was seated. "I see she got in all right. I wanted to walk in with her but—"

"She explained about that." Naomi chuckled. "Where's your dad?"

"He can't find a place to park so he had me come in to ask you if you'd be crushed if we didn't stay."

"Tell him he's done more than enough for today—you both have." She pulled the girl's thin body into a quick hug.

Ashley gave a sigh of disgust but did not pull away.

"Thanks, honey." Naomi swept Ashley's soft hair off her slouched shoulder. "And tell your daddy thanks, too—and that Gayle and I will take Miss Grace home."

"Okay." Ashley started to turn, then pivoted again to face Naomi. "Oh, um, hey, Miss Grace kind of gave me some stuff."

"Oh?"

Ashley stuck one hand in her coat pocket and withdrew some objects, which she held out toward her stepmother.

"Hmm, a plastic earring, the cap off of an old pen, a quarter, two nickels, and a lint-covered piece of ribbon candy. You got quite a haul." Naomi nodded to the young girl and extended her hand. "That means she really likes you."

Ashley dumped the contents into Naomi's cupped palm. "What are *you* going to do with this junk?"

"Oh, we have a collection." She leaned in as if sharing a deep secret. "Someday we hope to have enough to fund a museum where we can display the items."

"You're weird." Ashley laughed. "But kind of cool."

"Why thank you, Ashley. I think you're pretty cool yourself, going along to help with Miss Grace and all."

The girl shrugged, but pride in Naomi's approval shone in her eyes.

"See you later tonight," Naomi said.

"Okay. Bye." Ashley hesitated, then reached over and gave Naomi a hug so fast that if Naomi had blinked she'd have missed it.

But she didn't. Two miracles in one day! She felt all warm and woozy inside, the way you're supposed to feel at Christmas but so rarely ever do.

"Beautiful job, Rose, best ever."

"Gave me chills, it did."

"Thank you. Thanks." Rose shook hands and accepted the accolades as graciously as anyone could who was dog tired from the work yet curious as a cat to get across the fellowship hall to Gayle, Naomi, and Mrs. Grace Grayson-Wiley. Rose was dying to find out what had happened to bring the old lady to church today.

"Rose—a word with you?" Will's face was nearly gray with concern, his deepset eyes stormy.

"I...um...I..." She inhaled the aroma of sickly rich cake, cinnamon-spiked punch, and coffee brewed up in a pot the size of a canister vacuum. Children squealed and romped and cried and carried on throughout the room, the treat bags donated by the men's Christian fellowship clutched in their hands. The adults murmured and swayed to keep their eyes on whatever mattered to them at the moment; Brother Paul and his wife made the rounds, nodding, taking hands, laughing, sometimes stopping to chat, then moving on again.

Gayle and Naomi escorted Miss Grace through the fray like handmaidens bearing Queen Bathsheba to her throne, Rose noted with a smile. As for the "queen," well, Grace was eating up the homage like the kids ate the candy canes from their gift bags.

In the hallway, Will waited for Rose, one hand in his pocket, one held out to her. Sensing a lecture in the offing, Rose hesitated. She was too old for lectures and too stubborn to change anyway, no matter what Will had to say to her. Besides, her nerves had worn thin as tissue putting together this whole event, and now that she had a chance for the reward of rest, it tempted her mightily just to go in and sit herself down—right next to Grace, of course. She glanced at the old woman and the crowd huddling near her.

"Sit here, ma-yam. My mama says for me to fetch you over some cake and punch." Vhonda Faye gave her mother, who headed up the hospitality committee at the church, a big grin, then skipped away.

Aided by Gayle and Naomi, Miss Grace lowered herself into a metal folding chair that sat along the wall dotted with Sunday School attendance posters. As she settled down—with the gold, silver, red, and blue stars from the charts gleaming down on her—she announced to everyone, "I like that child. About time I ran across someone who didn't mutter in their beards when they talked."

"Rose? Rose!"

Rose faced Will. He was a good man, a decent man, and he'd certainly put up with more than his share of frustration from her this past year or so. She must have told the man a dozen times that she had no intention of marrying again, and yet he persisted in asking every few months "just to be sure she hadn't changed her mind." She hadn't.

But then, that shouldn't surprise anyone. Being contrary was hardly new territory to Rose. She had always railed against contrived expectations from her social set and her mother. She'd even gone so far as to fly in the face of tradition and wear a *black* dress with sequins on it to be feted at the Belle Gala.

That dress had made a statement about who she was and how she wanted to live her life. Now, at this age, she no longer wanted to have to fight against conventions or anything else— most especially Will Boatwright—just for the privilege of being herself.

"Rose? My dear, just a moment of your time?" He lowered his chin and gave her a long, sad puppy-dog look.

She glanced again at Grace, Naomi, and Gayle. Lucy, Dr. Ben, and his two children had joined them, not to mention Vhonda Faye's rapid approach with a slab of cake the size of a small ski slope. Rose sighed. They'd never miss her and they'd fill her in on everything that transpired later. Will wasn't asking her to relinquish her freedom here, he just wanted a word with her.

Smiling, she shook her head, gave one last parting look at the festivities in the chaotic fellowship hall, then turned fully toward Will. "Sure, sugar, let's slip back into the sanctuary. We can start collecting the jingle bells and gathering angels' cast-off halos."

"Well, I should have figured you'd put me to work in exchange for a few precious moments of your time." He grinned, then took her hand in his like a prince leading a princess onto a dazzling ballroom floor. "Nothing's ever easy with you, Ms. Rose Tancy Mason Holcolmb…"

He let the last name drag out as if tempted to add his own name onto the list, but too smart to try it even in jest.

"Never easy," he reiterated. "You know that?"

"Know it?" Rose, her chin angled up and hand in his, glided down the darkened corridor. "Darlin', I pride myself in it."

Ten

*D*ot and Daughters' on New Year's Day." Ted wrapped his arms around Gayle's waist and nuzzled the back of her neck.

Gayle leaned back into her husband's safe, strong embrace. The week between Christmas and New Year's had been like a second honeymoon for them with the law office shut down and no pressing requirements for kids, school, church, or charity. Gayle skimmed her fingertips over the buttery-soft leather of Ted's new aviator-style jacket. She inhaled the scent of it and the cafe's holiday buffet and Ted's own fragrance all meshed in some kind of warm, peaceful amalgam. Maybe...maybe Ted was just stressed over work before and everything would be all right after all.

"I haven't come down to this annual shindig since I was a kid," he murmured against her hair.

"Me, neither," she admitted.

"Blasphemy!" Taylor laughed from the parallel serving line, then slid his arm around Naomi. "How could you live in New Bethany and not celebrate New Year's Day here? We never miss it."

"Aren't *we* the lucky ones?" Ashley rolled her eyes.

"Tell me about it." Gayle's son, Nathan, poked at the dark green mass of collards swimming in glistening grease in a big pan before him.

"Yes, we *are*." Ted stepped forward and slapped a spoonful of the stuff onto his son's plate, then motioned him to move on.

"Lucky to have good food, good friends—"

"And the good sense not to eat like this every day," Gayle finished for him.

"Ham and greens and black-eyed peas—" Naomi tipped her nose in the air and shut her eyes "—and cornbread the way it ought to be made—in a cast-iron skillet. Even if it's just once a year, it's wonderful."

They each shuffled on, filling their plates with heaping spoonfuls and double helpings served from what had once been a salad bar—a leftover from the eighties and the foolish dalliance the daughters had with updating the cafe's image.

They crowded around two tables pushed together, Ted and Gayle and their two youngest children, then Taylor, Naomi, and Ashley. Lucy brought up the rear, showing all the enthusiasm of a bear rudely awakened from a very pleasant hibernation. Rose and Will were expected shortly and perhaps Rose's daughter, Stacey.

Gayle made a quick visual check to ensure that they had plenty of room for the latecomers then looked up at those ready to dig into their meals. "Um, I don't want to make anyone uncomfortable but...well, if Rose were here she'd make us say grace..."

"So, are you suggesting we *do* that or that we should simply take a moment to savor feeling like rebels for *not* doing it?" Ted grinned.

"That jacket has gone to your head, James Dean," she muttered back at him. Then she extended her hand. "And just for that, Mr. Smart Alec, you can be the one who gives the blessing."

All joined hands, Lucy and the two teenagers more reluctant than the others.

"Thank you, Father, for this food and for the company in

which we eat it. Thank you for your faithfulness even when our own faith wears thin. Thank you for the year behind us and the year ahead. Help us to use it to your glory. By his salvation and in his name—"

"Amen," came the response, in various degrees of loudness from around the table.

As if the starting bell had rung and the gate opened, everyone launched into their meal. Knives and forks scraped over the heavy white ceramic plates. Laughter flowed like iced tea from the big pitcher that Dawnetta brought by every few minutes to keep the glasses brimming. Everyone complimented her on their favorite dish—well, almost everyone, Gayle noted with a look at Lucy's glum expression.

"Eat up, Lillith, darlin'," Gayle told her nine-year-old who was stabbing suspiciously at everything but the cornbread. "You have to have your black-eyed peas and ham on New Year's Day."

"Why?"

"Well, the tradition holds that it brings prosperity." She touched one mauve nail to her child's pug nose. "You wouldn't want to go against a fine old Southern tradition, would you?"

"I would if it were a dumb one." Lillith's expression was mulish. "And I think this one is dumb as they come."

"Lillith," Ted said in his this-is-your-only-warning-young-lady tone.

"I think she has a point." Lucy laid her fork down and dabbed at the corner of her mouth with her napkin. "I've eaten ham and black-eyed peas every New Year's of my life and I haven't noticed much of any change from one year to another."

Lillith gave her mother a silent *so there.*

"We do not actually put any stock in superstition, Lillith. You know that. We just do it for fun."

"Yippee." Lucy swirled her finger in the air.

The three diners under fifteen laughed.

"What is wrong with Lucy?" Ted whispered in Gayle's ear.

"I'll tell you in a sec." She cleared her throat and turned to her children. "If you two aren't going to eat any more than that, why don't you all go up to the counter and have Miss Dawnetta fix you a sundae?"

"With sprinkles?" Lillith's eyes were now round in anticipation.

"Yes, with sprinkles." Gayle glanced up over her child's head. "Would you like to go, too, Ashley?"

"Ice cream's for kids."

Nathan bristled but had the good manners not to make a remark.

Ashley went on. "But it sure beats sitting around listening to grown-ups talk about how good the greens are while the black-eyed peas stare at me." She smiled with such affability that it entirely negated her earlier surliness.

Naomi and Taylor laughed.

Nathan relaxed a bit.

"C'mon, kid." Ashley motioned to Lillith. "Let's get extra sprinkles—and whipped cream."

Once the younger ones had hurried off, Gayle turned to Lucy. "So, Mary Lucille, to what do we owe this little-ray-of-sunshine routine of yours this afternoon?"

"I know," Naomi said, a piece of ham halfway to her mouth. "She's been that same beacon of joy and merriment ever since Dr. Ben took off out of town for the holidays. Surely you can cheer up now, though, Lucy, honey. He'll be back tomorrow."

"Dr. Ben?" Ted sort of straightened in his chair, appearing very interested all of a sudden. "Isn't he that new pediatrician in town?"

"General practitioner," Taylor corrected. "He takes care of Naomi and she swears by him."

"Hmm." Ted leaned his forearm against the edge of the table. "General practitioner, huh? That's good."

"Took over for Doc Glass, came highly recommended, too." Taylor said it as if he had personally checked out the man's references—and judging from the look of adoring protectiveness he wore when watching his wife, Gayle suspected he had.

"Doc Glass, huh? You know he delivered me? My sister, too, and most of my cousins. If this new man met Dr. Glass's standards, he'd have to be top drawer."

Gayle perked up at her husband's glowing endorsement. This was the most interest Ted had paid at the mention of a doctor in a long while. In fact, it seemed the more Gayle had been pushing for him to see someone, the less interested he became. She tried to convey with an anxious look and a subtle circling with her fork that it was time for Naomi to jump in to build up Dr. Ben's image.

"Well, if you're in the market at all for a new doctor, Ben Martin is the guy." Naomi sounded a bit like she was trying to get the physician elected to office instead of recommending him to a friend. "He's a young man, midthirties; he was part of a large practice in Nashville so he's up on all kinds of techniques, and—though I by no means say this as a put-down of our other local doctors—he does seem more open to new ideas and methods. And being as he's new, it's really easy to get an appointment with him."

"New ideas and methods are good and so is being able to get in quickly—if you need that kind of thing." Ted shook his head and chuckled, though not congenially. "I don't know, maybe it's a sign of age, but I'd have a hard time getting used to doctors that are suddenly so much younger than I am."

"Afraid they won't be as good as the old guard?" Naomi's expression was that of someone looking for grounds to refute Ted's objections.

"Won't be as good?" Lucy sounded outraged at any such inference. "Dr. Ben's…well, he's….he's just terrific, that's all."

"Oh, I didn't realize you were his patient, too, Mary Lucille." Ted folded his hands.

By that simple gesture, Gayle discerned that her husband had heard about all the professional puffery of Dr. Ben that he was going to take at one sitting. Still, it had been a beginning, one she could build on—and she thanked the Lord and her friends for that.

Lucy's face turned as pink as the fresh ham Dawnetta carried in to place on the serving table. She looked everywhere but at her companions, including a longing glance at the freedom offered by the cafe door. Then, her expression awash with instant relief, she perked up in her seat. "Oh, look, here comes Rose and Mr. Boatwright."

Sure enough Rose and Will came strolling through the door. They waved as they took their place in line.

"Actually, Lucy isn't Dr. Ben's patient, Ted, honey." Gayle gave her husband's arm a squeeze. "She takes care of his children at the day care and sometimes at her home in case of emergency."

"Oh, I see." Ted nodded to Lucy.

"That is all you do for him, isn't it, Lucy?" Gayle didn't even pretend the question came from anything but pure devilment and nosiness.

"Gayle!" Naomi choked on a mouthful of black-eyed peas.

"Don't act all innocent with me, Nomi. You've wondered the exact same thing. The gossip mill says Dr. Ben's car is in Lucy's drive sometimes as long as two hours after he is supposed to pick up his children."

"He stays for supper now and again. That's all." Lucy crushed her cornbread beneath her fork, the golden crumbs clinging to the silver prongs. "It doesn't mean anything."

"What's that saying? As the whale said when he laid eyes on Jonah. 'I ain't a-swallowing *that!*'" Gayle crossed her legs and her arms, settling in for battle. "If it doesn't mean anything then why are you such a grumpy-britches because you think he's gone off to spend time with his ex-wife over the holidays?"

Lucy speared a black-eyed pea and popped it into her mouth, her eyes narrowed.

"Why are you so sure that's what he's doing?" Naomi's question was directed at Gayle, not Lucy. "He could be visiting his folks or friends. For all we know, he doesn't even have an ex-wife. He could be widowed."

"He just checked the 'single' box under marital status on the forms he filled out at the day care," Lucy confided.

"Did you ever just ask the kids about their mother?" Taylor poked Naomi in the ribs for pressing the issue, but she ignored him.

"I couldn't do that." Lucy's silky blond hair went swinging, she shook her head with such vehemence. "I couldn't exploit my position as caregiver like that. Not to mention that if they have lost their mother, I might do some serious damage poking around."

"That's why you're so good at what you do, Lucy. You think of things like that." Gayle released the tight twist of her arms over her chest. "Those kids, Dr. Ben—all the kids in your care and their parents—they are so lucky to have you."

"Thanks." Lucy cast her gaze down. "But I'm not so special. If there were any other way to find out about Ben's true marital status, I'd do it in a heartbeat."

"You really don't have any clue?" Taylor repositioned the

fork in his hand. "Not so much as a hint, huh?"

This time Naomi poked him, but with a good-natured grin at his getting in on the act.

He smiled back at his wife with clearly adoring eyes.

"No. Nothing." Lucy sighed.

"And the children never even made a reference to their mom?" Gayle put her chin in her hand. "Not even when the other kids talked about theirs or when the other mommies came to pick them up?"

"Well, now, I never actually listened in for that kind of thing. I'm not sure I'd feel comfortable—"

Gayle chewed her lip, tipped her head to one side, then smiled and pointed. "Make Rose do it!"

"*Now* what?" Rose whined as she clunked her plate down in the vacant spot next to Lucy. "Whatever it is I have the feeling I'm not going to like it, and it's eventually going to lead to trouble, hard work, or weight gain. None of which I need at this particular juncture in my life."

"Leave poor Rose alone." Ted chuckled.

"Why? If I had it within my power to help Lucy solve this mystery I'd—"

"What mystery?" Will took the seat across from Rose.

"Wait one cotton-pickin' minute. There is someone here who could unravel this mystery easy as you please." Gayle snapped her fingers.

"*What* mystery?" Will asked again.

"Don't ask me, I just got here myself." Rose said with a shrug.

"Naomi?" Gayle wrung her hands in overplayed glee. "You see Dr. Ben regularly. You could just ask outright. Or maybe drop a hint here and there during your next visit. And voila, the mystery of Ben Martin's marital status is resolved."

"I could, but that doesn't mean I could share my findings with you all." Naomi smiled smugly. "Patient-doctor privilege and all that."

"Nuh-uh." Gayle, feeling so happy with her solution that she could hardly keep from giggling like a girl in pigtails. "That only applies to doctors talking about patients, not the other way around and you know it."

"I'll have to consult my attorney on that one." Naomi smiled at Ted.

"Oh, no." Ted scooted his chair back. "I'll take on desperate criminals, corporate raiders, violators of each and every constitutional right, and cheaters at any children's board game, but I will not—I *cannot*—stand between the noble women of New Bethany and a piece of gossip this juicy. It would be nothing short of suicide."

"Amen, brother!" Taylor slapped Ted's open palm.

"Oh, you think you're pretty funny, don't you?" Gayle grabbed Ted's knee and brought her face nose-to-nose with him. "But just remember this, bucko, if Naomi doesn't do this for us then we may be forced to send in a *spy*. And you know who I'd vote to do it?"

"I wish you the best of luck in your mission, Naomi." Ted gave Naomi a quick salute.

"And just how is every little thing over here?" Dawnetta whisked around the perimeter of the table as smoothly as if she wore roller skates, filling glasses and dispensing extra napkins from inside her apron pocket.

"Everything's perfect, Dawnetta."

"Delicious."

Ted and Gayle's sentiments were echoed by the others.

"I don't know if I ever thanked y'all proper for takin' on Miss Grace the way you did." Dawnetta filled Naomi's glass last, speaking most directly to her, then adding as an obvious afterthought a nod to the other women. "Heaven knows that niece a'her'n won't make the effort to extend a simple thank ya. No, they'll be serving devil's food cake in heaven before that happens."

"No need to thank us, Dawnetta. We actually enjoyed ourselves, what little we got to interact with the old girl." Naomi raised her iced tea to her lips, a drop of water trickling down the side of the glass to drip on the paper placemat below. "I guess she won't be needing our help anymore?"

"Miss Grace'll be off at the niece's 'til the end of February. Then I expect the niece will have hired another girl for her." The waitress lifted her pitcher as if making a toast, her smile looking strangely out of place in her lined, pale face. "Enjoy now, y'hear? And don't forget, the price of the meal is all you can eat. Go back for seconds or you'll hurt my feelings. And have dessert. I won't send a body out of this cafe today that hasn't had dessert."

When Dawnetta had gone on about her rounds, Naomi eased out a long, plaintive sigh.

"What's wrong, sugar?" Rose rubbed her friend's back in a slow, circular motion.

"Oh, it's just that it's been so nice today, being together. It was nice having the excuse to see one another every week, too. Now, with Miss Grace not needing us anymore, I'm afraid we'll drift apart again."

Gayle felt every bit as sad as Naomi looked. She despised the idea of losing touch again but she did not know what to do to stop it.

"It happened before." Rose swished her spoon around inside her tea glass, clinking it delicately to one side then the next.

"We just all got so busy," Lucy said, as if trying to excuse everyone's negligence.

"It's not like things are going to get any less hectic now." Gayle gazed at her dear friend Naomi, thinking of the baby due in five months and all the turmoil that would bring.

"True enough," Rose said, and Lucy agreed.

"Maybe you girls should think about having another prayer circle." Ted spoke with a potent mix of soothing fatherly assurance and Rhett Butler no-nonsense masculinity, complete with the lilt of a Southern gentleman's accent. It lulled Gayle for a moment.

"That's an absolutely lovely idea, honey. But I just don't see how we could manage. What with the circles forming in May, and Naomi and Taylor's baby due in June—"

"Oh, yeah." He stroked his finger over his chin.

No one else said a word.

The women stared at their plates or the children or out the window; the men sat back in their chairs, cleared their throats, or folded and unfolded their hands.

Finally, and Gayle readily pegged this as self-defense against a problem he could not readily fix for the woman he loved, Ted pushed back from the table and announced, "Didn't Miss Dawnetta say this was an all-you-can-eat affair? I don't believe I have eaten nearly all I can eat. How about you gentlemen?"

Will and Taylor practically leapt from their seats to follow him back to the makeshift buffet table.

"Cowards." Rose hoped her teasing accusation would serve as cover for the fact that she felt tremendous relief over Will's leaving the table. The two of them had reached a passable peace since the Christmas pageant, but the one thing that could ruin that faster than grease burns on a hot griddle was talk of Grace Grayson-Wiley. She turned her head to call out after the men-folk, using her jest as a means of keeping them away as long as possible, "Y'all are just afraid that if you sit here long enough we'll rope you into some far-fetched idea for preserving our little circle here. Like all of us taking a vacation together."

"A vacation?" Naomi put her hand to her cheek. "You know, that's not such a bad—"

"Hold it right there!" Gayle held up one hand. "You know I love you all—"

"Sure."

"Of course."

Lucy nodded.

"But I have to say that my friends and family are one of the reasons I *need* a vacation." Gayle fluffed her soft bangs with her fingers, her rings creating a flash of gold and glitter in the shaft of sunlight streaming in the grimy cafe windows. "This is not something I even want to joke about."

"What?" Naomi feigned disbelief.

"Going away together. I mean listen to what you're saying. The four of us going away together. Being 'round one another night and day for even a long weekend?"

Gayle gave them a moment to soak in the statement.

"I'd rather we just put on boxing gloves and duke it out in the school gymnasium." Gayle acted out throwing a punch. "It'd be a far quicker and less painful way to end our relation-ships—not to mention saving us thousands in travel expenses, hotels, sitters, and the price of dozens of T-shirts that said 'My friends grew to despise one another in Cancun and all I got was this lousy shirt.'"

Naomi and Rose laughed.

Lucy blinked. "I don't want to go to Cancun."

"No one is going to Cancun, Lucy," Rose whispered.

"Well, we have to do something. We can't lose touch again, not now. Not when—" Lucy twisted her napkin. "I'd just hate to lose your support, advice and…humor…and support."

"You said 'support' twice." Rose smiled gently.

"Yeah, well, I need a lot of support." Lucy put her hands in her lap. Her full lower lip poked out in a pout worthy of Vhonda Faye herself.

Lucy looked so lost and forlorn that Rose wanted to scoop her up like a little girl in a big squishy hug and tease her into smiling again. She wracked her brain for a funny take on the situation.

"Hey, I know." Naomi snapped her fingers.

Rose flinched.

Lucy gasped.

Gayle winced.

"What?" Naomi scowled at their overt reaction. "You guys act like you think I'll suggest something untoward or likely to land us in hot water."

"Can you blame us?" Gayle's voice cracked in mock shock.

Naomi wriggled in her seat, her head tipped up and her arms crossed. "When have I ever even encouraged any of you to do—"

"Having me sneak out in the middle of the night of the Belle Gala to spy on poor Miss Grace," Rose volunteered, her hand raised to testify.

"Walking out on my family Thanksgiving last year to come eat pie with you and Rose—though I actually enjoyed that. But some of those people still aren't speaking to me." Lucy wet her lips. "All right, I also sort of enjoyed *that,* too. Um, how about when you talked me into dating Dwayne Cobb, for my own good, no less?"

"Oh, I can top that. Going back to getting me in trouble in high school, talking me into trying a diet that still makes me sick to think of, a cake fight in the garden of Rose's old house…"

"Okay, okay, I get it. I'm a ba-a-ad influence." Naomi smiled. "But you kinda like that about me and you all know it."

They exchanged amused looks.

"Besides, I never get you into too much trouble and most of the time it works out pretty well, right?"

The looks they now exchanged ranged from skeptical to reluctant agreement.

"Okay, let's hear it." Gayle flattened her hands on the table. "What's your idea?"

"Ya'll heard Dawnetta say Miss Grace will be back at Sweet Haven the end of February?"

Rose broke a piece of cornbread in two and a damp curl of steam rose from its moist middle. Gratitude welled up within her that they'd shooed Will off before this bent of the conversation started. "We also heard that she'll have a girl to bring her out her cafe meal, too."

"Yes, but the last time we saw Miss Grace it wasn't about her meal. We'd gotten her into a church for the first time in years. We'd broken through, made contact. I'd hate to see her—or us—lose that."

"She does have a point," Lucy conceded.

"We're worried about not making time for one another. I'm also worried about our connection with Miss Grace, and hers with the outside world, slipping away." The legs of Naomi's chair screeched over the floor as she scooted it closer in. "So, why not combine the two? Easter is early this year, ya'll. What I'm proposing is that we all agree here and now to get together the Saturday before Easter to visit and catch up…and to call on

Miss Grace at Sweet Haven. We'll invite her to come with us to the sunrise celebration at the prayer grove Easter morning."

"That is—" Rose caught herself mid-harangue. The instant Naomi had made the suggestion, her own mind had filled with the disapproval Will would show. She thought of arguments and difficulties that what seemed a genuine Christian gesture might cause her. But when she saw the hopeful faces of her friends, she knew she needed a better solution, something else to distract them, not to simply deride Naomi's plan. "Um, sunrise service may be a bit much for all of us to manage, don't you think? And there's no guarantee it won't be too chilly and damp to get Miss Grace out."

"You don't want to do it?" Naomi's voice hinted at offense.

"Nuh-uh, now she didn't say that." Gayle glanced around them, her gaze landing on her children slurping down the last of their gooey, rich sundaes when her whole face brightened. "What if we invite her to the egg hunt Easter afternoon instead? More chance of it being warm and sunny and I think it'd do her good to be among the young ones as well."

"Oh, I vote for the egg hunt, too," Lucy hurried to say.

Rose thought them all terribly kind not to point out that this gave Lucy the perfect excuse to be where Dr. Ben and his children would surely also spend that afternoon. Now hers would be the only dissenting vote among the friends—and over what? Because she didn't want to help Miss Grace? No, because she did not want to rock the boat with Will. She pressed her lips together. Well, Will was a big boy—even if some days he seemed more of a big baby—and she would not live her life trying to please his arbitrary whims about "bothering" Miss Grace or any other thing.

"The egg hunt it is." Rose buttered her cornbread as daintily as a princess might lightly brush a scone at high tea.

"It's settled then." Naomi tapped her knife to the rim of her plate like a judge ringing down a gavel.

"What's settled?" Taylor asked as the men returned, their plates restocked and their curiosity clearly piqued.

"The date. We've all committed to meet on the Saturday before Easter," Rose hurried in to say, wanting to present the issue in vague but honest terms.

"Easter?" Ted sat back down. "Isn't that kind of a long way off?"

"It'll be here before we know it." Rose moved Will's tea glass to one side to make room for his plate and the side dish. "Besides, this gives us a definite date to aim for, to plan around."

"But why so far off?" Taylor reached out to caress the back of Naomi's neck. "Why not pick a date later this month?"

"Oh, January is always a crazy month at the day care." Lucy chattered a bit too buoyantly as if trying to divert attention from the fact that no man was returning to sit with her. "Some staff member always has a cold or the flu, and we have to hustle to cover schedules. I couldn't plan for a day in January. I guess we could do something around Valentine's Day."

"I have my own special plans for Valentine's Day." Will reached across the table for Rose's hand.

She let him take her fingers in his, dipped her eyes with all the coyness of a belle of the oldest school of Southern womanhood, then smiled like a modern woman full of fun and in charge of her own destiny. "Valentines Day, you say? Hmmm, might I make a teensy suggestion about that to you, sir?"

She had everyone's undivided attention, though no one appeared to be openly eavesdropping.

"What suggestion, my dear?" Will lifted her hand up as if to kiss it.

"I know what kind of plans you have in mind, Will Boatwright." She pulled her hand free, then patted his cheek with the sweetest of affection. "And I suggest you save them for another holiday."

"Oh?" His eyes twinkled. He lowered his voice. "Which one?"

She gave his taut cheek a pinch and laughed. "April Fools' Day."

"There you are!" Ben's leather-and-suede hiking-style boots rasped over the playroom floor of the near-vacant day care.

Lucy tugged her black cardigan on over her white turtle-neck. Her full pink skirt, which shrouded her hips while accenting the inward nip of her waist, swished over her white stockings as her black flats slapped out a rushed pace as she went to meet Ben.

"I'm sorry I didn't take the kids to my house yet. You're not the only late parent I've had today." Lucy pointed to Tiffany Crystal huddled over a table next to Alec. Paige looked on somberly as the older children worked away with construction paper and crayons.

"I drove past your place, and when it was dark I got a little worried." He ran his hand back through his hair and ducked his head sheepishly.

"No need to worry, Ben." She said his name softly, as she always did, as if it were not quite her right to use it. He had told her to call him that, of course, but while they had enjoyed one another's company regularly over dinner on Tuesday evenings, when either she cooked or he stopped and got take-out before coming, Lucy really had no clear definition of their relationship in her mind. In her heart, now *that* was a different matter entirely.

"You know the children are safe with me."

"Oh, absolutely." He put his hand to his chest as if taking an oath. "I wasn't worried about the kid's safety. I just thought maybe I'd forgotten some change in the arrangements."

"Nope. No change. Just waiting on Nikki to come and get her kids. Nothing new about that at all."

He smiled and nodded. "Yeah."

"Uh-huh." She nodded, too.

He put his hands in his pockets and nodded again. "Yep."

"Hmm." She started to nod yet another time, then checked herself, imagining the two of them looking like those bobbing head dolls that used to sit in the back windows of some cars.

"I wish she'd hurry up, though. I'd really hate for anyone to drive by and see the lights on and get the idea that the day care is open *tonight.*" Once she'd placed the extra emphasis on the last word, she wished she could gobble it right back up again. She had not intended for the world to remind him of the significance of this particular night.

"Yeah. Sure. Mmm-huh." He kept right on nodding then stopped. "Why? What's tonight?"

Was he kidding? Or was he just trying to put her on the spot in payback for having brought it up so tactlessly to begin with? How could he not know what tonight was, after all?

"Lucy?" His deep brown eyes fixed on her, causing the character lines in his face to furrow.

"It's nothing." She waved it off with a flit of her hand, then twisted her wrist so as to fan herself. She could only pray that she'd acted quickly enough to keep the heat of the blush she felt creeping over her cheeks from showing. "It's no big deal. It's just—"

The day care door swung open and a blast of February air swept in with Nikki Griggs behind it.

"Happy Valentine's Day, Mom!" Tiffany ran to her mother, the red construction paper heart in her tiny hand dripping a trail of glitter over the pale tile floor.

Ben groaned. "Valentine's Day! I should have known."

What was she supposed to say to that? Lucy's pulse fluttered. She tucked her hair behind her ear. "That's why I didn't want to stay late at the day care—for fear some parent might see the light on and assume I was staying open tonight and would want to leave their kids longer so they could have a romantic evening."

Not that I'm hinting, she wanted to add in haste, but she couldn't make herself say it. "I suppose I should have stayed open, though. I could have, since I didn't have any plans and all."

Also not a hint, she wished she had the nerve to blurt out. She had a knot in her throat as big as a softball and she thought that if she put her fingers to her face they'd come back singed. She pulled at her sweater sleeve. "I mean, it would have been a nice gesture to my babies' parents."

She called all the children in her care her "babies," but suddenly the term felt awkward on her tongue and made her wonder if it stung of desperation and classic old maidishness. Needing to combat the panic all these thoughts—and Ben's calm and smiling presence—created in her, she turned to the most unlikely ally she could imagine for help.

"Like, uh, like Ms. Nikki, here." She swept her arm out as gracefully as Miss Vanna White disclosing a puzzle on *Wheel of Fortune.* "I'm sure she and Ray would have loved to have used the day care tonight so they could go out on the town."

"Honey, Ray is already out." Nikki hoisted up Ray Junior, whom she had collected from his crib while Lucy had stood there stammering about the holiday, to lay his head on her narrow shoulder. The baby immediately drooled on her clingy red dress and the long coils of her hair, which was now so blond it seemed actually absent of any color at all.

Lucy had heard the rumors of trouble in Nikki's marriage, of course, but thought they could not possibly be true. Ray could not have backslid so much that he'd actually go out on his wife—with her so openly aware of it, no less. Ray had accepted Jesus, after all. He'd been baptized with Nikki right beside him in the river, two years ago come this Easter.

"Oh, Nikki, I'm—"

"Out like a rock, flat on his back on the couch, snoring." Nikki huffed.

"Well at least he's home," Lucy chirped before she could censor herself.

Nikki glared at her for a half a second, then sighed. "I guess I had that coming."

Lord, forgive me. And please control my careless tongue! Lucy shook her head, ashamed. "I didn't mean anything by it, I just—"

"Never mind." Nikki held up her hand. Her once professionally done, synthetic nails had given way to bitten-off nubs with peeling polish, Lucy noted, not sure if she felt sympathy or relief over that. "I know what folks say behind our backs. And I, more than anyone else, know why they suspect my husband of being unfaithful."

"So he's not running around?" Lucy wrung her hands, trying to find the median between curiosity and concern.

"Running? I'd pay to see that!" Nikki laughed, and it wasn't a pretty laugh. "Running, Miss Lucy? That man barely moves a muscle."

"Do you think it could be a health problem?" Ben stepped forward.

"Nikki, this is Dr. Ben Martin." Lucy gestured from Ben to

Nikki then from Nikki to Ben. "Ben, this is Nikki Griggs."

He reached out to shake her hand.

"So *you're* the new doctor in town." Nikki eyed him, holding onto his hand even when he tried to remove it from her grasp. "A doctor! And you come to pick up your kids at the day care! Isn't *your* wife the lucky woman?"

"Actually, I'm not married." He tugged his hand free.

"Oh, divorced then?" She arched a penciled-on eyebrow.

Lucy's senses went on defense.

"And you have custody." Nikki patted Ray Junior on the back, and he let out a window-rattling belch. Nikki didn't miss a beat. "Children are a lot of work, especially for a single parent. And on top of that—a medical practice? That's mighty impressive. Most men would never have even tried for custody under those—"

"It's not like that at all, Mrs. Griggs. I don't have custody. I'm not divorced."

So he was a widower, then, Lucy thought, pleased to finally know but sad for Ben's loss all the same.

"You see," he went on, his attention moving from Nikki to Paige and Alec still occupied at the art table. "Both my children are adopted. I've never been married."

Nikki shifted her weight from one bony hip to the other. "My, isn't that fascinating?"

Fascinating. Nikki had certainly picked the right word for it. Lucy had finally met a man who wanted children in his life as much as she did—but he had had the means and courage to take action on that longing. He'd adopted Paige and Alec. How wonderful!

Ben Martin's estimation as a man had skyrocketed in Lucy's eyes—and it had been almost stratospheric to begin with. And that only made the differences between them all the more pronounced. It served to show Lucy that a man like Ben could find nothing of interest with a dumpy, milquetoast woman like herself.

And if she needed further confirmation of that sentiment, she need only glance up and look at him. His head lowered, he huddled in intimate conversation with Mrs. Nikki Herndon Griggs, the woman who had already proved she had what it took to steal a man away from pathetic, pudgy Lucy Jewell.

Eleven

I can't believe you talked Nikki into watching Paige and Alec for a couple of hours." Lucy made tiny accordion pleats in her soft, flowing skirt.

Ben's reconditioned '67 Mustang smelled of old leather and new child seats. He backed it up with one hand on the gleaming steering wheel, his other arm extended toward Lucy so that his fingertips just brushed her shoulder. The evening, just fading to dusk, closed in around them.

The night's first star winked at Lucy from low in the lavender-gray horizon. *Star light, star bright...wish I may, wish I might...* The words echoed back from childhood. Lucy had grown too old and too wise for rhymes and wishes, she put her faith in the one who made the stars and not in childish games and yet——

She shut her eyes, then opened them. Ben Martin still sat there, his hair tousled and his off-white shirt ever-so-slightly rumpled after a hard day's work. He was looking at her—at *her*—and smiling.

What did she need stars for? She had everything she dared wish for here with her tonight. Life had taught her not to count on tomorrows where men were concerned, but today—tonight—she had that, and she would cherish it.

Ben backed the car to a halt in the street in front of Ray and Nikki's house. "Well, I did ask Nikki to take care of the kids. She agreed, and since you told me she'd keep a close eye on them——"

"Oh, Nikki is a good mama. The kids'll be fine."

"I know they will. But what about us?"

"Us?"

"Yeah, are we going to be fine?" He lowered his chin and looked at her with those compelling eyes half masked by his lids.

Even in the dim light, his five o'clock shadow intensified his features, showing the strength of his jaw, the whiteness of his teeth, and the sooty blackness of his eyelashes.

"*Us?*" The question came out in a squeak. Her fingertips felt like ice as she pressed them to her lips. Lowering her hand to touch the rounded collar of her sweater, she cleared her throat. "I wasn't aware that there *was* an 'us.'"

"There's not. Not yet, not exactly. But I'd like there to be." He touched her arm, then lifted his hand to push her hair back from her cheek. "How about you?"

"I'd like that, too." She was amazed the whisper made it out of her tight throat.

"So, is that it?"

She tensed, unsure of his unspoken expectations. "What?"

"Is it official?" He took her chin in his hand. "Mary Lucille Jewell? Are you my girl now?"

"Your girl?" She tipped her head, savoring the feeling of his fingers on her face.

"My valentine?" He rephrased it. "But not just for tonight."

For how long? her heart asked, but the words stilled within her. She nodded slowly. "Yes, I'll be your girl, Ben. Your valentine."

"Man, I'd love to kiss you right now, Mary Lucille. I've wanted to kiss you for a long time."

She raised her head, her lips falling apart as if she wanted to speak or find another form to communicate that she felt the same way.

"But this isn't the right place." He jerked the car into gear, and it lurched before purring down the road.

Forty-five precious minutes later, the door to the day care clacked open and Lucy reached in to flick on the lights.

"I should have known the town's two nice restaurants would be booked solid." Ben shook his head.

Lucy smiled, her thoughts flickering back to the one truly magical night she had known in her life until now. "Too bad neither of us is a member of Bethany Heights Country Club."

His answering smile was rueful. "And too bad there wasn't a red rose or a heart-shaped box of candy left to be had. He held up a bucket of fried chicken and a couple of cans of soda. "You know what they say: 'A bucket of chicken, a cold soda, and thou—who could ask for anything more?'" He slid his coat from his shoulders and it fell with a thud into a tiny wooden chair. He shook his head. "I wanted to give you a special night, Lucy, but I guess I really blew it."

"I would have been happy to cook for you." Lucy collected a big soft quilt from the playroom closet and unfurled it with a muted popping sound before sprawling it out over the cold floor for them. "I didn't expect anything, Ben. Just being with you is special enough."

"Yes, but I wanted to do more." He set the bucket down on the quilt, then placed the bag carrying the side orders and sodas beside it. His scuffed tennis shoes made no sound over the padded fabric as he came to her and cupped one hand along the side of her neck. "You deserve more, Lucy. You deserve starlight in your eyes, moonbeams in your hair, and waltzing in the gazebo on the courthouse lawn…"

Fighting back the sweet yearnings and romantic foolishness that his words and his touch inspired, she warned him, "You get fined for using the gazebo after dark without a permit."

His gaze swept over her. "I'd risk it."

"Why, sir, I do believe you are trying to scandalize me." She laid the accent on thick as Scarlet working her wiles. She tossed her head, and her hair tangled over his fingers. "Imagine the talk! The town's handsome new doctor caught alone at night in the gazebo, romancing the local old maid, day care provider…on the courthouse lawn, no less."

"You're no old maid, Miss Lucy. Not by a long shot." He inched closer. "You're young, young in your heart and in your faith and in the way you *come at* life. Like it's all still new to you, like you're just dying to sup it all up but not quite sure where to begin…or if you even dare to begin."

No one had ever described her inner most feelings to her so accurately. Her heart pounded in her ears. Her mind swirled with thoughts, none of which she could pin down. When she spoke it came just above a whisper. "Yes. Yes, that is how I feel. Like I've hidden away too long and I want to finally step out, into my life. How'd you know that?"

"By looking into those eyes." He moved closer still. "By seeing how you give all you've got with the children, yet how you hold yourself back around me. I wish you wouldn't hold yourself back so much, Lucy. I know you've got a great deal to give."

"I do, to the right person." Panic sent a quick shiver through her. This was Ben, a sophisticated doctor, a man of the world. His expectations might be as different from hers as…as…as every other startlingly real difference between them that she saw already. "Ben, you have to know something. Stepping into life does not mean trampling over my beliefs."

"I never expected it would." He stroked her cheek with his thumb.

Lucy wet her lips. "Those beliefs, they aren't very worldly.

In fact, they are the exact opposite of worldly."

"Lucy, are you trying to tell me that there are boundaries that you're not going to cross outside of marriage?" Ben cocked his head.

"Boundaries? Yes, boundaries!" A wave of relief swept over her. "And if that changes anything, well, I won't hold that against you—"

"It does." He pulled her into an embrace. "Lucy, it changes everything."

She tensed, her hands on his chest. "I thought it might."

"Are you telling me that to stay faithful to your beliefs, there are some things you simply will not indulge in before marriage?"

"Uh-huh."

"Then that has a profound effect on our relationship." He cocked his head.

Without intending to, she realized that she had mimicked his action. "It does?"

"Oh, yes." His lips quirked up on one side. His gaze dropped to her mouth, then met her eyes again, his lids lowered. "It means that we're going to have to hurry this courtship right along, Lucy. Because I can wait till we're married, but I don't want to wait too long."

"What are you waiting for?

Naomi spread her fingers enough to peek at the image glaring back at her from the full-length mirror.

"A miracle," she called back to her husband, whom she could just picture lounging on their big cherry wood sleigh bed. "Or shy of a miracle, a sudden, isolated power outage that plunges the bedroom into total darkness."

He laughed. "C'mon. It can't be that bad."

She lowered her hands from her face to confront her five-month pregnant body in Taylor's Valentine's Day gift, a black chiffon nightgown with red satin trim. By today's standards the lingerie practically rivaled a flannel nightshirt in tameness. Still, she decided, a nightshirt might have had room enough for all of her.

"Can't be that bad?" Naomi sighed. "Sweetie, I look like someone tried to smuggle two pounds of potato salad from a wedding buffet inside a ten-ounce evening bag."

"You? Look like potato salad? No way." He chuckled. "Caviar, maybe, but not potato salad."

"You, poet, you." She fidgeted with a twisted strap, her voice taking on that faraway, dreamy quality. "Ah, my love is like a...great big bowl of smelly fish eggs."

"You were the one who started the comparisons to food. I only wanted you to know that if you insisted on doing that, you should compare yourself to the very best."

"You really are too sweet." That's what she'd told him when he handed her the gold-wrapped gift box with the famous label on the seal. She had not meant it anymore then than she did now. Not that she was opposed to appealing to her husband. Not at all. She just wanted to be sure he found her appealing, not appalling.

"Aren't you ever going to come out in that thing?" Taylor called.

"I'm already coming out of it—in every direction." She slumped her shoulders forward, causing the gown's center split to fall open over the satin undergown like curtains parting over a late-summer melon.

"Come out *here*. I want to see you in it."

"Why? When we were in Maine last year you already saw

the whales. Just picture one of them in layers of sheer chiffon and red ribbons, and you've pretty much got the effect."

"The salesgirl said it was supposed to make you feel slinky, sassy, and self-assured."

"The sssalesgirl sssounds like a sssnake." She leaned toward the door as if that would hurry her words out more quickly, "And I don't mean that as a personal judgement."

"I know."

"I mean she probably had hips like one," she muttered to herself, her hands instinctively smoothing down along the growing curve spreading out from her once small waist.

"Naomi, darling, if you don't come out here I am going to come in and get you."

"You don't scare me, Mr. Boatwright." She laid her hand over her swollen belly, took a deep breath, and moved to the door. "I have already been gotten."

"Naomi Beauchamp Boatwright?" Her husband rose from the bed and came to her, nuzzling her neck, her temple, then pausing just before he kissed her lips. "You're still a knockout."

"Yeah, a regular heavyweight contender," she murmured even as she surrendered herself to the pleasure of her husband's kiss.

He pulled his face away from hers, his gaze penetrating and tinged with a sadness that cut her deep. "Just for tonight, Naomi, as my one true Valentine's present, could you just pretend you're not completely annoyed, inconvenienced, and unhappy about this pregnancy?"

Her breath caught in her chest like a fist closing low in her airway. She'd had no idea that all her attempts at making light of her feelings, of covering up, had been so transparent—and misinterpreted. She did not feel unhappy about carrying Taylor's baby, unsure, yes, and anxious…but—

"Oh, Taylor, I'm not. Knowing that your baby is growing

inside me is just so amazing. But being pregnant at this age, at this time in my life—it's more than a little overwhelming. Surely you can understand that?"

"I do." He placed his hands on the sides of her face and tipped her head back. "But tonight let's not let anything overwhelm us but our love for one another. What do you think?"

"I think that's the most lovely thing you've said to me since you compared me to fish eggs." She went up on tiptoe, placed her lips to his, and lost herself in her husband's kiss and love.

"Sure was nice running into Ted and Gayle at the restaurant tonight. Didn't she look wonderful?" Rose flipped the key in the lock of her townhouse door and pushed it open.

Will scowled. "I wish you'd let me do that, Rose. It just seems so ungentlemanly to allow a lady to unlock and open her own door."

She laughed and stepped across the threshold. "That's so old-fashioned, Will. In this day and age a woman handing a man her house key is like an invitation of a sort."

"I wasn't asking you to give it to me to keep, Rose." He followed at her heels.

"Besides, I'm perfectly capable of opening my own doors." She flicked on the inside light. "Hmmm, looks like Stacey went on to bed already. She felt a little blue about spending the big day alone, you know."

Rose flitted through the kitchen/dining room/living room area, leaving a trail of glowing sixty-watt bulbs in her wake. She placed her purse and bulky sweater in the coat closet, then extended her hand to collect Will's jacket, but he'd already draped it over the back of the armchair and settled down on the couch.

"I invited Stacey to come along with us—I knew you wouldn't mind—"

"Of course not."

"But she wouldn't hear of it."

"Thank goodness."

"Will!" Rose slid into her usual seat beside him, kicked off her shoes, and curled her legs up beneath her.

"Can I help it if I want to spend time alone with you on Valentine's Day?" He pouted like a silver-haired four-year-old.

She patted his leg. "You're alone with me now."

"Not really. *She's* in the next room." He folded his arms over his chest. "She's always around. If it wasn't for wrangling in on our dates, that girl'd have no social life at all."

"Why, Will Boatwright, that sounded positively ugly." She sat up. Things had not been "peachy-keen" between the two of them for some time now, but rarely did that result in a breach of manners and the overall lack of taste in making disparaging remarks regarding Stacey's presence.

"Well I didn't intend it as ugliness, Rose, I meant it as good advice from one parent of grown children to another. You coddle that child."

"When you'd rather I were coddling you?"

"Don't twist this around to a joke, Rose. Your daughter is taking advantage of you. She lives here rent-free, doesn't pay a food bill or a utility."

"Pay?" The fact that he was right only stung Rose's pride all the more. She tugged her collar up close to her neck and fiddled with the ends of her hair as if the whole bent of the conversation bored her. "How can she pay? She doesn't have a job."

"That was going to be my next point." He wagged a finger at her like a sturdy old schoolmarm. "She's been here since

November and has not once even tried to find a job. Not even extra work at a store during Christmas."

"Oh, you're just mad because you think she interferes with our private time." Rose waved it off.

"As if we need your daughter for that." He harumphed.

"What are you saying?"

"I'm saying it's always something, Rose. If not Stacey, then it's your work, someone from the church, one of the children, Lucy, or one of your other friends intruding on our time together."

"Why, Will, I—"

"Not that I blame any of them, Rose. They're only doing what you suggest." The normal congenial ruddiness of his face went deep red. "Join us. Come along. Will won't mind. Why even tonight at the restaurant you tried to coax Ted and Gayle into moving to our table."

What point was there in denying it? She'd done just that—but she'd had a perfectly sound reason. "I've been worried about them, Will. They've been through a rough patch and tonight Ted looked awful. Didn't you think Ted looked awful?"

"He did look worn down, for a fact." The taut grip of Will's twined arms relaxed.

"I just thought they might need another couple there to help siphon off some of the tension." Rose pulled her feet in tighter to her body with one hand on her ankle.

"He didn't look tense to me. He looked tired."

"Maybe so," Rose conceded. "I only offered for them to join us out of compassion, and they refused anyway. So I don't see why it matters."

"It matters because—"

"Lower your voice." Rose placed her finger to her lips.

"It matters because I can't even argue with you at a decent

volume level for fear of being overheard, anymore!"

"You're saying we don't argue enough? Or just not loud enough?" She laughed, hoping that would cajole him out of his grumpy mood.

He scowled.

"Oh, stop it, Will." She touched at her hair flirtatiously. "It's Valentine's Day, and instead of fussing over not spending enough time alone, let's enjoy what time we have together."

"I hate it when you're that right about something." He raised his arm, then lay it down across the back of the couch behind her. "You know that, don't you?"

"Then I must be a cause of constant consternation for you, sugar."

"It never ends." He kissed her cheek. "But I do have to say that things have certainly gotten better since you stopped that silly running out to Sweet Haven of a Saturday evening."

Rose pulled away. "Just because you didn't approve of what I was doing did not mean it was *silly.*"

"No, it was *silly* because it was silly." This time he laughed in a way that conveyed he hoped to jolly Rose out of her reaction. "Even you have to admit you didn't accomplish much by all that running out there."

"We got her into church, even if it was just for a children's program, and that's not nothing."

"Of course not. It was fine and noble, Rose, but now it's done." He sat forward, slashing his hand through the air like some high and mighty king sending out his proclamation.

"It most certainly is *not* done, William Boatwright." She pulled herself up, every inch of her posture as regal as his was arrogant. "Because we intend to go back out to Sweet Haven on the Saturday before Easter to try to encourage Miss Grace to join us on Sunday."

"Oh, no, you will not." There was a kind of rumbling laughter in his tone.

The patronizing effect did not sit well with Rose. Not well at all. "I will if I please."

"And you call yourself a Christian," he muttered, not meeting her gaze.

"What?" Intellectually she knew he'd hauled in the big guns to shore up his position, hit her in the place he knew she would be most quickly brought down. Emotionally, she could not fathom why this man, who had sat beside her in all manner of church services and programs and prayed with her over meals and knew that above all, she did, most certainly, consider herself a Christian, would fight so dirty. She reached for one of her linen handkerchiefs that lay on the table by the couch. She needed to fan herself or to dab the dampness from the back of her neck, she thought, but she balled the hankie into her fist instead.

All the while Will sat and watched her, his expression stern but not malicious. He looked quite earnest and, underlying that, upset, but he did nothing more to help her understand why he had said such a thing.

"I do call myself a Christian, Will." Her heart hammered so hard and high in her chest at that unwarranted sneer that she scarcely could get the breath out to ask, "Why ever would you want to imply otherwise?"

"I didn't mean it like that, Rose, dear." He took her hand and spoke like an old friend imparting a bitter truth or a father doling out discipline. "But, Rose, you know good and well the Bible gives some very specific instructions about how women and men should interact. Yet you choose to ignore them."

Her mind reeled, trying to make sense of this new tack without letting her stinging feelings control her reactions. "What are you talking about?"

"That verse—I'm sure you've heard even if you haven't taken it to heart—about how women are supposed to submit—"

"To their *husbands*," she finished for him. She sighed in quiet relief. Her whole world settled back to normal again, the pieces slowly drifting into place like the aftermath of shaking one of those charming Christmas snow globes. She actually found it within herself to laugh a little. "Will Boatwright, you are trying to pull rank in an army in which I am not even enlisted."

"Not for my lack of trying to recruit you." The sparkle in his eye told her he knew he'd overstepped his bounds. He took her hands in his, discovered the wadded-up handkerchief, and tossed it on the sofa beside him. "I'm sorry, Rose. I had no call to question your Christian sincerity, no call at all. I just feel so helpless when you refuse to even take into account my views on this whole Sweet Haven matter."

"But that's just it, Will." She searched his troubled gaze. "I don't know what your views on this *matter* are."

He pressed his lips together until they became like a pale slash across his grimly set jawline.

"Will, talk to me about this." She clasped his calloused fingers more tightly. "Explain the whys and wherefores, and maybe it will change my mind. We both know that isn't exactly what I'm famous for, but at least give it a try."

Neither her words nor her gentle self-admonition seemed to move him. She wanted to say more but waited instead for him to give some response, even if it were one she would not appreciate.

Finally, he shook his head, his downturned face in shadow, silver hair gleaming in the warm lamplight. "Can't my asking you not to go out there again be enough, Rose?"

She thought about it, then shook her head. "No, Will. I'm sorry. It can't."

"Oh, Rose, why do you have to be so obstinate?"

"Why?" She released his hands and looked away, took a deep breath and shut her eyes. "Will, for all our married life I let Curry make the decisions for the family, often with little input from me."

"You call throwing a rose bouquet in his face, hollering matches heard 'round the block, and locking him out on his own front porch 'little input'?" Will chuckled.

Rose cringed at the reminder of her very vocal and infamous clashes with her late husband. She lifted her face, her demeanor ruffled like cat fur before a hiss-fight. "Now you know for a fact, Will, that Curry was never mean nor violent nor abusive. And while I might have had a sassier tongue and a better turn of a phrase than he did, I wasn't either."

"Naw, everyone knew it was fire and passion with you two. That the fights were always about something insignificant— forgotten birthdays, missed dinners, the thoughtless remarks we all make to those we love. The rest of us snipped and snarled at our spouses for years over those minor infractions, but you two got it all out in one big cleansing row." He laughed.

"That's true." She laughed, too.

"Curry was a good friend to me, Rose, but I understand how he could provoke a person. I swear there were times when I'd have wished I could have just popped him a good one right in the nose. He could be that bullheaded."

"Bullheaded?" Rose snorted. "Will, if stubborn were a cash crop this man would have owned half the state."

"And you the other half, Miss Rose Tancy," he said in a low grumble.

216

"We were well matched, I'll give you that." She patted Will's leg.

It occurred to her that this is when someone, preferably her, should say that she and Will were also well suited—but in an entirely different way. She studied the courtly gentleman beside her. The tender assurances simply would not come.

She wanted to speak them. She cared for Will, cared for him a great deal more than she would ever admit to him, even more than she dared admit to herself. Still, something held her back. Something unfinished from her marriage, something that she would not see carried over into any other relationship.

"Will?" She staved off the pang of regret at what she had to do, but made herself go on. "Will, sugar, do you know the thing that Curry did that made me the maddest?"

"There are so many possibilities, I can't even begin to winnow out just one."

"Well, there was one." She cleared her throat. This was more difficult than she had expected. "He kept things from me."

Will visibly tensed. "Secrets?"

"Not exactly, though, yes, there were some of those, I suppose. But mostly he kept away unpleasantness. Money concerns, legal matters, even difficulties at his work. And do you know why he did that?"

"Because he loved you." The answer came so swiftly and he said it so firmly that Rose could almost hear Curry's own voice ringing in the phrase.

She sat back against the sofa, her hand over her heart. "I...I suppose that's what *he* would have said."

Will nodded as if he had no doubt of Curry's response.

"And I am not discounting his feelings about his actions," Rose hastened to add. "But the reason he told me he did that, Will, was *for my own good.*"

"He was protecting you." The sofa dipped and her cushion raised as Will shifted his weight. "When a man really cares for a woman, that's what he does. He cherishes and protects her, Rose."

"No man can completely shelter the woman he loves from life, Will. That wouldn't be healthy for either one of them. Then what happens if that man dies?" A strangled sob caught in her throat. Tears welled in her eyes, but she willed them not to fall. "Do you have any idea how angry I've been at J. Curran Holcolmb for *protecting* me into the safe little niche of wife and mother and then, just as the girls got grown up and gone, dying and leaving me with no one? After all those years of playing the role, of going along for my own good, I didn't even feel I had *me* anymore."

She sniffled, and Will handed her the hankie he'd tossed aside earlier. She dabbed at her nose and tried to present as ladylike a front as possible. Dignity was a woman's finest feature, her mother would have said to her right now. Rose angled back her head and sighed, reining in her emotions so that she could go on bravely. "I don't blame Curry. I went right along with it. And I would not have begrudged him his place as the head of our family, but I do wish he'd have just trusted me enough to share more things with me."

"I didn't know you felt that way, Rose." Will placed his arm around her. "I doubt that Curry did either."

She wanted to take comfort in Will's nearness, his compassion, but she could not until everything between them was resolved. "Well, I do feel that way. That's why I take such an affront to your ordering me not to go out to Sweet Haven, which you are doing 'for my own good' or simply as a means of exercising your control over me. Both are a bunch of nonsense, and I won't stand for them."

He met her watery gaze with steadiness and an air of someone caught in an inner struggle. He seemed about to speak, then shook his head and looked away, his shoulders rounded forward as if signaling resignation.

"So, whether you like it or not, Will, I am going out to Sweet Haven again."

He stood and for the first time Rose thought he seemed his true age, world-weary and worn down. He still would not meet her eyes. "I guess that's it, then. If you don't trust me enough to listen to me on this, to respect my wishes even if I can't tell you why—"

"And if you can't respect me enough to tell me why—" She stood too.

He started to say something, closed his mouth, then sighed.

This time her will alone was not enough to still a tear from falling.

He wiped it away with the roughened side of his thumb. "I'll think about what you've said, Rose."

"Thank you for that."

He leaned in to place a kiss on her forehead then gathered his jacket and left.

Standing with her back pressed to the closed door, Rose finally let her dignity slip and the tears flow. She'd made her choice, it seemed, and now she had to live with the consequences.

Twelve

*O*h, my goodness, what an Easter Sunday and it's not even over for me yet." Gayle reached the top of the stairs well before Ted, who took each step with plodding slowness.

He paused about halfway up, wincing as he fought to pull his new silk tie free from his neck.

Gayle clucked her tongue and went on ahead. "Can't you wait until you're in our room to do that, sweetie?"

"I swear this thing is trying to strangle me." Despite the tightness of his voice, it carried up to Gayle as she swept over the threshold to their bedroom.

"Well, at least you get to slip out of your good clothes. I only get to change my shoes before I have to take Lillith back out to the cemetery for the Easter egg hunt." Gayle flung open the door to her own personal walk-in closet. "You'd think she'd be too old for all that now, but she's really excited. Since this is the last year she can do it, what does it hurt to let her have her fun?"

Ted grunted from what sounded like the top of the stairs.

"Oh, sure, you pooh-pooh it when it's me doing the indulging but you do more than your share of pampering your baby girl and you know it." She kicked off her high heels, shut her eyes, and savored the feel of the plush carpet on the aching soles of her feet. "Besides, it's not like I'm going out of my way to take Lillith out to the egg hunt. Not after Naomi roped us into taking Miss Grace out there."

From inside her roomy closet, she heard Ted shuffling about in the bedroom. She imagined him tossing his tie and jacket in the chair for her to pick up later. She started to warn him against doing that, then clamped her jaw shut. Why start something? She didn't have time for another pointless argument now.

She knew the man she'd married. He'd laugh at her compulsion to relentlessly tidy all things within her small realm, to have everything in order. He'd laugh. He'd cajole. He'd charm. And in the end, he'd still leave his things all over for her to tend to.

Sometimes that man made her mad enough to...to...She couldn't think what, but it would not be ladylike, that much was for sure. She shoved her heels into the empty space reserved just for them among the pristine white cubicles of her built-in organizer, then paused to collect herself.

Selecting a pair of neutral-colored flats, she stood on one tired foot and then the other, determined to keep the mood light and avoid any unpleasantness on this special holiday. "Not that I mind getting Grace involved in the activity. Nuh-uh, not after seeing the old gal react to the invitation. Seems they've been having egg hunts in the cemetery since Grace was a little girl. I can't blame Grace or Lillith for their excitement, mind you, Easter is such a wonderful time, what with spring in the air and the promise of the resurrection in your heart."

A bump and a thud told her that her husband had dropped onto the bed and had taken off one shoe. The next would follow and both would be left for her to put away in his closet across the room. Gayle vowed not to let that spoil her enjoyment of the day.

"And wasn't that sermon just lovely?" She sighed, then began rummaging through the scarves dangling from a circular hanger near the back of the closet. "I always think Daddy gives his best sermons at Christmas and Easter. He says he feels he has to give 110 percent then because there are some folks who only just set foot inside a church on those days and he feels obligated to give them as much spiritual nourishment as pos-sible. And that sun-rise service! I've seen it done all my life and yet it still give me chills—especially when they play the trumpets at the exact moment the sun peeks over the knob and the soloist sings 'He's Alive.' Chills. Unsophisticated and sappy as it sounds, it posi-tively brings me chills. Doesn't it you?"

No response. No agreement. No laughing *harumph* for her corniness. Not even the sound of his other shoe dropping.

"Ted?" He'd probably just gone on into the bathroom to escape her chattering, she told herself before trying again, this time in tone that demanded a reply, "Ted?"

Nothing.

"Ted, are you listening to me?"

No reply.

That was it. All day he'd been grumpy and incorrigible and had put a damper on what should have been a precious day for faith and family. Gayle snagged one scarf off the hanger and spun around, her good intentions to keep things genial with her husband fallen away. The silky fabric whipped in her grasp as she marched out into the bedroom, then fluttered away in deceptive peacefulness as she let the scarf go the instant she saw her sweet husband. "No! Dear Lord, no!"

She rushed to where Ted's crumpled body lay on the edge of the bed, the duvet crushed in his white-knuckled fist.

"Ted? Ted, honey, what is it? What's happening? What do you want me to do to help?"

He made a sickening gurgling sound, spittle pooled in the corner of his mouth.

"No, Dear Father. God Almighty, no. You can't have him now. I need him, my children need him." The words poured out in halting anguish.

Ted stared at her, his eyes filled with pain and horror yet willing her not to give into her own fear. Whatever was happening to him, he clearly could not survive it without her presence of mind and quick action.

Blindly, she stumbled the few steps to snatch up the cordless phone, then brought it to his side, pressing 911 as she did. She slid to the floor, to keep her gaze level with his and waited for the system, which was not the same sophisticated operation of larger cities, to connect.

"Precious Jesus…" She stroked back her husband's thick hair. "Please don't let this happen. Extend your mercy on this wonderful husband and father. Extend your hand to hold up your servant, Ted."

When she said his name, her husband reached for her. She took his hand, amazed at the power in his desperate grip.

"911 emergency dispatch."

"Hello? Hello? This is Gayle Barrett." Even in times of the most extreme pressure her manners took over almost like an instinct as she paused to identify herself to the speaker before rushing on to say, "You must send an ambulance out at once to 217 Mitchell Lane. I think my husband is having a heart attack."

"Have you been to the hospital?" Rose rushed up to Naomi, arms open.

"No." Naomi clung to Rose like a child wanting reassurance. "Gayle's mother asked me not to come. She asked me to bring Lillith and Nathan on out here with me. Things are to seem as normal as possible for the kids, especially Lillith, until they know for sure what they are facing. Those are Gayle's orders."

"Well, Ted's a young man, athletic, in his prime. They don't really think it's his heart, do they? It's more what they call a warning, isn't it?" Even Rose's firm tone could not shore up her pronouncements beyond those two weak questions. She stepped back, aware of the sun on her face, the smell of the old cedars at the back of the cemetery, and the faint noise of children participating in the annual Easter egg hunt.

She glanced out over the rolling hills where generations of New Bethany's people lay in eternal rest. She squinted her eyes over the grayish-white stone markers, marred by time and the elements—the little lambs for infants lost, the angels for children, the plain but elegant slabs for the veterans. She turned to the "new" section, opened more than thirty years ago and slowly filling with the gleaming black and gray and even red marble markers, which now were more in vogue than the statuary of older days. Curry lay in that section, as did Rose's parents and Naomi's mama. Rose sighed, taking some sweet assurance in being among so many that she had loved in her lifetime. Cemeteries in the South were places of community and connection as well as solace and solitude. She folded her hands and looked again at the children running and laughing and the adults picking their way through the stones, reading names, stopping to visit with departed friends and with one another.

"Why, I don't really believe it's Ted's heart at all," Rose declared, strengthened by the beauty of the day and their surroundings. She shifted her low-heeled spectator pumps in the grass, which stood tall enough to switch against her ankles, causing an intermittent tickling sensation that made her leg twitch. "He's been under so much stress lately, you know."

She expected Naomi to nod but she just stood there, staring.

Rose choked out a watered-down laugh and shrugged her shoulders in an imitation of blithe dismissal, a refusal to acknowledge the worst of all possibilities. "Land's sake, this is just a wake-up call, a sign he needs to let up and relax a little more. Maybe he and Gayle can take an extended vacation and—"

Naomi looked down.

Rose clutched at her friend's arm. "Jump in here any time with an agreement, Naomi, because your silence is scaring me."

"That's because I'm scared, Rose." Naomi's normally olive skin, which had taken on a becoming maternal glow of late, now went ashen. Her hand trembled as she swiped back her curly black hair. "I've never heard Gayle like that before. Goodness, Rose, she was screaming. All the while her mother was giving me instructions on the telephone, I could hear Gayle screaming in the background."

"Screaming?" Rose couldn't imagine that at all.

"Well, maybe screaming isn't the exact word. Honestly, I've never heard a sound like it—something between a moan and a scream. Very…primal, I guess is the word, as if it were coming from the very farthest reaches of her being, like she was ripping the words out of the centermost place of her soul."

"Oh, my. What was she saying?"

"Mostly bargaining with God. Promising what she would do, who she would help, how she would change just to put everything right again. That, and blaming herself for Ted going so long without seeking help."

"Well, at least she still thinks *she's* in charge of everything." Rose said it not to poke fun at Gayle but because it was the first thing that popped into her mind. Besides, it made Naomi laugh a little and that posed a small comfort to them both. "No, really, Gayle knows who's in charge of everything. Her prayers are proof enough of that."

"I'm sure she does and—"

"What have you heard?" Lucy waved to them across the lush, green grass and bleached, white headstones of the old part of the cemetery. Sun glinted off her pale hair. Her flowing dress, the delicate color of a baby chick, made a sharp contrast to her reddened cheeks. Her eyes were clouded with concern.

"We haven't heard anything since the first call." Naomi extended her hand toward Lucy, who took it and Rose's as soon as she reached them. "I was hoping you might have heard something, maybe from Ben?"

Lucy shook her head. "Ben's still at the hospital. He said he'd come out to the egg hunt later if it wasn't anything too serious."

"So he didn't think it would be serious?" Rose knew she was putting words in Lucy's mouth—specifically the words both she and Naomi wanted most to hear.

"He didn't have time for suppositions, Rose. Just asked me to bring the kids to the egg hunt and said he'd be by later, if he could."

All around them the voices of happy children and doting adults filled the brilliant afternoon. The bright colors of over-sized Easter baskets and the new outfits in shades of petal pinks, sky blues, mint greens, downy yellows, and dazzling whites blurred in the corners of Rose's eyes.

"We should be with Gayle," Lucy whispered.

"We are, honey." Rose nodded firmly. "We're with her in spirit and in our love, and when she wants us, we'll go to her and hold her hands and do whatever we can to help. She knows that."

"There's nothing we can do at the hospital now anyway, Lucy." Naomi tendered a quiet smile.

Naomi appeared calm, but beneath that image Rose saw a frailness about her friend that she had not seen since the days after Naomi's mama had died. She wanted to do something for Naomi—and for Lucy—as much as she wanted to do something for Gayle. "You know, ya'll, there is something we can do. Something we got sort of good at last year—the very thing that brought us all together in the first place." Rose put her arm about Naomi's shoulders. "We can pray."

"I have been," Naomi said.

"Me, too." Lucy's voice cracked.

"But now we can do it together." Rose bowed her head and shut her eyes, her hands again reached for her friends' hands.

The breeze stirred. The grass prickled at her ankles. Beyond them the excitement of the afternoon dimmed to a hush, blotted out in Rose's thoughts by her own concentration on the task at hand. For several seconds she stood there, then she heard the quiet whisper of shuffling feet and felt Lucy's and Naomi's hands in hers.

Rose swallowed, took a deep breath of fresh, clean spring air, and lifted her face, her eyes still closed. "Oh, Father, our hearts open before you now. We are humble in the urgent hour of need. We see things through a glass darkly. We cannot know what plans you have laid for us or for our beloved friends, Gayle, and most seriously for her husband Ted. But we know your mercy and goodness go beyond our means to comprehend, and so we come before you now with just one earnest plea. Father, be with Ted and Gayle and even as we pray without ceasing for Ted's healing, be in his every heartbeat and grow stronger in him even as he is strong in you—be Ted's strength and Gayle's courage and give us hope and peace. We ask it all to your glory and by your will and in the name of Jesus—"

"Amen," Naomi said, firmly.

"Amen," Lucy echoed.

"Amen." The word reverberated in the sudden stillness of the afternoon, gentle as a wave rolling out from a pebble dropped into a pond.

Rose looked up to see the cluster of people who had stopped and joined in, unbidden but surely welcome. The sight buoyed Rose's spirits, and she felt as if she'd experienced the presence of angels. She smiled to think that Ted and Gayle might feel the same.

The Johnson sisters, Marguerite and Princess, came up to ask if they could do anything to help. Rose marveled how quickly news spread through the town proper and through the religious community in particular. With Gayle's father being a minister and this being Easter Sunday, the word of Ted being rushed to the hospital must have gone through New Bethany like a fire through dried briar.

Marguerite and Princess had heard of it from their minister's wife, they reported, and she wasn't the first to catch wind of it, to their understanding. All of them were glad to offer up a prayer for the Barretts along the way, as well. At times like these, Rose was pleased to note, differences like race and social standing seemed to hold no bearing. The Johnson sisters' round, dark faces were set off by fine red hats. Their full bodies were adorned in dresses of colors so bright they made your heart light just to look at them. And their boisterous personalities were about as far removed from the Barretts—especially Ted's people, who were very much "old South"—as east was from west. Or more specifically, black from white.

But the women showed not the slightest hesitation to go

before the Lord on Ted's behalf or anyone else's for that matter. They knew that in God's domain worldly distinctions held no meaning, and Rose often wished she had the kind of faith the sisters showed the world on a daily basis. She gave them each a hug and felt confident in thanking them on Gayle's behalf for their offers and their prayers.

When Rose, Naomi, and Lucy stood alone again, none of them seemed ready to leave, yet they couldn't give a reason to stay. Finally Lucy wrung her hands and looked to them, as if for guidance, "Now what?"

Naomi looked expectantly to Rose.

Rose opened her mouth, not knowing what she would actually say.

"Over here by this here big 'un, Miss Grace," Vhonda Faye Womack hollered in a voice that seemed to come from the tips of the child's toes.

Grace toddled after Vhonda Faye like a sprightly child, a basket slung over her bony twig of an arm. The old gal tip-toed past a towering Irish cross that had settled with a pronounced list over time. Spying something on the ground, she squealed with delight, and Vhonda Faye joined right in.

Nearby, Dr. Ben's little ones ran and tumbled pell-mell over their shiny new shoes. They giggled, gawked, then grabbed up the foil-wrapped candy eggs that Lillith and Nathan had pointed out to them.

"Now, Lucy?" Rose laid a hand on her friend's back and smiled. "Now we go on with life. And we hope and wait and have faith."

"Still no word?" Taylor slipped his arm around what little remained of Naomi's waist.

With the last of the participants gone, they walked the now vacant cemetery, making sure no colored eggs had escaped the zealous eyes of the children. Colored eggs, either the dyed or the candy variety, were not something anyone wanted left out in the weather, exposed to heat and rain and acting as beacons for critters to invade the peaceful cemetery.

Naomi laid her head on her husband's shoulder, keenly aware that Gayle could not do the same with Ted. Drawing the vibrant spring air deep into her lungs she held it while she watched Lucy's car, with Paige and Alec Martin and Lillith and Nathan Barrett in it, rounding the corner out of sight. "We had hoped Dr. Ben would come out before the egg hunt ended."

"It could be good that Ben didn't show up, you know." Taylor stroked her hair as they walked along. "Could mean he just had to run a few routine tests, and not that he had to call in a specialist."

"It could." Naomi didn't even try to couch her doubt of that with a gentle tone. "Not likely, but it could."

Taylor stopped, squinted, then bent down to pick up a lavender egg with a cross and lily decal on it. He plopped it in the basket in Naomi's hand. When they resumed their walk he said, "Sure was nice of Lucy to take Lillith and Nathan with her, wasn't it?"

"Well, they were getting such a kick out of helping with Ben's kids, and it seemed good for them to feel they had a purpose in the scheme of things. Besides, we volunteered for egg reconnaissance duty months ago. We had to stay for this, and the last place I wanted Nathan and Lillith today was in a quiet cemetery."

They walked on in silence for the length of an entire row of headstones, pausing only long enough to poke through weeds here and there to check for strays.

"Let's see, they started out with ten dozen hen eggs, of which one hundred and ten were found. Do we have a count on the candy ones?"

"No, we're just supposed to pick any up we see if they get left behind. At least they won't turn into stink bombs."

Taylor nodded as if she had just shared some great mystical truth. Though he hardly knew Ted, it was clear he felt genuine concern for the man's condition. Caring ran deep in Taylor and a respect for all of God's creation. When someone was hurt, it brought out his protective streak—the same streak that made him an attentive gardener, a devoted father, and a wonderful husband.

Naomi took his hand and drew her strength from him as they wandered over the grounds together.

Twenty minutes later he tallied the collection in the basket. "Ten colored hen eggs and various and sundry remnants of candy and wrappers. Looks like our job is done, then. Are you ready to go home?"

Naomi paused and looked around. For the first time she actually took note of where they stood. Her heart stopped cold in her chest. She inched up her chin and the breeze blew back her hair.

"We're near Mama's grave."

"So we are." Taylor moved close to her, his eyes gazing outward toward the section where her mama was buried. "I'd had my mind so set on the egg count I hadn't noticed."

"Me, either."

He pressed his hand to her back. "Shall we pay our respects?"

Naomi hesitated. She hadn't been to Mama's grave since the marker was set. Not since the weekend she'd returned from Maine as Taylor's wife. Something always kept her away after that. She took a step back, balking at going over even now. "It's late."

"She won't mind." He took Naomi by the elbow.

"That's not funny." She tugged her arm away. "Besides, I'm…I'm tired."

"Too tired to walk a few feet more?" He moved forward.

Naomi stood her ground like a mule stuck in mud.

"You're really not coming?"

"I…" She shook her head. Her throat clenched tight as a fisted hand. Tears warmed her eyes but a shiver crept over her skin. "I don't…I can't…I don't want to see her name carved in a headstone like that. It'd just make it all so…"

"Honey, is this because of Ted? Because you don't want to think what might happen if he—"

"No." She twisted her head away so she wouldn't have to face him when she told her husband the truth. "It's not about Ted. It's about me, Taylor."

He shifted his weight, saying nothing, waiting on her to fill up the brittle silence.

A thousand thoughts went through her mind. Emotions came so fast she could not single out any one to comprehend and deal with it. The early evening breeze swirled around them, flattening her full maternity dress over the new fullness of her belly. Tears that had only blurred her vision before now fell—first one onto her cheek, the next rolling down along her nose so that she had to brush it away across her face, probably smearing her makeup in the process.

In the distance the Tennessee hills stood gray and somber. From where she and Taylor stood, they could see a swath of Old Seminole Cemetery Road, which led in one direction to Boatwright Nursery and in the other back to town, emptying out at Ray's Bob's Cone' and Coney King. Closer still, the kudzu leaves rustled where twining tendrils covered the rock walls at the far side of the cemetery.

Taylor came to her, his arms open but he did not pull her into an embrace. Rather he made himself available for her—physically and emotionally. "What is it, Nomi? Help me to understand what's going on."

She swallowed, shut her eyes, and shook her head. How could she explain to him what she herself did not fully understand?

Taylor set aside the basket of eggs then came to take first one of her hands and then the other. "Please, Nomi. I'm trying to help you. I want to help you. I just don't know how. If you could just tell me—"

"Oh, Taylor, how can I bring a baby into this world who will never know Mama?" The level of her own anguish, not the question itself, startled her. She had mulled the question over in her mind almost daily since the doctor's confirmation of her pregnancy. She exhaled a hard, shuddering breath. "Do you know how many times I've picked up the phone these last few months to call Mama, to tell her that the baby moved or to ask her for advice?"

He combed back her hair, his eyes full of empathy. "Your mother *knows*, Naomi. She knows about the baby and she's always with us, you have to believe that."

"Yes, but some days that's just not enough. I want to hear her voice, Taylor. I want to touch her hand and feel her put her arm around me. I want our baby to know this remarkable woman who raised me, and whom I so loved and respected, in more than photographs and my pale stories about her." She wound her arms around her husband's chest.

His heart beat strong and steady beneath her ear, and the rhythm of his breathing soothed her jagged nerves. "I *am* scared about Ted. I won't deny that or pretend this emergency

234

has not heightened the feeling of loss for me."

She felt him nod. "I know. Of course, it would."

"But it's missing my mama that has really robbed me of the joy of this baby, Taylor. I wish I had a way of connecting with her again, of making her a part of our baby's life and his or her history."

"You do." He tipped her head up with one finger. "Through your faith. When we share our faith, the faith of our mothers and fathers and theirs before them, we not only give our children a sense of unity, we help them to find eternity."

"I know that and I believe it with all my heart…"

"But?"

"But I wish with all my heart and—" She pinched her thumb and finger an eyelash width apart "—just that much more that I had a way of knowing that bond between the generations of women in my family would endure."

"Then do it."

"Do what?"

"Find a way, Nomi. If there was ever a woman alive who could figure out a way to make that connection for herself, for her child—for half the township of New Bethany, Tennessee, if you so chose—it's you. So my suggestion is, stop wishing. Keep praying, but stop wishing and start doing what it takes to make that happen."

"You understand you may live to regret giving me that advice, don't you?" She gave him a sly grin, her spirits lifted, her mind already racing with ideas.

"I understand you need to do this." He gave her a hug, laughter rumbling in his strong chest. "And heaven help anyone—man, woman, or otherwise—who would try to stand between Naomi Beauchamp Boatwright and her determination to get something done."

Thirteen

"We're keeping him in ICU at least for tonight, and then we'll talk about moving him to—Gayle? Are you listening?"

Gayle battled fatigue, confusion, and relief to bring her focus back to Dr. Martin. However, after his initial "It looks like Ted's going to be all right," everything else took on a faraway, fuzzy quality. She saw him speaking—even heard his words—but it was as though she stood at the bottom of a dim, deep well and he were calling down to her.

All right. Not out of the woods yet, but it looks like he'll be all right. That's how Dr. Martin had put it, like some doctor from a prime-time drama, complete with the long, compassionate gaze, the encouraging nod, and the hand on her shoulder. Ben could not have given a more cliched performance if he'd tried—and still Gayle thought she had never heard nor seen anything more glorious in her life.

For hours—hours that had dragged by like days—she had waited and prayed. Her parents had stayed by her side until she asked them to go. She needed them to take care of her children, to call her oldest daughter at college, to hold up the home front, as it were. Ted's elderly, widowed mother had wanted to come down but she really was in no condition for the grueling wait. In the end, Gayle had persuaded Ted's sister to drive down from Kentucky. They set up a kind of command post, a "Barrett Central" for receiving calls and casseroles and what have you. This allowed them to feel useful and occupied, but out of Gayle's hair, as they all awaited the outcome.

In truth, Gayle wanted to be alone when she got the news, whatever it was. She did not want anyone, not even her mother—most of all her mother—to see Gayle lose control if the news were bleak. Or worse.

But it wasn't bleak. Gayle took in a breath and for the first time in forever actually felt her lungs fill, the oxygen fresh and revitalizing. She felt the forced air of the waiting room on her face, smelled the odors of the sterile surroundings, heard the swish and swoosh of the nurses' thick shoes and of doors swinging open and shut like the flutter of great wings. An impromptu image of the stained-glass window on the door of Sweet Haven sprang to mind.

"Beneath the wings of angels." She felt for all the world that she had just stepped from beneath those wings, that she had spent the day under the shelter of God's care and the cover of the heartfelt prayers of her friends and family.

"What's that, Gayle?" Ben watched her carefully.

Ted would be all right. Her heart virtually sang it. Her pulse thrummed. She felt the blood humming through her veins. Her skin prickled.

"Gayle?"

She ran her trembling hand back through her hair. "I want to see him."

She collected her purse, glanced around the pale vinyl seat and, finding nothing of hers lying about, began to stand. Just as quickly, she dropped back to her chair again. She shook her head. "Guess I got up too quickly."

"Gayle—"

She held her hand up to still whatever worry Ben wanted to express and tried again to get to her feet. Her legs quivered. The room tilted and spun. Her vision blurred. This time she sank down slowly.

"Whoa." Ben had caught her beneath the elbow to help her control her descent.

"I want to see Ted now."

"You just stay put, Gayle." Ben's hand, far more powerful than one might have suspected, pressed down on her shoulder. "You cannot see Ted just yet. That's what I've been trying to explain. When you first brought Ted in, I told you I wanted to call a friend, a cardiologist. He's originally from here and wants to move back? Dr. Clemmons? Mark Clemmons?"

She shook her head. The only thing she really remembered about this whole day was the first sight of Ted in soul-rending, horrific pain. "I'm…I'm not sure…I—"

"Well, I called him and he agreed to come out here. He wanted to check out the hospital and the area again, anyway." Ben fidgeted with a pen in his lab coat pocket. "He's just arrived. He's going to examine Ted and maybe run a few tests. After that he and I will want to have a consultation, and the nurses will need to get Ted situated for the night. *Then* you can see your husband."

"When will that be?"

"An hour, forty-five minutes." He bent at the knees to put his calming gaze level with hers. "I suggest you use that time to get something to eat and to clear your head. I'd prescribe a quick catnap, but I venture you won't go for that?"

"Nuh-uh. No sir." She shook her head, which made it throb with dull, persistent pain in each temple and across her burning eyes. She put her fingertips against the pounding pressure points at the edge of her scalp. "But I think I will get that bite to eat. All I've had today is a handful of jellybeans and a swimming pool full of coffee."

Ben checked his wristwatch. The silver band glinted as he rotated it first toward himself then toward Gayle to show her the glow-in-the-dark numbers illuminated against the blue watch face. "The hospital cafeteria is already closed for the evening. Looks like you'll have to go out."

"That settles that then." Gayle tipped her head back to rest half against the wall, half on the squared cushion behind her. She shut her eyes. "Even if I were in any shape to drive, I don't have a car here. I came in on the ambulance with Ted."

"Oh, I don't think finding a ride is going to present much of a problem, not as long as you've got that caliber of friends."

"What caliber...?" She squinted up at him.

He inclined his head just a hair toward the window in the nearest door. "They weren't allowed here in the ICU waiting room, since they aren't Ted's family. But they've been just outside for the last couple of hours."

Gayle gazed out on two women she had known most of her life but who, until a little over a year ago, she would have only deemed as long-time acquaintants, a part of her personal history in New Bethany, no more significant than her high school math teacher or senior prom date. Now they were her lifeline.

The weariness and concern of the day was etched in their faces like the wrinkles in the clothes they'd had on since the sunrise service more than twelve hours earlier. Rose sat, straight-backed, her head cocked, her neck twisted at an odd angle, her gaze fixed on the elevated television in one corner of the room. Naomi, shoes off and legs kicked up to rest her feet in Rose's lap, had one hand thrown over her eyes and the other resting over the swell of her tummy. The sight warmed Gayle in a way she did not expect.

For all her devices and schemes to be alone today, she never really had been. The prayers of many, the presence of God, and these two good friends had thwarted that plan completely. She had never been so happy to see the evidence of God's love manifested in his followers.

"They showed up right after their egg hunting duties concluded." Ben chuckled. "I know Lucy wanted to be here with them but she's taking care of Paige and Alec."

"That's important work, too." Gayle stood judiciously, bracing herself with one hand on Ben's arm as she did so. "I understand she had my two younger children for a while today as well. That Lucy, she might not look it at first glance, but she's a gem, you know. A regular diamond in a dime store, as my grandfather might have said."

"Yes. Yes, she is." The man practically beamed.

"Tell Lucy when you see her how much I appreciate what's she's done for me, won't you?" She gave his hand a pat and started toward the door.

"You can count on it."

Head bowed, she used the walk to the door to pull herself together—and to express her gratitude for all she had received today. *Thank you, dear Father, thank you for this second chance. I've been awful and I know it, unworthy of Ted's love or your wonderful mercy. Lord, your salvation and goodness are more than I could ever deserve with my doubts and shallow selfishness. You gave a second chance, on the cross and now today with Ted. My thanks are not enough but with my whole heart, they are yours.*

"Oh." Gayle stopped in her tracks then turned slowly to face Ben again. "And thank you, Dr. Martin. Thank you for everything you've done today, from taking Ted on when he hadn't even ever come to see you before, for hunting down his medical records from his last physician, and for calling in your friend for a consultation."

"Would it sound too corny if I said I was just doing my job?"

"Entirely."

"Then I won't say it." He winked. "Now you go get something to eat before you faint from hunger and bonk your head on this hard floor and I have to take on another Barrett as a patient."

"Oh, you'll rue the day you fretted over not having enough Barretts as patients. After today, you'll have all the Barretts you can bear, and the Shorters as well. Those are my folks and our people, and who knows how many there are from Ted's law firm, and—"

"Whoa. Hold on there. Maybe *I'm* the one who should get something to eat. It sounds like I'm going to need to keep my strength up." He laughed.

"Then may I bring you anything when I come back?"

"Actually, I'm going to scoot on over to Lucy's to check on the kids while the tests are being run. I'll pick something up."

"Then I'll see you back here in about an hour." She did not pose it as a question but rather, a commitment. And she did not dally for him to hem and haw and tell her how imprecise test running can be and so on. She'd give them an hour, no more—and then she was going to see her sweet husband's face, if she had to raise the roof to do it.

"An...an...an...God bless Mizz Rose an, an, an...Von'a Faye an...an....an Tiff'ny an...an...an God bless, God bless, God Bless-s-s-s...Mr. Woobie Bear at th-the-the day care an...an..."

"And let's wrap it up now." Lucy opened one eye to peek at Alec.

He ventured a peep at her the same way, his hands still folded under his chin for good-night prayers.

The little boy looked so angelic and small lying in her big bed next to his drowsy sister, Lucy almost didn't have it in her to nudge the nighttime rituals along. But it was already past the pair's bedtime, and it had been a big day, what with two worship services, dinner out with Lucy and their dad, the egg hunt and all. For Lucy, the added burden of worry over Ted and

Gayle and wishing she could do more had taken its toll.

How easy it would be to sit here in the dim light of her room and let Alec drone on asking God to bless everything and everyone he could imagine. How easy not to go out and face the emptiness of her house waiting for Ben to come home— come *back*, she corrected herself. This was not Ben's home, not yet. Perhaps not ever.

Despite his bold proclamations on Valentine's Day, nothing much happened to make Lucy think her relationship with Ben was progressing. Sure, they ended their nights with a kiss and held hands openly and snuggled a bit as they watched TV, but nothing substantial had changed in Ben's attitude or treatment of her. Though he was still thoughtful and kind and just look-ing at the man still unleashed a flutter that unnerved her to the very core, little else gave Lucy any indication that he was ready to take their relationship forward.

Please, dear Lord, don't let this be another disappointment. Don't let me waste away any more of my youth and hope on some-one who will only use it up then toss it aside. I've waited so long, oh Lord, and been so good, please, don't let it be for nothing.

Her past experiences, she told herself, were to blame for her fears and concerns. She'd simply been taken for granted far too often to trust that it could not—that it *was* not—happening again. Her own judgement, not Ben's action, called it all into question. But in the end she had to face the facts, after the first thrill of their romantic Valentine's Day, Ben had fallen into a nice, comfortable rut and obviously felt his presence was effort enough for a girl like her.

A girl like her, after all, deserved so little and should be thankful for whatever she got. She'd learned that lesson from her father. Ray Griggs and Dwayne Cobb had only served to hammer it in.

The sharp slap of reality in that thought brought out the responsible side of her personality. It won out over the mushy mama wannabe, and she touched one finger to Alec's pug nose. "Quit stalling and get to the amen."

"What's *stalling*?" he asked in an exaggerated whisper.

When he fixed those huge eyes on her, widened in innocent denial, it wiggled under her trained day-care-lady exterior and melted her to the core.

"Stalling is trying to put off for as long as you can something you know is going to happen. Like you stretching out your God blesses to try to keep me from turning out the light right away." *Or like me hanging onto one failing relationship after another hoping that something would be different this time.* She pushed the thought away. "You can't get away with that kind of thing with me, kiddo. I'm the queen of dealing with stalling males and I have had my fill of it." To her surprise she meant it. Pulling herself up straight she shook back her hair and concluded, "I simply will not put up with it one minute more."

"The *queen*?" His voice was filled with hushed reverence.

"Say amen. *Now* Alec."

"But you—"

"Amen."

He stuck out his lower lip in a pout, but obeyed her request. "Amen."

"Amen." Softened by the close of the prayer and by his genuinely sweet expression, Lucy bent down and placed a kiss on Alec's forehead. "And good night, sweetie-pie."

"Night," Alec mumbled.

"Good night, Paige." She smoothed the blanket out over the tiny girl, then kissed Paige's forehead, too.

The cherub-faced child roused, her eyes unfocused and her

lids looking too heavy for her to keep open. She smiled at Lucy.
"Miss Lucy?"

"What honey?"

"'S'a happy day."

"Yes, it was." Lucy stroked back the downy curls on Paige's
temple. "You had lots of candy and excitement and fun and—"

"You." She raised one finger slowly to point at Lucy. "Paige
likes be wif *you.*"

Lucy liked to be with the children, too, more than she
wanted to let herself admit. It was a potent thing to love a man,
to want to spend your life with him, and to realize that dream
might remain forever just beyond your reach. But to also love
his children? To long to see them grow, to guide and pray for
them, to give them a happy home, perhaps one with other sib-
lings born of your love for their father? The hopes—and even
more so, the fear of having those hopes dashed—were almost
too much to bear.

"Thank you, sugar." Lucy could not dredge up enough
voice from her aching being to say more.

Alec squirmed.

Now it was Lucy who was stalling. She should leave and let
the children go to sleep, but her legs would not carry her away
just yet. She stole one more moment to caress Paige's cheek.

The child's plump fingers lightly brushed over Lucy's hand.
"Um lo'b'es you."

Paige did not pronounce the words clearly but they still cut
through Lucy's lifelong defenses with the accuracy of a finely
honed knife's edge. A knife that twisted in her heart when she
looked at the pair with their guileless gazes fixed on her.

"I love you, too," Alec hurried to add.

"And I love both of you, as well," she managed to choke
out.

Lucy sat there in the glow of the moment for as long as she could without breaking into tears. Clearing her throat, she fixed on a this-time-I-mean-it face and adjusted the covers just so. "Now that the stories and the prayers and the lovefest are over, it's time for you two to go to sleep."

She stood, then on impulse bent to kiss Alec one more time.

"You smell good," Alec announced.

She stopped to inhale, laughing when she caught a whiff of the vanilla icing she'd used to frost cupcakes earlier. She inhaled again and this time found the sugary aroma muted by baby shampoo and flannel pajamas. "You smell good, too."

She leaned over to kiss Paige again, starting when the child threw her chubby arms around Lucy's neck.

"Wish you was tuck me in eb'ry night." Paige returned the kiss on Lucy's cheek.

"Me, too." Alec wadded the covers up in both hands over his chest.

"Me, too." Lucy's eyes stung.

"Then it's unanimous."

She spun around. Her eyes locked on Ben's extraordinary gaze. Her heart stopped. Heat rose in her neck and her face, even making her scalp tingle. She garbled something about not realizing he was there.

He smiled.

Usually that would have been *it*. Flash that look, hand her that smile, and he could have carried her home in a pitcher. Not this time.

With sorrow over past mistakes and the yearning for a life with this man still all welled up in her chest, she would not melt this time. Her mind called up Ted and the fleeting property of life itself, and that stiffened her spine and gave her courage.

But before she rallied that courage into action, she had to ask. "How's Ted?"

"He's going to do all right, I think. We're still watching and monitoring. I've called in a specialist. You remember me talking about Mark Clemmons, the cardiologist who grew up in New Bethany and first put the idea of moving here into my head?"

"Sure."

"Well, he's with Ted now. I'll have to go back in a bit to go over the test results with Mark. If you don't mind keeping the kids tonight?"

"Of course not."

He mimicked her curt nod to show his gratitude. "Overall, though, it looks good for Ted. Very good."

Lucy pressed her hand over her drumming heart and shut her eyes for a brief but earnest prayer. "Thank you, Father."

"Amen."

Though outwardly very private about it, Lucy understood the depths of Ben's faith and that, too, gave her the mettle to go forward. She lifted her hand to fuss with her hair, but stopped herself. Neither did she straighten her collar or pull at her skirt...she simply folded her hands together and strode across the bedroom floor. At the doorway, she leveled her gaze on Ben.

"Lucy?" He tipped his head.

She could feel the warm dampness of his coffee-laced breath, see his pupils dilate in the dim light from one room to the next. She heard the rustle of cotton on cotton as his lab coat rasped over his baggy scrub pants. He still smelled of the hospital and of the soap that made his fingertips perpetually pink and his nails white from rigorous scouring.

Lucy loved this man. She wanted to step into his arms even

now, and in that place where just the two of them existed, forget her hurts of the past and her hopes for the future and just love him. And accept his love, such as it was, in return without question.

Her steely reserve of just seconds ago began to waver. She really should let him know how she felt. She should tell him she wasn't in the market for yet another man to ignore her needs and assume she'd always be there—preferably in the background—when he needed a meal, a hug, a sounding board, or, in Ben's case, a baby-sitter.

"Lucy are you okay?" He curled his fingers under her chin.

Look at him, her mind chided, *worn to a frazzle after a day of literally life-saving effort and facing going back for more of the same. Yet he still cares enough to ask if you're okay.*

Her lips twitched. She batted her lashes. "I'm fine."

"You sure?"

No, I'm not sure. That's what she should have said. Then she should have launched into a strictly unemotional, long overdue discussion about where this relationship was headed and what they each expected from one another.

Instead, she brushed back a wayward strand of brown hair that fell over his furrowed brow. "Why don't you go in and kiss the kids good night, Ben? I'll go fix you something to eat. Then if you have time, maybe I can give you a neck massage before you head back to the hospital."

"It is now official." Gayle propped her elbows up on the weathered table at Dot and Daughters', then put her head in her hands. "I am just one tacky, rotten, petty person."

"Don't be so hard on yourself, hon." Naomi slid into the booth beside her old pal and gave Gayle a spirit-bolstering squeeze. "You're not all *that* tacky."

"Oh, thank you very much." Gayle lifted her head enough to huff out a derisive laugh.

Naomi nudged her friend, just itching to cajole her from her dark mood. "C'mon, Gayle, lighten up. Ted is going to be fine. What on earth could you find to feel badly about in light of that?"

"See?" Gayle threw her hands up. "That just proves it. I'm a small, small, petty person."

Rose strode up to the table and plunked down her pocketbook. "Who's small?"

"Certainly not me!" Naomi rubbed her protruding belly. "It's Gayle. She says she's small and petty and tacky and...what was that other thing, Gayle?"

"Rotten." Gayle grimaced. "Rotten as an eight-week-old hard-boiled egg."

"Well, here, you old, rotten egg." Rose extended her monogrammed linen hankie. "You've got runny mascara all over your shell."

"Have I?" Gayle dabbed under each eye. "I imagine I look a terrible fright. I haven't been near a mirror since..."

She didn't have to say since when. Naomi took the hankie away and began to wipe away the most obvious of the black streaks on Gayle's flawless golden skin. "You're a mess, all right."

"A mess. Now there's the perfect word for me."

"It's an unwritten law, sugar." Rose reached over the table to take Gayle's hand. "On the day your husband has a heart attack you are allowed to be a mess."

"But at midnight of that day you've got to change back—" Naomi wriggled her fingers with a flourish "—*pftt*! Into the picture perfect model of control we all know and depend upon."

Gayle straightened and lifted her chin, donning a grim mask of serenity. "You're right, of course. You're *both* right."

"No, hon, I was teasing." Naomi gave her friend a shake as if that might bring her to her senses.

"Well, you made a valid point nevertheless. People are counting on me for strength and solace. I have to provide that for my children and for—oh, my goodness! Ted's Mother!" She pushed against Naomi's side, straining to get out of the booth. "I forgot to call Ted's mother to tell her he's all right."

"Just you stay put, Gayle." Rose held up her hand. "I already called and told Ted's sister. I also promised to call her back when we knew when he could have visitors. That's what I was doing while you two found us a table."

Gayle slumped back, her disheveled pink Easter outfit a pale contrast to the shiny red vinyl cushion with the silver-gray duct tape patch. "I should have thought to do it. It was my responsibility."

"Hey, it's not midnight yet." Naomi doled out the laminated menus. "You've still got a few hours to mess things up."

"Hours?" Gayle took the menu and began to fan herself with it, her gaze distant. "I've been messing up for a lot longer than that, for days—months, if you get right down to it. When was it I first told you I thought something was amiss with Ted?"

"Oh, I don't know." Naomi scanned the cafe specialties for something even remotely within her diet. "Right around the time of the Belle Gala, I suppose. But you couldn't have known this—"

"I knew *something* was wrong. And petty selfish person that I am, what did I do?" Gayle shut her eyes and tears beaded on her lashes. "I made it all about myself, about *my* fears and insecurities. Ted said it was about his health. You said it was about his health." She churned her open hand in Naomi's direction.

"But what conclusion did I jump to? That my dear, God-fearing, honorable, Christian husband was having an affair!"

"Now, Gayle." Rose set aside her menu and glanced around for the waitress. "You are hardly the first wife to jump to a hasty—"

"Did I say jump?" She gave a most unlady-like snort, snatched up Rose's hankie again, and swiped away the dampness under each eye. "Ya'll, it wasn't a *jump*. It was more like one of those daredevil leaps you see on TV, where some fool ties a rope around his ankle then hurls himself off of a suspension bridge over a river gorge. Dazzling and terrifying and… *stupid, stupid, stupid* all at once."

"Don't be so hard on yourself."

"On myself? Hard on *myself*?" The edge of desperation in her voice made other diners nearby perk up and pay attention. "What about how hard I was on Ted? He drove himself to the dropping point day after day, and I never even saw it. I only saw how the things it did to him affected *me*. I was so afraid of losing him to another woman, I almost lost him to all eternity."

They had nothing to say to that. What could they say? Naomi did not have it in her to disagree with Gayle's assessment. The dark look in Rose's eyes said she knew too well the crush of emotions of a woman who wondered what role she had played in her husband's hardships.

"All I could seem to pray today was that I would get a second chance." Gayle opened her mouth and drew in a breath that caused her thin body to shudder. "Even if it only lasts a short while—and I am praying it lasts much, much longer than that—I am so grateful to the Lord for what he has given me. So grateful."

"Well, amen to that, honey." Marguerite Johnson came up behind them.

She opened her arms to Gayle who obliged by scooting from the booth to accept the offered sympathy.

"Come here, baby girl." Marguerite wrapped Gayle up in the kind of hug that could take a person back to childhood and being folded in a grandmother's arms.

Not that Marguerite was old enough to be Gayle's grandmother, or even her mother, for that matter. Though no one knew for sure, and Marguerite would rather go to her grave than tell, Naomi figured the elder of the Johnson sisters to be a year or two younger than Rose.

"Sister and I have kept your Ted at the forefront of our prayers today." Marguerite rocked slightly, her embrace still all encompassing. "I hope you know that."

"And I hope you know how much I appreciate that, Sister Marguerite." Gayle clung to the woman as if, at last, she had found haven in her turmoil. "I felt it, too." Gayle pulled away then and looked at them all, her eyes shimmering, the tip of her nose red. "All day I felt buoyed up. My mind and my body told me I couldn't possibly survive, I couldn't face whatever I had to face or last another minute without some resolution. But my spirit had its resolution. I knew somehow that because so many good people like y'all and—" She sniffled and gave a welcoming nod as Marguerite's younger sister approached "—and like Sister Princess, here, and others were praying, that I could face it."

"The peace that passeth understanding." Marguerite pronounced each syllable crisply. "It comes from more than knowing others are praying for you."

"Yes." Gayle sniffled again.

"I don't mean to bust up your big chance at a brush arbor meeting and testifying extravaganza, here, now, Sister—" Princess stepped up, with a kindly smile on her lips and an impish gleam in her eye "—but if we hope to get our supper home before it gets cold…"

"You're right." Marguerite sighed, then took both of Gayle's hands in one of hers. "We have to get a move on, but that doesn't mean we won't still be praying. And if there is anything we can do for you, don't even stop to think—just ask. We can run meals over to the house or since I'm not working anymore, I'm free to help with the children or even sit with your precious husband in the hospital if you should need a break."

"Thank you." Gayle smiled, but the sadness in her eyes made Naomi's heart ache. "But Daddy's church will have us up to our armpits in ham, pies, and frozen casseroles. And I think we'll have enough folks around to watch the younger kids. As for sitting with Ted, well, I can't even do that. For the time being, he's going to stay put in the ICU unit."

"Not for long." Marguerite said it as if she had the inside track on Ted's recovery. Given the woman's closeness to the Lord, Naomi thought she just might.

"We'll see." Gayle's response was guarded. "Dr. Martin has called in a cardiologist to look Ted over, a friend that Ben says is actually from New Bethany originally."

"Oh?" Obviously that piqued Marguerite's attention. Well, why not? The woman knew absolutely everybody in town and they her.

"Yes, now what was his name?" Gayle's brow crimped down. "Um, Clinton? No…"

"Sister, the pasta will go all gummy."

"Just a minute, Princess." Marguerite waved away her sister's impatience, her focus remaining on Gayle's struggle to recall the right name.

"Was it…Campbell? No." Gayle snapped her fingers repeatedly, sort of creating the sound effect for her mental checking off a list of possible names. "I know it started with a *C*, though, and the first name was…"

"Sister, I'm hungry," Princess whispered. "And my feet hurt. No disrespect to the gravity of your situation, Sister Barrett."

"None taken." This time Gayle's smile reflected throughout her expression. "The specialist's name isn't important, and I only think it starts with a *C*. For all I know I could be way off the mark…Oh, that's it!"

"What?" Naomi asked.

"The doctor's name." A look of smug relief crossed her face. "It was Mark."

"I'm going on out to the car." Princess patted her sister's shoulder. "Don't hurry…unless, of course, you *mind* your dashboard being used as a buffet table."

Naomi and Rose chuckled.

Marguerite pursed her lips, obviously rising above her sister's jab.

"I'll keep you and yours in my prayers." Princess gave Gayle, a comforting pat.

"Thanks."

Princess walked on past.

"I can't believe I forgot that doctor's name." Gayle stepped toward Marguerite. "Mark. That's it."

Naomi waved good-bye to Princess as she reached for the door a few feet away from them.

Gayle hit her open palm with her fist. "Mark Clemmons. Dr. Mark Clemmons, that's the specialist's name."

Thuwmp.

"Oh, my goodness, Princess!" Rose leapt up.

Gayle gasped.

Naomi blinked, then looked to Marguerite for some explanation as to why her sister had just yanked the cafe door smack into her own nose and yet stood staring at Gayle as if she had no idea she'd done it.

"Mark Clemmons?" The sack in Princess's hand crinkled in her tightening grip. "Mark Clemmons, who used to live in New Bethany? Oh, Sister, could it be?"

"What?" Gayle asked in a whisper to Marguerite standing next to her.

Marguerite's jaw set firm, her gaze narrowed and went cold. "Mark Clemmons, formerly of New Bethany, Tennessee, just happens to be the name of the one and only man who ever broke my little sister's heart."

Fourteen

So Mr. Johnson put his foot down and forbade Princess from ever seeing the young man again." Rose's soft-soled shoes hardly made sound on the flat-napped carpeting of the hospital corridor.

"All because Clemmons proposed to Princess and gave her a ring without asking her father's blessing first?" Will tapped his chin with his crooked knuckle.

"That, and the fact that Princess was only sixteen at the time. Her father feared that with Mark away at college they'd not be able to wait until she finished high school to marry. Then Princess might never have gotten a diploma or gone on to further her own education."

"I can see his concern. We southern daddies are pretty protective of our daughters." He leaned toward Rose so that their foreheads touched for just a moment. "We're pretty protective of all our girls, you know."

Rose closed her eyes to share a fleeting, good-natured laugh over that, then straightened away. "Curry was like that, too."

"Yes, he was." Will scowled, his gaze downcast. "Sometimes to a fault."

It struck Rose as odd, the way he added that. She wasn't sure if Will was making a judgement on how Curry treated her as his wife or if, perhaps, he was making an inference that her girls were too coddled, a sort of sideways jab at the situation with Stacey still living at home.

Will's response went from odd to downright peculiar. "But

Curry was a good man, despite his sometimes autocratic tendencies. A good friend to me, for sure. I still cherish and honor that friendship, in more ways than you realize, Rose."

Not knowing what to make of what Will had said, she hoped to spur him on to deeper revelation with a hint of gentle teasing. "Well, aren't you the cryptic one tonight?"

"Me? Cryptic? Not one bit." He chuckled. The subtle self-effacing shake of his head, the way the lines on his face deepened around his sparkling eyes and framed his languid grin worked their way through the defensiveness of Rose's skepticism. He shrugged. "I'm just a silly old fool trying to do his best with what God gave him."

"Doing a fine job, I might add." She reached out to take his hand. She lost herself in his nearness just as her cold fingers became enveloped in his powerful, warm grip. They stood there in the dimly lit hall just beyond the ICU unit for several seconds before she broke their intimacy with a long sigh. "Thanks again for coming down to keep me company tonight. Despite the fact that what I really want most in the world is to be safely tucked in my bed at home, I have to stay available to Gayle through the consultation and until after she finally gets to see Ted. I have a feeling when that's over, *that*'s when all this will really hit her."

"Of course. It's right you should be here for her. And we couldn't let Naomi stay down here 'til all hours. She needs her rest—got to take care of my grandchild." Will curled Rose's hand to his chest. "Besides, I'm kind of fond of the company. And it's my first chance in forever to have you all to myself."

"Ah, there's the reference to Stacey still living with me. I knew it was coming, I just didn't know when or how you'd manage to work it in." She dropped his hand. "But I could foresee its coming sure as a pig seeks out a bog in summer."

"Tempting as it is to make a joke about a certain young lady being as content as a hog in a mud hole, I'll refrain. Both of us are too tired and the circumstances far too stressful to wade into *that* territory right now." He snatched her hand back up again. "Let's pass the time talking on safer subjects. Like this suddenly surfaced tale of Princess and her long lost love."

"All right. Fair enough." She walked with him over to a bank of chrome and vinyl chairs against a gray-papered wall with tiny pink and green abstract flowers dotted over it.

Rose sank into her seat, not realizing until her knees bent and her back fit to the sighing cushion just how much the day had exhausted her. She tipped her head back and shut her eyes, physically drained but pushed beyond the ability to doze or even relax enough to sit quietly and wait.

"You know it's a funny thing about the Johnson sisters." She was content to babble on about something that took no emotional or intellectual investment.

"What's that, dear?"

"All the years I've known them, mostly through church services and community functions, I have to say I know almost nothing about their private lives."

"My, in *this* town, the gossip factor being what it is, that's something akin to a minor miracle."

"Absolutely." Rose smiled.

"However, I do know that Miss Marguerite ran the Westside Nursing Home for years. The whole time she was administrator at that place, she had an account with Boatwright Nursery to keep the grounds." Will laid his arm over the back of Rose's seat. "Then she had some kind of accident that was apparently the responsibility of the home because they paid out a rather large settlement and she receives some kind of disability payments."

"Was that about the time Princess went from fulltime to parttime as secretary at their church?"

"Well, she stayed home to care for Marguerite at first, but since that settlement paid for the house outright and provided a nice nest egg, she never had to go back to full-time work. Though in truth, you know, she works far more than half-time hours, but she considers it a donation to the church."

Rose sat back and blinked. "My word, William Boatwright, the things you know about folks."

A slow grin broke over his face. "Hairdressers might pick up all the hearsay, but the gardeners unearth all the dirt."

Rose laughed. She hadn't realized how much she needed to do that until it came freely from her lips, bubbling up from deep within her. "I'll remember that."

He pressed his fingers into the taut muscles at the base of her neck, and Rose surrendered to the sweet pangs of pressure on just the right spot. She shut her eyes—shutting out, as she did so, all thoughts of Stacey, the difficulties with Will, Princess's poignant love story, Gayle's guilt…even Ted's crisis melted away. Rose's breathing slowed, and she became aware of the blunted sounds around her. Nearby, elevators whirred and occasionally dinged as the doors clattered open. People passed, their voices never raised above a whisper, their footsteps hushed and hurried.

Rose put them all out of mind until a new sound intruded. She sat up in time to see Ben Martin pushing through the swinging doors that led from the ICU unit, his brown hair mused, his jaw stubbled, but his stride upbeat.

"Mark and I just finished talking with Gayle. She's on her way in to see Ted now."

"Been a long day." Will stood.

"Yes." Ben rubbed the back of his neck. "Yes, it has. I'll be glad to get home tonight."

"Guess it's going to be just a little longer." Rose wagged her finger at Will to prevent his thinking this meant *their* work was done. "Because I intend to wait until Gayle is done seeing Ted before I leave."

"That won't be too long." Ben raised his hand to bid them good-bye. "They'll only let her stay with Ted for ten minutes."

Rose returned the wave. "Well, if I know Gayle she'll make the most of every second."

"Ted." Gayle moved her lips. She felt his name resonate through her, but heard nothing.

Her eyes fixed on the man lying in the midst of the monitors and machines. The single fluorescent light above his headboard created an eerie, flickering halo effect in the otherwise darkened room. An almost inaudible blip, then quiet, then blip measured out the beating of her husband's heart.

Ted. She loved him even more than she had known until this very moment. Now realizing how close she had come to losing him made her shudder. Lose Ted? She tried to swallow down the fear closing up her throat. What would she do? How would she go on?

Everyone always thought of her as the strong one, the foundation of their family. They thought Ted, with his easy wit and charm, always deferred to her in order to keep harmony in the home. That simply was not the case.

Ted was her lodestone, her anchor, her haven in a world when such things no longer meant anything to many people. He made her feel safe and loved and important, even when she did not deserve those feelings. He gave her laughter and a sense of perspective when she got her nose out of joint about things over which she had no control. He gave her a home—

not just the bricks and mortar and an address in one of the town's finest neighborhoods, but the essence of what that means: a place to belong no matter what. He shared her faith and had given her love, respect, and three wonderful children.

Lose Ted? That would be tantamount to losing her very life. The life she had made for her family and worked hard to preserve. A clutching in her chest forced out a tiny gasp. Ted stirred, then turned only his head to face her.

The features of his face remained in shadow, yet she did not need to see them to know their sweetness. He extended his hand. Her fears fell away.

She had not lost him, and she would not. Her fervent prayers had been answered, praise the Lord. The life she loved would stay intact, her home and family whole.

"Ted." The clacking of her heels on the cold tile floor echoed in the quiet stillness of the room. She reached his side, her hands seeking his as though in taking them she would be rescued from the day's uncertainty.

But Ted's fingers skimmed over hers until he grasped at her forearm, gripping as best he could, then clinging. His damp palm slid downward, then twisted around her slim wrist, burning her skin with a strength that belied the reality of his physical weakness. He said nothing, but the dark hollows around his eyes gave a haunted, desperate quality to his otherwise calm expression.

"Ted?" She reached over him with her free hand and swept back the sweat-thickened hair plastered over his forehead. "Ted, honey, it's all right now. The doctors say it's going to be all right."

He neither met her gaze nor let go of her arm. The crisp cotton of the pillow rustled as his head bobbed in a faint nod.

Her pulse lurched as if mimicking the awkward stops and

starts of countless unnamed emotions within her. The fear she had expected to fully abate once she laid eyes on her husband had only subsided a little. Now doubt and confusion rushed in to mingle with the more predictable feelings of relief and tempered happiness.

She wanted him to look at her, to speak to her…to reassure her. When that did not happen, a tiny shiver of near panic flared in the pit of her stomach. *Say something!* she wanted to demand of him. *Tell me you feel tired but hopeful, that you know it will all be fine and life will be back to normal soon. Make everything normal again for me, Ted.*

Blip. The monitor counted out her husband's heartbeat, blunt and unwavering in its constant rhythm.

Gayle blinked, shame in her neediness scalding her cheeks. Biting her lip, she pulled her shoulders upright, drawing her face back into the dimness beyond the unnatural glare of the headboard light. With a serenity she did not feel, she forced herself to say, "Dr. Ben told me everything they put you through. It's no wonder you're worn out from it all."

Blip.

"You do look plum tuckered out, as Miss Grace would say." She curled her hand against his cheek.

Ted shut his eyes and turned his face into the half-closed palm of her hand. The gesture touched Gayle, a loving salve on her jangled nerves. Still, she wished he'd speak to her, she wanted to hear his voice, to hear from him that this wasn't going to defeat him or alter their lives in any significant way.

Blip.

"I think half the town was praying for you today." She didn't dare say more.

He peered at her with one eyebrow cocked, as if to ask, *"Only half?"*

Gayle smiled. "The other half were all folks you'd bested either on the courts or in them, of course. But who wants the prayers of bad seeds or bad tennis players anyway?"

It was a lame attempt at humor, but he chuckled anyway, a dry, coughing chuckle that ended in something between a whimper and a wheeze.

Blip.

"Mathina's come home from college." She rushed on to fill the dismaying silence. "She's with Nathan and Lillith, and your sister's come to care for your mother. They'll likely all be up tomorrow to visit as they can, but you know in ICU they only allow one visitor at a time, ten minutes every hour."

Blip.

"Ten minutes, Ted. That's all."

He looked up.

She stepped back into the circle of light to make sure he could see the tenderness and raw emotion in her eyes. "In fact, they're going to chase me out of here in a couple minutes. But I can stay. I can come back in an hour to see you again if you want me—"

He shook his head. The sheets hissed over his skin as he stretched his legs out straight.

"Oh."

Blip.

"I guess you really prefer your rest."

He groaned out a hum of agreement.

"Okay, then."

His grip loosened on her wrist but he did not release her.

Gayle found strange comfort in that. She turned her hand to weave her fingers into his, a perfect fit.

He looked at the spot where their hands meshed as though he might find some answers there.

She laid her free hand on top of their heartfelt grasp.

He hung on to her.

Blip.

And she to him.

His gaze found hers.

Tears trembled on her lashes. How she found the voice to speak, she did not know, but somehow she did it. "I love you so much. So very much."

He squeezed her hand with more power than she ever suspected he could muster to tell her he felt the same way. That was all the reassurance she needed. Her spirit light, she cleared her throat and bowed her head. "Thank you, Father, for the miracle of this moment, for the care of skilled doctors, the concern of kind friends, the love of our families, and the goodness of your grace. In Jesus' name, amen."

Ted murmured something—or perhaps it was nothing at all. When Gayle opened her eyes, his were still closed, and she thought she heard the faint buzz as he drifted into a much-needed sleep.

Sniffling, she pulled the sheet up high on his chest, mindful of the tubes and wires, then bent over him to kiss him good night. His lips felt like coarse-grade sandpaper, his hair smelled of sweat and his hospital gown of some antiseptic that made her nose tingle. When she lifted her mouth from his he let out a rude snort of a snore. Gayle could not remember having cherished a kiss more from this man in her whole life.

He loved her, and he was going to live. She wanted to laugh out loud! Instead she touched his cheek, his forehead, then kissed each of his fingers where they were still locked in hers.

"That's right, sugar, you rest tonight."

Blip.

"I'll be here first thing in the morning. It's going to be all right, you know. You'll rest up—first here—then at home for a while—pretty soon things will get back to normal, you'll see."

"Mrs. Barrett?" A heavyset nurse with her hair in a long braid, peered in. A shaft of light from the hallway cut a pie-shaped swath in the darkness. "Time's up."

Gayle nodded to her. "I've got to go now, honey."

Blip.

She slid her fingers slowly from his, memorizing every sensation, from the smell of the room to the sound of his snoring to the feel of his clammy skin sliding from her touch.

"Mrs. Barrett? I understand your wanting to remain here, but the rules are—"

"I'm well aware of the rules." Her eyes were on Ted's face. "Just let me say good night. It won't take a moment."

"Of course, but you'll have to wrap it up." The door swished shut. The room beyond the bed went dark again.

"Get your rest, sugar." She stepped backward once, paused, and then stepped back again. "It'll all be all right, you'll see. You get your rest and before we know it, you'll be back on your feet like none of this ever happened."

Ted stirred. The blips on the monitors picked up speed ever so slightly.

Gayle hesitated, unsure if she should go to him or call the nurse. Her own heart raced.

Ted struggled to lift his head. "Gayle?"

"I'm here." She hurried to his side. "Hush, now, don't strain yourself."

"I can't—"

"Can't what?" She gulped down the swell of fear threatening all reasonable thought. "Can't breathe? Can't…can't what?"

"I can't let you go—"

A wave of joyful relief washed over her. She laughed, but

before she could tease him or tell him once again that she'd stay if he wanted her to, he coughed into his fisted hand and exhaled loudly.

"I can't let you get out of here thinking that."

"Thinking what?"

The door creaked open again. "Mrs. Barrett? I have to insist—"

Gayle waved her away, willing to risk being escorted out by security to hear the rest of what Ted had to say. "Thinking what, Ted?"

"That after this, anything can be like it was before. I thought I was going to die today, and I didn't. I got a second chance at everything, and I won't waste it. That could very well mean, honey, that *nothing* in our lives will ever be the same again."

"It's the medication talking, that's all. And the scare. The medication and the scare." Rose set a silver tea tray down by Gayle's bed.

Will had driven them to Gayle's home, then gone on home. Gayle had not argued when Rose insisted she was spending the night. Not leaving loved ones alone in times of distress was an old and honored Southern tradition. From her present vantage point, Gayle understood and appreciated that custom more than she'd ever dreamed possible.

She scrunched up the plump, quilted comforter in both her hands and drew it to just beneath her chin. In the middle of the large four-poster bed she usually shared with her husband she suddenly felt small, almost childlike. Rose's fussing over her and bringing up a tray of hot cocoa in the good china cups with a delicate plate on the side piled with Easter candy only abetted that perception.

"I couldn't find any of those little miniature marshmallows around the house, so I pilfered some of these bunnies from Lillith's Easter basket." The cups and spoons clattered softly as Rose retrieved a white linen napkin and shook it open with a resounding pop. "I don't think she'll mind, she had so much…Gayle? You listening?"

"Nathan was too old to have a basket this year, you know." Gayle rotated a grainy yellow, marshmallow chick held between her thumb and forefinger, scrutinizing it from every angle but not really seeing it at all. "We still gave him something—his favorite jellybeans, a chocolate rabbit, and a video he'd hounded us for, just enough to let him know we'd thought of him. *I* wanted to still use the basket we've had for him for umpteen years but Ted said no, it would embarrass the boy. Called it so much sentimental rubbish."

The faint sound of Rose's chuckling penetrated the fog of Gayle's thoughts. Obviously Rose knew before she had to say it how this story would turn. That Ted was a kind and gentle man who would do anything to make his children happy.

Gayle sighed. "So, last night when he saw Nathan's treats just lying on the table next to Lillith's fancy fare, well, he nearly had a fit. What had he been thinking, he asked me—but he still refused to let me use that old basket for a boy Nathan's age. He decided we had to find a compromise."

Compromise. The word mocked Gayle as she considered the last thing Ted had said to her before she was forced to leave the ICU. "*Nothing in our lives will ever be the same again.*"

Her heart ached. Her stomach knotted. Compromise seemed the furthest thing from Ted's thoughts now. What that meant for her and the family she could only guess—and she dared not attempt that or she'd drive herself mad with worry.

"So the basket was out of the question…" Rose prompted.

Gayle pulled her knees up closer to her chest and plunged on with her story. "Do you know what that man did instead? Last night he hopped in the car and drove over an hour round trip to go to a certain all-night discount store so he could buy a Vols baseball cap for us to use in lieu of a basket."

"Ted would do anything for his family, there's no disputing that." The edge of the bed dipped down where Rose sat at Gayle's side.

"He even insisted we send Mathina a kind of Easter care package since her college didn't allow time off for the holiday." Gayle pinched at the yellow confection in her hand, tearing away a piece to expose the gooey white center. "I gave her a new spring outfit and some homemade goodies, but before he'd let me seal up the box, Ted just had to put in his own touch. A sugar egg—you know, the kind with the tiny Easter scene inside? He's given her one every year of her life since she was a toddler. He said it just wouldn't be Easter if he didn't give her one."

"What a sweetheart your husband is, to think like that."

"Last week he thought like that. He cherished our family traditions, wanted to do whatever it took to provide those precious extra touches for his children's happiness…" Gayle tossed the candy chick onto the tray, then swiped the sugar off her fingertips with brisk, slashing passes of the napkin. "Today he says nothing in our lives will ever be the same."

Rose handed her one of the brimming cups. "He probably won't even remember he said it in the morning."

Gayle could only nod stiffly and accept the cocoa with a grim smile. She didn't believe Rose. Didn't believe her for one minute. Not that she thought her friend was lying, but Rose had not seen the look in Ted's eyes when he'd made his proclamation. He meant it. She'd stake her life on that. He meant every word.

Rose opened her mouth to say something, made an abrupt little sound, then shook her head. She reached for her own cocoa cup, raised it to her lips, and took a sip.

They sat there together, sipping cocoa in thoughtful silence for several soothing seconds until a sharp rapping on the bedroom door intruded. "Mom? It's me, Max. May I come in?"

"Of course, baby, come on in." Gayle called out. She set her cup back onto its saucer with a distinct *clink*, and Rose did the same.

"I've fixed your mama some hot chocolate, honey." Rose went gliding across the floor to welcome Mathina in, the picture of Southern grace and solace. "Would you like me to bring some up for you?"

"Yes, thank you. That would be just lovely, Miss Rose."

Gayle smiled. She'd had her reservations about sending her oldest child off to a fancy eastern college. She'd worried that the move might spawn radical ideas about politics, personal appearance, and, heaven forbid, encourage ill-manners. She was happy to see that after a semester and a half away her child had not forgotten her upbringing and tried to address Rose on a first name basis without the deferential *Miss* in front of it.

"I'll be back shortly, then." Rose gathered the robe borrowed from Gayle's closet about her and hurried to the door. She stopped only long enough to give Mathina a quick hug. "I'm sorry that seeing you again has to be under these circumstances, darling. But now that the worst has past, maybe you and your mama can have a good visit. I think you could both use a little reassuring about now."

"That's true." Mathina returned the hug, then pulled away and allowed Rose to slip on out the open door.

"Come on in and sit down." Gayle patted the bed beside herself. "I haven't hardly got to share two words with you since you got in this afternoon."

Mathina hurried to her mother's arms—just as she had when she was little and came scurrying into this very room seeking shelter from a bad dream.

Gayle closed her arms around her child, pulling her close. For one brief moment time vanished and she was cuddling her baby, her firstborn, the little girl she would always cherish within her heart even when that little girl had children of her own. A wave of warmth enveloped her and she shut her eyes against the realities the day had thrust upon her and just savored the bond between mother and daughter.

Mathina clung to her, ducking her head so that her cheek rested on Gayle's shoulder. "All the time driving home I just kept thinking two things, Mommy. First, I prayed and prayed and prayed that Daddy would be all right."

"You weren't alone in that, sweetie," Gayle murmured against her temple.

"Then, secondly, all I could think was, if I could just get home to Mommy. I felt like if I could just get to you again and let you hold me, that everything would be all right. You wouldn't let any bad things happen to me or to our family, I just knew that. I wanted you to hug me and make all my dreadful fears go away." Mathina let out a shuddering breath. "Do you...do you think that was terribly immature of me?"

"If it is, then you're in good company." Gayle took a deep breath and the familiar scent of her child's hair brought tears to her eyes. "More than one time today I wanted my mama to just hold me and make all the pain go away. I called her to come up to the hospital three times today just to cry in her arms."

"You did?" Mathina craned her neck to peer into Gayle's eyes.

"Yes." Gayle sniffled. "I did."

"You don't know how glad I am to hear you say that!"

"Why?" Gayle managed laugh. "You cotton to the idea of your mama being a great big crybaby?"

"I don't think you acted like a baby at all. I'm just glad to know it doesn't mean *I'm* one."

"Everybody needs someone, a mother, friend, family, and, of course, faith in the Lord and his presence, especially in time of crisis. I think people who don't seek that out are the immature ones. Those are our roots, our grounding. If we don't have any roots we're just like tumbleweeds, with nothing to hold onto when a mighty wind stirs up."

"Holding onto your roots is one thing, I think, but letting them hold you back, now, that's not good either."

"Hey, when did you get so wise?" Gayle smiled through the quick peck she gave her daughter on the head. "What's that old saying? The greatest gift we can give our children is roots *and* wings?"

"Oh, Mom, I'm so glad you said that." She snuggled up closer. "I wasn't going to say anything with Daddy so sick and all. But now that we know that he's going to be all right and all and since I know you understand, well, I think there's something I want to confess to you."

Startled, Gayle braced herself. A mental checklist of possibilities whizzed through her brain and each was instantly dismissed. She was not utterly naive, but she did know her child and felt certain it wasn't one of the foremost problems parents dread: pregnancy, drugs, or legal difficulties.

"It's about college." Mathina twisted a strand of her hair around her finger.

"College." They'd sent her child off to college with reservations about the distance from home, but when they saw the confident young lady her child had become, they no longer had had any regrets. Mathina's schooling had cost them dearly but they'd done the right thing in sending her. She was a strong, intelligent, moral young woman, and whatever mistake she had made at college, Gayle told herself, they could fix it. Tutors could be hired to raise low grades, alternative housing arrangements made if her roommates were the problem.

"Maybe this isn't the best time to tell you, but...

This would not get her down, this, among all the things in their lives that Ted said would never be the same, could remain unaffected. Mathina would stay at the beautiful, ivy-covered eastern college and get a highly regarded degree. Then the world would be hers.

Gayle tightened her grip around her daughter's shoulders and lay her cheek on the girl's soft hair. "That's okay, honey, we can deal with this. Just tell me what it is so we can get your education back on the right track."

"Um..." Her legs jiggled beneath her long nightgown. She cleared her throat. "My education is on the right track, Mom. I'm just not sure you're going to agree with the direction it's headed."

From the corner of her eye, Gayle noticed that Rose had appeared at the bedroom door, a steaming cup of cocoa in her hands. She'd come just in time to hear Gayle's oldest daughter sit up on the bed and announce, "I'm dropping out of college to go to missionary school. Mom, I'm going to become a missionary."

Fifteen

"Ben! What are you doing here? It's...why, it's five o'clock in the morning." Lucy didn't know where to begin to try to tidy herself. She started to finger comb her hair, then decided she'd best rub any traces of sleep from her eyes, then changed course again and clasped at the edges of her robe to make sure it sufficiently covered her thick cotton nightgown. "What are you doing here at this hour?"

"Lucy, I know we agreed to let the kids just stay here and have you take them into the day care this morning, but there hasn't been a day in their lives since I adopted them that I haven't been the one to wake them up." He cocked his head and made great big puppy-dog eyes at her. "I want to see my children this morning, too."

"But it's 5 A.M., Ben." The whine in her voice gave way to a jaw-stretching yawn. If her fresh-from-REM-sleep appearance didn't scare the man away forever, then her uncouth behavior surely would!

"Yeah, I know what time it is and I'm sorry about that, but I couldn't sleep. The house just seemed so quiet without Paige and Alec. I kept thinking about Ted and how he and his family must feel to face this morning, after what almost happened..." He rubbed the scruff of his neck, then let his hand sort of plop downward as if it suddenly weighed too much to hold up. "Anyway, can I come in?"

"Ben are you crazy? It's five—"

"A.M., I know, I know. Actually..." He paused to steal a peek

275

at his wristwatch. "It's almost a quarter after. Guess there goes your shot at that job announcing the time on the telephone."

"Very funny." She clamped her hand down over the glowing face of his watch and pushed his arm away. "But then I'd expect that kind of flippant answer from a man who hasn't thought his actions through any better than you have tonight."

"It's morning."

"Well, exactly." She folded her arms with sharp, deliberate movements.

"Exactly?" He gaped at her for a beat then broke into that effortless laugh of his. "Exactly what?"

"Exactly *what* will the neighbors think? That's what."

"Neighbors? What do they mind what goes on at your house?"

"Oh, my, you still have a lot to learn about living in a small town. Neighbors not only mind, they meddle. Worse yet, they talk."

"You make them sound like a bunch of nosey old snoops." He laughed again.

"Your point?" She deadpanned. "Besides, they don't think of it as snooping. They consider it just looking out for one another. When they start coming out to get their newspapers and see your car parked out there, as if..."

"As if?" He raised an eyebrow.

Heat rose from Lucy's cheeks to her scalp. Her gaze went to his car parked in her drive, all dark and looking dangerous with its chrome gleaming in the porch light. She moaned inwardly. Her neighbors would have a field day with this, spreading their speculations without really saying anything defaming, allowing folks to draw their own dubious conclusions. Lucy could just hear the phone ringing off the hook now—and the very first call of all would be to her mother.

Lucy swallowed down the seething anxiety rising in her chest. Her mother would not readily believe the worst of her only child, but she would certainly chastise Lucy about putting herself—and her mother and her father's good name—in this position. Only Lucy hadn't done anything, Ben had come over uninvited and just assumed it was all right to do so. She clenched her jaw and her fist at the same time. It was the kind of thing Raymond Griggs would do. Lucy's skin crawled.

"They'll come out to get their papers and see my car parked in your drive as if what, Lucy?" He obviously relished toying with her in a most charming, innocuous way.

She clutched her robe in a vice grip at the base of her throat and whispered, "You *know* what."

He shook his head. "But nothing happened. We know that, God knows that, isn't that all that should matter?"

"You'll *think* that's all that matters when my mother descends on you to lecture you about propriety, common decency, and the way a man behaves toward the women with which he is involved."

"Loves." The correction came with a quiet conviction that struck a chord in Lucy's already strained emotions as real as someone plucking at a taut harp string. "You meant to say how a man behaves toward the woman he loves."

Did she? She blinked. *Love?*

She simply had not wholly embraced the idea that this man loved her. He said that he did. And she supposed that, for a girl like her, that ought to be more than enough. Ben was a doctor, after all, a man of faith, kind and gentle, a wonderful father of two children whom she adored. He'd even spoken of marriage without any demanding or wheedling from her. Seeing as she'd never been good enough to sustain the affection of any man from her father through Dwayne Cobb, the words alone should be enough, more than enough. She knew that. And yet…

A man did act a certain way toward the woman he truly loved. Whether or not he agreed with the small-town sentiments about situations that might be looked at askew, out of regard and…love for her, Ben ought to respect them. He ought to respect her, not just love her. His actions in the past and even at this moment made her wonder if he did.

She'd been hit by this bus before and finally after all this time, maybe she had learned to look out for herself before she stepped off the curb.

"Whatever you call it, Ben, the appropriate conduct remains the same. You really should not have come here like this. It just looks—"

"You're right." He held up one hand and ducked his head like a boy caught stealing a pie from the windowsill. But Lucy didn't let her heart give way. It was easy to feel repentant once the damage had been done. "You are absolutely right. You warned me about keeping everything above reproach on our very first official date on Valentine's Day, and I should have taken that more to heart. I'm wrong and I'm sorry."

All thought, including any form of response just went whooshing out of Lucy's mind. She wasn't sure why until her consciousness came creeping back. She didn't think she'd ever heard a man apologize and admit to her that he was wrong before. She stared blankly ahead and made a sort of scoffing gurgle in the back of her throat that she felt sure, the instant she heard it herself, Ben would take as a careless belch.

Regaining her composure, she covered over her momentary lack of poise with a stern shake of her head, a lift of her chin, and a raising of her hands to the heavens. "All right, Lord, I'm ready. You can take me now."

Laughing, Ben asked, "What's that about?"

"Well, I've now heard a man admit that he's wrong and even say he's sorry. The way I see it, I haven't got much else to live for." She broke into a big grin.

He narrowed one eye, lowering his head and his voice. "Oh, Lucy, my love, you have no idea what you have left to live for! Fact is, if we weren't standing here on your front porch in full view of *CNN*—"

"Of what?"

"Concerned Nosey Neighbors." He winked.

She giggled.

"If we weren't where prying eyes could see, I for sure would give you a small sampling of what it is you have to look forward to in your life with me."

"Oh, yes, that would certainly stir the stew pot, now wouldn't it? For someone to spot us kissing on my doorstep at this hour, me in my nightgown. Then you driving off?" Lucy leaned out to make a quick perusal of her street. No lights shone from any windows yet. She straightened up again. "As my friend Gayle would say, nuh-uh. No sir."

"Funny you should mention Gayle." His whole demeanor shifted, went pensive. His emotions seemed suddenly to rise to the surface and shine in those incredible eyes. "It was seeing how everyone rallied around her, and Ted, of course…seeing how much you all are there for one another, how genuine your affection is for one another, and how strong your faith is when put to the test…well, it made me feel so good, so proud to be here and a part of this community and…so very glad I have you, Lucy."

"Oh, Ben." She stepped forward to throw her arms around his neck, but he retreated, his hand up to stop her.

"No, Lucy. It really *wouldn't* look right. I understand that now. Let's not jeopardize either of our reputations that way." He stepped backward again and thrust both his hands in his pants pockets. "Clearly I shouldn't have come over this morning but I—"

"It's all right." She felt light as an angel. Sudden surges of hope that your relationship was going to work out after all could do that to a person, she reasoned. "Really, it is."

"No, it's not. I should have known better than to think I'd get invited into your home under these circumstances." He hung his head, then raised it just enough to show the glimmer in his eyes as he said, "However—"

"Oh, I do not like the sound of that." This time she backed up a step, even though her tone remained playful.

"Well, just because I can't come in doesn't mean you can't come out."

"Out? Out where? In my nightclothes?"

"Out to breakfast, silly. You'll probably want to wear considerably more than a nightgown—it's still chilly out, you know. 'Course if you want to kick up a real cloud of controversy over at Dot and Daughters', you can just wear your—"

"No sir! We will not be parading ourselves into Dot and Daughters' for breakfast with the first-light-of-day coffee crowd. Why don't you just ask if you can hang my house key from your belt as a trophy. That's what it will look like! And don't you kid yourself, either, my mother would be down there before you could wash back the last bite of your grits, looking for a trophy of her own. I think your head would look mighty nice grinning down from over her den's mantel between the deer antlers and Texas longhorns daddy put up there years ago."

He roared out a wicked laugh. "All right, all right. So Dot and Daughters' is out of the question. That doesn't mean we can't still have a nice breakfast with the children, does it?"

Did it? She chewed at her lower lip.

"How about this." He ran his hand back through his hair. "You go get dressed and get the kids up—I'll run over to the Dixie Dazzler Party-Mart and Bait Shop, pick up a box of those little white powdered donuts, some coffee, and a bottle of juice for the kids, and be back for you all in twenty minutes. That'll still leave plenty of time for you to eat and get to the day care on time, won't it?"

"I don't have to open up until seven, as long as I get there a few minutes before that—"

"Good." He clapped his hands together. "Then we'll have time to drive around until we find a spot where we can sit and watch the sunrise over the prayer tree grove."

"You mean the water tower?"

"Really?"

"Well, yes. What you just described—a place to watch the sun come up over the prayer grove—is the water tower."

"Hey, cool, except one thing."

"What?"

"We can't exactly take the kids up on top of a big, tall water tower, now can we?"

"Up? On top of?" She covered her mouth with her hand but that could not contain her laughter. "You must have seen the water tower hundreds of times, it stands on one of the knobs at the edge of town. You don't have to climb anything for the view. You only climb up the tower if you want to profess your undying love in three-foot-high, neon-orange letters."

"Oh."

"You weren't planning on picking up any spray paint at the Dixie Dazzler, now were you?"

"Um, no."

"Then we'll all be fine, safe on the ground.

"We will? So that means you're going?"

"Ben Martin, there *are* some issues about which I will never compromise. However, eating a lovely breakfast with you and the children on a glorious spring morning is not one of those."

"That a yes or a no?"

"It's a yes. Now git. I've got three people to get ready, and you have grocery shopping to do."

He started down the porch steps, then paused and looked back at her. "I can't think of anyone I'd rather share a sunrise with, Lucy. You do know that, don't you?"

She knew that's what he thought, at least for today—and since today was all her tender heart had to give anyway, she smiled at him and nodded.

A pink glow pushed back the drab remnants of the long night. Naomi flattened her palm to the cold glass and gazed out at the view of New Bethany from the third-story hospital window.

She'd come down around 5 A.M., when the vague discomforts of her stage of pregnancy awakened her, and she called to check on Ted. As Naomi tried to get some kind of answer, the charge nurse told her that Gayle had just arrived. Taylor, always an early riser and eager to get to Boatwright Nursery a few hours before they opened so he could catch up on paperwork, had driven Naomi to the hospital only after she promised not to overdo.

Gayle said she shouldn't have come, but Naomi doubted that anyone in the waiting room believed it, especially when Gayle caught her friend up in a hug and refused to let go. Later, when the waiting for the next interlude to see Ted left Gayle restless, bored, and feeling helpless, Naomi persuaded her to take a walk.

So far, they'd toured the basement and learned the cafeteria would not open for another half hour. They wandered through the main floor lobby where they poked fun of the tacky gift shop fare. They scouted out the vending machines to find the best for future reference, rating them on a scale of one to ten, with the top number going to those with the richest cache of chocolate.

Eventually they'd ended up on the fifth floor: maternity. The windows would not be opened in the nursery until 6 A.M., so they could not stop to *ooh* and *ahh* over the babies. Instead, the two of them decided to find a window with the best view of town and watch the sun come up until it was time for Gayle to see Ted again.

Naomi glanced at her friend beside her.

Gayle folded her arms, unfolded them, folded them again, cocked her hip, then sighed.

Naomi placed her hand in the middle of Gayle's back. She could feel the tension in the other woman's muscles, feel the weariness that seemed to permeate every fiber of her being. Wishing she had the right words to lend cheer or comfort, Naomi rubbed her open hand lightly between Gayle's shoulder blades. "Well, honey, it's a whole new day."

"Day?" Gayle huffed. "From my vantage point, Naomi, it's a whole new world!"

Naomi tipped her head to put her temple next to Gayle's.

"And I have no idea how it is I fit in this new world, Nomi, no idea at all."

They stood in silence then, looking out the window.

Naomi closed her eyes. *If there is something more I should do or say, show my now, Lord. Please show me now. Gayle has been through so much and I need to be a blessing other now. Show me how.*

Naomi racked her brain for the right words of encouragement, but none came. Ted's illness and Mathina's surprise announcement had knocked Gayle's well-ordered world off its streamlined track twice in one twenty-four-hour period. On the heels of that, what words would seem adequate?

Naomi tipped her head. Her gaze fell on the glory of God's creation in the dawn of the new day. Peace and his presence filled her soul and she could only sigh and take Gayle's hand. "It's beautiful, isn't it?"

"Hmmm."

"Nothing like watching the sun rise to really feel a new appreciation for the wonder of God's creation, is there?"

"Mmm."

"Don't you think it's lovely? Why, look there, at the old Christian church. Look how the light has cast it all kind of pinkish, and how the steeple looks tipped in gold by the morning sun. Breathtaking, isn't it?"

"I suppose."

"And beyond that…You can see the turnoff to Old Cemetery Road. That's the way I always take to go out to see Taylor at the nursery. It's always so peaceful that way. Wonder what he's doing about now?"

Gayle shrugged.

"They're at the start of their busiest season, you know. Opening back up after the winter off and suddenly deluged with seedling sand saplings and—"

Gayle nodded, her eyes fixed toward the horizon.

"He told me they have orders for three more prayer trees this year. That's good news, isn't it?"

"Sure."

"Hey, I think if you stand on your very tippy-toes you can make out some of the trees on the western-most edge of the grove from here."

This time she shook her head, but her gaze did not waver.

"Yes, you can. There's a cedar and a willow." Naomi squinted to feign picking out the different kinds. "Gayle, you have to go up on tiptoe to see—"

"No thanks."

"Can't you even appreciate it a little, Gayle?" Naomi knew she was pushing, but she felt she had to do something to get her friend to open up. To hold her emotions in the way she was doing wasn't good. Last year long pent-up guilt and emotion had almost cost Gayle her marriage and her self-worth. Naomi would not stand here and be a party to that happening again. "C'mon, pep up. It's a new day and Ted's all right, doesn't that make you feel even a teensy bit like celebrating? Like reaching out and grabbing up life with both hands?"

"I'll tell you what I'd like to grab with both hands—whoever put this fool idea into Mathina's head about dropping out of school. The missionary part I could support…eventually…I suppose…when she was ready…but to drop out of college to do it?" Gayle shook her head, sighed, then checked her watch. "We'd better head back, Naomi."

Naomi frowned. Why hadn't she been able to reach her dear friend? Why couldn't Gayle do as the Bible asked and rejoice in the day the Lord had made? Naomi felt just awful that she had not offered any better encouragement. Her disappointment must have showed, too, since Gayle suddenly put on a bright expression.

"Just think, next time we're up on this floor, maybe we'll be visiting your brand-new baby son or daughter." Gayle gave Naomi a squeeze, but as her arms fell away with a leaden heaviness, the darkness of her mood resurfaced. "But in the meantime, I'm going to spend the next few days balancing ten-minute visits with my critically ill husband with trying to convince my oldest child not to throw away her life."

285

Sixteen

"So, did the girl go off to become a mish'nary?" Grace practically bounced with anticipation.

Naomi smiled back at the small figure of a woman, dwarfed even more by the expansiveness of the Cadillac's monotone tan backseat. Grace seemed almost childlike with her tiny, gloved hands folded neat as the pressed hankie beneath them in her lap. Her dress, in an exact same shade of pink as a certain stomach remedy, accented with huge white polka-dots had a white Peter-Pan collar that Grace had adorned with a ruby and gold starburst pin. If Naomi hadn't already seen Grace's slightly stooped posture, she might have accused that pin of pulling the old woman's shoulders down with its weight.

Grace adjusted her feet in her clunky, off-white shoes on the hump in the floor. While true white would have better matched her outfit, it was not yet Memorial Day and that simply wasn't *done*. Naomi grinned. If there was one thing Miss Grace had proved, it was that she *knew* convention. And the old gal certainly knew her own mind, Naomi thought, her grin broadening a bit as she glanced at the older woman as she shifted her feet again. Despite their protests, Miss Grace insisted on sitting squarely in the middle of the huge backseat—so she wouldn't get left out of the conversation, she'd said. Naomi suspected that while this was certainly a consideration, Miss Grace also liked the idea of being perched there like a princess in a horse-drawn coach, equally accessible for both sides to peer in and see her.

Grace touched her parrot-blue hat. She moved the rolled brim just so until the cluster of blue roses and brilliant red cherries she's obviously pinned on herself fit jauntily to one side. The motion caused the trembling fount of seed pearls bursting out from the center of the decorative piece to bob up and down like some alien antennae sprouting from her head.

Naomi would have told her how comical that looked, but the woman's eyes sparkled with such enthusiasm and pure joy, she didn't have the heart.

Rose maneuvered the car in lurching fashion, trying to ease it into the small but slow moving lane of traffic pulling away from the prayer grove.

They'd spent the day with Miss Grace, she and Rose—with a harried visit by Lucy and a gracious but fleeting moment with Gayle—at the grove on the edge of town. This was the day the women of New Bethany—and many of the men—gathered to celebrate the planting of new prayer trees. Today, they honored those who served the year before and encouraged those who volunteered for the coming year of community service through prayer for others. It was this tradition which had brought Naomi, Rose, Gayle and Lucy together just two short years before.

When Miss Grace confessed she'd never been to one of the services, Naomi had been appalled—until Rose reminded her that most folks in town thought of Miss Grace as a whole smoked ham shy of a full picnic. She would not have been readily included, certainly not invited to participate in a prayer circle or the ceremony,…before they came into her life.

It still thrilled Naomi to think of it. Her hopes for this venture had proved far more fruitful than even she could have dreamed. Not only had they begun to whittle away at the prejudices the town had against Miss Grace, they had brought the dear old soul into a whole new world of experiences and people that had been just beyond her door, yet always beyond her reach. A person had to feel well pleased about a thing like that. And Naomi did.

She felt as content as a milk-fed cat curled up by a fire. She crossed her arms lightly over her enormous tummy and sighed.

"Well?" A persistent tapping on Naomi's shoulder broke through her self-congratulatory warmth. "Did the girl git herself off'en to mish'nary school, or what?"

"Um, no." Naomi gave her head a sharp little shake as if that would snap things back into a clearer perspective. "No, Gayle prevailed."

"As she usually does," Rose muttered, then hastened to add, "Often to her credit, of course."

Naomi grinned at her friend, then twisted her head around to address Miss Grace. "Gayle persuaded Mathina to go back and finish this year then they'd discuss any future plans this summer."

"Sounds right proper." Grace nodded like a monarch issuing a pronouncement. "Now then, what about Sister Marguerite's baby sister?"

"Sister Marguerite's…?" Naomi scrunched up her nose, trying to imagine where that reference came from. "You mean Princess?"

"Yes, Princess!" Grace brought her hands together in one delicate, muffled clap.

The gesture sent a cloud of richly floral day cologne into the recycled air, making Naomi glad to be past the stage where that kind of thing could churn her stomach.

"Yes, yes, *Princess.*" Grace cocked her head. A few strands of her thin white hair fluttered around her forehead and cheeks. Her hat tilted heavily to one side like a boat listing as it took on water. Her seed beads wobbled, and she sighed like a young girl hearing a fairy tale for the very first time. "That's the one— the one what had her heart's one true love come back after all so many years."

The hush of her words accompanied by that placid Southern turn of a phrase and the faraway look in Grace's eyes made Naomi smile. "Where'd you hear about that, Miss Grace?"

"Oh, 'twas only all over the grove, my dear. The word flitting in one body's ear and out their flapping lips almost all at the same time." Grace opened and closed her fingers and thumb as though working a hand puppet's mouth. "I know Sister Marguerite, know her well, I do. So I took an interest in the story."

"How come you to know Sister Marguerite?" Rose demanded in a provincial expression that would have sounded quite odd without the thickness of her accent.

"Know her from the nursing home. Done some charity work there years ago."

"You did not," Rose blurted out.

Naomi gasped.

Rose blanched. Not many things made ol' Rose blush or flustered her, but if anything could it would be the kind of blatant display of bad manners toward an elder that she'd just exhibited. "Th-that is…"

"Rose. Stop!"

Rose gave Naomi a sudden harsh glance.

She pointed to the stop sign they had finally reached at the corner where Grove Street met a road that officially had a number for its designation, but everyone simply called it Town Road.

Rose stomped on the brakes. Then whipped her head around so quickly, Naomi wondered that she might sprain something. "Are you all right, Miss Grace?"

"I'm all in one piece, if that's what you want to know."

"Good."

"*All* in one piece, Miss Rose." Grace tapped her gnarled finger against the side of her head. "Now, Sister Marguerite, she never treated me like anything less. That's why I come to do so much for her at the home. She's good folks."

"Yes, she is," Naomi agreed.

"And that's why I took such an interest in what happened with her baby sister and that Doctor-man what had the nerve to show his face back here all these years gone by and take to courting her again."

"Well, it sounds like you've pretty much gotten the whole story, Miss Grace." Naomi glanced over at Rose for confirmation.

"I don't know any more than that, except..." Rose's voice trailed off as if she were unsure whether or not to go on.

"Except..." Naomi and Grace echoed in unison.

"Well, I have heard a thing or two from Ben when he has come by the day care, but I hesitate to—"

"He who hesitates is lost, my dear." Grace's fervor and authority rivaled that of a Baptist preacher at a tent revival meeting. "Tell!"

Rose chuckled a bit. "All right, it's not much, though. All I know is that Dr. Clemmons, that's Princess's once—and if he has his way—future suitor is looking for a house here in town and hopes to move his practice here this fall—if and only if Princess will consent to be his bride."

"Rose, I can't believe you kept that from me!" Naomi grabbed her friend's arm for a second, careful not to crush the silk fabric of her pale purple, tailored blouse. "How long have you known this?"

"Since yesterday." She shrugged. "I thought I'd catch you up on it later but since Miss Grace here wants in on the whole story let me tell you one more thing."

If they had been in a rowboat, it would have suddenly dipped down and to one side, that's how fast Naomi and Grace scooted toward Rose, anxious to get in on every morsel of information.

"What is it?" Grace clutched at the back of the seat, probably more to steady herself than because she was that overwrought to grasp at the news.

"Well, Princess has never said this outright, but ya'll know how close the bond is between those sisters, right?"

"Yes," Naomi said.

"When Sister Marguerite left her job and the home, Princess quit her full-time job to take care of her and Marguerite paid off their home so Princess would never have to worry over a mortgage." Grace nodded firmly.

Rose inclined her head in agreement. "I've heard that."

Naomi made a mental note to quiz Rose on what other interesting tidbits she might be withholding.

"Well, given the sisters' closeness, their kind of long-standing interdependency, if you will," Rose went on, not in a condescending tone but like someone explaining an intricate set of circumstances, "you can understand that Mark has complained outright to Ben and made it known to others that he does not think Princess will ever marry him unless she feels she can do so without abandoning Marguerite."

"Ahhh." Grace nodded slowly. "I can see that. I can see how someone might feel that way fo' sure. I *certainly* understand all about family obligations and sacrifice, if nothing else."

More than the news about Princess, that piqued Naomi's curiosity and she turned around in the seat to peer over at Miss Grace.

Before she could get a word out to pursue it, Miss Grace held up her hand. "But now that's enough of that. I declare you are taking the long way about to get to Sweet Haven, my dear."

"Soon as we get up another mile or so it will fall off and we'll be sailing on home."

"Home." Miss Grace said it like it was honey on her tongue. "I do love my home, I have to say so ladies. And I don't like to stay away too long."

A light went off in Naomi's mind at that. If Miss Grace was unwilling to speak anymore about her obligations and sacrifices, at least the old woman might finally turn lose of a bit of information about her home—perhaps even invite her and Rose inside. "You know, Miss Grace, my mama was born in your home—right there at Sweet Haven."

"She was? When?"

"Oh…well…" Naomi did some fast calculations in her head. "I'd say about ten years before you were born. My grandmother came to the house to have her baby at the insistence of your great-grandmother, Miss Sable."

"Let's see, ten years before I was born, that would have been right around the year Granny Sable died."

"Yes, my grandmother, her name was Minnerva Sweeney, looked after your great-grandmother in her dotage—no offense intended, that's the way my mama always put it."

"None taken. And I'm sure my grandmother took great pleasure in seeing a birthing right before her time to go on home to Jesus. What a joy and comfort it must have been to her, seeing the full seasons of God's goodness before her eyes, new life even on the very brink of her own death." Grace leaned forward and put her hand on Naomi's shoulder. "And now you're going to have a baby yourself. Aren't we women lucky to be so intimately entwined with the Creator's blessings?"

Pain shot through Naomi as real as an arrow piercing cleanly through her chest at Grace's observation. Why had Mama not been given at least what Miss Sable had? To have glimpsed her grandbaby? To have allowed them to complete the circle of mother and child, and child becoming a mother? Why couldn't Mama have seen the full seasons of God's goodness before her time to go home?

Naomi put her hand on the swell of her stomach. She tried to swallow down the lump in her throat, tried to shut away the tears that threatened to wash over her lashes. Her mother had been there for her when her son came into the world twenty-one years ago, and she had tried to console herself with that thought but it did little good.

"Wouldn't it be perfect—" Grace looked skyward, resembling a wistful angel surveying heaven for inspiration. "Oh, but they don't do that anymore, do they?"

"What, Miss Grace?" Rose asked because she understood Naomi did not have the voice for it.

"Well, I was just thinking, probably quite selfishly, how wonderful that must have been for Granny Sable to have life born right into Sweet Haven like that and for that baby to get birthed beneath the wings of angels."

Naomi sniffled.

"And I can't help wishing…" Grace folded her hands and blinked her eyes at Naomi. "I just thought it might be very lovely if your baby was born at Sweet Haven, too."

Naomi's pulse fluttered. Her breathing grew shallow. She heard laughter in her own voice as she touched her friend's arm. "Rose, do you think—"

Rose guided the car onto the dirt roads that would lead them to the grand old white house. She did not even look at Naomi, but her mouth had a grim set and her brow creased.

"Dr. Ben would never go along with that, nor would your husband."

"But people do it all the time now, they call it home birth and they—"

"*They* are young women or women who have had a lot of babies or—"

"Or perfectly healthy older women. If he's told me once, Dr. Ben has told me a hundred times, I'm having an extremely healthy pregnancy. He does not foresee any trouble."

The tires crunched over dirt clods but the graceful car never joggled its passengers, much as Rose did not flinch or give any telltale signs of stress in her voice as she said, "Usually, it's the trouble they can't foresee that poses the greatest danger, Nomi. Now you put that foolish idea right out of your head."

But Naomi could not put it out of her head or her heart. She'd wanted a way to connect with Mama, to give her child a unique part of history that came from that woman she held so dear. This could well be it.

If she could just get herself inside Sweet Haven to check it out and then persuade her husband and doctor to go along with it. That was, if Miss Grace wasn't just churning up some elaborate fantasy that would turn into the threat of buckshot should Naomi actually try to follow through on it.

"Miss Grace, are you serious?" Naomi wet her suddenly dry lips. "Would you really let me have my baby at Sweet Haven?"

"Would I have offered if I didn't mean it?"

"You might." This was no time for mincing words. "I still don't approach your door without checking for a place to duck should you decide to come out on your porch with your guns blazing."

Grace let out a self-satisfied little cackle. "Smart girl. Mighty smart. But you don't have nothing to be a-feared a if I've extended my hospitality to you up front. A lady would never go back on an invitation like that. It just isn't done. Not by a Grayson. It's—" She crinkled up her button of a nose and it astounded Naomi to see even more wrinkles appear on that heavily lined face "—common."

Naomi curled her lips over her teeth to keep from blubbering out a big ol' guffaw. This woman, with her hat askew, antennae quivering, and her junk jewelry flashing—not to mention her reputation for nutty behavior—was worried over what might be thought unseemly etiquette?

The urge to laugh faded quickly when Miss Grace's eyes grew quiet and she lowered her head so that she caught Naomi off-guard with a guileless, longing look. "Now that you know that, tell me, would you really consider having your baby in my home?"

Naomi drew in a deep breath, hardly aware of the car swerving gently into the long drive at the very house they had been discussing. The house where her mama was born and where, if Naomi had her way, her child would soon come into this world. "With all my heart, Miss Grace. I'd love to have my baby at Sweet Haven, just like Mama was born there. It's perfect for more reasons than—"

"Looks like you've got company, Miss Grace." Rose cut Naomi off, the big car slowing noticeably as they rolled along the drive up to the big, white house. She pointed to an elegant sedan sitting smack in front of Sweet Haven and the woman standing beside it with her arms crossed and her face glowering. "Who is that?"

Grace squinted, leaned forward, then squinted again. "Whoo, don't that take the biscuit? I never thought she'd do it. No siree, never thought she would."

"Do what?" Naomi's gaze bounced from the woman in the

backseat to the woman standing at the end of the drive then back again. "Who is that, Miss Grace?"

Grace folded her arms like some petulant child and thrust out her lower lip. "My baby sister's only child."

Rose and Naomi exchanged knowing glances and Rose mouthed the words Dawnetta might have used, "The niece."

Naomi turned again to the older woman, almost afraid to ask but knowing she had to. "And just what is it you didn't think your niece would do?"

"I never thought she'd have the nerve. She dangled the prospect afore me the whole while I was at home with them for the holidays but I never imagined she had the gumption to try it."

Rose's impatience was showing as they coasted to a stop just a few feet from the other parked car. "Try what?"

Grace sat up straight as a board on the backseat, clasped her hands together in her lap and situated her pointed chin at a lofty angle. "If that one has come all this way, ladies, there is only one thing she has on her mind. She's come to take Sweet Haven away and send me to the nursing home."

Seventeen

"I s he asleep?"

Gayle looked at Naomi, who was eyeing her warily, then peered in at her husband. Ted lay there, draped like some warm, damp towel across the dark green leather sofa in his den, his eyes shut and his robe knotted sloppily over his cotton pajamas. The color in his face had returned now, weeks after the scare, but the sparkle had not come back to his eyes. She studied him, his stubbled jaw and the thick hair that needed cutting and a good shampoo, and she pressed her lips together. The sight created a snarl of emotions in her—relief at having him home and safe, fear over his listlessness, anger at his seeming indifference to helping himself.

Bowing her head, she pulled the door three-quarters closed and stepped back, her hand still clenched on the knob. A steady gaze on Naomi, she spoke loud enough to insure Ted heard her. "I don't think he's sleeping. I think he's playing possum."

"Ted? Never! Why just look at him, Gayle, he looks so cute and innocent." Naomi's lips puckered up as she spoke in a cooing baby talk, done—Gayle knew full well—purely for Ted's benefit, to rouse him to acknowledge her visit.

Ted did not move a muscle.

"Sure, all husbands look perfectly precious when they're sleeping, Nomi. But don't let that fool you." Gayle sighed and turned her back to the door, dropping her voice. "When he wakes up he'll bite your head off."

Naomi walked so close that with every step her very pregnant belly rubbed Gayle's arm. "That bad, huh?"

"Nuh-uh." Gayle stopped to let her friend walk into the sunroom, where they'd be having lunch and lemonade. "That's the *good* news, hon. At least when he's snapping at people he's interacting, he's expressing *something*—something besides the hangdog blues and a poor-pitiful-me refrain."

"Really? It's that bad?" Naomi settled into the chair Gayle held out for her and Gayle tried not to show any difficulty in pushing the seat in with her friend's added weight.

"I expected some depression, of course. I'd been warned he'd have emotional highs and lows after…" She cleared her throat rather than say *it* again. At this point she was so sick of the term—or of any reference to Ted's heart, for that matter—that she thought she'd tear her hair out, hundred-dollar highlight job and all, if she heard it one more time. That sentiment did not exactly make her feel good about herself, but at least it was honest.

She inhaled and savored the unique smell of the room with its wall of windows and lush plant life in every corner. The dank, earthy smell of soil mingled with an exotic but faint floral. Both were overpowered at the table by the sweet smell of an elaborate fruit salad with Naomi's favorite dressing, a mix of cream cheese, fruit juices, and tiny colored marshmallows.

"Dr. Clemmons says Ted is fine, that he should be able to resume his routine—his new routine—soon." Gayle scooted her own chair up and picked up a fork. She wasn't the least bit hungry but as the hostess, her role demanded she take the lead. She spotted a luscious looking strawberry, red as a valentine heart and shaped like one somewhat. Gayle gritted her teeth and stabbed her fork straight through the innocent piece of fruit. "The trouble is, I think Ted may have already resumed his new routine."

"You're not going back to that crazy affair notion, are you?" Naomi took a forkful of banana chunks and blueberries.

"No, no. Nuh-uh. Not that." Gayle stared at the morsel glistening on her own fork. It dripped with sticky white goo and had a pink glob of half-melted marshmallow clinging to it. "I mean his new routine seems to be nothing more than lying around, moping, keeping to himself—feeling sorry for himself. It's just...it's just so not like Ted."

Naomi nodded. "Hmmm."

Wild as some of her ideas could get, when Naomi shut up and stayed put she was the world's best listener. Unlike Rose, who's first impulse would be to jump in and tell Gayle how to handle things, or Lucy, who would wring her hands and look away, Naomi knew to just listen. While Rose and Lucy might eventually offer some wonderful support and advice, and Gayle would trust them with anything, especially to pray about, she needed Naomi's ear now.

Her heart filled with gratitude. *Thank you, Lord, for the gift in my life of all my friends, but especially for Naomi, for bringing her back to me just when you knew I would need her the most. Let me be as good a friend to her as she has been to me.*

She met her friend's pensive gaze. "That first day in ICU, when Ted said nothing in our lives was going to be the same, I never thought this was what he meant, Nomi." She eased out a shuddering sigh and put her fork down with the distinct clink of silver striking a fine crystal bowl. "His first day home he announced that he would quit the law firm, liquidate his assets, and buy up a live bait and boat rental operation."

Naomi tried to stifle her laughter. Gayle gave her credit for that.

"Whatever did you do?" Naomi's expression was all solicitous concern—probably to conceal her amusement.

301

"I pointed out to him, of course, that he knew nothing about either live bait or boats, which sent him into a tailspin of regret over all the things in life that he knew nothing about, all the experiences he'd missed." Gayle threw up her hands. "Nomi, he ranted on for an entire afternoon about how could a good Tennessee boy have grown to manhood not knowing a blessed thing about live bait!"

"Not really?"

"Oh, yes, really." She pushed at the rim of her bowl with her thumb. "I tell you, I was about ready to put him on a hook and dangle him off a pier by the end of it."

"But you got past that urge, I assume?"

"Gracious, yes. Let's see, after that he decided he would stay at home and become a regular Mr. Mom, thus allowing me to go out and be family breadwinner and realize my full potential, of which he had robbed me by expecting me to stay home with the children."

"To which you said?" The gleam in her friend's eye clearly showed her skepticism in Gayle's ability to win a crust of bread, much less the whole loaf.

"I said fine. I am not without resources, you know, Naomi. I am not helpless."

"No one every accused you of that, sugar." Naomi reached over to pat her friend's hand.

"Thank you—I think. Fact is, I'd have agreed to anything Ted proposed about then. At least he finally had a plan. At least we were seeing forward movement."

"So you'd have gone out to work, then?"

"Like any good Southern woman, I'd have done what needed doing to keep hearth and home together, hon." She lifted her head envisioning Scarlet swearing she'd never go hungry again. Then she looked down again and sighed. "Anyway, that doesn't matter because a few days into plan number two, Ted tried to run the house while I spent the day helping Mathina get ready for her trip."

"Oh—I forgot about that. She's gone off with that church group for six weeks doing work in Appalachia, hasn't she?"

"Left four days ago."

"And called home how many times already?"

"Only five." Gayle smiled slyly. "And not once have I chided her that if she were away in the mission fields she couldn't call home that often."

"Such restraint! They are polishing gems for your crown in heaven, my dear." Naomi laughed. "Now back to the tale of Ted, house husband extraordinaire. You left him home for the better part of a day and—"

"And I returned to find him watching TV, sitting on top of a pile of dirty laundry. Nathan was nowhere around, and Lillith was wearing her T-shirt inside out, her hair caught up on top of her head in a peculiar ponytail that made her look like a drunken whale spouting water."

Naomi chuckled.

Well, she could afford to chuckle, Gayle thought. She'd have had a good snicker at it herself if that had been all she'd found. She started ticking off the offenses one-by-one on her fingers. "The was dinner ruined. The kitchen a disaster area. The carpet spattered with an unknown agent which is either the spray from a shaken can of red soda pop or the aftereffects of a nick in a major blood vessel. Oh, and a black smudge on the *ceiling,* the origins of which I believe my family has obviously sworn to take with them to their graves."

"Ouch." Naomi took another bite of fruit salad.

"You bet *ouch.*" Gayle raised an eyebrow. "So, after another few days brooding over his less-than-sterling attempt at household management, Ted finally decided he knew what he did best. When Dr. Clemmons gave him the all clear, he would resume work at his practice, slowly at first, and never go back more than three-quarter time."

"Well, that sounds excellent."

"Oh, it was music to my ears to hear him say that, believe me. He needs to work, Naomi, for his own good more than our financial needs. Ted needs to feel like he's a useful and contributing member of society, that's all there is to it. That's what drove him so much at work, why he drove himself so hard—he felt it both contributed to his family's needs and that he was a cornerstone in the practice's entire operation. Not to mention the good he felt he did others with his representation. He felt useful, *needed.*"

"So what's the problem?"

From down the hall, Gayle heard the sound of the TV in the den switching on. She bit her lip to keep from calling out to Ted to join them, knowing he would ignore her request.

"The problem is, his partners came calling yesterday." Gayle wadded up the crisp, white napkin in her lap and laid it on the iron and glass table. "And thinking they were alleviating stress for him, no doubt, they announced they'd divvied up his clients and caseloads so successfully that he could take as long as he wanted to return. No rush, they said, everything was fine without him."

"Oh, dear."

"I think I used stronger words." Gayle jerked her head toward the soft buzzing of the television from the other room. "You saw the results of that visit yourself. He's entirely unmotivated. Useless. He doesn't have a single case or client that seems to need him, and it's devastated him."

Naomi blinked. She looked about to say something, then

304

snapped her mouth closed. She strummed her fingers on the tabletop, cocked her head one way then the other, started to speak again, and again stopped herself.

"Heavenly father, give me strength." Gayle leaned back in her chair. "Oh, Nomi, sugar, I recognize those signs in you. You are cooking up an idea, aren't you?"

"Well…"

"I cannot believe these words are coming out of my mouth, but…" Gayle shut her eyes. Her neck felt hot and her pulse skittish. "I'm beyond reasonable tactics, here. I've given it over to the Lord and promised to trust whatever he sent my way to help Ted. I love you like a sister, Nomi, but you, of all people, know how wary I am of your schemes. So you, of all people, understand how hard it is for me to ask this. Still, I have to do it for Ted's sake. So what's your idea, and if it even remotely seems like it will get some life back into my husband, when can we get started?"

"What a terrific way to spend a Saturday, eh, Lucy?" Ben went striding past with a load of cleaning supplies in a bucket. He landed a sharp pat on her back just before he slipped inside the open door of Sweet Haven.

A pat on the back. Lucy harumphed, realized how that must sound, then cleared her throat. She straightened up, hoping no one mistook her reaction to Ben's causal neglect of her feelings as disdain for the work. She reserved her disdain for a certain handsome doctor and felt none towards the job they had come to do, which was to help keep Miss Grace and her home out of the clutches of that self-serving niece, Eve Kimbro-Tattersall.

Ted had taken an immediate and unflagging interest in the case as soon as Naomi told him of it. He'd determined it easily won with a little legal maneuvering on his part, a lot of elbow grease by able-bodied friends and neighbors, and—the wild card—some good behavior on Grace's part. Once Ted had done the preliminary work—staving off any action on the part of Mrs. Tattersall and getting a quick court date set for a judge to determine Grace's competency—Naomi had made the calls.

Despite the fact that she was harrowingly near to her due date, she'd rounded up the old prayer circle and a few other volunteers and gathered the needed supplies. She'd even arranged for Nikki to watch over Ben's children for both this Saturday and the next to let Ben pitch in. He'd already given Miss Grace a free medical checkup and written a letter on her behalf. Of course they'd all written such letters, at Ted's request, so that was not a special effort on Ben's part.

Lucy sanded down the windowsill before her with a vengeance, releasing a gritty cloud in her wake. She clenched her teeth and glared in the direction Ben had just gone, still keenly aware of the place his hand had met with the middle of her back.

A pat. Like she were a dog. Things had gotten so much better for them for a while, right after Ted's heart attack. But then as Ben's patient load picked up, he'd come for the kids later and later, usually worn to a frazzle. He promised things would get better when Mark Clemmons moved to town—*if* Mark Clemmons moved to town, that was—that they could share on-call duties, which would free Ben up more.

Lucy had her doubts, but she kept those to herself. Why rock the boat when you're not sure if you're booked for a long-term passage? Besides, she'd grown increasingly sensitive to the murmuring that winged its way through town regarding her relationship with Ben. She'd done the "talk of the town" thing once when Ray Griggs had made a fool of her, and she was not interested in a repeat of that brand of heartache and shame if things ended poorly.

Just the suggestion of things ending between she and Ben made her choke back a gasp. She wet her lips and touched her hand to her hair, sincerely trying to recall the feel of Ben's hand on her—even on her back—as reassurance.

"Yes, ma'am, I'll get right on it. Thank you, ma'am. Yes, I will." Ben's voice carried to Lucy over the scritching of the sandpaper she was still employing with absentminded swipes and the slap-slap-slap of paint brushes at the railing behind her.

The last thing she wanted was to be caught mooning over the man, especially by that very man, when she should be busying herself with altruistic endeavors. She looked around the weathered wraparound porch, making sure she spoke loud enough for any and all nearby to hear. "Yes, sir. I couldn't think of anything I'd rather do than help out Miss Grace. And isn't it the perfect day for it?"

Taylor, his daughter Ashley, and Gayle and Ted's son, Nathan, all mumbled some form of agreement without even a pause in their work. The pungent odor of fresh paint stung Lucy's nose and made her eyes water—or at least that's what she'd tell Ben if he asked. If he even noticed she was weepy at all.

"Yes, ma'am, Miss Grace. I understand." Ben pivoted just as he reached the front door, which stood propped open by a cast-iron figurine of a pig wearing a daisy. Framed by the gorgeous oval of stained glass, he glanced from the interior of Sweet Haven to Lucy, then to something in his cupped palm.

She blinked up at him.

"Um, Lucy—hey, are you all right?"

"It's the dust." It was the best her mind could come up with, stunned as she was by the fact that he had noticed what she suspected were her red-rimmed eyes.

"You sure?" He peered at her.

"Of course I'm sure." She looked away, feeling very unsure about anything at that moment. Her gaze fell on the box of "decorations" Rose had brought for Sweet Haven today before any of them had known what they would find inside the house. Lucy had taken a moment earlier to flip through a *Proverbs For Daily Living* Calendar, stopping to read some of the verses. One in particular sprang to mind now: "My mouth speaks what is true, for my lips detest wickedness."

With that in her thoughts, she knew she must either tell Ben the truth or find a way to avoid the subject altogether. Collecting her composure as delicately as a lady gathers up her skirt on a windy day, she sniffed and pretended total fascination with the peeling sill. "Was there something else you wanted to ask me?"

"Uh…oh, yeah." He moved his hand and it's contents jingled softly. "Miss Grace had a fit over the idea of her physician scrubbing her toilets, so she demanded my job should be to go over to Dot and Daughters' and pick up an order of food for everyone. She said she'd call ahead so it'd be near ready when I got there."

"Sounds good. So what's the problem?"

He shook his head, jangled the things in his hand again and whispered, "As I was walking past, she pushed this onto me. I think she expects me to pay for it with this."

Lucy stood and leaned over to check out Ben's haul. "Four nickels, a quarter, a ball bearing, and a golf pencil."

"Don't you think that's a little odd? I mean, Lucy, we've all just enlisted ourselves in the cause of proving that woman is competent to take care of herself and then she expects me to pay for a wagonload of food with this?" He thrust his hand out.

Lucy laughed. "She doesn't expect you to pay for anything,

Ben. I'll wager when you get there, Dawnetta will have either put it on Miss Grace's account or she will have donated it toward the cause."

"The why did Miss Grace give me this?" He stared in confusion at the collection.

"Because she *likes* you, honey." Lucy held her hand under his open one. "'Round these parts when someone likes someone else they look for ways to let that person know it."

"Well, then." His face brightened. His eyes filled with fun as he turned his hand to empty his goods into her palm. "This should show you how I feel about you, Miss Lucy. I want you to have my treasures."

The gesture touched her far more than she should have allowed, but when Ben leaned in to plant even a chaste kiss on her lips, that she did not allow.

"Ben." She tuned to present him with her cheek. "People will talk."

"Lucy, I…" He lingered, his face near hers, his eyes flooded with some emotion she could not hope to fathom.

She swallowed hard, one had to swallow hard to gulp down feelings as strong as those she had for this man. She shook back her hair. "What is it, Ben?"

"I…"

"What?" The frost in her tone was for the benefit of any nosey onlookers, she told herself, but it chilled Ben's expression just the same.

He sighed, then straightened away. "I still think that if Miss Grace continues to do things like give people this kind of worthless junk that we may be in for a tough fight."

She nodded.

He stepped back, started to walk away, then paused and turned just his head to say softly over one shoulder, "But then

I'm not the kind to walk away from tough fights if they bring me the results I dearly want—and I hope you aren't either, Mary Lucille."

He bounded down the stairs and out to his car. Lucy did not take her hopeful eyes from him until the last puff of dirt from his tires had disappeared down the long, tree-lined drive.

"This place is really shaping up fast." Rose plunked her hands on her hips as she looked around the parlor. The residence had hardly changed in decor since she had lived here when it was a boarding house over thirty years earlier. The rooms, made dimmer and smaller by their heavily-patterned wallpaper, were cluttered but surprisingly clean. The crystal beads on the chandeliers all needed a good ammonia soak, the rugs could use a steam clean—or to be tossed out completely—and the knick-knacks begged for a thorough dusting...but at first glance, Sweet Haven's interior needed nothing more remarkable than that.

A man would be out Monday to tell them if the house had any significant structural problems that might preclude Miss Grace continuing to live there. However, Ted and Ben and Taylor had already walked the place top to bottom and declared it sounder than most modern homes. Rose would have put more credence in that assessment if Will had been in on it.

Will. Just thinking of him made her ill at ease. She shifted her weight, scarcely ruffling her work clothes—one of Curry's old golfing shirts she hadn't been able to throw out and a pair of elastic-waist pants that practically ballooned out like riding jodhpurs they were so large. Ludicrous as the outfit must have looked, Rose did not care, she'd come to work not to give a fashion show. She'd come without telling Will, too, and that played on her conscience.

Will had not approved of her coming out here just to deliver meals. How would he respond to know she was here now? Rose didn't dare think about it. If she did think about it, she'd have her answer and that answer could do nothing but widen the rift already growing between her and Will. If only he understood her, respected her wishes in this. If only he wasn't acting so much like…like Curry, doing things without explanation, supposedly for her own good.

She put her dust cloth to her neck like a linen hankie before she even realized her mistake. When the coarse fabric, thick with furniture polish, touched her skin, she started, her gaze darting quickly to see if Naomi had caught her mental lapse. Naomi did not even seem aware of her at all. Lost in thought, her very pregnant friend stared at a large glass case topped with porcelain figurines of eighteenth-century ladies with tall, powdered wigs, broad skirts, and tiny feet. In the case itself was an odd but amusing collection of pigs—dancing pigs, fiddle-playing pigs, sows and piglets, spotted hogs, and pigs dressed like everything from farmers to doctors.

"Isn't this place just fascinating, Rose?" Naomi put her fingertips to the glass. "I'm so happy that Ben, Taylor, Miss Grace, and I came to a compromise regarding having my baby here."

"Having your baby *shower* here, don't you mean?"

Naomi sighed. "I wish it were more, but yes, having my shower here will be nice won't it? Having it here where Mama was born, among all these old treasures and in the very same rooms my grandmother walked when she was here."

"Yes, Sweet Haven sure has its history and it's a lovely place. I knew what to expect inside, since I'd lived here before, but most folks would be surprised to find it not very showy or grand, really, compared to the kinds of antebellum homes one sees in movies and such. I'm glad you're not disappointed."

"Disappointed? Oh, no. I love this place, Rose. It's like touching a piece of my personal past, as well as the town's. Besides, I never expected showy, myself." Naomi's eyes glittered with excitement and a faraway dreaminess. "After all, Sweet Haven is, first and foremost, a home."

"A home in far better condition than I ever expected to find—judging purely from the rundown appearance of the exterior." Rose peeked out the window at the progress of the porch painters. A new coat of paint on the old place, a patch in the roof, and some boards replaced on the steps and they'd hardly recognize the house. "Of course, the grounds have always been meticulous—no telling how Miss Grace accomplishes that—but I did think we'd find far more dirt and cobwebs and who-knows-what on the inside."

Naomi turned to Rose, or more precisely, moved her burgeoning body in slow agitating movements like a washing machine chugging away with a burdensome load. "From hearing Eve Tattersall talk I'd expected a real health threat. And, yes, thanks also to my own healthy imagination."

"Well, we have to remember that Miss Grace's niece, regardless of what we think of her, has hired people in to look after Grace for some time now."

"Leave the food on the doorstep, my foot. This place was not kept in order by Miss Grace, nor by anyone who's only job was to plop down dinner on the front porch, I tell you, Rose."

"Well, amen to that." Rose glanced around the parlor then into the adjoining anteroom with its hardwood floors still gleaming from her run with the dust mop. Then her eyes fell on the great, swooping staircase that she knew Miss Grace could not have climbed for years. Even the upstairs beyond those graceful flowing steps was neat as a pin and needed only superficial cleaning to ready it for a court-ordered home assessment. Grace had had plenty of help with this place, and who knew how many other things, in the past. Sweet Haven's condition stood testament to that even when Grace herself denied it. "Naomi?"

"Hmm?"

"In all the flurry of activity to get this place polished up, have you ever stopped to wonder if we're doing the right thing? That maybe Miss Grace requires far more help than we realize, and Eve has a point in trying to get her out of here?"

"Are you asking me if I think it's right to allow that dear old woman—already unjustly maligned by most of this town—to continue to live in the home that has been in her family for five generations? Are you thinking it's better for her to move to some nursing home and to have all the ridiculous gossip confirmed by letting that snooty niece of hers declare her mentally incompetent? Can you really stand by and let that happen, after we've come to care so much for Miss Grace, Rose? Where's your sense of pride in Southern womanhood and all it stands for? Where's your sense of decency? Where's your moral outrage?" Naomi tipped her head to one side and put her hands on her hips, her elbows bowed out.

"My moral—" A flashfire burst of laughter cut off Rose's response, which she immediately got under control. "I have just as much moral outrage as—" This time she could not control her laughter. "Naomi, honey, I simply cannot have a discussion about moral obligations, decency, and Southern womanhood, much less about Miss Grace or anything serious at all, with you standing there like that."

"Why not?"

"Because with your arms sticking out and your head tipped

to one side, I keep thinking you look like a round little sugar bowl that had its lid handle broken off then glued back on all whomper-jawed." Rose chuckled at the image her mind created.

"That may be so, but there is more than sugar in this bowl and don't you forget it." She feigned a fierce scowl that did not fool Rose for one moment. "Now would you kindly get back to work, Miss Rose, ma'am? I would dearly love to have this place looking shiny as a new dime before Sister Marguerite arrives."

"Sister Marguerite?" Rose tucked her cleaning rag into the pocket of her baggy work pants then leaned the heels of her hands on the wine-colored brocade chair that sat at the parlor door. "Is she coming 'round to help out today?"

"She's coming 'round, all right. But not just to help out today...not if I have anything to do with it."

"Oh my." Rose crept over to her friend's side, reached out and pinched up the white cuff that circled Naomi's upper arm.

"Rose! Have you lost your mind, just what are you doing?"

"I am trying to see just what it is that you've got up your sleeve, sugar."

Naomi broke into a slow, puckish grin. "You don't have to sneak a peek, Rose. I'll tell you what I've got up there outright. Only the perfect solution for absolutely everyone's problems, that's all."

"That's *all?*" In just the short time they'd known one another—short measure in New Bethany time, which meant anything less than a second generation of family acquaintance—Rose had learned to take Naomi's ideas with a healthy dose of skepticism. "Let's see now, you've already helped Gayle get Ted out of the mulligrubs, started us all to rescuing poor little Miss Grace, and now you're going to do something for Sister Marguerite?"

"And Sister Princess and Dr. Clemmons, too."

"Oh, dear." Rose sank into the brocade chair, threw her hands over her eyes, and tossed her head back against the tightly padded bolster. "Wake me when it's over."

"Ha ha. Very funny. But we'll see who's laughing when this all works out." Naomi settled into a matching chair across the way. "I tell you, Rose, it will benefit everyone involved and it isn't just my idea. It came from something Miss Grace said about how well she and Sister Marguerite get along. Add to that the fact that Princess won't marry Mark because she won't leave Marguerite alone and—"

"I see where this is going, and Naomi, I have to say you really shouldn't get so—"

"Oh, it's not just me. I've dragged Dr. Ben in on this one and he thinks it's a fine idea. So does Dr. Clemmons. In fact, Mark has already talked it over with the sisters. That's why Marguerite will be over later, to look around and have a nice, long talk with Miss Grace about the arrangements."

"Really?" Rose sat up, genuinely interested now. "So Dr. Ben thinks this might fly?"

"Like an angel through the heavenly firmament." Naomi skimmed her hand through the air. "Think of it, Rose, after all these years, Princess will get to be with her one true love, Marguerite won't be alone, and how better to convince the judge Miss Grace is well cared for than to show she's living with a former nursing home administrator?"

Rose shook her head, not sure what to make of it all. "Naomi, hon, I have to say it. You have raised meddling and scheming to an art form—a pure art form, I tell you. If you pull this off—"

"If I pull this off—" Naomi's smile could only be called smug "—the only one left for me to meddle with will be you, Miss Rose."

Eighteen

o! Go! You can do it!" Ashley, perched precariously on the arm of Naomi's chair, cheered Lucy on in the baby shower's big contest. The instant Lucy signaled she had accomplished her assigned task, Ashley depressed the stopwatch in her hand. "That's the fastest time yet!"

"Well, of course." Lucy gave a curtsey, her blond hair swinging as she added a gracious dip of her chin.

Naomi laughed to see Lucy accept the accolade with such confidence. Ben and his children had been good for Lucy. And she had been good for them. Now, if there were only some way to get them to do something about it.

"No fair, that's just the kind of thing she does for a living. She's a professional. A ringer!" Gayle carried on in mock outrage as she escorted Miss Grace to center stage of the crowded room.

Grace had wanted to have the shower in Sweet Haven's parlor, or at least the smaller drawing room, but Naomi would not have any part of that. She wanted to be in the room where her mama had been born, and in the end Grace had relented. Taylor and Sister Marguerite had moved the furniture out—none of that was here when her mother had been born, anyway—and brought in a narrow, decorative table that had been in the hallway to hold the punch bowl, cake, plates, and silver.

Naomi glanced around her at the pink and blue netting Gayle had draped over the large, sun-brightened windows, complete with twinkling white lights. Naomi's gaze lingered on the now-yellowed wallpaper—stripes and roses—that would have been new when it greeted her mother into the world. Then she looked to the fresh and friendly faces all around her—Rose, then Lucy, then Ashley by her side.

Ashley had not wanted to attend the shower, but Taylor had put his foot down and the girl had come along, sulking most of the way and muttering about "a bunch of women I hardly know doing goofy things and eating cake that tastes like a sponge soaked in sugar and iced with lard." Naomi studied the girl, a young woman, almost. She never knew where she stood with Ashley, never knew if Taylor's daughter would ever accept her as a friend, much less a mother figure.

"Okay, next contestant," Ashley called out, her leg swinging. "You want to try it, Nomi?"

That she called her by the endearment used only by those very close to her brought a lump to Naomi's throat. She smiled and shook her head. "You'd have to get a winch and pulley and hire a team of men to hoist me up out of this chair, hon. I think I'll just stay put. Let someone else have the...honor."

"All right, then." Ashley looked all around her, making a show of hunting up the next victim. She gave Sister Princess a one-eyed squint, then moved her discerning gaze pointedly to Rose's daughter, Stacey, who made a snarling face to warn her off. Ashley played up passing over Opal Parks, who had worked for her daddy forever, then came back to her. Opal shook her head. Ashley clucked her tongue in a sound of total teenage frustration. "Doesn't *anybody* want to go next?"

Naomi jabbed her stepdaughter with her elbow and whispered. "Miss Grace. Ask Miss Grace."

The girl gulped down a squeal of delight at the very idea, then tested Naomi's seriousness with a somber glance.

"Do it. I'll back you up, I promise."

Ashley licked her lips, tossed back her long, dark hair, then gave a nod. She stood.

Naomi scooted forward in her chair, the sudden demand on her dormant muscles causing a spasm to flare in her back. She held her breath to keep from letting out an audible gasp, but winced at the sudden grip of it. It quickly passed, though, and she exhaled and got comfortable on the edge of her seat.

"Our last competitor, then, before we give out the awards will be none other than—" Ashley swept her hand out, taking in the whole of the room as if any one of them could be the next one nabbed "—our hostess, Mrs. Grace Grayson-Wiley!"

Grace clapped her hands to her cheeks with all the poise and excitement of a beauty pageant entrant just being named "Miss Sweet Corn Queen." "Me? Oh, I couldn't! No! Why I don't have the foggiest notion how to go about it…"

"That's okay. We'll coach you." Gayle motioned to Rose to get up and help her prod Miss Grace from the brocade chair that matched the one Naomi sat in.

The twin chairs, Naomi noted, nestled among the elegant but sparse Chippendales carted up from the dining room, left no doubt which two women were the day's focal points. As Miss Grace allowed Gayle and Rose to assist her up from her chair, she looked like the grand duchess arising from her throne to go out amongst the little people. A grand duchess wearing a peachy-pink chiffon party dress and a decidedly orange sherbet hat, complete with a small flocked pear and a pair of feathered doves stuck front and center of the thing.

Ashley stepped back and resumed her perch at Naomi's side.

"You know the first thing Sister Marguerite should do when she comes here to live next month after Princess' wedding?" Naomi whispered to Ashley as they waited for Grace to assume the centermost spot in the room. "The first thing she should do is take Grace hat shopping."

"And shoe shopping and dress shopping," Ashley added, without a trace of criticism. "Any and all of those—but please tell her not to go *fragrance* shopping."

The girl had a point. As Grace toddled to her place, she left an almost visible vapor trail of an opulent perfume. Naomi wanted to laugh but got a stitch in her side that stopped that activity cold.

"Now here's what you have to do, Miss Grace." Rose spoke loudly, articulating each syllable. "You take this baby doll here."

Gayle handed Grace the plastic doll, which only served to make the doll look enormous or Grace even more childlike—Naomi wasn't sure which.

"And you take this bathroom tissue here." Rose's expression gave a clear message: "In *my* day we would never have used toilet paper in a party game." Still, she took the white roll from Gayle, then handed it to Grace, who smiled as sweetly as if she'd just been presented with a canned ham as a prize at the county fair. "And you have to fashion a baby diaper on the doll—in less time than it took Miss Lucy to do it—to win."

"I see." The old dear looked like she didn't have the slightest idea how to proceed, but she seemed game for it, Naomi had to give her that. The feisty woman ought to win a prize for sheer pluck, if nothing else.

And while they were handing out those prizes, Naomi thought, she ought to earn one herself for not complaining about how uncomfortable these chairs were. She shifted and swore she felt the baby swoop off to one side as if it were performing some kind of water ballet inside her belly. Of course— she looked down at her girth—the child certainly had room for water sports in there. She put her hand on Ashley's leg to provide leverage to situate herself better. Her back cramped again, and her leg went numb for just a second, but when she found a more cushy position, both eased.

"The only catch is…" Gayle came up behind Miss Grace, creating a comical contrast between the tall, thin, tanned woman and the pale, elderly imp. Gayle lowered a leopard spotted sash down before Grace's face. "You have to diaper the doll blindfolded."

"Oh, blindfolded!" Grace lifted her head as Gayle went about fastening the cloth in place. "Just like in blind man's bluff."

"Sort of, only you don't chase anyone around with a stick in this game. You are perfectly clear on that point, aren't you, Miss Grace?" Gayle mugged her pretend horror over Grace's imagined antics.

The group chuckled.

"Yes, dear. No sticks."

"Good." Gayle looked quite smug and started for her seat.

Grace tucked the paper roll beneath one arm, took the doll by both ankles, then proceeded to swing it like a baseball bat behind Gayle's retreating back.

The group laughed.

Gayle smiled graciously as if she were the cause of the humor and sat down.

"Okay, Miss Grace, you can staaaaart—" Ashley stretched the word out until the stopwatch was readied "—now!"

Face scrunched up and the tip of her tongue poked out to one side, Grace tackled the job, twisting the doll one way and then the other, toilet paper flying.

"Now, you behave yourself for Auntie Grace, you ol' baby, you," Grace ordered as she flipped the doll over and promptly began diapering its head…

The crowd laughed again.

Naomi swallowed in an effort to push down a wave of queasiness. It had to be because of the toxic blend of high sugar punch, rich cake, and Grace's thick perfume. Still bracing herself on Ashley's leg, she leaned forward in her seat, trying to get the baby to move enough to relieve the intense pressure on her lower back.

"Isn't Miss Grace just adorable?" Ashley bent down to put her mouth to Naomi's ear. "I think she's cheating, though. Should I tell Gayle that I can see one little eye peeking out from the...Nomi? Nomi, you're hurting me. Nomi!"

Naomi had had no idea how tight her grip on Ashley's leg had grown until she heard the squeak of pain in the girl's voice. "Ashley, hon, I'm sorry. I was just—" She swallowed the last of her words in one heaving gasp.

"Oh my word! Miss Gayle! Miss Rose, get over here, quick! I think Naomi is going into labor."

Labor? The very idea was ridiculous, and Naomi would have told all the gawking faces just that had she been able to straighten up and speak. Instead, she blew a long, cleansing breath out through her rounded lips, waiting for the engulfing wave of pain to pass, then relaxed as much as she could under the circumstances.

"Lucy, run get a cool rag." Rose was all commanding efficiency.

"Shouldn't I boil water or something instead?" Lucy blinked like a deer caught in the headlights.

"A cool rag will do, Mary Lucille." Rose's Sunday school teacher voice, which could send grown men scurrying, did the trick. Lucy scampered away, with Rose's admonition right behind her. "Now hurry!"

"Naomi, is this true?" Gayle knelt to put her face in Naomi's line of vision. "Are you in labor?"

Was she? Naomi's mind refused to imagine the possibility. "I can't be. The baby isn't due for ten days. Besides, I only had the one pain, and it was nothing like the contractions I had when Justin was born."

"Every birth, like every baby, can be completely different." Rose smoothed back Naomi's bangs. "Do you think we should head off for the hospital?"

"We're going to the hospital?" Lucy wedged her way into the knot of onlookers. "Here's the rag, Rose. Should I call Ben?"

"Good idea, Lucy." Gayle patted the young woman's shoulder. "Tell him to meet us at the hospital."

"No, not the hospital. That's just plain silly. Even if I am in labor, which I seriously doubt, it's far too soon to go bundling off to the hospital. They'll only take one look at me, tell me I'm not having a baby, and send me home. I'd rather stay here."

"Nuh-uh! No ma'am. Not on *my* watch, this is not going to happen." Gayle stood and Naomi could have sworn she was ten feet tall. "Naomi Beauchamp Boatwright, you are not going to trick us into dallying too long here so that you have to give birth at Sweet Haven."

That thought had not crossed Naomi's mind, but now that Gayle had planted it there—

"Nuh-uh. Isn't going to happen." Gayle's image became of blur of lightly streaked short brown hair, heavy gold jewelry, and a voice that could have come from straight out of the mouth of thunder. "I will not let you put yourself and your baby in jeopardy for some wild hope that it might make you feel closer to your mama to stay here."

"Your mama knows what's going on and her love will be with you whether you're at Sweet Haven or at the hospital, Naomi." This from Lucy.

"And make no mistake about this, you'll be at the hospital." Gayle turned. "Lucy make that call to Ben. Ashley, sugar, there is a phone in my car you can use to call your daddy. Tell him we're on our way to the hospital and to meet us there."

"Don't either of you make a move or a phone call. I am *not* going to the hospital. I'm fine, I tell you. I'm just having a—" The next wave hit out of nowhere, with no buildup to warn her it was coming. It took away her breath, her words, her very thoughts of anything but the claw that was twisting in her back and the band of pain tightening low in her abdomen.

"You're just having a baby." Gayle's tone was dry. "And you're not having it here."

Naomi was aware that someone was holding her hand, but not until Ashley actually spoke did Naomi realize it was her. "Nomi, please, listen to Gayle and Rose. They know what they're talking about. Please don't do anything that might risk you or the baby. Please."

Naomi tried to wet her lips, but her mouth had gone dry as the desert. Between the emotion surging up in her and the effects of her discomfort, she could not make a sound except a short, hacking cough. She hoped her eyes would be enough to convey how much Ashley's concern meant to her.

"I know I was a brat about it at first, and that I haven't always been really nice to you since you and Daddy married, but I really love you and I really depend on you."

"I love you, too Ash, I really do. You're such a good kid. I'm so proud of you." She managed to smile weakly as the last traces of the contraction faded.

"Then please, go to the hospital now. I can't lose another mother, and I don't want to lose my baby brother or sister, either. Please go." Tears glistened in Ashley's eyes.

"You want a tie to your mama?" Rose spoke softly, still

stroking Naomi's head. "There it is. Your mother's history is not in this room, Naomi, or in Sweet Haven. It's in these children. Your children. And the way to serve your mother's memory is not by a sentimental gesture, but by taking care of yourself and being the best mama to them that you possibly can be."

Rose wasn't saying anything that Naomi didn't already feel welling up in her own heart. The connection Naomi had so desperately desired had been made, with Ashley, not through the imagined pieces of her mother's life. The faith and love that Mama had instilled in Naomi would pass on through her to Ashley and to the new baby. They were all a part of the circle, of the seasons of God's goodness, and they would go on.

Naomi exhaled, shut her eyes, and gripped Ashley's hand tightly. "Lets go to the hospital then. Our family is about to get a little bit bigger."

"Is that the most perfect baby you have ever seen or what?" Ben laid his arm over Lucy's shoulders as they stood back from the crowd that was admiring Taylor and Naomi's new daughter. Ben had but a few minutes before he was expected with another patient, but he had said he couldn't go back to work before he came out to see the baby, shake a few hands, and give Lucy a hug. "The most perfect baby, except for Alec and Paige, of course."

"I'll have to take your word for that."

"I wish you had been there, Lucy. I wish you'd been a part of this family from the very start. I'd love to see you with a little baby in your arms."

"You can see that any day of the week, just stop by the day care." She laughed, though she did not feel like laughing.

"Yeah, but those aren't your babies, Lucy. Not for keeps.

And I know you want one of your own for keeps."

Yes, that was her, all right, with her biological clock ticking ruthlessly away like a terrorist time bomb strapped to her hips.

He nuzzled her hair. "So I guess you know what that means."

Kablooey, she thought, lacing her arms around her middle.

"I guess that means that you and I are going to have to get married so you can have Paige and Alec and then a baby of your very own."

She blinked up at him. "You mean we'd adopt another baby? Like you did with Paige and Alec?"

"W-well, we could. I sort of thought we'd try the...um, other method first, though."

She heard his words—she'd heard words like them before—Ben was very free with alluding to marriage and very forgetful when it came to actually doing anything about it. Usually she let him get away with it, but today she had to say something, to let him know, in some small way, that she wasn't one to take for granted forever. "You mean we'll try the...other method...after we're married, of course."

"When else?"

A nurse came to the swinging door and waved to him to come. Ben raised his hand to tell her he understood.

"When, indeed." Lucy was unimpressed with the man's big talk or his mad dash to leave again.

"Why, Lucy, you sound suspiciously like a woman fed up with waiting." He grinned at her. "If I didn't know better, I'd think that might be a Lucy-style ultimatum."

"Ultimatum? Are you kidding?" Girls like Lucy did not make ultimatums. Girls like Lucy knew better than to do anything that foolhardy. "That's not what...I would never..."

"I know." He put his hand under her chin. His eyes, behind

his glasses, were serious and yet held a merry glint in their depths. His breath was warm and his touch warmer.

Lucy felt her resolve beginning to melt.

"But I sure do wish you would, Miss Mary Lucille."

"W-would what?"

"Marry me."

Yesterday those simple words would have reduced her to a puddle. Today, Naomi had had a baby. Naomi, who was almost ten years Lucy's senior, who had not even known Taylor as long as she and Lucy had known one another, short time that that was, was married and had a baby. With that rigidly implanted in her craw today, Lucy simply did not have it in her to dissolve over Ben's sweet nothings.

"Marry you? Ha! You say that, Ben. You tease me with it and thrill me with it, but then nothing ever comes of all your talk."

"That's not my fault if it doesn't. I'm waiting on you."

"On *me?*" If he had slapped her she could not have felt more surprised. "To do *what?*"

He leaned down low to put their gazes level. "To say yes."

"Say yes to what?" She stepped back, keeping her tone calm so that she wouldn't draw attention. "You've never really asked me anything definite."

"You've never acted like you wanted me to, Lucy. Believe me if I'd ever just get one sign that you were ready—"

"Well, if I'd ever just get one sign that you were seriously asking—"

"That I…? What would it take? You want me down on one knee?" He stared to lower himself.

"No! Not here, not like this! Not with everyone watching."

"No one's watching, Lucy." He made a point of looking over at the cluster of people cooing at the nursery window. "But maybe you should open *your* eyes."

"Dr. Martin? You're needed as soon as possible." It was the nurse who had beckoned him before.

"I'm coming."

"My eyes are open. Ben." More than he probably knew.

"Good, then maybe you can take a good long look at yourself, Lucy. You say I've not asked you proper to marry me, and if that's so, I can correct it. And when I do, I guess we'll *both* see for sure, won't we?"

"See what?"

He walked backward the few steps to the swinging door, his eyes never leaving hers, then paused. "We'll see exactly which one of us is really avoiding marriage in this relationship."

"Aren't they a lovely bride and groom?" Rose leaned close to Naomi but kept her eyes on the TV monitor in the darkened judge's chambers. The beaming faces of Princess and Mark Clemmons, fresh from their late-August nuptials, were replaced by a multitude of joyous guests videotaped during the reception at the newly rejuvenated Sweet Haven. "And look, there's little Chloe Faith's first outing. She's so tiny there, it's hard to believe she's over four month's old now."

Familiar faces continued to flash across the small screen, but Rose refrained from commenting on them all. Even though Ted, the judge, and the attorney accompanying Eve Tattersall had all stressed the casual nature of this informal hearing, Rose hesitated to say anything that might reflect poorly on Miss Grace. So when the camera passed by a group shot of Gayle, Lucy, Naomi, and Rose with all their families gathered round them and it struck a harsh chord in Rose to see again that Will was not beside her that day, she said nothing.

What did it matter if Will had declined the invitation,

claiming that he would feel too much like a party crasher among people he hardly knew? Still, when she saw her friends standing close to the men they loved—and then herself with only her long-faced daughter at her side—it mattered. She raised her chin, unwilling to give in to the immediate sense of loneliness and loss that threatened to overwhelm her.

If only Will could see things her way. If only he did not insist on trying to protect her from unseen and imaginary hurts. If only he had come here today, that might have gone a long way to bridge the ever-growing gap between them. If only Will were not such a stubborn old—

The hiss of the tape ending startled her away from that thought. She blinked, suddenly self-conscience about her drifting thoughts, and straightened up in her chair.

"As you can see, Judge Brakke, things have changed dramatically for Miss Grace and her home in these last few months." Ted depressed the power button on the sleek black VCR in the deep mahogany bookshelves that lined the spacious room.

Ted looked handsome today, younger and more rested than Rose believed she'd seen him look for a good two years. The simple cut of his dark suit, the vivid whiteness of his shirt against his tanned skin, and the sun streaks in his hair only added to the picture of vitality he presented. Despite the fact that this gathering was only to see if Eve had enough evidence of Grace's incompetence to support further action by the courts, Ted appeared ready to take on the Supreme Court if need be to win his cause. Championing the underdog certainly seemed to agree with that man.

Gayle smiled adoringly at her husband as he moved to take the seat between Gayle and Grace in the front line of chairs arranged in three short, neat rows in the room. But beneath

Gayle's smile lay a grim determination that only a close friend would perceive. Rose wanted to ask Naomi if she saw it, too, but didn't dare risk disrupting the session.

"So, Judge Brakke, you have seen the video evidence, have heard the reports of several upstanding New Bethany citizens—" Ted swept his strong hand toward the people Miss Grace had selected to come today: Marguerite, Rose, Gayle, Lucy, Ben, and small but vocal Vhonda Faye Womack, whom even Ted had thought added just the right touch of humor and sentiment to the proceedings "—and you have numerous letters of endorsement and support from as diverse a group of individuals as Dawnetta Mudd, owner of a local business, and Brother Paul Underwood, pastor of the Second Antioch Baptist Church."

The judge adjusted his glasses with one hand while he flipped open a file folder in front of him with enough force to cause the stack of handwritten letters to flutter.

"Clearly, Your Honor, the conditions under which Mrs. Tattersall first made this complaint no longer exist. Therefore any further inquiry into this matter should be halted." Ted tapped his finger on the arm of his chair, just lightly enough for emphasis without any unnecessary drama. "Right here and now."

"Well, hmmm…yes…" The judge glanced over the first few pages of the file, then looked up, removed his black reading glasses, and honed his gaze on Grace's niece. "Have you anything more to add to this, Mrs. Tattersall?"

"Yes, Your Honor, I have." Eve Tattersall rose from her chair with the same regal bearing that Rose most associated with Grace.

Rose found herself wondering if the petite, cultivated woman, with her already thinning chestnut brown hair and blue eyes the same shade of the aunt she sought to have put away, would appreciate the irony of how much she favored that very aunt?

"First I want to thank the people who have taken on my aunt's case of late. They've done a beautiful job with the house and provided some much needed services." Eve smiled and gave a sort of bowing nod to the people seated on Grace's side of the room.

In that moment Rose saw distinctly the difference between Grace and her aunt. Miss Grace had an innate sense of joy tempered with graciousness; she embodied it even when she was misbehaving. Eve's attempt to even broach that wondrous quality fell short and came across more as stilted civility over thinly veiled disapproval.

"I also would like to point out to these people, however, that I have been providing for my aunt's care for the past four years, since my mother's passing. I suggest that perhaps I do know more about what truly goes on with her than they could grasp in the short time they've known her."

"Go on," the judge said.

"Perhaps what these thoughtful folks have failed to take into account is that my aunt has had plenty of support and help in the past, all arranged by myself or my mother before me."

"What did I tell you?" Rose nudged Naomi. "I knew she had a lot of help with that house."

"So she needs help in her home, if that were a cause to question folk's sanity we'd all be locked away," Naomi countered.

"The fact is that no matter who I hired, how good their references, or how much I paid them, Aunt Grace always found some reason to chase them away. One time it was because she didn't like the way the girl smelled—"

"Like cheap toilet water over even cheaper liqueur." Grace's tone was disdainful

"And another one she let go because Aunt Grace said the woman mishandled her pigs!"

"Excuse me, did you say pigs?" The judge tipped his head to one side.

Eve shut her eyes and heaved out a sigh. "This...this horrid, tacky collection of—"

"They ain't tacky, they's cute." Vhonda Faye Womack looked like she'd like to get up and stomp Mrs. Tattersall right on the pointed toe of her expensive shoe. The six-year-old wasn't the only one harboring such sentiments.

"She has an irrational attachment to them, sir." Eve gave Vhonda Faye a glare.

"The collection was given to me by my late husband, Hamilton Chester Wiley—of the New Jersey Wileys." Grace made the comment simply, as though it would mean something to those gathered. Then she looked at the judge. "His nickname was Ham, Your Honor. Thus the collection."

"Ah." The judge smiled.

"I never knew that," Naomi said.

"Why do I have the feeling we are going to find out several things about Miss Grace we didn't know before?" Rose wasn't sure that was a good thing.

"If you ask me. To fire a perfectly good caregiver because of the way she dusts your pigs is beyond the pale, it shows a distorted sense of priorities." Eve's nose rose a tad higher into the air.

"Those things are precious to me as a memory, Eve. I don't want to see them destroyed by sheer carelessness."

Vhonda Faye Womack raised her hand and in doing so brought her little body right out of her chair.

The judged indulged the child. "Yes, dear?"

"Miss Grace lets me play with them pigs, sir. She says it's okay for me to do it when my mama comes to read to Miss Grace oncet'a week. My mama teached me that when you handle other folks's treasures, you show the same respect like they was your own."

"That's very good advice, young lady, and it appears to me that if I had someone in my employ who did not follow that standard, I'd let them go, too." Grace beamed.

"But you're missing the point, here, Your Honor. This isn't about pigs, it's about keeping Aunt Grace safe in her home. And the fact that a handful of people who've only known her a few months can't possibly comprehend what that entails. Aunt Grace has maliciously fired everyone I have sent, and I, for one, have no doubt she will do the same to her new caregiver, sir."

"I will not." Grace folded her hands over her new dress. She lifted her head as if she knew the gesture would make her perfectly matched new hat create a subtle halo effect around her professionally coifed hairdo. "The main difference between those women and Marguerite is that those women treated me like a helpless ol' fool. They were only there for the money Eve paid them, and sometimes what they could skim off the household accounts. Marguerite has come to Sweet Haven to make it her home. She is not simply a caregiver, she is not my *employee*. She is—as are all these people trying to do something for me here today—my friend."

"That's so." Marguerite nodded firmly.

Everyone else offered a quiet affirmation.

"World of difference, Your Honor," Ted reiterated.

"But there is one last thing that we have not addressed here. One thing that not even friendship can overcome, Your Honor." Eve bent at the knees to lower herself without so much as a wobble, into her chair. Everyone's attention fixed on her and it seemed to Rose that everyone held their breath, probably because they knew what she was about to say so well they felt they could say it with her. "A little matter, Your Honor, about Aunt Grace's behavior regarding a certain celebration—the Splendor Belle Gala, I believe it's called."

Naomi reached over and took Rose's hand without looking at her. Rose leaned close to hear her friend's whispered words. "I know Ted said we had to get this meeting in before the Belle Gala, Rose, and that he chose this day for his own reasons, but I wonder if he didn't make a tactical mistake? With the Gala being tomorrow night and all, it's at the forefront of everyone's thoughts. And so is Miss Grace's story."

"Now might be a good time to offer a little silent prayer," Rose suggested. She, herself, did just that—praying for guidance for Ted, for mercy and understanding from the judge, and for peace and resolution for Grace—and perhaps a little for herself, as well.

"You know the story of my aunt and the Belle Gala, don't you, Judge? How she's gone out on her porch every year on that night for the last fifty-something years?"

"I daresay Miss Grace goes out onto her porch many, many nights in a given year, but no one in town seems to take note of that, only this one." Ted spoke directly to Eve, then turned to the judge. "And last I heard, Judge Brakke, it was not yet against the law for us Southerners to enjoy the pleasures of sitting on the veranda of a pretty evening."

"Heaven forbid." The judge chuckled.

"Yes, but on this night she wears…that dress." Eve glowered.

"What evidence do you have of that, Mrs. Tattersall, besides the rampant gossip of a few people who may have passed by Sweet Haven? Now, as anyone who has done so can tell you, those folks could not have seen for sure what Miss Grace was wearing without actually trespassing on her property. Is there someone like that you wanted to call to support your story, ma'am?"

Eve's lawyer waved off the question without a word. It was the first thing he'd done all day to indicate he wasn't comatose.

"Seems like Eve has a knack for hiring people who don't do much," Rose muttered.

Naomi hid a snicker behind her hand.

"So it seems, Judge, that Mrs. Tattersall has no real evidence of anything odd occurring at Sweet Haven on the night of the—"

"What about the flowers?"

"The what?" There was a sly smile on Ted's lips, as though Eve had just walked into his meticulously laid trap and he was about to snap it shut.

"The flowers. Your Honor, my aunt sends herself a corsage every year, pretends it's from the boy who stood her up all those years ago and puts it on to sit out on her porch and wait for him. Now that's just crazy, plain and simple. I'll bet there are records at the town florist of her ordering those corsages dating back for years that will prove she does it, too."

"There are no such records, Your Honor." Ted stood, went over to Grace, put his hand on her shoulder. "Sir, I, myself, did not learn the whole truth of this story until just a few hours ago when a certain person came to me, with Grace present, to tell me they could not let Grace risk ruination if they could stop it. But first and foremost, this person insisted that this was Grace's story to tell, no one else's, and if she did not want any of it revealed, then nothing more would be said. Ever. It's a debt of honor, sir, the kind of thing one rarely sees these days and a measure of great character both on the part of this individual and the part of Miss Grace, who has long kept a secret which might have redeemed her reputation long ago."

Rose was on the edge of her chair now. In fact, the whole room seemed to have grown smaller from everyone edging inward toward the core of the action: Miss Grace.

Ted knelt just enough to put his gaze level with Grace's. "Well, Mrs. Grayson-Wiley? What do you think? Shall we go forward? Do you want to tell your story?"

"Yes, I do."

"Then will you start by telling us why your niece will never find any record of your having sent yourself a corsage every year on the night of the Splendor Belle Gala?"

"Because I never did do that, sir." Grace spoke to the judge, then turned in her seat to Eve. "Sweetheart, I'm not crazy and I'm not lost in the past. I never sent myself any flowers because I never had to—no matter where I was, even when I lived in New Jersey those few years—one thing I could always count on. The first Saturday in November, the man who had stood me up all those years ago and carried the tremendous guilt of thinking he had cost me my chance to save our family sent me the same kind of corsage that arrived the night he failed to show up himself."

"And—" Ted prompted.

"And…that man…" Grace twisted in her chair to face Rose and Naomi. "I should have told you this before now but, well, it all seemed so silly to me. I loved the corsages and felt that if they gave him some measure of absolution for the act of a reckless young man, then what did they hurt?"

Rose stared at Miss Grace as the truth struck her. *Oh, my word, she's talking to me!* "Will?" she heard herself whisper, then louder still without thinking before she spoke. "Will sent you those flowers?"

"No, honey." Grace shook her head. "Well, yes, he did,

these last two years, but only to uphold the promise he made to someone else, that I'd continue to receive those corsages the rest of my life."

"Curry!" Naomi said aloud the name forming in Rose's mind. "Rose, when Will didn't want you to go out to Sweet Haven, it was because he didn't want you to know—"

"He was protecting his best friend's honor, Rose, and my privacy." Grace's expression was filled with understanding and compassion.

"Yes, I know." And suddenly Rose did know: Will's aversion to Rose being around Miss Grace had nothing to do with sheltering Rose from the stigma of Sweet Haven, or even from learning of her husband's part in the drama—that all happened long before Rose knew Curry, when Rose was still a baby, for goodness sake. Will had acted as he had because a decent man like him could do no less. He'd simply been protecting a woman's honor and privacy. How could Rose have misjudged him so?

She looked at Miss Grace, and her perspective broadened. How could they all have misjudged Miss Grace as well?

"There's only one more thing I want to say before you make your decisions, Your Honor." Grace lifted herself up from her chair to step forward, then pivoted in her new, sensible but stylish shoes and put herself in the precise spot where she could address both the gathering and the judge. "Since we're all here, and since so much of my life and my secrets are already out, I think this would be the perfect place and time for me to completely exonerate myself. To prove once and for all to everyone that I am not crazy or temporarily insane or that I get moonstruck one night a year or whatever the current gossip says about me. Judge, if I may?"

"Certainly." He nodded, his face the very picture of curious awe.

Grace folded her hands like a schoolgirl reciting a memory piece, acknowledged those listening with a dip of her head, and took a deep breath. "Now, once and for all I'd like to say, for the record, why it is I *do* go out on my porch every year in my old gown—remade from my mother's wedding dress—on the night of the Splendor Belle Gala."

Nineteen

*S*ee, there! I told you she went out on that porch in that dress. Didn't I tell you?" Eve pointed an accusing finger at Grace.

"Hush up, child." Grace spoke as though she were talking to an infant. "And do sit yourself down. I know you are only up here for the day and that you are paying that there man sitting beside you enough to bankrupt the riches of Solomon—by the hour, no less. So it seems to me it would be in our best interests if you'd settle down and let me get this over so we can both just go on home."

Eve scowled, not in scorn or anger, but more in petulance, Naomi noted, maybe more from embarrassment than anything else.

When her niece had taken her seat, Grace nodded, as if asking some imaginary conductor to strike up the band. She drew in her breath, then raised one hand and thrust the other, palm down, toward the Bible which rested near the judge's forearm. "Am I supposed to take an oath?"

"No, ma'am, that won't be necessary." The judge patted her tiny hand. "This isn't a formal deposition. We trust you to tell the truth."

"That I will. Finally, after all this time." She turned, her expression a bit sheepish as she looked at Rose. "It feels good, too. I never held it again Curran that he didn't show up that night. Years later he wrote me a letter explaining that he'd asked out of obligation to my brother, who'd been lost in the war. But when word got out to some of his friends that he was taking me, and with the whole of the town knowing my beloved mother was counting on me to land a rich catch at the Belle Gala and save the family, well…conclusions were drawn, shall we say?"

"Ah-ha!" Naomi slapped her hand over her mouth, wishing she'd have thought of that sooner before she'd made a fool of herself.

Grace ignored the interjection. "Being only seventeen at the time, your late husband, Rose, got scared. Obviously he felt quite badly about it, and I have to say that I, myself, have one regret regarding the whole thing—that I never told him what I am about to say here. That I never thanked Mr. Holcolmb for what he did that night, nor told him how well things turned out despite his actions."

This is going to be good. Naomi just smiled at Rose, keeping her excited thoughts to herself.

"Your Honor? If I may?" Grace cocked her head and picked up the Bible lying on the judge's desk. "Are you familiar with the Scriptures?"

"I can't quote chapter and verse as I should, but, yes I'm familiar. Is there any one in particular I can help you find, ma'am?"

"Oh, no, I have this one memorized, but I wanted to read it today, if that's all right?"

"By all means."

"It's found in Second Corinthians, and this here is the King James, so it might sound a bit…well, here goes." She tipped her nose up and adjusted the book.

"Would these help, ma'am?" Judge Brakke offered her his reading glasses.

Grace tried them on, broke out into a grin, then began to

read. "'And he said unto me, "My grace is sufficient for thee; for my strength is made perfect in weakness. Most gladly therefore will I rather glory in my infirmities, that the power of Christ may rest upon me."'"

Judge Brakke accepted the book back from Grace. "That's very nice, ma'am, but I'm not sure I understand..."

"Well, neither did I, sir, not until that long ago night of the Splendor Belle Gala when I thought I had lost everything, not just for myself, but for my family as well. I sometimes wonder if any of us truly understands and appreciates those words until we've come up against our biggest fears and finally come to understand that in our weakness, God is strong? His grace is sufficient to carry us through, if we would let him. I am so glad I learned that at an early age, sir. It carried me through a lot of dark times and sad times and even happy times when I wondered how I would go on if that happiness would begin to fail me."

Naomi knew it was true. She's seen it in her own life and in the lives of others.

"What a wonderful testament," Lucy murmured behind them.

Naomi glanced back to see that Dr. Ben had taken Lucy's hand, and while she had not pulled away from the display of affection as she often did, the young woman did not return it, either. She simply sat there, her eyes focused on something no one else could see.

"But the dress? Why on earth do you need to humiliate yourself by putting on that old dress?"

Naomi could hardly fault Eve for asking as she'd wondered the same thing herself.

"I don't find it one bit humiliating." Grace angled her chin up and sniffed like the queen in a storybook who was about to cry out "*Off with her head!*" "Not anymore humiliating than I would find wearing a paper hat at a birthday party, shooting off fireworks on the Fourth of July, or staying up late and singing that song that not a soul really understands on New Year's Eve."

"Birthdays? Fourth of—" Eve shook her head "—Why, those are entirely different, Aunt Grace, and you know—"

"Not to me, they're not." Grace pulled herself up to her full height—which still wasn't very substantial. "The night of the Splendor Belle Gala is all those things to me and more—my birthday, my independence day, my new beginning. That first night I waited on that porch I thought my world had come to an end, but any one of you with eyes in his head can see for yourself that just did not happen. I knew I could never be strong enough to do what needed to be done, but I also realized that night that I would do it, whether I thought I could or not. And from that point on I never looked back over what might have been."

Grace gave Rose a reconciliatory wink, as if to say, "Please don't carry on your husband's guilt in this," then she went on. "As you all know, I did not marry a wealthy member of New Bethany society. I did not do any of the things the women of generations past had done in our family. I didn't study abroad, become a patron of the arts, or travel extensively. Neither did my sweet baby sister. But we were happy and healthy and did all right for ourselves, marrying good men, making good lives." Grace looked at Eve, who managed a smile at that. "And while Sweet Haven and its lands were never returned to their former glory, the house remains in our family and beneath the wings of angels to this day."

"Remarkable." The judge nodded slowly.

"So on the night of the Belle Gala, you will find me on my porch, sir, in my gown and wearing my corsage. It's the evening when I walk out there and say, 'Yes, Lord, I trust you. You've taken me this far in my weakness and I know you will carry me the rest of the way. No matter what comes, I'm going to make it.'"

"Doesn't sound one bit crazy to me, Your Honor." Ted stood.

"Me, neither." Instead of ringing a gavel, the judge tapped the corner of his reading glasses on the leather cover of the Bible and gave one curt nod. "Mrs. Tattersall?"

Eve sighed. "I don't think we need to go on with this anymore, Your Honor."

Naomi wanted to jump up and shout, but refrained herself long enough to let everyone congratulate one another and hug Miss Grace. On the way home, she whooped a few times, laughed out loud, then put her thoughts on tomorrow and her own plans for celebrating the Belle Gala.

The twinkling lights of the Bethany Heights Country Club never looked more sparkling and festive, even though, as Ben's Mustang rolled up the long drive, it was not yet dark.

Lucy fussed with the neckline of her dress, with the clip in her hair, with her full, green taffeta skirt. She wondered if anyone would know it was the same dress, though remade, she'd worn the night she was feted at her own Belle Gala fourteen years ago. Naomi had talked her into it, but Lucy had to admit something in her liked the idea of taking the dress she had worn the one time she had imagined she'd won her father's love—and updating that dress to reflect the woman she had become. Now that they were driving up to the club in Ben's classic car, though, she felt a little sad about her choice.

"Lucy, last time we came here, the valet dinged my car." Ben frowned. He wasn't typically the motorhead type, overly concerned with not letting anyone touch his precious machine, but this was a classic automobile and the valets were notorious for haphazard driving. "Would you mind if I let you off by the door, you can go in and wait and I'll be right there."

"Sure. That's fine."

He pulled up to the door, hopped out, spoke with the valet, then rounded the car to open Lucy's door for her. Escorting her under the canopy, he kissed her cheek. "Did I remember to tell you how gorgeous you look tonight?"

Her heart raced. Her? Gorgeous? The two words did not belong in the same sentence. "I…uh…"

"Well, you do. And in case I haven't told something else tonight…" He turned her to face him, his forehead against hers. "I love you, Lucy Jewell. With all my heart."

He gave her a quick kiss, then pivoted away, rushing to get the car before a zealous valet tore off in it. "Wait for me."

Forever, she thought, wondering if that valet could get a wheelbarrow and scoop up her now liquefied body to roll her inside. Ben loved her.

She turned to face the entrance to the country club. *Ben* loved her. "What do you think of *that*, Daddy?"

"I beg your pardon, miss?" The valet cocked his head.

"Um, nothing." Lucy wet her lips and turned toward the club's impressive doors. Suddenly she felt eighteen again. She definitely had come full circle.

She inhaled, expecting to fill herself up with the wondrous scents remembered from childhood, but found only car exhaust and stale cigarette smoke from those banished to the steps to indulge in their habit. A passing car radio blared out the hoopla before a high school play-off football game—and Lucy's thoughts went immediately back to last year's gala.

Full circle? Had she really done that or had she just been going in circles all along and now, at last, she had the chance to stop the dizzying pace? Ben *loved* her.

He'd told her so before, but it just had not seemed possible that he could really mean it. Now, as she stood on the edge of the country club, she felt the hollow victory of coming back in triumph over her father's disdain, Ray's betrayal, and Dwayne's indifference.

And suddenly she knew what she had to do.

Just as Miss Grace had known the truth on that night long ago, Lucy understood she had to get past her fears and trust that, no matter what, even if things went terribly wrong with Ben, God's grace was sufficient to cover her weakness—all off her weaknesses. No matter what happened, because she had the Lord, she would survive.

"Ready, Lucy?" Ben strode up to her, smiling as always.

She reached out to take his hand. "When did you first fall in love with me, Ben?"

He blinked as if she'd just asked him to do advanced algebra in his head, then slowly his sweet smile crept back over his lips. "Lucy, I think I fell in love with you the first time I ever saw you."

"Before I did anything to earn your love? Even though you saw I was chubby and plain and a horrible mess?"

"You're none of those things to me, Lucy." He pulled her close. "To me you're kind and sweet and caring and cute and funny and...all the things you were that very first moment I laid eyes on you."

"Really?"

"Don't you believe me?"

What would happen if she did? What would happen if she surrendered her fears as Miss Grace had suggested and put her faith totally in the Lord?

Ben loved *her.* She loved him. What would happen if she let God take over from there? "Ben? Why don't you ever ask me to marry you anymore?"

"Would you laugh at me if I said it was because I'm scared?"

"No."

"I've been waiting for a sign, Lucy. Something unmistakable. Because last time we talked about it, I made it clear that when I asked again I would expect an answer, and I dearly want it to be yes."

"A sign. I see."

"Why?" He peered into her eyes. "What's going on in that head of yours, girl?"

"Ben, how disappointed would you be if I said I didn't want to go to the Gala?"

"What do you want to do instead?"

"How about a picnic?"

"Under the water tower?"

"Sounds terrific," she murmured. "But there's something I have to do first. Can you meet me there at ten?"

He gave her a pensive look. "Kind of late for a picnic, isn't it?"

"What's the matter, Doctor? Afraid you'll be scandalized?" She grinned.

His answering grin was decidedly delighted. "Ten it is, then."

"William Boatwright? Come out here." Rose hadn't spoken to Will since Grace's revelation. She simply had no idea what to say to the man. Not, that was, until now.

"Rose? Rose, hon! It's good to see you. I didn't think you'd be speaking to me—not after you learned that I'd kept that secret from you for so long." He stood inside his door, squinting into the late-afternoon sun.

"Keeping a secret from someone and keeping someone's confidence are two entirely different things, Will. Even an old hothead like me can see that. I should have guessed it anyway, what with Sweet Haven's grounds always so well groomed. Only Boatwright's nursery does that kind of fine work around here. Then knowing you were just enough younger than Grace that you couldn't have been her mystery man, I should have put it together. Besides, Curry always did try to smooth things over with flowers."

"Except with you. That took chocolate." He smiled tenderly. "I was thinking about sending you some of that, myself, but I found out they don't sell it by the ton. I figured it'd take that much just to get you to say 'boo' to me again."

"Will?" She leaned against the doorframe, putting them almost eye-to-eye.

"Yes, Rose?"

"Boo." She smiled.

"Just like that?" He gave her a suspicious look. "No chocolate transaction involved?"

"None whatsoever. You did the right thing, Will. How could I be mad at you for that?"

"Well…"

"And now it's time for me to do the right thing."

"You going to make an honest man out of me?"

"Oh, there aren't enough angels in heaven or hours in the day for that." She groaned, laughing, then grew serious. "No, hon, I'm here for the corsage."

"What? But—"

"It was Curry's gift to Grace, and it's my responsibility now."

"Oh, Rose, I don't know, I…"

"You do have it, don't you?"

"Of course."

"Then why don't you give it to me? I still have to run by my house for something and then make another stop and…" She did not want to discus this to death. She knew what she was going to do and no one would dissuade her. And after it was done, then she and Will could talk…and talk…and talk. "Let me do what I have to do tonight, Will, and tomorrow…"

"Tomorrow, why don't you and Stacey and I go to church together and then out to eat?"

It touched Rose that he would include Stacey in the invitation after all they had been through. That and the knowledge of what he had done for Grace and Curry made it easier for her to smile at him coyly and whisper, "It's a nice thought, honey, but after church tomorrow, Stacey is going to be far too busy for eating out."

"What's she going to be doing?"

"Looking for her own apartment."

"Rose, really?" Hope gleamed in those kind, old eyes.

"Why not? She's a grown girl, and while she doesn't have as high a paying job as she used to, she's smart and capable. Besides, God's grace is sufficient. She'll be just fine."

"If you are going to go back to looking out the window at the moon, Nomi, hadn't you better ought to wait until it comes out?"

Naomi angled her shoulders toward her wonderful husband. A soft rustling came from under the robe she had cinched around her finally thin-again middle. "I'm not waiting on the moon, Taylor."

"Then what are you waiting on, sugar?" He came up behind her, his arms stretched out, but before he could actually hug her a sound drew Naomi's attention.

"That's what I'm waiting on." She pointed to Rose's big luxury car idling in the drive. She spun around and laid her hand on her husband's tanned cheek. "You can watch the baby for me, can't you?"

"Well, I suppose. But where are you and Rose off to?"

"It's Belle Gala night, sweetie." She tugged at the belt of her robe and with one whoosh, it fell open to reveal an awful pink and lavender creation, all chiffon ruffles and rose print.

"What is that?" The question came out in a squawk.

"Well, I couldn't make over my mother's wedding dress for a gown, so I made over the dress she wore when they celebrated their twenty-fifth wedding anniversary in 1967." She did a little turn for him. "Don't you like it?"

"It's um…"

Honk. Honk.

"Rose is waiting, honey. I don't have enough time for you to think up a not-too-cutting adjective." She planted a kiss on his cheek. "I won't be late getting home tonight."

"Getting home from where?"

"Now where do you suppose?"

"Well, you behave," he called after her as she scooted down the stairs.

"Now, *there's* a much-needed warning. You know how out of control Rose and Marguerite can get—and that wild, party animal, Miss Grace? Alert the police to be on standby!"

"I wasn't worried about their influence on you, Nomi, but yours on them!"

"This is not that kind of get-together, thank you." She knew he wanted to ask what kind of get-together it was, but she never gave him the chance. She just darted out the door and on her way before he could utter another sound.

Ted fell back in the chair by his side of the bed. He looked beaten down and exhausted. Grim. He'd gone into the office today around eight in the morning to refamiliarize himself with some files and cases. Those had been his words: "refamiliarize myself."

"Only for an hour or two just to prep for starting back full time come Monday," he had said. Ten hours later he had dragged himself back home, all gray around the gills and beaten down. He sighed and kicked his shoes off his feet.

Gayle started to go over and pick them up, then stopped herself. She stared at the shoes laying there, much as they had been that awful Easter morning…and for an instant her mind flashed on the sight of Ted, struggling to breathe, fighting for his life.

A shudder seized her body. Is this what she'd come to? Is this how little faith she had in her Lord and her husband that she would let Ted push himself like this, that she would prefer him miserable, unhealthy—or worse—rather than have her delicately balanced life altered? Her hand froze just above the empty shoes and she recalled the verse Grace had read to them. God's grace was sufficient. He would be their strength no matter what came their way.

Gayle straightened. "You'll have to get those yourself, Ted."

"Okay. Sure."

She drew in her breath, and with it the smell of Ted's fading aftershave, dinner on the stove, the understated elegance of outrageously priced candles she never let anyone actually light…the whole familiar package of their life together. Hard as it was for her to do, she exhaled and fixed her gaze on Ted. "Things are going to change around here, you know."

He huffed, placing his hand absently over his heart as had become his habit the last few months. "Change? I thought they already had."

She crossed her arms. "Well, they are going to change again."

"Back to the way they were before—" He didn't have to say before what, they both knew when.

"Nuh-uh, no sir." She shook her head. "No way am I going to go through that again, Ted Barrett. I love you too much to see you like that ever again."

He narrowed his eyes at her. "Then just how is it you want to see me, Gayle?"

"Happy." She moved to him, going onto her knees and taking his hands in hers. "Like you were yesterday, the way you were the whole time you were helping Miss Grace."

"That kind of law doesn't pay the kinds of bills we have, Gayle." He spoke softly, sounding as though he felt he had no choice in this matter.

"Then we'll change the kind of bills we get, Ted."

"That's not as easy as you may think. It would mean drastic cutbacks. The kids' college funds would be safe, but everything else would be subject to cutbacks."

"I don't care. We'll scale down everywhere. Get a smaller house. Live more simply. I grew up a Methodist minister's daughter, and even though Mother's people came from money, we never had much of it. I don't mind, Ted. If it's what you want to do."

"It's too much to ask, Gayle." His eyes searched hers, hopeful and filled with longing for so many things Gayle could not imagine them all. "Leaving my practice would not just mean less money, it would mean we'd have to invest some of our savings in my new practice. And most of it we might never see again. I couldn't ask it. It would be too much, it would be too hard for you and the children."

"Is it harder than living without you?" Tears sprang to her eyes. "I don't think so."

"Gayle, do you know what you're saying?"

"Yes. I do." She went to him, curling up in his lap, her arms around his neck. "I'm saying God's grace is sufficient, Ted. We can handle whatever comes."

"I love you, Gayle." He nuzzled the back of her neck. "And if I weren't so tired, I'd show you how much."

"You rest. You can show me later." She kissed his temple. "Right now I think I know how to start simplifying our lives."

"How?"

"Well, you know how you complain that I have all these fancy dresses that I won't throw out but I never wear again?"

"Uh-huh."

"Well, there's one that's been up in a box for a couple decades now—I saved it because I thought Mathina might want it." She sighed and slowly stood up. "Somehow I think my old formal may be a bit out of place on the mission field."

Ted laughed. "So what are *you* going to do with it?"

She waggled her eyebrows at him. "I am going to a party. A little Independence Day-birthday-New-Year's-Eve celebration. I think it will do me good."

Twenty

"Why, Sister Marguerite, don't you look pretty this evening?" Naomi leaned back against the porch rail.

Marguerite fluffed the gaudy yellow bridesmaid's dress she had worn just a few months ago at Princess's wedding. "I look a fool, but then I see—" She paused to make a long, pointed study of Naomi's attire "—I'm not the only one."

Naomi laughed. "This just sort of fit the character of the evening, I thought."

"Well, these are outfits for a couple of characters, I will grant you that." Marguerite adjusted the large, sparkling applique that almost covered her ample chest. "I know my sister fell in love with that man when she was sixteen, and their love is ever youthful, but I do wish she had considered the passing of time when she picked out this dress. Worse yet, she actually told me she thought I could wear it again."

"And you did!" Naomi wagged a finger in warning. "And because you have worn it tonight you'll have to start wearing it every year on the night of the Belle Gala!"

"Oh, my, no!" Marguerite shook her head, her eyes glittering with fun. "Well, if that's the way it's got to be..."

"Got to be." Naomi confirmed it. "We're starting a tradition."

"Well, I didn't know what *else* to wear tonight." Marguerite got up and lifted the lid on a thermos of warm apple cider, which instantly saturated the air with the rich, damp aroma of fruit and spice. "I didn't have any old ball gown to wear. For obvious reasons, I was never one of the belles at the Belle Gala."

"I was never feted there myself—unless you count ill-fated." Naomi waved her hand. "Been that more times in my life than I care to think of—but I don't suppose that counts, does it?"

"No, I don't think so." Marguerite laughed.

From inside the house, big band music began blaring. That had to be Rose's signal that Miss Grace was ready for her entrance.

"Just give me a moment, Miss Grace, to get out onto the porch." Rose stepped out the door, her gorgeous black dress rustling. It did not have sequins on the petticoats, she'd lamented to Naomi, as her first gala gown had, but it did have plenty of sparkle across the top and it looked wonderful on her. Rose turned to them. "Miss Grace is just about ready to come out, and she looks adorable—like the tooth fairy or something!"

"Land-a-Goshen," Marguerite muttered, half laughing, half in disgust. "That is what she looks like, isn't it? I've been trying to place it since she got dressed this afternoon."

Naomi looked from one of her companions to the other then back again, but neither of them said more.

"Here I am. Here I am." Grace's raspy voice carried out through the screen door, but she did not show her face. The music, a brassy dance tune, played on, and Naomi suspected Grace was waiting for it to end and something more pleasant to begin before she came wafting through the door with the stained-glass window as a backdrop. "Now don't start any of the fun without me."

"Or me!"

"Gayle!" Naomi opened her arms, her heart actually skipping with near giddiness at having her oldest pal there to join the celebration. "I never imagined you'd show up here tonight!"

"Well, where else would I be? At that stuffy old country club?" Gayle gave Naomi a breath-stealing squeeze, then pulled away and snapped her fingers. "That much for those old snobs. I want to be where the *truly* beautiful people are tonight."

"Why? Do you want to ask them for fashion tips?" Naomi stepped back to...*admire* Gayle's gown. "What *is* that you've got on?"

"Don't you like it? It was my gala gown."

"Honey, it looks like a flower child got mugged by a devotee of haute couture." Naomi plucked up some of the wheat-colored lace overlay to expose a swath of the heavy gold satin skirt. "A flower child with very, *very* bad taste."

"Thank you." Gayle made an exaggerated bow that actually seemed in keeping with the princess cut of the dress.

"Bad, bad taste." Naomi whisked her fingers through the velvet ribbons that fell almost to the floor in front, at the back, and at the elbow just where the fabric poofed upward to Gayle's shoulder and belled downward to her wrist. "A flower child with a maypole fixation, perhaps."

"Oh, you are one to talk fixations, aren't you? Miss More-Ruffles-Than-A-Bedskirt?" Gayle giggled. "And Sister Marguerite! You look...you look..."

"I look like a canary who swallowed a basketball, and I know it."

The music faded to a soft crackle and popping sound.

"This is it." Rose clapped her hands.

Naomi grabbed Gayle's hand to pull her around so they could both get the full effect.

Soft music, something Naomi could only describe as

swooping and swaying, began. A shadow fell across the stained-glass image of an angel's wings. Despite the levity of the evening so far, Naomi felt a lump in her throat. When Gayle's hand closed around hers, she felt the tingle of threatening tears. Rose stepped up, one hand on Marguerite's back, her other arm coming to close around Naomi's shoulders, her fingertips touching Gayle.

They had all been through so much in their brief but wonderful relationships, and finally they had come to the place where they could all stand together, hand in hand, and celebrate that they still had their faith and their friendship—and promise they would always support one another in both.

"I wish Lucy were here." Gayle summed up what Naomi did not have the voice to say.

"Wait! Wait!"

Lucy's voice apparently carried far enough to reach Miss Grace, who called back. "Well, get a move on, girl, I can't stand in here all night!"

"All right, I'm coming! Just give me one second."

"Did she plan that, or what?" Elated, Naomi pulled back enough to open a space for Mary Lucille, who was even then rushing up the newly refurbished stairs.

"Nuh-uh. You should know by now, our Lucy doesn't plan anything." Gayle lifted her arm to let Lucy slide into place.

"Shows how much *you* know." Lucy beamed at them, then nodded to Rose and Marguerite. "I have a plan for tonight, and it's a doozie!"

"Did you put ideas in that sweet child's head, Naomi?" Rose gave her a mock glare.

"Not me. What is it, Lucy?"

She grinned. "You'll find out tomorrow."

"Tomorrow?" Naomi's jaw dropped. "I can't wait until to—"

"If y'all are done fussing out there, I'm ready to make my appearance."

"Yes, Miss Grace," they called back, more or less in unison.

"Good." Grace stepped up.

Naomi gasped.

For one fleeting second, with the forgiving haze created by the door's screen softening her features and the evocative effect of the light on the stunning stained glass, Naomi could imagine the girl Grace had once been. "Oh, Miss Grace, you look absolutely lovely."

The door screeched, though not as much as it used to, and Grace came out onto the porch.

"She looks like—" Lucy cocked her head "—the tooth fairy."

Gayle tried so hard to hold her laughter back that she began to choke.

Rose offered a none-too-subtle pound on the back.

Marguerite moved to the table with the punch and paper cups, shaking her head. "I told her that crown was a leftover from a child's Halloween getup, but she insisted we buy it. 'Oh, no' she says. 'It's a hat and I'm going to wear it this year on the night of the Splendor Belle Gala.'"

"I think it's perfect." Naomi went over to give Miss Grace a hug, careful to avoid the corsage the old woman wore like a medal of honor high on her frothy, white dress. "Tell us what we're supposed to do now, Miss Grace."

"Do?" Grace scrunched up her nose. "Well, I've never 'done' this with anyone else before, but my usual routine is to sit on the porch swing with a cup of cider in my hand. I say right out loud the biggest fear that I have faced this past year, then I tell myself that with God's help I'm not going to let it best me."

"Let's start with that, then." Rose already had a cup of cider in her hand for Miss Grace.

While Rose helped the older woman to the porch swing, the others solemnly accepted their drinks, then took up places around the swing, either sitting or standing. They left the chair by the window for Marguerite, who claimed it once she'd served up her own cider.

"I'll start," Miss Grace announced. "My greatest fear this year was that I would be alone these last years of my life, without even the comfort of my home and the memories it holds around me. But when, in a moment of sheer weakness—and what I then suspected as the onset of lunacy—I opened my door to you ladies that fall afternoon, God stepped into my life and lifted my fears from me."

She raised her glass, setting the swing rocking gently as she did so, and signaled for the next person to speak.

"I've been afraid to move forward this year," Rose began. "I have not been a shining example of trust in either the man that I love or the Lord that I serve. It humbles me to know that both are bigger than my shortcomings. That God's grace is even bigger than my capacity to be a great big donkey's hindquarters."

Quiet laughter welcomed Rose's confession, and she raised her glass too.

"My fear..." Lucy hesitated, looking around as if asking if it were all right for her to go next. When everyone gave her encouraging nods, she heaved a deep breath and smoothed one hand down her green gown. "My fear was that I did not deserve to be loved. The thing I think I learned this year was that probably none of us *deserve* it, but isn't the greatest miracle of all that we *do* love one another despite that very fact?"

"Amen to that." Rose gave Lucy a watery smile.

Lucy raised her glass.

"Though I never pictured it as a fear, my ladies, I was powerful distressed that after all my years of giving to others, and seeming this self-sacrificing spiritual person, that I would be the thing that stood between my baby sister and happiness." Marguerite paused to collect herself. "I did not want to rattle in a house by myself or become the lone Sister Johnson. My life needed more purpose than that. And just when I should have lost it all, the Lord brought me here." She looked toward the oval in the door that depicted the starry sky and a tree's branches—all magically transformed into an angel's wing. "'He shall cover thee with his feathers, and under his wings shalt thou trust.'"

She raised her cup.

Gayle shuffled her feet forward. "Well, I'm just a whole big mass of fears, ya'll."

They chuckled at the unlikely admission, though deep down, Naomi felt they all saw the bare-bones honesty of it.

"Now, I'll tell you right now, I have not given them all up, either. I'm learning to, but it's not as easy as you might think to let go of the things that you have been clinging to for dear life—even if those are the very things weighing you down. But that's what I'm going to do, ya'll, and I am going to have faith that it will be all right. And if it's not all right, I will say absolutely that no matter what comes, my faith will abide and I will go on."

Naomi smiled at her friend as Gayle raised her glass.

"I guess that leaves me, and I know you all here know what my biggest fear was this year and how wonderfully God and my friends helped me face it. So I just have one more thing to say." Naomi looked down into her cup, then raised her gaze to speak to each member of the circle, her heart poured into each look and each word. "I love you—all of you. I'm so proud my daughter—my daughters—will grow up with such fine role models, such truly good and caring women. I'm so glad to have found you all. You are a blessing to me, and I will be thankful for you and everything you have taught me, given me, suffered with me, and hoped with me, for the rest of my life."

Naomi raised her cup.

"Amen," the women murmured as if they had just all joined in prayer—and in a way, Naomi supposed, they had.

They all passed the rest of the evening laughing and talking.

All, that was, except for Lucy, who excused herself early.

"Where you hurrying off to, sugar?"

Naomi was as curious as Rose about the answer to her question. To their utter shock, Lucy broke into an ear-to-ear grin.

"I've got a plan. You'll understand tomorrow. I promise." And with that she hurried off, Naomi supposed to put said "plan" in motion—leaving Naomi and the others to wonder what tomorrow would reveal.

Whatever it was, from the amazing twinkle in Lucy's eye, Naomi had the distinct impression that her young friend was about to outdo even her in outrageousness.

Lucy reached out to take Ben's hand, still unsure herself, but confident in her newly bolstered faith. She cleared her throat. "You said you needed a sign."

"That I did." He pulled her into his arms. He searched her face, then settled his gaze in hers.

She smiled, her heart thumping, tempted to just stand there and savor his nearness without asking for anything more from him. But that's not why she had come—and to do anything less than ask him outright for his answer would be a slap in the face to the vow she had made on Miss Grace's porch. She let her gaze drift upward, then back to meet his twinkling eyes. "So, then, your answer is—"

"Yes." He cut her off. Then he proved just how much he meant it with a long, sweet kiss.

Epilogue

he next morning the entire town discovered Lucy's plan when they looked up to find the words "Will you marry me, Ben?" painted in sprayable chalk on the town water tower.

Naomi stood there, staring at the bold message, smiling from ear to ear. There was never a dull moment in New Bethany. Nor would there be for quite some time, she thought as she slid into her car and started the engine. Nuh-uh, no sir. Dull was not in the plan. In the coming months, big things would be brewing. She glanced back at the water tower. For one thing, there would be a wedding to plan. And Gayle would need help selling her house—Naomi giggled—and having her very first ever tag sale. Rose would need constant reminders, Naomi knew, that Stacey was a big girl and would not starve if Rose didn't provide her meals or go naked if Rose didn't do the child's laundry. As for her and Taylor…well, they had a new baby and a newly formed family to tend to.

Life is good. The thought swept Naomi as she drove out to Sweet Haven to pick up Miss Grace for church. And even when it wasn't, God was always faithful.

Thank you, Lord, her heart sang out, *for that and for the friends and family you have given me. It's not enough, I know, my meager gratitude, but you see my heart and you know how much your gifts*—images of her friends, her mama, and Taylor and the girls drifted through her mind, bringing quick tears to her eyes—*and you* truly *mean to me. And in your grace, I think I am finally beginning to understand how much I mean to you.*

In that instant Naomi could feel the presence of her mother, of her friends, and of God's goodness…his *sufficiency*. And at last she understood. For all the times she'd felt alone, she hadn't been. Not ever. Nor would she be, ever again.

"'My grace is sufficient.'" She murmured the verse, savoring its truth for the past, for today, for always. "Amen, Lord. Amen."

Dear Reader,

I had not intended to extend the story begun in *The Prayer Tree* to a second book, but as the story of that first year of service came to a close, I felt a tug. Maybe it was the sense of loss I felt for a town and four friends (and their families) that I had grown to love, or maybe it was the urge to find out if Miss Lucy ever did have those children she so desperately wanted.

I think now, as I have finished *Saving Grace* (a thousand thank-yous to my editor, Karen Ball, for that title) that the tug was actually more of a nudge—from the Lord. There really was one more thing to say about these characters that reflected on all of us as Christians as we go about our daily walk, facing challenges big and small: God's grace is enough. We have everything we need in the gift of grace to face whatever comes our way. So many times we want to judge our deeds—and one another—by the sum total of our sins and forget the magnitude of Christ's salvation. His blood is enough to cover all our sins, enough to carry us through anything. What an amazing realization.

When I look at people whose faith has really moved me, I can see this understanding at work. And I have to ask myself how much more could I accomplish, how much better an instrument of the Father could I be, if I could truly begin to walk and talk and act in the trust and faith that God's grace is sufficient for everything? And so I brought the friends I came to love—Naomi, Gayle, Rose, and Mary Lucille—through another year. I let them come up against life in good times and bad. And their stories brought them to the point where we could *all* know that no matter what happens to them—or to us—God's grace is sufficient.

Blessings!

Annie Jones

ALABASTER BOOKS
Fiction that speaks to a woman's heart

Homeward, Melody Carlson
Redeeming Love, Francine Rivers
Enough, Gayle Roper
Tangled Vines, Diane Noble
(who also writes as Amanda MacLean)
The Invitation, Nancy Moser
The Prayer Tree, Annie Jones
Saving Grace, Annie Jones
Arabian Winds, Linda Chaikin
Lions of the Desert, Linda Chaikin
Valiant Hearts, Linda Chaikin
Where Yesterday Lives, Karen Kingsbury

COMING IN 1999
Mixed Signals, Liz Curtis Higgs (February)
Highland Call, Sharon Gillenwater, (March)
sequel to *Song of the Highlands*
The Quest, Nancy Moser, (June) sequel to *The Invitation*
The Long Road Home, Karen Kingsbury (July)
Deep Dixie, Annie Jones (August)
Distant Bells, Diane Noble (September) sequel to *Tangled Vines*

Homeward, **Melody Carlson**
ISBN 1-57673-029-8
Meg Lancaster returns to the hometown she left in anger twenty years before, but what she finds there is far from the peace she'd hoped for. Instead, Meg uncovers secrets that have been hidden for decades—secrets that force her to confront the family she ran away from and to reevaluate the beliefs she's held her entire life.

Redeeming Love, **Francine Rivers**
ISBN 1-57673-186-3
California's gold country. 1850. A time when men sold their souls for a bag of gold, and women sold their bodies for a place to sleep. A time when two people are brought together by an all-knowing, all-loving God—and neither will ever be the same. A powerful retelling of the book of Hosea; a life-changing story of God's unconditional, redemptive, all-consuming love.

Enough! **Gayle Roper**
ISBN 1-57673-185-5
Molly has had enough of her children's lack of respect. And so she stages a walkout: no cooking, no laundry, no cleaning, no chauffeuring. No *nothing* until her kids learn to treat her with the honor God commands children to show a parent. But how much time—and pandemonium—will it take before the kids cry "uncle"?

Tangled Vines, **Diane Noble**
(who also writes as Amanda MacLean)
ISBN 1-57673-219-3
When K.C. Keegan's aunt, well-known but eccentric mystery writer Theodora Whimple, disappears, K.C. risks everything to find her—even joining forces with her ex-fiancé, Sheriff Elliot Gavin. Following Theodora's trail, they come to an elegant winery in the sun-drenched Napa Valley, where something is going on…something far more sinister—and dangerous—than either K.C. or Gav can imagine.

The Invitation, **Nancy Moser**
ISBN 1-57673-115-4
Four ordinary people receive anonymous invitations to a small Midwest town they've never heard of. Each dismisses the invitations as a prank—until strange, even miraculous, things start happening. Soon all four embark on a journey that will test their mettle—and their faith—to the breaking point.

The Prayer Tree, **Annie Jones**
ISBN 1-57673-239-8
Naomi, Gayle, Rose, and Mary Lucille are Southern, born and bred. So when New Bethany's fine tradition of praying for others is threatened with extinction, they step forward as a group to plant the town's last prayer tree. Characters all, each woman has a secret reason for taking part in the prayer circle. But what none of them realize is that God, not their agendas, has called them together—and what he has in store for them is beyond their wildest imaginings.

Saving Grace, **Annie Jones**
ISBN 1-57673-330-0
Though Naomi, Gayle, Rose, and Mary Lucille are as close as sisters in their hearts, the bond they share has grown fragile. Can a loony old lady bring them together again? And just who—as the women appoint themselves guardian angels over the old dear—is really helping whom?

Arabian Winds, **Linda Chaikin**
ISBN 1-57673-105-7
British field nurse Allison Wescott finds herself face-to-face with—and at the mercy of—the enemy, handsome and cynical Major Bret Holden. But there's something odd about this German soldier, something that makes Allison think the major isn't what he'd like her to think he is. An exciting tale of espionage and romance in World War II.

Lions of the Desert, **Linda Chaikin**
ISBN 1-57673-114-6
Allison and Bret are caught up in a sinister plot that pulls them into an unexplainable murder, a search for treasure, and frightening encounters that make Allison wonder if she can trust anyone—even Bret. The thrilling sequel to *Arabian Winds.*

Valiant Hearts, **Linda Chaikin**
ISBN 1-57673-240-1
The story of Allison Wescott and Bret Holden concludes as the Great War breaks across Palestine. As a field nurse, Allison must follows the Australian Lighthorse Cavalry to capture Beersheba—and then on to take Jerusalem from the Turks! But love flares to life again when Allison unexpectedly finds Bret wounded—and they end up trapped together behind enemy lines.

Where Yesterday Lives, **Karen Kingsbury**
ISBN 1-57673-285-1
At thirty-one Ellen Barrett has already won a Pulitzer Prize, but her skill as a reporter far surpasses her ability to sort out a troubled past. When her father dies, she returns home, where she must reopen old wounds before true healing can begin—and where a long-lost love unexpectedly reappears, drawing Ellen to make peace with her past—and put Christ in her future. A stirring novel that is the basis for an upcoming 1998 Hallmark Hall of Fame Movie.